UNSPEAKABLE

A Deadly Secrets Novel

OTHER TITLES BY
ELISABETH NAUGHTON

Deadly Secrets series
Repressed
Gone
Protected

UNSPEAKABLE

A Deadly Secrets Novel

ELISABETH NAUGHTON

Published by Montlake Romance, Seattle

www.apub.com

Amazon, the Amazon logo, and Montlake Romance are trademarks of Amazon.com, Inc., or its affiliates.

ISBN-13: 9781503904903
ISBN-10: 1503904903

Cover design by Caroline Teagle Johnson

Printed in the United States of America

This one is for Kristina Campbell,
a Pacific Northwest girl, a lover of all kinds of books,
and a fellow Beaver alum.
Thank you for loving the stories your crazy aunt
spends countless hours writing.

CHAPTER ONE

On a good day, Russell McClane could handle a family party. He looked forward to the chaos, to watching his pathetic brothers make fools of themselves bending over backward for their wives, to hearing his five-year-old niece Emma's high-pitched shriek and the way the sound set his youngest brother, Thomas, on edge. He didn't even mind the inevitable bickering that always accompanied a McClane family event or the dozens of ways his brothers would razz him for being single in his midthirties.

But today Rusty wasn't in the mood for family or laughter or teasing. Today, every second that ticked by until he could leave was torture, like plucking his chest hairs out, one by one, with tweezers. Just a giant, in-your-face reminder that he didn't belong in this family. That he wasn't honest and good-hearted like the people surrounding him. That the really awful things he'd done in the past—not years ago but as recently as last night—made him the outcast. The black sheep. The sinner.

"I swear . . ." Hannah McClane swept through the patio door and shook her head as she moved around the kitchen island to where Rusty was standing, slicing tomatoes for the burgers his dad was supposed to be grilling outside on the deck. "Your father is getting harder of hearing by the hour. I told him fifteen minutes ago to start the barbecue, and he's only just doing it now."

Rusty glanced through the wide windows of his parents' house on the edge of Lake Oswego outside Portland, Oregon, and watched his dad toss Thomas a football as he slowly backed his way toward the barbecue where he was supposed to be playing grill master. All of Rusty's siblings were out on the deck, along with their significant others, chatting in the late-spring sunshine. Somewhere around the corner, out of Rusty's line of sight, his niece Emma squealed and yelled, "I get it, I get it!"

"Told ya you should have put Alec on grill duty," Rusty said.

Hannah huffed as she set another cutting board and a head of lettuce beside him before turning to grab a bowl from the cabinets. "Alec burns everything when I assign him to the grill."

"On purpose so he doesn't have to work the grill," Rusty muttered under his breath, focusing on the tomato in his hand.

His mother moved back beside him, pushed up the sleeves of her black cardigan, and reached for a knife from the block with a smirk. "Perhaps. But he's too distracted by their news today to be trustworthy. I'm afraid he'd burn his hand off if I put him near a flame."

Their "news" was Alec and his wife Raegan's announcement that they were expecting another baby—the reason for this impromptu family party that Rusty couldn't wait to get out of.

When he didn't respond, his mother glanced sideways at him, her sleek, dark hair cut into a stylish bob swaying near her ear. "Aren't you excited for your brother?"

"Sure." Rusty moved the tomatoes he'd sliced to the tray and went to work on the onion. "Why wouldn't I be?"

"I don't know. You just seem quiet today. I wasn't sure if the baby was the reason."

The baby was not the reason. He was happy for his brother—thrilled, even. Alec and Raegan deserved some joy after everything they'd been through. Though Rusty was sure a new baby was going to cause his brother serious anxiety both before and after it arrived next fall.

"I'm fine, Mom." He made quick work of slicing the onion and arranging it on the tray. Moving to the sink to rinse off the cutting board and knife, he added, "I'm always quiet, in case you forgot."

He worked up a half smile as she watched him, one that did nothing to alleviate the worry in her amber eyes. At fifty-five she had no wrinkles and not a strand of gray hair. She was still as youthful as she'd been the day he'd met her nearly twenty years before when she'd come into his life and she and Michael had eventually adopted him. Too bad he felt a million years older.

"I haven't forgotten. Doesn't mean a mother doesn't worry."

"You don't have to worry about me. I've told you that before." He shook the water from the cutting board and set it on the rack to drain. "I'm fine."

"I do, though. Especially when you show up with bandages on your hands like that."

His hands stilled on the dish towel as he looked down at the bandages covering the backs of his knuckles. The sounds of fists cracking against bone echoed in his head, reminding him just how he'd gotten those injuries last night. But just as quickly, he remembered the lie he'd told to cover for it.

He resumed drying his hands, then tossed the rag on the counter. "Not a big deal. I already told you."

"Yeah, I know." She sliced through the head of lettuce with a sigh. "Just everyday scrapes working on the vineyard. I'd still feel better if you let me look at them just to make sure you don't need any stitches."

Yeah, not happening. He did not need his physician mother inspecting his injuries because she'd know immediately his story was crap. She'd always been able to see right through his bullshit. Which was another reason he wanted out of this damn party *now*.

He pushed away from the counter. "Anything else you need me to do?"

"No, grab a drink and go on outside. This salad's the last thing, then I'll be out."

He moved around her and headed for the patio door.

"Rusty."

He stopped a foot from fresh air and freedom and glanced back. "Yeah?"

She set her knife on the block and reached for the hand towel, drying her hands as she moved around the island to stop in front of him. "I haven't told you this enough—*we* haven't told you this enough—but your dad and I are very proud of you."

A feeling he didn't like bubbled up in his gut. A familiar stab of shame and regret he wished he could ignore. He glanced down at the floor.

"It's true," his mom went on. "I know you think I was disappointed when you dropped out of college. I wasn't. I realize college isn't for everyone. And I know you think your dad and I were against you buying that property with part of your trust fund, but we weren't. We were just worried you were taking on more than you could handle." She reached for his hand and squeezed his fingers, careful to avoid his bandages. "But everything you've done with that property, planting the grapes, starting the vineyard, getting the loan to build the winery . . . It's amazing. *You* are amazing. You surprise me every single day with your resourcefulness. You've overcome so much in your life. I know you can do anything you set your sights on."

Shit. His eyes grew hot, and that uncomfortable feeling jumped from his stomach to his chest.

His mother smiled. "I'm not trying to embarrass you. I just want you to know that I'm proud of you. And I know I have no reason to worry because you have a good head on your shoulders and you only make good decisions, but I always will worry. I'm a mom, and that's what moms do. Because I love you."

Guilt swamped him. This was so not what he needed today. If she knew what he'd done last night, she wouldn't be proud. If she had any idea what he'd been up to for the last six years, she'd be horrified.

Not that he had any intention of telling her. All he wanted to do was get the hell through this damn party and get back to his property, where he could be alone with his memories.

"I-I love you too, Mom."

Her smile widened. "I know you do." She wrapped her arms around his waist and hugged him, pressing her cheek against his shoulder and filling his senses with the scent of lilies.

Fucking lilies. He closed his eyes and held her close, drawing in the scent that had first made him trust her, remembering that day so long ago when he'd been in the ER and she'd pulled back the curtain and stepped into his room.

He'd been thirteen, physically and emotionally broken, and she'd smelled like lilies when she'd bent over him in her blue hospital scrubs and white doctor's coat to look at his burns. He'd flinched at the touch of every other adult that day, traumatized by an event he still had night-mares about, but he'd told himself someone who'd smelled like his most favorite person in the world couldn't be bad.

He'd let Hannah McClane save his life that night, all because she'd smelled like a flower. And today, he fought back the guilt as he savored the scent and let her hug him. Some days he wished she'd smelled like Betadine that night he'd first met her. It would have made things so much easier. It would have made his *life* a helluva lot easier. He wouldn't be feeling like shit now if she had. He wouldn't be feeling anything now.

"Okay." She drew back and smiled up at him. "Enough mushy stuff for one day." Letting go, she said, "Go on outside and tell your father everyone's hungry."

He watched her turn and head back into the kitchen, feeling like a fraud, feeling lucky that she'd found him that night, wishing like hell he could be like his other siblings who'd all moved beyond their troubled pasts. But he couldn't. He was still stuck in the middle of his nightmarish upbringing—this time by choice. And there was no way he was going to drag her into it by confessing things she didn't need to hear.

He turned for the patio door just as it opened. His pint-size niece, Emma, burst into the room, darted behind him with a squeal, and wrapped one arm around his left leg. "Potect me, Unca Rusty!"

"Gosh dangit, Emma!" The youngest McClane sibling, Thomas, a senior in high school who was only a few months away from graduating, burst through the door right after her, nearly mowing Rusty down. "Gimme back the damn football!"

Laughter echoed through the open door from the deck. In the kitchen, their mother Hannah exclaimed, "Thomas! Language!"

"Sorry," Thomas muttered. But his apology was cut off when he spotted Emma behind Rusty. He twisted to the left to grab the football she'd tucked under her arm. "I said, give it back, Em!"

Emma squealed in delight again, thrilled with the keep-away game she'd started, and shifted behind Rusty's other leg so Thomas couldn't reach her.

Rusty wasn't so thrilled. He wasn't in the mood to play referee, even if it did involve his favorite five-year-old. Not after last night, and not after the last few minutes.

"Dude." Pressing a hand against the teen's chest, Rusty pushed Thomas back a step and pinned him with a hard look. "Chill out."

"You chill out. We were playing catch out there, and she had to ruin it, like always." When Thomas darted in the other direction to tear the football out of her arms, Emma shrieked, wrapped her chubby arms around the football, and raced for the kitchen.

Thomas shifted to run after her, but Rusty stepped in his path, blocking him. "She's five, Tommy Boy. Ruining things is what little sisters like to do."

Thomas huffed and glared past Rusty's shoulder. "She's not my sister."

"That's right. She's your niece, which means she can get away with being a brat, and you just have to deal with it."

Thomas scowled, and his shoulders slumped. "That's not fair."

Rusty rolled his eyes and shifted his hand to squeeze Thomas's shoulder. "Life's not fair, kid. The sooner you accept that, the better off you'll be."

A lesson Rusty had learned long ago.

Thomas's scowl deepened, but the kid was smart enough not to argue.

Behind Thomas, Emma's mother, Raegan, moved into the house along with Rusty's brother Alec and tucked a lock of auburn hair behind her ear. "Sorry about that, Thomas," she said. "Emma thinks it's a game."

"Yeah, deal with it, butthead." Alec tapped the back of Thomas's head as he moved past him toward the kitchen, ruffling Thomas's shaggy hair. "She wouldn't mess with you so much if she didn't like you. Don't you know anything about women?"

Raegan rolled her eyes.

The rest of the family filtered into the house to refill drinks and help Hannah take items out to the patio for lunch. Even though it was only late March, the weather the last few days had been unseasonably warm, and their mom had wanted to eat outside.

The doorbell rang. From the kitchen where she was still hiding behind her grandmother, Emma heard the sound, dropped the football with a thunk, and raced toward the front door. "I get it!"

Hannah shot a quick look at Alec. "Intercede. Fast."

Alec was already moving toward the foyer. "On it. You expecting anyone else?"

"No. But if it's a door-to-door salesman, she'll order ten of whatever he's selling before we know it."

"My kid? Never." Alec chuckled as he disappeared around the corner.

The room was filling up with too many people. That familiar feeling of being boxed in surrounded Rusty. Instead of joining in the conversations starting up around him, he ducked behind his brother Ethan and sister-in-law Sam and headed out to the patio, making a beeline straight for the cooler. Just as he'd hoped, his dad had loaded it with ice and craft beers from their favorite local pub.

He popped the top on a red and took a long pull. From the grill behind him, his dad said, "Is your mother almost done in there? These burgers are going to be ready in about two minutes."

Rusty lowered the bottle and raked a hand through his hair, itching to get on with the meal because it would mean he was that much closer to being able to leave. "Yeah. They're all grabbing stuff now."

"Good." Michael McClane glanced over his shoulder toward Rusty, then refocused on the burgers in front of him. "Your mother get done grilling you about those hands?"

Rusty's gut tightened. He lifted the bottle back to his lips as he said, "Yeah, she did."

His dad shook his head. "You got her all worried again. Gotta stop doing that, son."

And there was the guilt once more. Rusty's fingers flexed around the beer bottle. "I'll keep that in mind."

"Hey, Russ." Alec stuck his head out the patio door. "Can I talk to you for a minute?"

Rusty did not want to go back inside right now. Not with all the chaos happening in there. "Go ahead and talk."

Alec's worried gaze darted toward their father, then settled on Rusty. "There're two guys here to see you."

Rusty's brow lowered. "What two guys? No one knows I'm here."

"Uh . . ." Alec stepped out onto the deck, again glancing warily toward their father's back as he flipped the burgers. But it was the tense line of his shoulders that caught Rusty's attention and told him something was wrong. "Just a couple guys I think you work with. Come in here for a second."

None of the guys Rusty had hired to work on his property would stop by his parents' place on a Sunday afternoon. Spine tingling, Rusty moved toward his brother. As soon as he got close, Alec slapped a hand on his shoulder and ushered him into the house with a whispered, "What the fuck did you do? Two detectives are outside the front door, asking for you."

Every nerve in Rusty's body went on full alert. "Shit."

"'Shit' doesn't exactly put me at ease," Alec mumbled.

Setting his beer on the table with a sweaty hand, Rusty followed Alec around the rest of his siblings and significant others who were busily grabbing items from the kitchen and headed toward the entryway.

"Alec," their mother called just before they could disappear around the corner unnoticed. "Who was at the door?"

"Oh. Uh." Alec all but pushed Rusty into the entryway as he looked back at Hannah. "Encyclopedia salesman. No one special."

Emma was standing in the foyer playing with the hem of her shirt with her chubby little hands, yacking away at the two men in suits on the other side of the screen, when Rusty turned the corner. Her mother, Raegan, glanced over her shoulder when she heard Rusty's footsteps. "There he is." She shot Rusty a worried look as she reached for Emma's hand. "Come on, Em. Let's let Uncle Rusty talk to the nice policemen."

Raegan quickly brushed by Rusty, squeezing his forearm as she passed. The reassurance did little to ease the ball of stress suddenly building in his gut, though, because he could think of only one reason the police had tracked him down.

"Mr. McClane?" the shorter of the two men asked. He was only about five seven, late forties, with dark hair and eyes and a brown suit that looked as if it had seen better days.

"Yeah." Rusty tucked his hands into the front pocket of his jeans, trying to stay as relaxed and unintimidating as possible. "Who's asking?"

He flashed a badge. "I'm Detective Simms." He nodded at the second man, taller and older with salt-and-pepper hair and wearing a gray suit, as he slipped his badge into the inner pocket of his jacket. "This is Detective Pierce. We're with Portland Police. We'd like to ask you a few questions, if you don't mind."

"About what? I'm kind of in the middle of a family party here."

"Oh, this won't take long," Simms said. "We're just hoping you can clear up a few things for us regarding a case we're investigating."

Nothing was ever routine with the police. And Rusty didn't miss the way the man refused to answer his question. "I don't know how I can—"

"Could you please step outside, Mr. McClane?" Pierce asked.

Rusty's gaze shot toward the guy in the gray suit. His blue eyes were easy and relaxed, and there was no warning in his expression, but Rusty didn't trust the guy. There was something in his body language that screamed he was waiting for Rusty to say or do the wrong thing.

Good cop, good cop. Rusty had been baited by that before, and he didn't like where this was headed. He knew what they were doing. If he refused to move out onto the porch, it would raise suspicion, give them a reason to wonder. If he did, and he said something they didn't like, they could haul his ass in.

Before he could decide what to do, tiny footsteps echoed on the hardwood at his back, followed by Emma's small voice, yelling, "Unca Rusty!"

She threw herself at him and latched onto his leg with a death grip. As Rusty reached down to try to pry her free, footsteps sounded on the hardwood again, followed by Raegan's worried voice. "I'm sorry. Emma, come here." She disentangled Emma from Rusty's legs. Hauling her daughter up into her arms, she said, "I told you to leave them alone, sweetie."

Voices echoed from the other room. He could hear his mother questioning Alec about who was really at the door and what was going on, followed by his dad, who'd obviously abandoned the grill when he'd realized something was happening.

Shit. Whatever these yahoos wanted from him, he didn't want them to ask it in front of his family. Especially since he had a pretty strong hunch it had to do with last night, where he'd been, and what he hoped no one knew he'd done.

He pulled the screen door open and moved out onto the porch, shooting Raegan a secret message he hoped she caught.

Raegan nodded and reached for the door. "I'll just close this so she doesn't bother you again." To the detectives, she said, "Sorry about the interruption."

"No worries, ma'am," the taller one said with a half smile that didn't reach his eyes.

When they were alone on the porch and Rusty was sure no one inside could hear him, he folded his arms over his chest. "So what's this about?"

The shorter of the two detectives pulled a photograph from his breast pocket and held it up. "We're looking for a girl. Any chance you've seen her recently?"

Rusty's gut dropped like a stone as he focused on the blonde in the picture. She looked nothing like she had last night. Instead of wild curly hair and heavy makeup that made her look twenty-five, her hair was pulled back into a ponytail, her skin was pale and clean, and she was smiling in a head shot like the kind taken for a school yearbook.

A thousand thoughts and reactions pinged around in his head as he studied the photo. If he lied and they caught him in the lie, he could find himself in deep shit. But if he told the truth, there was no guarantee that wouldn't lead him to the shit either.

"Mr. McClane?" the taller detective asked.

"Uh. Yeah. She looks a little familiar."

The shorter detective jotted notes on a pad of paper Rusty hadn't seen him reach for. "Any chance you were at an establishment known as Leather and Lace in Portland last night?"

Double shit. They wouldn't be asking if they didn't already know the answer. Perspiration dotted Rusty's spine. "Uh—"

"It's a strip club," the taller detective cut in. "In case you can't remember."

"I know what it is." Rusty worked to stay relaxed. "Yeah, I was there. It's a legal joint. What's this all about?"

The shorter detective pocketed the picture again. "This girl was reported missing by her employer. We're checking in with anyone who might have come in contact with her last night."

Fuck. Rusty's mouth went dry.

"What happened to your hands, Mr. McClane?" the taller detective asked.

Rusty's adrenaline shot sky-high. Before he could answer, though, the front door of the house jerked open.

"What's going on out here?" His mother pushed the screen door open. "Rusty?" Her worried gaze darted from the detectives to Rusty and back again.

All that guilt came rushing back. He didn't want to do this in front of Hannah McClane. Not in front of the one person who believed in him more than anyone else ever had. He moved quickly to her side. "It's fine, Mom. It's nothing."

"It doesn't look like nothing." Voices echoed behind her. More of his family filled the entryway, questions already flying.

"Mr. McClane," one of the officers said in an irritated tone.

Rusty turned back to them. "I'd rather do this somewhere else."

The officers exchanged glances. The taller one looked back at Rusty with a superior expression. "We can do this down at the station if you'd prefer."

That was not what he'd prefer, but it was better than this. "Fine."

Shock widened his mother's eyes. "Rusty—"

"Right this way, Mr. McClane." The taller detective stepped back and held out his hand toward the blue sedan parked in the drive.

Hannah grasped his arm tightly. "Russell McClane, you tell me right now what's going on. Are you in trouble?"

He hoped like hell not. But something in his gut said that was wishful thinking at this point.

He kissed his mom's cheek, desperate to reassure her but also to get away from her and the rest of the family before one of these officers spilled something he didn't want them to know. "I'm fine. This is no big deal, and it won't take long. I promise. Go on and eat without me."

He twisted out of her grip before she could do something to keep him at her side, and he didn't look back at his siblings all whispering in the foyer as he crossed the drive and slid into the back seat of the sedan like a common criminal. He also didn't look up as the taller officer slammed the door, climbed into the front, and the car pulled out of the drive. Because he knew what each and every one of them would see in his eyes if he met any of their gazes.

They'd see guilt. A guilt he hoped like hell he could figure out how to cover before these detectives tore into him at the station.

CHAPTER TWO

True evil was hidden. Most never knew where it lurked, when it was a threat, or how it consumed. But Harper Blake did. She knew all about the trappings of evil because she'd seen it up close. And because even though she tried to deny it, something inside her was attracted to that evil on a very basic level.

She hit "Rewind" on the tape and waited while the image scrolled backward, then pressed "Play" again, this time narrowing her eyes as she watched Russell McClane's body language as he answered the detective's questions in the interrogation room at the Portland Police Department.

"Look," McClane said, running a hand through his dark hair in obvious frustration. "I already told you I don't know where she is. I didn't spend all that much time with her. It's not like I knew her well enough to know where she went after work."

"But you confirm you were alone with her."

"Yeah." He dropped his bandaged hand to the table and leaned back in his chair, meeting the detective's gaze head-on. "Check with the bouncer if you don't believe me. We left the VIP area together. He saw us. I went back into the club and got another drink. I have no idea where she went after that."

Harper hit "Pause," this time not to look at McClane but so that she could see the detective's face.

Noah Pierce.

Her blood hummed at just the sight of his familiar features on the screen. A friend at the PPD had given her the tape. As an investigator working with the attorney who'd been hired to represent McClane, she hadn't expected much when she'd popped it in the machine. She just wanted to get a read on McClane before she had to meet with the man. But she definitely hadn't planned on seeing Noah up close and personal. That had thrown her for a loop and stimulated all those evil receptors inside her all over again.

Her intercom buzzed. Turning quickly, she crossed the floor toward her desk and pushed the button. "Yes, Tina?"

"Mr. Renwick and the client are ready for you, Ms. Blake."

Shit. Go-time. "Thanks."

Pointing the remote at the screen, she powered down the TV, then reached for her blazer from the chair behind her desk. After slipping it on, she turned and checked her reflection in the small mirror on the wall.

She hated that seeing Pierce on that screen had rattled her. Smoothing her straight locks back from her face so they fell midway down her back, she breathed slowly and forcibly relaxed the muscles in her face so she wouldn't look like a crazed bitch when she met with the client. But Pierce had a way of getting under her skin, of making her feel self-conscious and old—way older than her thirty-two years.

So what if he thought her hair was muddy brown and her eyes were an unremarkable green? She didn't care what he thought of her anymore. She didn't even care that he'd used her to further his career, then tossed her aside when he didn't need her any longer, because one day soon, he was going to get what was due to him. One way or another, she was going to make certain of that. She just wasn't sure how yet.

"Enough," she muttered. Pushing thoughts of Pierce out of her head, she drew one last deep breath, turned and grabbed the file she'd read earlier from her desk, and headed for the conference room.

As far as gigs went, hers wasn't too bad: a private office on the twenty-third floor of one of Portland's tallest buildings, an amazing view of the city and the Willamette River, a flexible boss, and the ability to set her own hours. The pay wasn't anything to grumble about either—twice what she'd been making on the force. Of course, back then she'd been digging up evidence to put rapists and murderers behind bars. Now she was looking for ways to defend them.

"Innocent until proven guilty," she muttered to herself as she headed down the corridor, her heels clicking along the slate floor. It wasn't her job to decide guilt or innocence. It was her job to investigate and find evidence one way or the other for the attorney. What he did with that evidence wasn't her concern. Yet something in the back of her mind wasn't thrilled with the fact she knew he buried some of the information she brought him. Things the prosecution wasn't devious enough to find themselves.

"Still not a bad gig," she reassured herself. At least here she didn't have to deal with backstabbing, treacherous, blackhearted people like Noah Pierce. As for Russell McClane? She hadn't decided what he was yet.

She stopped outside the conference room, told herself not to think of Noah again, and knocked. A split second later, Andrew Renwick's voice called, "Come in."

Harper pushed the door open and stepped into the room. Daylight spilled through the wall of windows overlooking the river. An oval table surrounded by leather chairs filled the space. At one end of the room was a bookshelf lined with legal tomes; at the other, a whiteboard someone had recently wiped clean. Her boss, Andy, sat at the far end of the table, looking as unintimidating as a lawyer in his late fifties could look: his salt-and-pepper hair slightly ruffled, he was dressed in slacks and a pin-striped dress shirt rolled up to his forearms, his tie loosened and slightly askew. With clients, she knew he liked to come across as relaxed and easy to talk to so they'd be more open and honest with their facts. In a courtroom, he was the exact opposite—polished and professional, a total shark when the moment called for it.

"Right on time," Andy said, pushing back from the table.

"Thanks for including me in your meeting." Harper glanced toward the dark-haired man sitting to Andy's right. He pushed to his feet as she moved along the opposite side of the table and pulled out the chair on Andy's left. Her first impression was tall. Her second was way hotter than he'd been on tape.

Setting her folder on the table, she reached for the hand the man offered. "Mr. McClane, I'm Harper Blake."

"Ms. Blake is the firm's investigator," Andy said as he sat again.

Russell McClane didn't answer, only nodded slightly before taking his seat once more and looking back at Andy. But Harper hadn't missed the jolt of electricity that had shot up her arm when he gripped her hand, or the way those receptors inside her tingled with awareness like they used to when she was on the trail of something intriguing.

"As I was saying," Andy went on, glancing back at the papers in front of him. "It's all circumstantial at this point, but you're definitely a person of interest in the disappearance of Melony Strauss. The club has you on their security footage entering and leaving the premises. They also have footage of you alone with the girl." He flipped through his documents. "I don't think they've interviewed the bouncer yet, but they will. If his story doesn't match yours—"

"It will."

Harper sat quietly and watched Russell McClane as Andy went through the evidence he'd gathered. His face was all chiseled angles, his eyes like coal, his jaw covered in a dusting of dark scruff that matched his black hair. He was handsome but not classically so, more rough and rugged in his long-sleeved black Henley, dark jeans, and heavy work boots than slick and gorgeous like a lot of men she saw come through this office. And though his answers were convincing and confident, she sensed he was a man who'd seen and done a thing or two in his lifetime—and not all innocent and good things.

Something primitive stirred inside her. Something she recognized as attraction. She had a tendency to be drawn toward the bad boys, and Russell McClane had "dark and brooding bad boy" written all over him. That was a warning flag for her. That and the fact this case for some reason stimulated her evil receptors.

"Well." Andy closed the folder in front of him and leaned back in his seat. "At this point you're not being charged with anything. But it was smart of you to hire representation just in case. It's your word against the club owner's word at the moment." He glanced down at the scabs on McClane's knuckles, then up to his face. "He doesn't have a stellar reputation, so that's a plus in our favor. But the fact you don't have an alibi after leaving the club doesn't look good. We'll try to find the bouncer and see what he has to say."

McClane didn't answer. Didn't even flinch. Another thing Harper found interesting.

"Ms. Blake?" Andy turned toward Harper. "Is there anything you'd like to add at this point?"

"Nothing to add. I just have one question."

McClane had barely spared her a second glance since she'd entered the room, but he finally looked her way. There was no friendliness in his coal-black eyes when they met hers, though. Only indifference.

She didn't let that deter her. "Did you make arrangements to meet up with Ms. Strauss after she got off work at the Leather and Lace Club?"

His eyes narrowed. And something dangerous filled their depths. Something that told her she was right to be suspicious. "I don't know where she went after she left that club."

"I didn't ask that. I asked if you made arrangements to meet up with her."

He hesitated, as if considering his answer, then said, "Whether I did or didn't doesn't change the fact that I don't know where she went that night."

"It will if the police find her body."

"They won't."

Oh yeah, he was definitely hiding a lot. "You seem fairly confident."

"I am." With a last contemptuous look, he pushed back from the table and glanced toward Andy. "I have to get to work."

Andy rose and shook McClane's hand. "We'll be in touch."

McClane didn't look her way again. Just headed for the door without another word and disappeared into the hall.

When the door snapped closed behind him and they were alone, Andy dropped into his seat and met her gaze. "So? What do you think?"

"I think he knows a whole lot more about that missing girl than he's letting on."

Andy sighed and leaned back in his chair. "Agree."

Harper opened her file folder and pulled out a paper, which she slid across the shiny table toward Andy. "I did a little digging. Mr. McClane likes strip clubs. He's visited twelve in the last three weeks. The employees I talked to at each club confirmed he's also only interested in the youngest girls."

Andy studied the information she'd tallied with an unreadable expression. "What about Melony Strauss?"

"Not much there, I'm afraid." Harper pulled out another paper and handed it to him. "She lived in a dive apartment with a couple of the other girls at Leather and Lace, but according to them she kept to herself. Her employment records list her as turning eighteen three months ago, but I can't find a driver's license or any other identification anywhere to confirm that. I did get a recent photo of her."

"And?"

She handed him the picture she'd printed. "And there's no way that girl is eighteen."

Andy frowned as he studied the image taken of Strauss dancing in the club. "Damn."

"I'm thinking fifteen, maybe sixteen tops."

He looked back at the information she'd gathered, listing the clubs McClane had frequented in the last few weeks. "You've seen your fair share of shady characters. You think he's one of them? That he's some kind of predator?"

Harper thought back to McClane's dark eyes and his chiseled good looks. She knew first impressions could be deceiving. She also knew evil came in many different packages and that she wasn't always the best at recognizing it at first glance. Noah Pierce was a perfect example of that. "I'm not sure what he is. But I'm fairly certain there's more to him than meets the eye."

"In this case, I'm inclined to agree with you." He set her papers down and pinned her with a hard look. "I did some of my own digging. Strauss isn't the first dancer to go missing from a Portland club in the last year. Word on the street is that a handful of girls—all on the young side—have vanished recently. In most cases they're not reported because they're too young to be working in the clubs to begin with. Owners don't want to draw any unwanted police attention. But there's definitely something going on."

Harper's eyes narrowed. "How many girls are you talking about?"

"At least eight."

Shit. Eight was not a coincidence. "Are the police investigating this?"

"Not that I'm aware of. But it's interesting, especially considering this case. Wouldn't you agree?"

Yeah, it was more than interesting. She suddenly had a burning need to know where those girls had gone and if McClane had visited the clubs where they'd worked. "You think it's possible McClane is involved in these other disappearances?"

Andy shrugged. "I'm not speculating one way or the other. I can tell you I've known the McClane family for years. It's amazing what they've done with those kids. Rusty, though . . . well, he's always been a loner and a bit of an unpredictable character. Hannah and Michael did their best with him, but considering his background . . ." He sighed and shook his head.

Harper's instincts went on alert all over again. She knew from her research that Hannah and Michael McClane, both doctors, had adopted all five of their children—four boys and one girl. Three of the boys, including Russell McClane, had been adopted when they were in their early teens. They'd adopted the daughter when she was about ten, and the last sibling, also a boy, had been adopted only recently and was about to graduate from high school. All had come from questionable backgrounds, and all seemed to have straightened out their lives after joining the McClane family. All except Russell, it seemed.

"You think this missing girl is somehow linked to his past?" she asked.

"I'm not sure. It's our job to defend him, though, should this missing person case turn into something else. And to do that, we need to know Rusty's motivations."

Which meant he wanted her to dig into McClane's background and find out why the man seemed to have a thing for underage strippers.

Harper gathered her papers and pushed back from the table, her mind spinning with options and scenarios. "I'll see what I can find out."

Just before she reached the door, Andy called, "Oh, one more thing."

She paused and glanced back. "Yeah?"

"Be careful with this one. The people who run these clubs aren't exactly on the up-and-up. Most are involved in some pretty shady stuff."

"You don't have to worry about me. I used to work homicide, remember?"

"Yeah, but you always had a partner back then. Now you're going it alone. That concerns me. If you need help—"

"Andy." His concern touched her. "I'm a big girl who can take care of herself. I also know what I'm doing."

"I know you do. Just promise me you'll be careful."

A small smile curled her lips. "I will."

He held her gaze a long beat, then waved his hand and looked back down at his papers. "Okay, then. Go get on with it."

She pushed the door open and headed toward her office, a long-forgotten tingle of excitement stirring inside her. One she told herself had nothing to do with her attraction to the dark and brooding bad boy, McClane, and everything to do with the fact this case made her feel like a real detective again.

One whose life wasn't a total waste of time.

———

As soon as Harper was gone, Andy leaned back in his chair and rubbed his throbbing forehead.

He didn't like lying to Harper. He liked sending her into harm's way even less. But he needed answers, and she was the only way he was going to get them.

Stomach rolling at what he had to do next, he reached for the burner phone in his back pocket and dialed. He didn't want to make the call, but he knew if he didn't share what he already had, his life could be in even worse shit than it already was.

"Yeah?" A voice answered on the second ring. A familiar voice. A voice that sent the hair on Andy's neck standing straight up.

"I think I might have a lead on Robin Hood."

"Really? That's the best news I've heard all day. Tell."

"My investigator is looking into it. I picked up a client who's a person of interest in the missing stripper case at Leather and Lace."

"Name?"

Bile rose inside Andy's chest. "I-I can't divulge that yet."

"I want Robin Hood. If he escapes because you wouldn't give up a name, I won't be happy. And you know what happens when I'm not happy."

Fear spiked Andy's blood pressure. "As soon as I know for sure if it's him, I'll let you know. I promise. I'm looking into it. If it's him, I won't get in your way. But . . ." He knew he was walking a dangerous line here, but he didn't want to see anyone dead. Especially because of him. "But if it is him, it might make sense to let the cops deal with him. If this case goes where I think it might, he could be looking at spending the rest of his life in jail."

"I don't want Robin Hood in jail. I want him dead. And if you get in the way of that, he won't be the only person on my list."

Andy swallowed hard. "You know I won't."

"Good. Call me when you have more."

The line clicked dead in Andy's ear. Hand sweating, he dropped the burner phone on the table, rested his elbows on the shiny surface, and braced his palms against his eyes.

He'd gotten wrapped up with the wrong people long ago, all for a quick buck and a better life. And even though he'd turned things around and worked his ass off to stay on the straight and narrow ever since, he was still paying for that one fateful mistake.

His only hope now was that Harper would find the connections he'd laid out in front of her. And that it would be enough to get him off the hook once and for all.

Rusty wasn't in the mood to work. Or talk. But since it was almost noon on a Monday, he knew there was no way he was getting out of either. If he'd been smart, he'd have waited an hour to come in. By one o'clock Abby, his part-time office manager, would have been gone. But he'd already wasted half a day on that stupid meeting, and he knew he was likely going to waste at least another hour on his computer researching Harper Blake and whatever burr was stuck up the woman's skirt.

Bypassing the construction crew hammering away on the old barn he was converting into a new tasting room, processing facility, and office for his winery, he jogged up the three steps of the portable trailer he was currently using as an office and pulled the door open. Just as he expected, Abby was busy at work, hunched over some papers, her dark hair streaked with silver falling into her eyes.

"Hey." She looked up when he entered and adjusted her too-big glasses on her small nose as she shook back her wayward locks. "Was wondering when you'd show. I didn't see your truck at the house when I came in this morning. Dare I guess you had an exciting weekend?"

"Exciting" was not how Rusty would describe his weekend. And he wasn't about to get into any of it with his motherly assistant who took an unnatural interest in his personal life. If she had any clue what he'd been up to . . .

He moved past her desk, pulled open the small fridge in the corner of the room, and grabbed a soda. *Not going there.* He was already trying to figure out how he'd explain things to his real mother. He didn't need to explain things to Abby as well. "Nothing eventful. Just family stuff. Anything important going on here?"

"Nothing I can't handle." She handed him a trio of phone messages. "You need to deal with these this afternoon. Oh, and the guys up at the barn need you to walk through and mark where you want the electrical outlets."

Easy enough. "What about in the vineyard?"

"Pruning was finished this morning. Will and Ian are cleaning up, then taking off for the afternoon."

Rusty nodded. Will and Ian were college kids he employed part-time to help him manage the twenty acres that made up his vineyard. His operation was a small one. For the last five years, he'd focused on perfecting his biodynamic farming techniques by growing mostly pinot noir grapes and selling them to other wineries for processing. Now that he'd made a name for himself with a vineyard that had eliminated the need for chemicals but consistently produced high-yield fruit of exceptional quality, it was time to expand. Things would pick up once the winery and tasting room were complete, but for now it was just him, Abby, Will and Ian, and a handful of seasonal workers during the busy months.

"I'll take care of these." He moved past Abby, carrying the phone messages. "You heading out soon?"

"Yes. Just finishing paying some of these bills." She turned as he pushed the door to his office open. "Oh, and the bank wants you to call with an update on the construction progress sometime this week."

He knew that. It was already on his calendar. The bank that had given him the loan for the expansion was pressuring him to keep the construction on schedule. "I'll get to it. Have a good afternoon, Abs."

"You sure everything's o—"

He didn't hear the rest of what she said. The door clicked closed before she could finish her sentence. Which was completely fine with him. He liked Abby. She was efficient and gave him the space he needed. But she was friendly with his mom. At this point he didn't need to say or do anything that would make things worse for him with Hannah McClane.

The hammering from the construction crew echoed through the thin walls of the portable, making his nerves vibrate as he moved around his desk, dropped into his chair, and flipped open his laptop. He had half a mind to tell them to stop, that he wasn't in the mood for the incessant noise today, but he couldn't. Everything was riding on keeping to the construction timeline. If he didn't, the bank was going to come down on him hard, and he did not want to have to dip into the trust fund he'd gotten from his biological mother again. As soon as he could, he was paying back what he'd already borrowed. He didn't want the stench of that money on his hands any longer.

An image of the old arched double doors that led to the caves lit up his laptop screen, instantly relaxing him. Aside from the portable and the old barn, there was a small farmhouse on the corner of the property where he lived. But it was the caves he really considered home. They were what had sold him on this property almost fourteen years before. They were the reason his life had taken a major detour.

The caves had barely been anything back then—just cutouts, really, where the previous owner had stored farm machinery—but he'd known the moment he saw them that they could be more. So he'd dropped out of school, taken a big part of his inheritance to buy the land, and started a vineyard. Hannah and Michael had told him he was nuts, that he didn't know the first thing about owning property or being a farmer, and when he was twenty-one, they'd been right. But he hadn't cared. He'd had a vision, and he was determined to see it through. He'd struggled. He'd nearly worn his fingers to the bone—multiple times. He'd worked odd jobs to keep the place afloat. And now, almost a decade and a half later, he was months away from seeing his long-ago vision turn into a reality; from transforming a barren piece of ground into a real-life working winery.

If, that is, his extracurricular activities didn't catch up with him and land his ass in jail first.

Frowning, he tapped the keypad and pulled up a search engine. After typing in "Harper Blake," he waited while the sites populated and then scanned what came up.

He definitely wasn't feeling comfortable after that meeting with Renwick and his investigator. Renwick he was okay with—though the man wouldn't have been Rusty's first choice in attorneys for this particular situation, he knew his parents had set up the meeting because Renwick had handled Rusty's legal affairs since the time he'd joined the McClane family back when he was just a teen. He didn't particularly like Renwick knowing any of the shit he was into today, but he hadn't given the lawyer anything that could incriminate him. And the cops were operating on leads, nothing more. He knew they were never going to find that girl. None of that was what bothered Rusty. No, what bothered him was the man-hater vibes he'd picked up from the shark in heels who'd eyed him across that conference table as if he were a predator she couldn't wait to stab with her fancy pumps.

Portland Detective Resigns Amid Affair Scandal.

Rusty clicked the first link that popped up and started reading. And before he'd even gotten through half the article, he knew his assessment of the slim brunette with the hazel eyes had been right. She definitely didn't like men.

According to the article, she'd risen to the rank of detective after only a few short years on the force, not an easy feat for a woman. Part of that had been due to her name—her father had been the deputy chief of police until his death roughly two years before, and he'd been well respected throughout the city. But a bigger part had been due to the name she'd made for herself by being tough and unemotional at crime scenes, for getting the job done, and, more importantly, for solving her cases. Some in the department had even thought she was on the fast track to one day becoming chief of police. But her career had taken a serious nosedive when she'd been caught making a move on her very married partner one night after hours. She'd claimed it was a mutual attraction. He'd cried reverse sexual harassment and that she'd used her legacy with the department to try to intimidate him.

For a while, it had looked like a "he-said, she-said" case that would result in no more than a slap on the wrist for both of them. Until, that is, her previous patrol partner had stepped forward to inform the powers-that-be that she'd done the same thing to him. That she'd manipulated him into an affair he hadn't wanted by claiming she'd report him for sexual harassment if he didn't sleep with her and that no one would believe him if he told anyone since her daddy was the deputy chief of police.

Rusty sat back and frowned. Oh yeah, she was a definite man-hater. Not just because she'd lost her job, thanks to a man, but because two had called her out for being a black widow.

He definitely did not need a woman like that digging into his past and the fucked-up things he was doing after hours now. Especially not with the way she'd looked at him earlier today. She hadn't believed a word of his story. She'd branded him guilty of that girl's disappearance without a shred of evidence. And that meant he needed to stay as far away from Harper Blake as was humanly possible.

Shoving his laptop closed, he pushed to his feet and headed for the door. He was feeling too claustrophobic to sit in this dingy office and return calls. He'd check in with the construction guys, walk through the vines and inspect the pruning job, then visit the caves. That would settle him down. And when he was feeling more in control, then he'd figure out how the fuck he was going to keep his ass out of jail.

After, of course, he'd started researching which girl would be his next target.

CHAPTER THREE

Harper could count on one hand the number of friends she still had within the Portland Police Department. And she could count on one finger the number of friends in the PPD she trusted.

As she sat in the back corner of the coffee shop in downtown Portland, nursing the sorry excuse for a cappuccino in front of her, she hoped like hell she could still trust that one friend. And that she wasn't screwing herself over by talking to him now.

The front door to the trendy shop opened with a jangle of bells, and Brett Callahan stepped into the café. He spotted her in the back with one look, but no reaction showed on his weathered face—no smile, no frown, no nothing. Not that his nonreaction surprised her. Brett had always been hard to read.

Since he'd been promoted to detective only a few weeks ago, he was dressed in a gray suit that hung off his shoulders instead of the blue uniform she was used to seeing on him. Her stomach tightened as he pushed the hair off his forehead and wove around afternoon shoppers on a caffeine break and headed her way.

Sitting up straighter, she slid the mocha she'd ordered for him across the table, then looked up with a half smile as he drew close and pulled out the chair across from her. "Hey, Callahan."

"Blake." He sat and reached for the paper cup she'd left for him. "Thanks." He took a long sip of the chocolaty drink, then closed his eyes and sighed. "Needed this. Coffee downtown is shit . . . as I'm sure you remember."

She did. But, damn, she missed that shit.

"Thanks for meeting me," she said. "I hope it wasn't too much of an inconvenience."

"You're never an inconvenience. I'm just glad I had the time. Robinson's got me on three different cases that are keeping me pretty busy."

Daryl Robinson was the captain in charge of the detectives division at PPD and ran an extremely tight ship. He'd been promoted only about three months before Harper had been asked, not so eloquently, to resign, and she had very few fond memories of the man. In fact, he was one of the people on her list she couldn't wait to see go down because he hadn't had the balls to stand up for her.

She lifted her coffee and sipped, knowing better than to bring up any of the past today. "I'm sure you'll make the best of it. How's your new partner?"

"Stark?" He sipped his mocha again and set the paper cup on the table. "Eh. Kind of a pain in the ass, but we get along okay." He pinned her with a look. "How 'bout you? I'm sure talking about the department's the last thing you want to do. How's the new gig? Still enjoying it?"

Fake it till you make it. That had become her personal mantra the last year. "Good. Plenty to keep me busy too."

Callahan's eyes narrowed as they held hers. And a heartbeat of silence passed before he said, "Liar."

If there was one thing she could count on from Brett, it was the fact he could see through the bullshit. Even hers.

Sighing, she leaned back in her chair and gripped the warm cup in her palm. "It's a job. Is that better? It pays well, and I've got an office with a great view, unlike your little basement hovel. I also don't have Robinson breathing down my neck."

Brett chuckled and lifted his cup again. "Got me there. Your boss hiring? Maybe I should look into a new gig."

He was joking, of course. Brett would hate her job. He loved being out on the street where the action happened. That was where he felt most alive. In that way, they were alike.

"Sadly for you, this one's all mine." She took a big sip to wash the bitter words down.

Brett was silent for a few seconds, then said, "Give any more thought to opening your own PI firm? My buddy O'Donnell says there's plenty of work for PIs in this city if they're willing to—"

"We've talked about this." It was her turn to pin Callahan with a look. "I'm not interested in chasing after cheating husbands, which is the bulk of work a female PI in this town will get."

Brett frowned. "You don't know that."

She did. Hell, it was the bulk of work she was getting in Renwick's firm.

Not wanting to think about that too much, she shifted in her seat. "Don't worry about me. I'm fine. Besides, my occupational status is not why I asked to meet with you."

"It's not?"

"No. I wanted to thank you for the tape you passed my way. And to ask if there's anything else you can tell me about the Melony Strauss missing person investigation."

Brett tensed and leaned forward to rest his forearms on the table. "I'm assuming this is off the record?"

"Of course."

His eyes narrowed. "What's your interest in this case?"

There was no sense hiding anything. "Russell McClane is a Renwick client. I'm digging into his background for Andy but was curious if you had any new info on the investigation."

"Ah."

She wasn't sure what that meant. "You've given me info before."

"This time's different."

"Why?" She hoped it wasn't because he was now a detective instead of a beat cop.

He glanced around the coffee shop, checking to see if anyone might be listening. Appearing satisfied that they weren't being watched, he faced her again and said quietly, "Because I'm connected to this case, and as such, I'm not supposed to be involved in it."

That triggered her interest receptors. She leaned forward. "How are you connected?"

He shot a look around the coffee shop again. "My buddy O'Donnell? The one who runs that security company I told you about before? He's engaged to Russell McClane's sister."

Shit. She hadn't realized that. "How'd they connect you to O'Donnell?"

He huffed. "Do you not read the papers? O'Donnell and Kelsey McClane were caught in the Goldman Building collapse last month where they used to tape *Good Morning Portland*. She's a big-time fashion designer. Her name's been everywhere since that bombing. I played intermediary between her and O'Donnell and the FBI when they were being questioned."

Harper definitely remembered the bombing. It had been national news and a huge deal here in the Rose City. But she hadn't paid much attention to the players.

She tipped her head as she looked across the table at her friend. "Considering your connection, it makes sense they're keeping you off the case. Of course, it also would make sense if you're keeping tabs on the investigation."

His frown told her, yep, he totally was. "I don't know Russell McClane personally."

That actually made things easier for her. "I'm not interested in your personal interpretation of the man. I'm curious about the facts of the case. Strauss is not that girl's real last name, and we both know it."

Brett frowned again and looked around the coffee shop. "You're gonna get me into trouble, you know that? And I haven't even been at this job a full month yet."

She had him. The tension in her belly eased. "No, I won't. Just tell me what you know. I promise no one will find out I got the info from you."

Brett sighed and met her gaze. "PPD's still trying to find her. But yeah, Strauss is an alias. Best working theory at this point is that she was a runaway, probably living as a homeless teen on the street before she got roped into working at Leather and Lace."

"Do the detectives have any idea where she came from?"

He shook his head and swallowed a mouthful of coffee. "Not yet, but they're not looking into her background too hard. They're more focused on finding her body."

"So they think she was killed? What evidence do they have?"

"None."

"But you said—"

"Listen carefully." He leaned forward and lowered his voice. "Have you heard any whispers on the street about a character named Robin Hood?"

"No. Should I have?"

"You're going to. We've had four dead prostitutes turn up in Portland in the last six months, on top of eight missing, underage girls. And working girls we've interviewed have whispered about a guy who goes by that name. Up until now, the department hasn't been able to connect him to these murders, but with this case, they're hoping to."

"How?"

"However they can."

Her gaze narrowed. "You think McClane is this Robin Hood character?"

"I don't. They want to pin that name on him, though."

Harper's brow wrinkled. "I don't understand. You just said you have no concrete proof tying him to Melony Strauss's disappearance."

Brett shook his head and glanced around one more time. "You're not following me. It doesn't matter if they have proof. The string of dead prostitutes has drawn some national media to the city. And with all the bad press Portland's received lately because of its sex-trafficking situation, it's only a matter of time before the press connects this missing girl. The mayor's pressuring the department to solve the case before it blows up on the nightly news. He's planning to run for governor, if you don't already know. An unsolved serial killer case is the last thing he needs at the moment."

That all made sense to Harper. "But why McClane? If there's no hard evidence linking him to Strauss—"

"Think back, Harp. Where have you heard the McClane name before? And I'm not talking about that bombing. There was another McClane in the news over a year and a half ago. Connected to a huge scandal here in Portland."

Harper's mind spun. A year and a half ago she'd been pretty consumed by her own personal chaos. She couldn't quite remember what scandal had happened in the ci—

Her eyes widened when she made the connection. "Oh shit. Miriam Kasdan. The socialite who went down for child trafficking. There was a McClane connected to that case, wasn't there?"

Brett nodded. "Alec McClane. A reporter. Kasdan was implicated in his daughter's abduction. McClane and his ex-wife were the ones who blew the lid off that whole case and are the reason Kasdan and her son are now sitting behind bars. Guess which politician Miriam Kasdan was a huge donor to?"

Harper's stomach pitched. "Gabriel Rossi. The mayor of Portland."

"Bingo. Millions of dollars in his political coffers, gone because of the McClane family. When Russell McClane's name turned up in connection with Melony Strauss's missing person case, you can only imagine what the mayor's reaction was."

Yeah, she could only guess.

"The mayor's putting pressure on the detectives working Strauss's case to find her body. And when they do, it wouldn't surprise me if they find a way to tie McClane to her death. He doesn't have an alibi."

Harper's stomach pitched. Guilty or innocent, no one deserved to be targeted simply because of a name. But her vision turned red when she remembered Noah Pierce interrogating McClane on that tape. "Please tell me someone has the smarts to take Pierce off this case."

Brett frowned again, looking sick himself before he tossed back the rest of his coffee. "Sadly, I can't tell you that."

Her jaw clenched hard.

"I know." Brett lowered his empty cup to the table, reading her reaction even though she fought like hell to keep her face neutral. "Now you know why the guy is basically fucked."

Yeah, she did. Pierce had no morals and wouldn't give a shit about falsifying evidence to please his boss. He'd fucked her over, and she'd been his damn partner. To get ahead in the department, he wouldn't even think twice about framing an innocent man. When she'd watched that tape yesterday, she'd had no idea it could be this bad.

Not that she was convinced Russell McClane was innocent or guilty of anything . . . but just knowing that Noah Pierce was itching to pin this on McClane made her that much more determined to uncover the truth.

The bells above the door jangled, distracting Harper from her anger, and she glanced that way to see two uniformed police officers step into the café. They didn't immediately see her and Callahan, and for that she was thankful. "I think that's your cue to go."

"Yeah." Brett rose and pushed back from the table, stepping to the side, out of the officers' line of sight as they moved toward the counter to place their orders. "I need to get back to the office anyway."

"Thanks for the info. I appreciate it."

"No problem. I can't tell you if your client is guilty or innocent, but I can tell you that everything I know about the McClanes is on the up-and-up. They're a good family."

Harper knew looks could be deceiving. She also knew that everyone had secrets. Her included. "Thanks. I'll keep that in mind."

"Find the girl, Harp. Dead or alive, that's the only way you're going to be able to help McClane." With one last glance back at the officers who still hadn't seen them, Brett tugged his coat on and headed for the side door.

Alone, Harper looked out the wide windows and watched as he jogged across the street in the late-afternoon light, stepped onto the sidewalk, and disappeared around a corner. She didn't really care if Russell McClane was innocent or not. It wasn't her job to judge a client one way or the other. But if the department was trying to frame him, that made the man all the more interesting to her. And, she had to admit, that made this current case a thousand times more appealing.

For the first time in months, she was actually excited about her job. Which was more emotion than she'd felt in a really long time.

———

Rusty knew it was probably a safe bet to lay low for a while, but he'd never been one to listen to logical advice—from others or his own conscience. And his current project was too important to ignore.

He checked the picture he'd printed off one last time, memorized the details of the photo in the neon lights illuminating the dark street from above, then stuffed the picture into the inner pocket of his jacket. Clouds had moved in during the afternoon, and the temperature had dropped dramatically. Shrugging deeper into his denim coat, he moved down the damp sidewalk and slowed as he approached three women loitering near the entrance to a dark alley.

All three were dressed in skimpy skirts, high heels, and short jackets that kept their arms and torsos somewhat warm but didn't hide their bodies. And all three were dolled up with heavy makeup, big hair, and gaudy jewelry that marked them as working girls.

He recognized the bleached blonde puffing on a cigarette while leaning against the side of the building. The other two were new. Or new to him.

"Hey, handsome," the blonde said, her dull-brown eyes brightening as he drew close. "Haven't seen you 'round here in a while." She drew a long puff of the cigarette and pushed away from the wall. "Thought you'd gone and forgotten 'bout lil ol' me."

She blew smoke all over his face with her last words, then smiled up at him with a crooked Cheshire grin.

"Been busy." He glanced past the blonde toward the brunette and redhead watching him closely. "New friends?"

"New, but not nearly as good as me." The blonde cupped his jaw with long, red-tipped fingers, drawing his attention back to her. "You lookin' for a good time, honey? You come to the right place. Barbie's got ya covered."

The brunette huffed and crossed her arms over her ample chest, cocking her hip in what Rusty knew was meant to be a seductive move but fell short because she was too thin. "Her name ain't really Barbie, and she don't have no clue what a good time is. You want a real good time, sweet cheeks, you come on over here and let Minx take care a ya."

The blonde shot a glare over her shoulder. "You shut your mouth, Minx, or I'll make sure you never work this town again."

The brunette's whole body tensed, and she dropped her hands to her sides and curled them into fists with a glare that could stop traffic. "Oh, you wanna piece a me? Come on, then."

The redhead, leaning up against the building on the other side of the alley, rolled her eyes as if she'd seen this drama too many times to count and didn't give a rip who won or lost.

"Now, ladies." Rusty had watched this scene unfold more than once himself, and he really didn't want to get in the middle of a catfight again if he could avoid it. "No sense fighting over me. Sadly, I don't have time for a good time. I'm just looking for a little information."

The blonde glanced back at him and frowned. "Information's still gonna cost ya. Ya know that."

Rusty did. He pulled three twenties from his pocket and held them up. "I'm looking for a girl. Strawberry blonde, young, new to the scene."

The brunette's eyes lit up.

The blonde, however, only frowned deeper. "You tryin' to save another one, honey?"

Rusty didn't answer. Tugging the photo from his inside jacket pocket, he held it up so the women could see, then said, "Seen her recently?"

The blonde and the brunette studied the picture. In the silence, Rusty could see they were both trying to figure out a way to convince him they recognized the girl so they could take all the money.

The blonde shifted in her sky-high heels. "Yeah, she's familiar. I mighta seen her yesterday."

"No, I'm the one who saw her yesterday." The brunette tensed as she stepped closer. "Barbie only pays attention to the guys. But I know I seen this girl."

"Shut up, you bitch." The blonde shot a glare at the brunette before looking up at Rusty with big eyes. "You know I always tell ya the truth, honey. Don't listen to Minx. What ya wanna know about the girl?"

They were both lying. Rusty stuffed the picture back in his jacket pocket. "I need to know where she is. Tonight."

Wheels spun in both the women's eyes. The blonde licked her lips and glanced at the brunette. "I-I'm pretty sure I saw her a couple streets over. Isn't that where we saw her, Minx?"

Minx shot Barbie a glare, then her eyes widened, as if she'd just clued in to the game. "Oh yeah. That's right. We saw her over on Third, right? Near Voodoo."

Voodoo was the famous Voodoo Donuts shop in downtown Portland.

"Yeah. That's where we saw her." Barbie nodded encouragingly, clearly thinking she could scam Rusty over and they could split the cash. "She's workin' Burnside."

"Yep." The brunette nodded emphatically. "Workin' Burnside."

Wrong. The girl wasn't working any street. At least not yet.

The redhead leaning against the wall huffed.

Rusty glanced her way. Her back was to the wall, one knee bent, her high heel braced on the bricks behind her as she stood with her hands stuffed in the pockets of her fake fur coat and a bored expression on her face. She looked to be in her late twenties, thin but not overly so, and her skin was clear and healthy, showing no signs of the drug use so many in this line of work were known for. "You disagree?"

Barbie and Minx both turned icy glares toward the redhead.

The redhead frowned at the women. "Not necessarily."

The other two relaxed and looked back at him with expectant expressions.

"They mighta seen that girl near Voodoo earlier," the redhead said, "but she isn't there now."

"How do you know?" Rusty asked.

"Because she walked by here about an hour ago, and I paid attention to where she went."

Rusty pulled out the photo once more. "And you're sure it was this girl?"

The redhead pushed away from the wall and stepped forward, focusing on the photo. And as she drew close he saw that she wasn't quite as old as he thought. Maybe early to midtwenties. And in her cleavage where her fake fur coat fell open, he noticed the faint end of what looked like a surgical scar on her sternum. "Yep. It was her. Don't often forget a girl that young going where I saw her go." Her gaze lifted to Rusty's face and narrowed. "What's a guy your age doing looking for a girl that young?"

Rusty tucked the photo back in his pocket. "Here." He held out the sixty bucks. "This is yours. Just tell me where she went."

Minx and Barbie both huffed in disbelief. The redhead only stared at the money but didn't take it.

Slowly, her gaze lifted back to Rusty's. "Look, I don't have a problem with a kid lying about her age to wait tables. We all have to do what we have to do, to survive. But I'm not going to be a party to someone taking advantage of stalking a kid all becau—"

"You've got the wrong idea," Rusty said. The redhead might make her living on the street, but she was smart, and she wasn't one to be easily deterred. "I'm not trying to take advantage of her. I'm trying to help her. She doesn't know what the people she works for are planning."

The redhead's gaze held his, searching, he knew, for some kind of verification that what he was saying was true. And in her green eyes he saw not only skepticism but also something that marked her as a survivor. "If I find out you're lying—"

"You won't." Rusty added protective to her list of attributes. He liked the redhead immediately. "Now where'd she go? She might not have a lot of time left."

The redhead pursed her lips, then nodded to her left. "She's at Assets. She was with that dickhead with the accent. I don't like that guy. He gives me the creeps. I'd have gone in and told that girl not to be in a place like that myself, but the bouncers won't let me in."

Rusty glanced down the street where the neon sign for the strip club known as Assets flashed roughly two blocks away. Adrenaline surged in his veins.

He turned back to the redhead and pushed the cash into her hand. "Thanks." He also tugged a pen and a blank card from his inner pocket and jotted his cell number on the card, then handed it to the redhead as well. "You ever want to get off the street and get a real job, you give me a call. I'm hiring."

The redhead narrowed her eyes on the card, then on him. "What kind of job?"

Definitely a survivor. Just like him. She simply needed someone to take a chance on her. "Wine. Lots and lots of really good wine."

Pulling out two more twenties, he turned and handed one to each of the other two women. "You all were a big help, ladies. I appreciate it."

He made it two steps down the sidewalk before the redhead called, "Hey! You're not that guy all the girls have been talking about, are you? The one they call Ro—"

"That guy?" Rusty winked. "Don't have any idea what you're talking about."

He didn't wait around to hear the redhead's response. With the sound of the three women's whispered voices at his back, he pulled a baseball cap out of his jacket pocket, pulled it on so the brim hid his face from any cameras that might be scanning the outside of the strip club, and moved quickly down the street. But he seriously hoped the redhead considered his offer and called him.

Assets was just like the club he'd been in the other night. Dark, smoky, and reeking with desperation. As he stepped through the doors and moved into the club, his stomach churned as he scanned the patrons at small circular tables in front of the stage where girls in various stages of undress were wrapped around poles, gyrating in the flashing lights. A heavy dance beat pounded out of speakers and vibrated through the floor.

He narrowed his gaze, checking each face for the one in the picture. None on the stage matched. He searched each of the waitresses in skimpy outfits, serving drinks and clearing empty glasses from tables, but still none fit the description. Growing desperate, he glanced toward the back of the club, where the VIP area was located behind a half wall. Seeing several shadows moving behind the wall, he headed in that direction, only to slow his steps when he spotted a door open off to his right.

A bouncer was stationed outside the door with his arms crossed over his chest. As one of the dancers drew close, leading a man by the hand, the bouncer gave the man the once-over, then nodded and stepped to the side, allowing them to pass. Rusty only caught a glimpse of the hallway before the door closed behind them, but he instinctively knew that was where he needed to look next.

A quick check of the VIP area told him he was right. The girl wasn't there. Which meant the guarded door was his best bet. Only there was no way he was getting through that door alone. Scanning the room again, careful to keep his head tipped down so his face was shadowed by the brim of his cap, he zeroed in on the closest stripper looking to make a quick buck and headed her way.

The brunette was dressed in a skimpy white bra, matching short skirt, and four-inch platform stilettos. Flirting with two guys at a back table nursing beers, she was clearly trying to get their attention so they would follow her to the VIP area. Both men—decked out in jeans and flannel shirts, sporting heavy beards—were too busy ogling the dancers on stage to pay the brunette much attention, though, which was perfect for Rusty.

He touched her arm at the elbow. Her gaze swung his direction. And one look was all he needed to see she was stoned out of her mind.

"Hey, handsome." She stumbled his way with a crooked smile. "You lookin' for a good time?"

She all but fell into him, and as he reached out to make sure she didn't take him down, he recognized the scents of cigarette smoke, gaudy perfume, and hairspray.

She righted herself with a giggle, held on to his arms, and straightened. "Oh, you're strong. And hard."

"Uh-huh." She wasn't particularly attractive—or all that young. Up close the lines on her face made her look closer to forty than the twenty he'd assumed from a distance, and her skin had that leathery, blemished quality from years of drug use.

"*Mmmm.* I like dancing for strong men." She pursed her lips and squeezed his biceps as she shimmied closer. "How 'bout you and I go back to the VIP area and I show you just how hard I can make you."

That definitely wasn't going to happen. But he wasn't opposed to using her to get what he wanted.

Continuing to hold her up at the elbows so she wouldn't fall, he nodded and glanced past the VIP area toward the dark hallway that led to the secret area of the club. "What if I want something more than just a dance?"

Her gaze darted to the dark hallway, then slid back to Rusty, and when her eyes met his, he saw a spark of excitement. Only this excitement had nothing to do with attraction and everything to do with cold hard cash. "I don't know what you mean, handsome." She winked. "We only give dances here."

He leaned close, fighting back a wave of nausea when her smoke-filled hair brushed his cheek, and pressed a wad of bills into the palm of her hand. "I'm pretty sure you know exactly what I mean. And what I want."

The brunette sucked in a breath and carefully glanced down at the two hundred-dollar bills in her hand, keeping them out of sight from anyone else in the club.

"You give me what I want," Rusty whispered into her hair, "and there's more where that came from."

Her gaze shifted from the cash to his worn Romeos, then slowly lifted to his jeans, gray T-shirt covered by a flannel shirt, denim jacket, and, finally, to his face. And oh yeah, there were definite dollar signs in her eyes now. "Hmm." In a move that was anything but sexy, she rubbed her breasts against his chest and sighed. "Looks like tonight is your lucky night."

Rusty wasn't convinced of that yet, but if she got him behind that door, he hoped it would be soon.

Slipping the hundreds discreetly into her bra, the brunette dropped her hand to his and pulled him behind her toward the dark hallway. "Follow me, good lookin'. I'm about to rock your world."

The bouncer was a big guy, at least six five and close to three hundred pounds. As they drew close, Rusty knew he was memorizing every inch of Rusty's face.

"Heya, Jay," the brunette said with a wink as they approached.

The bouncer tensed, lifting his shoulders at least another inch. "Destiny. You ain't supposed to be back here tonight. You're not on the schedule."

The brunette only rolled her eyes. "Relax, would ya?" Tugging a twenty out of her bra, she slipped the bill in the bouncer's front pants pocket and said, "No one has to know but us."

The bouncer's jaw clenched, but as the brunette maneuvered around him and tugged Rusty with her, he didn't try to stop them. Just turned after them and said, "I'm serious, Destiny. If the boss man finds out—"

"He won't," she tossed over her shoulder. "Because you're not going to tell him, are you, Jay?"

Jay frowned and shook his head. As he turned away from them, the brunette mouthed to Rusty, "Sphincter police. Ignore him."

Rusty wasn't entirely sure what that was all about, but as soon as they made it past the bouncer, he didn't care. The hallway curved to the left and then to the right, and they followed it like a maze through the building before it dropped to a set of stairs that led down a flight and finally opened to a wider hallway illuminated by an eerie red light.

Doors were spaced every ten feet or so down the long corridor on both sides. Some kind of heavy metal echoed out of speakers hidden in the ceiling, drowning out noises coming from beyond the doors. But as the brunette led him through the hallway, checking each door she passed to see which one was unlocked, Rusty didn't miss the unmistakable sounds of sex oozing around him—hinges squeaking, walls rattling, grunts, and groans, and even a high-pitched female scream now and then that sounded more practiced than pleasured and not the slightest bit arousing.

Halfway down the hall, Destiny pushed a door open and pulled Rusty into the room after her. "Come on in this way, big boy."

Rusty was barely listening. His gaze was already fixed on the door at the end of the hall, the one that was partway open and through which he could just hear muffled voices.

He itched to follow those voices, but he knew he'd never make it very far if he didn't take care of the woman currently tugging on his arm first.

Destiny closed the door at his back. The room was nothing special. A box with a cement floor, a bed covered by a shabby-looking red comforter, and bare walls but for one rectangular mirror opposite the mattress.

"So." Destiny let go of his hands and slinked closer, pressing her palms to his chest and rubbing her lower body against him. "What do ya like?"

Definitely not that. But Rusty knew better than to push her away too quickly.

Ignoring what she was attempting to do with all her rubbing, he leaned down until his face brushed her sprayed-stiff hair. The scents of cigarette smoke and cheap perfume filled his nose. "Where's the camera?"

She stopped her useless rubbing. "I-I don't know what you're talking about."

"Yeah, you do," he said so only she could hear him, not anyone else who might be listening outside in the hall. "I don't care if your boss is a perv. I just want to make sure he doesn't take a cut of your money."

That seemed to relax her. She turned her head his way, causing her hair to scrape his cheek, and smiled. "On the top of the mirror."

Rusty shifted his gaze that direction without moving his head and spotted the small camera on the upper right corner, likely unnoticed by most of the clients who ventured into this room. "How often does he check the feed?"

"Only at the end of the night. He's too busy out on the floor, making sure no one's stealing from the dancers."

Perfect.

Rusty peeled off his coat and dropped it on the bed, then tugged off the flannel button-down he'd worn over a gray tee and threw it in the direction of the mirror. The shirt hooked the right corner, covering the small surveillance camera.

"Nice." Destiny's grin widened. "You've got talent." She reached for the hem of her skimpy bra-top. "Now, why don't you show me your other talents?"

Before she could get it off, Rusty placed a hand on her arm, stopping her. "Thanks." He kept his voice low. He was pretty sure there were no microphones in the room—sound was an extra surveillance piece he was sure her boss wouldn't spring for in a joint like this—but he wasn't about to be stupid, just in case. "But that's not what I came for."

Destiny glanced at his waistband and shrugged. "It's your money."

She started to drop to her knees, but Rusty grasped her by the arms, pulling her back up. "I'm not here for that either." Confusion crossed her face as he let go of her and reached for the photo from his jacket pocket. "I just want information. I'm looking for this girl. Have you seen her in here tonight?"

Destiny scowled. "You said you was gonna pay me."

Rusty glanced toward the camera to make sure it was still covered, then looked back down at her. "I will. The deal hasn't changed. You tell me what I want to know and the money's yours."

Skepticism filled her eyes. "Without any action?"

"No action necessary. Just information."

She tipped her head and eyed him warily. "You gay or somethin'?"

Rusty smirked. He'd been asked that before. "Not gay."

"So ya into virgins?" She nodded at the photo with a scowl. "Cuz I guarantee that one doesn't know how to take care of a man."

She clearly felt threatened. "My reasons for looking for her are my own." He held the photo higher so she was forced to look at it. "Focus if you want the cash. Have you seen her tonight?"

Destiny snatched the picture from his hand and brought it super close to her eyes, squinting as if she had eyesight problems. "I don't know. Maybe."

"Maybe?"

Scowling, she shoved it back at him. "I saw her in the club earlier tonight."

"And?"

She heaved a sigh and crossed her arms with a roll of her eyes.

Rusty pulled out another hundred. "And?" he asked again.

Her eyes locked on the cash. "And that prick they call Mihail brought her back here about a half hour ago." She snatched the bill from his fingers and stuffed it in her bra with a self-satisfied smirk. "You want more, you gonna have to pay more."

"Do you know more?"

"Course I know more. I pay attention. I ain't stupid like some o' the girls."

No, she wasn't. She obviously knew her working days were coming to an end and was doing whatever she could to make a buck. He pulled out another hundred. When she reached for it, he tugged it away from her hand. "Not so fast. Tell me what else you know. Who's Mihail, and what did he want with the girl?"

"Besides the obvious?"

Rusty didn't answer. They both knew whoever this Mihail was, he wasn't dragging the girl back here for sex. She wouldn't have been advertised on that website for thousands of dollars if her handler was simply going to pimp her out in the back of a seedy club.

The brunette sighed and glanced toward the hidden camera. Lowering her voice even more, she said, "Look, if I tell ya, it's gonna cost ya way more than a measly hundred. I could get in serious trouble for giving this up."

"Giving up something you're not supposed to know?"

She smirked. "Yeah, that."

He tugged out two more hundreds. "Okay, spill."

Her eyes lit up. This was probably more money than she'd made in weeks. "I don't know exactly who Mihail is, I just know he only shows up when the boss gets his hands on a really young girl. If she's pretty, the boss man usually gets the girl to wait tables for a couple weeks, then Mihail shows up, he heads back here with the girl, then no one ever sees her again."

"Where does he take the girls? If they come back here, they have to leave somehow."

She rolled her eyes as if he were a complete moron. "The tunnels. Duh. There's a set of stairs back here that run down there. The tunnels run all over under the city. Haven't you ever taken one of those tours?"

Shit. He hadn't even considered the Shanghai Tunnels. Didn't know they were still in use by anyone except tourists.

"Pretty sure they get 'em out that way."

"How do they avoid being spotted by the tours?"

"Beats me." She eyed the money with a frown. "They proly don't go where the tours go. Now look, I gave you the info you wanted. You gotta give me the money, or I'm calling Jay down here."

Rusty had no intention of running into Jay the bouncer again. And he definitely didn't want Jay to know where he was heading next. He handed the brunette the hundreds, tugged on his coat, then pulled out one last hundred. "Stay here for at least fifteen minutes, make whatever kind of noises you make with a client, and then you can leave."

He pushed the money into her hand and turned for the door.

"Hey," she whispered at his back. "Where you goin'?"

With one hand on the door handle, Rusty glanced over his shoulder. "Nowhere. And if anyone asks, we never met."

She stuffed the extra hundreds in her bra and flopped back on the bed. "Fine by me. I never seen ya in my life."

Rusty fixed the collar of his coat as he stepped out into the dimly lit hall. The sounds of sex echoed around him, but he ignored them, focusing only on the door at the end of the hall he'd spotted earlier.

He had no idea if that door led to the tunnels or even if the girl from the picture was down there, but he'd come this far and he wasn't leaving until he checked it out for himself. His adrenaline pulsed as he headed down the corridor, and in the back of his mind, he hoped he wasn't too late.

CHAPTER FOUR

Harper was pretty sure this night was going to end up as one giant bust.

She'd covered twelve blocks downtown on foot, hitting most of the places where working girls tended to congregate. Not a single one had seen Melony Strauss in the last week, and none had shown any kind of reaction that led Harper to believe they even recognized the girl. She was cold and damp now, thanks to the light rain that had decided to fall in the last thirty minutes, and her feet hurt like a bitch. The next time she got the bright idea to hit the streets in search of information, she needed to remember to wear comfortable shoes instead of her trendy boots.

Deciding this location would be it for the night, she crossed the wet, empty street and headed toward the trio of girls camped out near an alley. The blonde was leaning into a car parked against the curb, her ass all but hanging out of the short skirt. The brunette was walking back and forth in front of the alley, shouting at any guy in her line of sight. And the redhead was braced against the wall as if she were bored out of her mind.

Not wanting to get in the way of a transaction, Harper ignored the blonde and headed toward the other two. "Good evening, ladies. I was hoping you could help me with something."

The brunette froze, her eyes growing wide and her expression turning wary. "We don't know nuthin'. And there ain't nuthin' illegal about us standin' on a sidewalk, neither."

"Relax. I'm not a cop." *At least not anymore.* Harper ignored the bitterness that thought triggered and tugged the photo from her jacket pocket. "I'm just looking for a girl." She held up the photo of Melony Strauss. "Either of you know this girl?"

No recognition passed over the women's faces, but the brunette narrowed her eyes. "What if we did? What's in it for us?"

"Nothing. Except my not calling my friend at PPD and telling him where you're working."

The brunette's eyes narrowed in a glare.

Pushing away from the wall, the redhead stepped forward and reached for the picture. "No, I haven't seen her." Releasing it, she added, "But it's been a busy night for people looking for young girls."

Harper's gaze lifted. "Someone else was asking about this girl tonight?"

"Not that one."

The brunette hissed. "What the hell ya doin'? You gotta make them pay for information, bitch. She's bluffin' about callin' the cops. If she was serious she woulda done it already. You ain't never gonna survive down here."

The redhead rolled her eyes and looked back at Harper. "A different girl." She eyed the picture with a disgusted expression. "Just as young, though."

Excitement stirred in Harper. She tugged the other photo from her pocket and held it up for the redhead to see. "It wasn't this man, was it?"

Recognition flashed in the redhead's green eyes just before a nervous expression crossed her face. "I . . . I've never seen that guy either."

She was lying through her teeth.

"Look," Harper said, trying not to show her excitement. "I'm not a cop, and your friend is right. I'm not going to call anyone. But I do need to know where you saw this man and where he went."

The redhead's eyes narrowed. "Why?"

Because if he's a serial killer hunting little girls, I'm gonna stop his ass. It might go against her current job description, but Harper had already decided if Russell McClane was into young girls, she wasn't going to play any part in defending him. She'd take everything she found straight to Brett Callahan at PPD. "Because I think this girl's life might be in danger."

The redhead studied the picture of McClane again, then met Harper's gaze. "He's not a threat."

"And how do you know?"

"Intuition."

Harper nearly snorted. "Intuition is often wrong."

"Mine isn't." She nodded at the photo still in Harper's hand and stepped back toward the wall where she'd been leaning. "He's a good guy. You should leave him alone."

Frustration welled up inside Harper. This hooker knew nothing about Russell McClane. She'd clearly been fooled by a rugged face, but then that wasn't a surprise. Most of the girls out here on the streets were not that bright. "You don't know a thing about this guy. He's already been linked to one girl's disappearance. Do you want another missing one on your conscience?"

The redhead eased her back against the brick wall. "He didn't hurt that other girl, and he won't hurt this one. You should try having faith in people instead of assuming the worst about them."

Harper's mouth nearly fell open, but before she could argue, the brunette stepped between her and the redhead. "I seen that guy tonight too."

The redhead stood upright. "Minx, don't—"

"You give me fifty bucks, and I'll tell you where he went."

Harper tugged a twenty from her pocket. "This will have to do. It's all I've got," she lied.

Minx huffed but snatched the money. "Figures."

"Where'd he go?" Harper asked.

"Minx." The redhead shook her head. "Don't tell her—"

"Assets." Minx nodded down the block. "He went down there lookin' for some young ass."

The blonde, who'd been flirting with someone in the car, climbed in the front seat with a wave to her friends. "See ya bitches later."

The car pulled away with a squeal of its tires, but Harper barely noticed. Her gaze was fixed on the flashing neon sign down the block where Russell McClane had gone in search of another victim. "Thanks for the information."

She made it three steps before the redhead called, "Watch your back in there. That guy isn't the one you have to worry about in that place."

Harper glanced over her shoulder. The brunette was already halfway down the block in the other direction, shouting at a group of guys across the street. The redhead, though, looked genuinely concerned.

For her safety? Or McClane's? Harper wasn't sure. And she really didn't care enough to find out. "I know how to take care of myself."

The redhead frowned with a shake of her head, but Harper was almost sure she heard her mutter, "Famous last words."

Harper tugged her jacket tighter around her to cut the chill as she crossed the street and headed for Assets. The redhead was once again leaning against the brick wall, not giving off any working-girl vibes. Yeah, she was dressed in the right clothes, but she wasn't flashy, wasn't blatantly advertising herself. She also didn't have the attitude of a girl who'd worked on the streets for any length of time.

Why did it bother Harper if the redhead thought McClane was innocent? The redhead didn't know the guy. Frowning, Harper wrapped her arms around herself to stay warm. And if the redhead *did* know the guy, then what did Harper care if McClane had hired the redhead for her services? Harper did not give a rip what the man did. Except . . .

Pressure condensed beneath her chest. A pressure she didn't like. One that told her she was disappointed by the idea of McClane with a prostitute. With his looks he could get any girl he wanted. Why would a guy like him turn to a prostitute for companionship?

"Yo. Lady. You comin' in or not?"

Harper blinked and focused on the man to her left, a burly-looking bouncer seated on a stool at the doorway to Assets, the club she hadn't even realized she'd stopped in front of.

"Cover's ten bucks," he said around a toothpick.

Shit. She was totally lost in her own head, thinking about things she should not be thinking about. Reaching into her pocket, she pulled out two fives and handed them to the bouncer. But as she stepped toward the door, she couldn't stop herself from looking back.

The redhead was gone. Harper glanced up and down the street but could no longer see her. Had no idea if she'd left with a john or if she'd called it a night. Or if she'd gone looking for McClane herself.

And, damn, that was a lingering thought that left a bad taste in the back of Harper's mouth.

"Sheesh. Get your head on straight," she muttered with a disgusted shake of her head as she moved into the smoky club. "Do not go getting all stupid because of a ruggedly handsome face."

She'd met plenty of ruggedly handsome men in her day—Noah Pierce had been one, and look how that had turned out. She wasn't dumb enough to get sucked in by looks again. Been there, done that. Men like Russell McClane were not worth the trouble. In her experience, all of them turned out to be assholes.

She cleared her mind of any lingering stupidity and scanned the dimly lit club as she moved deeper into the establishment. It was like others she'd visited while working homicide—dingy and dark with pulsing lights and heavy music and women of all shapes and sizes in various stages of undress.

Harper scanned the face of every girl in the club, searching for Melony Strauss, but none fit the girl's description, not that Harper expected any to. Strauss was either long gone or dead. And at this point, Harper had no idea which.

Her gaze strayed to the VIP section, but a quick search confirmed what she suspected. McClane wasn't there. Standing in the shadows at the back of the club, she zeroed in on the giant bouncer with his arms crossed over his chest in front of a door she'd watched a few dancers disappear through with men from the audience.

If she was a betting woman—which she wasn't—she'd put her money on that door leading to where she'd find McClane and the girl he seemed so focused on locating.

Options flittered through her mind. The bouncer was a problem. The guy was huge, and his stone-cold expression told Harper he didn't take crap from anyone. Getting past him wouldn't be easy. She wasn't a dancer, she didn't work here, and she had no reason to be behind that door alone. And there was no way she wanted to go back there with anyone else. Which meant the only way she was getting past the bouncer was with a diversion.

"Shit." Her gaze scanned the crowd again; the club's patrons were intently focused on the show in front of them, not on her lurking in the background. The moment she spotted the drunk guy in the corner getting frisky with one of the waitresses, she knew she had her way in.

A dancer in four-inch platform heels and a skimpy sailor outfit stepped past Harper, heading for the bar. Reaching out, Harper touched the woman's elbow, drawing her attention.

She was short—only around Harper's five foot six, even with the sky-high heels—and so blonde her hair didn't match her olive skin tone. Her dark eyes settled on Harper, and her expression changed from annoyed to pure business with a crook of her lips and cock of her hips. "Well, hello there, honey. Don't often get women all alone in here. You lookin' for a little fun?"

"Not really. Not unless you count catching my cheating husband fun."

A shocked expression crossed the blonde's face, but Harper ignored it. Tugging a hundred from her pocket, she held it out and added, "Speaking of which. See that guy over there?" She nodded to her left where the guy at the corner table—not far from the bouncer—was playing "grab ass" with the waitress, who wasn't doing a whole lot to deter him. "That's my SOB husband. This is yours if you go dump a bucket of ice water over his head and tell him his loving wife hopes he's having fun."

The blonde turned to look at the guy in the corner and snickered. "That prick's in here three nights a week."

Even better. "Is that a problem?"

The blonde glanced back at Harper and snatched up the hundred. "Not for me. He's a douchebag. Always trying to get a freebie. You sure you just want ice water? I could have the bartender mix up something that would make his eyes sting for a week."

Harper liked this girl more than she probably should. "Sounds even better."

The blonde winked and turned on her heel. "Wait here in the shadows where he can't see you. This is gonna be good."

Harper hoped so. Because if it wasn't she might have to proposition the blonde for a good time just so she could get behind that door.

A good five minutes ticked by as she waited for the blonde to return from the bar with whatever concoction she'd convinced the bartender to cook up. Five minutes during which she kept checking her watch and glancing toward that door to make sure she didn't somehow miss McClane coming back out. Then the blonde appeared with a pitcher full of some kind of bubbling brown liquid, winked Harper's way in the shadows, and wove her way toward the corner table and the unsuspecting schmuck who'd made himself a target.

Harper knew she should probably feel somewhat guilty for what was about to happen, but knowing the guy was a freeloader helped ease her conscience.

Her gaze narrowed as the blonde approached the table. The waitress still flirting with the guy looked up. Some kind of words were shared between the two women. The waitress stepped back, clearly frustrated by the interruption, and the guy glared up at the blonde. From Harper's spot at the back of the club, she couldn't hear a thing said among the three—especially not over the thumping bass. Then the blonde upended the entire pitcher over the guy's head. Dripping, he jerked to his feet and lurched back. And the minute whatever was in that concoction hit his mucous membranes, he howled and flipped the table over, covered his eyes with his hands, and started screaming.

All eyes in the club shot their direction. Even the dancers on stage stopped their gyrating to watch the unfolding scene. The waitress's eyes were wide with shock, but the blonde only laughed—until, that is, the man blinked uncontrollably, spotted her, and went after her.

Commotion exploded in the club. Tables and chairs went flying. The blonde screamed and lurched back. And then it happened just as Harper had hoped. The bouncer guarding the door saw what was happening and bolted from his spot to make sure the guy didn't get his hands on the blonde.

As amusing as the scene was, Harper didn't wait around to see it play out. As soon as the door wasn't guarded, she made a beeline straight for it and slipped into the darkness on the other side.

The thumping music echoed in the hallway as well, but the flashing lights were gone, this space dark. Heart thundering, Harper followed the hallway as it wove right and left and dropped a set of steps. The music was different down here, a faster beat she didn't recognize, but the minute she stepped into the lower hallway illuminated by an eerie red light, both sides flanked with doors, she knew what it was attempting to cover up. Grunts and thumps and screams that were the sure signs of sex.

Her blood warmed. There wasn't a damn thing sexy about this place. But for some reason she couldn't stop herself from imagining

McClane behind one of those doors. Making those sounds. Covered in sweat. And what his ruggedly masculine features would look like just before he climaxed.

Something hard smacked the other side of the wall to her right, and the sound was so loud it jolted her out of the fantasy she'd just tripped into. Giving her head a swift shake, she reminded herself these were hookers. And if McClane was behind the walls with one of them, making all that noise, he wasn't worth fantasizing about. If he was down here at all, he wasn't worth even thinking about.

"Good God, pull your head out, Blake, and focus," she muttered.

Disgust rolled through her as she reached for the door handle to her right, but she found it locked. Partly relieved but also partly frustrated because a locked door wasn't going to help her find McClane, she tried the door to her left; it was locked as well. She made her way down the hall, checking one door after another. The only ones that opened led to empty rooms that were just as shabby and depressing as she'd expected. Just as she reached for a door halfway down the hall, footsteps sounded on the stairs.

A male voice echoed from the stairs—two male voices, muttering something about a woman. Heart rate shooting up into the triple digits, Harper twisted the door handle and silently rejoiced when it turned in her hand. The voices from the stairs grew louder, but she slipped into the room before they turned the corner and closed the door softly, flipping the lock in the process, then freezing with her back against the flimsy wood.

A woman in a skimpy white skirt and lacy bra top sat straight up on the bed and shot Harper a glare. "What the—"

Harper jerked at the sound of her voice, but one quick look around the small room told her the woman was alone. She lifted her finger to her lips and mouthed, "Shh." The brunette stilled and glanced toward the wall, where footsteps and voices were already echoing in the hallway.

Blood pounded in Harper's ears as she stared at the brunette. She had no idea who the woman was, if she was waiting for one or both of those men, or what she planned to do. The door was thin. If they tried to come in here, they'd be able to knock it down without much effort even if she was leaning against it. Her adrenaline surged. Against her hip, the Glock 26 she'd tucked into the concealed holster grew heavy.

"Are you sure she came down here?" a male voice asked over the thump of the music.

"I saw her when Jay went to help Violet with that prick. I swear she's down here somewhere."

"Shit. Start checking rooms, then."

Harper's hand darted for the lock, double-checking it was flipped. Her other hand reflexively moved to her hip, just in case, but she didn't push her leather jacket back—at least not yet. The brunette's eyes grew wide where she still sat on the bed.

Shit. You could be home with a glass of wine and a good book, you dipshit. Harper's heart thumped hard and fast as she turned toward the door, bracing herself for the inevitable. *But no, you had to chase McClane down to some seedy strip club where you might get your ass clipped. And for what?* Her hand settled over her weapon atop her jacket.

The door handle rattled. Heart in her throat, Harper stepped back and was just about to pull her piece when the woman on the bed started moaning. Loudly.

"Oh yes, right there. Don't stop . . ."

Harper's hand froze against her gun, and her head swiveled to the right. The brunette nodded encouragingly but didn't stop her groaning. "Oh yeah, big boy, you're making me *sooooo* hot." She shuffled to her feet on the mattress and started jumping, causing the springs to squeak and the bed to thump against the wall. "You like it when I do that, don't you? You like it rough, don't you? Like that?" She slapped a hand against her bare thigh, making a cracking sound that echoed through the room. "You're such a naughty boy."

The door handle stilled. Harper's gaze darted back to the door. And from the other side, she heard one of the men say, "Shit, that's just Destiny."

"I thought she wasn't supposed to be down here tonight."

"You wanna go in there and interrupt her? 'Cause I don't. Let her finish him off, whoever he is. We'll get our cut when she comes up."

Footsteps sounded, but the voices faded as the men moved away. Seconds later there was nothing but the thump of the music out in the hall and the bed squeaking behind her.

A thunk sounded at Harper's back. She looked toward the bed to find the brunette—Destiny?—standing behind her with her hands perched on her hips and a curious expression on her face.

"Someone had a hard-on for you," Destiny said in a low voice.

Harper dropped her hand from her hip so as not to scare the girl. "Just someone who doesn't want me down here."

"Clearly."

"Thanks for—"

Her words cut off as Destiny bent and reached for something from the floor at Harper's feet. The girl's eyes narrowed, then widened, recognition flaring in their dark depths as she continued to stare at what Harper realized was the photo that had fallen from her pocket. "Do you recognize that guy?"

"Yeah. He was just here with me."

Bile rose in Harper's throat, but she swallowed it back and reached for the photograph of McClane. "How long ago?"

"'Bout ten minutes. He gave me extra to stay in here for a while and make it sound like we was goin' at it." She nodded toward the photo. "What are you doing with that picture?"

Harper tried not to be disgusted by the thought of McClane getting it on with this stripper but failed. Miserably. She stuffed the photo back in her inner jacket pocket. "Looking for him."

"You the wife or somethin'?"

She huffed. "Not even close. I just need to ask him a few questions."

The brunette crossed her arms over her chest and drew back a step. "You're a cop."

Harper forcibly relaxed every muscle in her shoulders and face so as not to give off a threatening impression. "Not anymore. I was fired."

"For what?"

There was no sense holding back. Not when Harper needed this woman to tell her where McClane had gone. "Sexual harassment."

Destiny's lips curled in a full grin, and the tense line of her shoulders relaxed. "No shit?"

"No shit. I think my accuser called me a praying mantis."

Destiny laughed. "Was it true?"

A bitter taste burned the back of Harper's mouth. She shrugged. "Depends on who you ask. Me or the dick with elephant balls."

Destiny laughed harder.

At least someone was entertained by the situation. "Now the guy," Harper said, hoping to get the woman back on track. "Any idea where he went after you . . . you know, finished?"

"Oh, we didn't do nothin'."

"You didn't?" A hope Harper did not like lifted her voice a full octave. She quickly cleared her throat, hoping the stripper didn't notice.

"No. He wasn't interested. Not that I didn't try." She held up a hand as if telling a secret. "Between you and me, I think he might be gay."

Russell McClane . . . gay. The thought tumbled through Harper's mind.

No way. He didn't give off the gay vibe at all. And her opinion had absolutely nothing to do with McClane's rugged good looks and dark and mysterious persona.

She gave her head a swift shake, trying not to imagine him naked and in the throes of passion all over again. "So if he didn't bring you down here to get busy, why were you in this room with him?"

Destiny shrugged. "He wanted information."

"What kind of information?"

Destiny bit her lip, her expression growing serious and somber.

Harper knew where this was going. She reached into her pocket and pulled out a fifty.

Destiny frowned. "He gave me hundreds."

"Of course he did. He's probably a criminal. I'm ex-law enforcement. You can either take this fifty and tell me what you told him, or I can call my friend at PPD and tell him about this classy establishment."

With a scowl, Destiny swiped the fifty from Harper's hand. "You didn't have to go getting all bitchy. We was having a nice conversation till you brought in your cop friends."

No, they were having a long conversation. One she didn't have time for. "So what did you tell the guy in the picture?"

Destiny heaved out a heavy sigh. "He was lookin' for a girl. A young blonde."

"And?"

"And . . . I told him everything I knew. That sometimes we get young girls waitin' tables in here, and then they disappear."

"Disappear, how?"

Destiny pursed her lips.

Harper tipped her head. "C'mon. All I have to do is make a phone call."

"All I had to do was tell those goons you were in this room with me."

Shit. She was right. "Why didn't you?"

"Because they're pricks. I don't like 'em."

Harper blew out a breath and pulled three twenties from her pocket. "This is all I have left."

Destiny's eyes brightened, and she plucked the bills from Harper's hand. "That'll do." Tucking the bills into her bra, she said, "I told him I saw the girl in the club about a half hour ago and that I saw her come down here with him."

"Him who?"

"Mihail."

"Who's Mihail?"

Destiny shrugged. "Another prick. But you can't miss him. He's got a shaved head and a weird accent. Anyway, I told that guy in the picture where Mihail probably took her, and he gave me more cash to hang out in here alone for a while without him, then he left."

Harper's pulse picked up speed. "Where did you tell him they went?"

"Into the tunnels. That's how Mihail gets all of 'em out."

Holy shit. Harper glanced back toward the door. "How do I get to the tunnels?"

"There's a door at the end of the hall that takes you to—"

"Thanks." Harper reached for the door handle, already thinking ten steps ahead, hoping McClane and that girl weren't so far in front of her she'd never find them. "I really appreciate all your help. You're all right, Destiny."

"Of course I am. That mean you ain't gonna call the cops on me?"

Harper grinned. "Definitely not."

The hall was empty when Harper peeked out from behind the door. The heavy bass was still thumping, and people were still going at it on the other sides of the walls, but she barely noticed this time. Her attention was fixed solely on the door at the end of the hall that was thicker and heavier than all the rest.

Her heart beat hard and fast as she moved toward it. She half expected it to be locked from the other side, but when she reached for the handle, it turned easily. Quietly, she tugged the door open a crack and peered into nothing but darkness. Glancing down, she spotted a cement platform roughly four feet square and a metal ladder that descended into the abyss.

Her instincts told her not to go down there alone. She had no idea what she was walking into. But before she could step back and close the door, voices echoed from the stairs at the other end of the hall again. Voices that sounded eerily similar to the ones who had been looking for her.

Before she could change her mind, she moved onto the cement platform and tugged the heavy metal door closed behind her. Then she drew her gun and hoped like hell this wasn't the dumbest thing she'd ever done.

CHAPTER FIVE

Harper shivered in the dark tunnel where she'd stopped a good thirty yards from the ladder to wait and listen.

It was pitch black down here. The ground was dirt, the walls some kind of brick or cement blocks, she couldn't tell which without a light, but she wasn't about to flip on her phone, not until she knew she hadn't been followed. No one had come down the ladder after her—not that she'd been able to tell—but she wasn't completely convinced she was alone. Leaning against the cold wall, she held perfectly still with her weapon drawn and pointed back the way she'd come as she'd done for the last five minutes.

An eternity seemed to tick by. An eternity where the only sound was the thump of her heartbeat pounding in her ears. When another few minutes went by without a single sound, she finally lowered her weapon and let herself breathe.

Her gaze strayed the other direction, deeper into the pitch-black tunnel. These had to be the famous Shanghai Tunnels of Portland. She'd heard about them, of course. Everyone in the Rose City had heard of them, but she'd never seen them in person. She glanced up at the ceiling she couldn't see, remembering what her father had told her. That back in the mid-1800s, Portland had been called the Unheavenly City because businesses had installed trap doors, known as "deadfalls," that led to the tunnels. The deadfalls were used to drop unsuspecting victims into the Portland Underground, where they were often held in prison cells before being tossed onto ships leaving the city, where they were used as free labor.

Supposedly, the tunnels had been boarded up back in the 1940s, all except for a few that were still open for tourism. A shiver rushed down Harper's spine at the thought that a new, vile criminal element now existed in the city's underbelly, using the tunnels not to transport people into forced servitude on ships but to abduct and move innocent young girls into the sex trade.

Harper knew all about Portland's sex-trafficking statistics. The city was a national hub for traffickers for a multitude of reasons. First, the location was a boon. Two interstate freeways ran right through the city—one running east, the other running north and south, from British Columbia to Mexico. Portland had a major port, receiving ships from all over the world thanks to the Columbia River and easy access to the Pacific. And it also housed an international airport with multiple flights leaving the country on a daily basis. On top of all that, the city was well known for having a tolerant attitude toward the sex industry, with more strip clubs per capita than Las Vegas and a lax attitude when it came to sex workers, both legal and illegal.

Dan Rather had once famously called Portland "Pornland," and Harper knew the news anchor hadn't been far off the mark. But that was a dangerous thing when you took into account the city's other major attraction as a hip and progressive metropolitan area that attracted a number of youths. Not just twentysomethings right out of college who were searching for work in an open-minded job market where marijuana was legal and every lifestyle you could imagine was encouraged, but also runaways and homeless kids. Kids, Harper knew, who were naive and innocent and could be easily sucked into the high demand for sex workers in the city.

A sick feeling rolled through Harper's stomach. If McClane was involved in any of that . . .

She swallowed hard, not wanting to think about McClane's role in the trade, especially if his "role" included recruiting underage girls. Yeah, she knew good looks sometimes masked an evil monster, but tonight she wasn't chasing that monster into the dark. She wasn't stupid. If she had stumbled onto an underage sex-trafficking ring, she was not dumb enough to get herself kidnapped as well. Then she'd be no help to Melony Strauss or any other unsuspecting young girl who'd crossed McClane's path.

Telling herself she'd find another way to figure out just what McClane was up to, she turned back toward the ladder. But she drew up short when a female scream echoed at her back.

Harper pulled her gun and pointed the weapon into the darkness with both hands wrapped around the grip. Her adrenaline surged, and her heart kicked up in her chest. The scream died out, leaving nothing but an eerie silence that made the hair on her nape stand up straight.

Shit. She hadn't imagined that. The scream was still ringing in her ears, even if it had been silenced. Which meant whoever had made it—*the young kid*—was closer than she thought.

Shit.

Instinct screamed at her to leave, to come back with help. Releasing the gun with one hand, she fumbled through her coat pocket for her cell, powered up the screen, blinking at the flash of light, then hit Callahan's number.

"No signal" flashed on her screen.

"Dammit."

Her phone's light illuminated the dirt floor, scattered rocks, and brick walls. Above her, wood braces held up the ceiling.

Indecision warred inside her. She glanced back the way she'd come, and at the ladder that led to freedom.

Another scream echoed from the opposite direction and was again abruptly cut off.

Her heart thundering in her chest, she stared down the tunnel as far as her light could shine. By the time she got above ground where she could get a signal to call Callahan, the girl would be gone. She knew it in her gut. Vanished into thin air, just like Melony Strauss. She couldn't let that happen. Not when she could do something to save her.

Even though it went against her better judgment, Harper braced the phone against the side of her weapon so its light shone ahead of her, and she slowly headed down the tunnel toward the sound of that scream. She was careful as she walked, watching for rocks or boards or anything that would cause her to trip and fall and give herself away. The tunnel narrowed until it was only wide enough for two people, the walls changing to cement blocks rather than bricks. After traveling what she suspected was several blocks in nothing but darkness, the tunnel curved to the left, and she spotted what she thought was a light ahead.

Her adrenaline soared. Slowing to a stop, she hit the light on her phone and tucked it back in her pocket. Gripping the gun again in both hands, she shifted closer to the cement wall and inched her way toward the corner and the light, which was growing stronger with every step.

The tunnel widened again. The walls here were brick once more, the ceiling arched instead of flat. Muffled voices drifted her way. She couldn't make out what they were saying, but she recognized the low timbre, telling her whoever was speaking was a man.

A whimper drifted to her ears. A whimper that sounded as if it had come from a woman. Or a girl. Followed by a man's voice saying, "Leave her alone. You want to deal with someone, deal with me."

Holding her breath, Harper stepped closer to the wall and peered around the corner. And nearly gasped at what she saw.

McClane stood not twenty yards away, in the middle of the tunnel with his hands up. Beside him, a girl with auburn hair who looked to be no more than fifteen stood cowering, her hands up as well, her head hunched, her shoulders shaking from fear. Across from both of them was a slim man with a shaved head, holding a flashlight in one hand and a gun in the other.

Harper only had a split second to assess the situation. The guy with the gun was yelling in a language she didn't recognize. If she didn't do something fast, the girl was going to get hurt.

She stepped out from the behind the corner, gun held high and trained on the shooter. "Drop it. Now."

Heads twisted her direction. She saw the way McClane's dark eyes widened when he spotted her. But her focus was locked on the other guy. On the one who was already shifting his gun in her direction.

She recognized the wild look in the man's eyes. She'd seen it on the street before. His finger moved to the trigger of his weapon. She lifted her gun. "Don't do i—"

His light went out, dousing the tunnel in darkness. The girl screamed. Harper's pulse raced, and she fumbled for her phone in her pocket. A grunt sounded ahead. Then a crack. She wrapped her hand around the phone in her pocket, and—

Something hard slammed into her side, knocking the air from her lungs. She stumbled and flew forward.

Shouts echoed in the tunnel. Her body hit the far wall with a whack. Her weapon flew from her fingers, and her head smacked hard against the unforgiving stone, sending pain spiraling across her skull. Dazed, Harper slumped to the ground, groaned, and tried to push herself up from the dirt floor. Some kind of commotion was happening in the darkness. She could hear grunts and cracks and the sounds of a fight coming only feet from her. She managed to stagger to her feet in the darkness. Squinted to try to see. Then felt two hands close over her shoulders just before a menacing voice at her back muttered, "Stay down, bitch."

———

Rusty plowed his fist into the jaw of the man he assumed was Mihail—the one who'd had that fucking gun trained right on him and the girl. He couldn't see a damn thing in the dark, but he wasn't about to give this prick a chance to get the upper hand.

Pain exploded across his already-battered knuckles and up his arm, but holding the dick by the shirtfront with one hand, he drew his arm back and threw another right punch that landed solidly on bone.

The man grunted. Behind him, a shuffling sound echoed. He slammed his fist into the guy's face again, part of him pissed at what the guy'd planned to do with the girl, and another part—a part he didn't like—even more pissed that Renwick's investigator had followed him down here.

Who the hell did she think she was?

A gunshot echoed through the tunnel like a bomb blast, bringing every thought to a halt. Rusty released the dickhead he'd been beating on and whipped around. The guy slumped to the ground at his feet. Eyes wide, Rusty looked for the girl, only it was too dark to see shit. He scrambled for the phone in the pocket of his jacket, flipped the light on, and sucked in a breath.

When Mihail had killed the lights, Rusty had known it was their only chance, and he'd thrown himself at the man. The gun had gone flying, but he hadn't cared. Now he did, though. Now, the girl held it in both of her shaking hands as she backed up several steps with wide, horrified eyes. Feet away, a second man—who must have shown up in the middle of the chaos—was lying facedown in a puddle of blood.

Fuck. Me.

He glanced quickly down at the guy at his feet, bloody and bruised and barely moving. Confident he was no longer a threat, he stepped over him and moved toward the girl.

She whipped his way, the gun shaking in front of her, and pointed the weapon right at him.

"Whoa." Rusty held up his hands. "Careful there. I'm not here to hurt you."

"I-I don't b-believe you." Her whole body trembled. She backed up another step. "S-stay away."

Rusty knew all about trauma. What this girl was going through now was bad, but it could have been a thousand times worse. "I know you're scared," he said calmly, taking another step her way. "But you can trust me."

"Stay back!" She scrambled away from him, stumbling on a rock, then righting herself with one hand on the cement wall. The gun in her hand shook harder, and a wild look filled her eyes. "I mean it!"

"Okay." Rusty stilled, not wanting to do anything to send her into a panic. Or rather, a worse panic. "Okay, whatever you want. I know you've been through a lot, but all of that can be over now. All you have to do is trust me."

"Trust you?" She stumbled back another step, and her eyes grew so wide the whites were visible even from ten yards away in the dark. "Trust *you*? So you can try to kidnap me too?"

"That's not—"

"You're sick. All of you. Even her. Trusting sick fucks like you almost got me killed."

For the first time since that gun had gone off, Rusty remembered Blake had shown up. He glanced over his shoulder and spotted Blake motionless on the ground against the wall.

Fuck.

He didn't know if she'd been shot. He was pretty sure he'd only heard one gunshot, but he couldn't be sure. And in the dim light—and from this distance—he couldn't tell if she was bleeding.

His gaze darted to the motionless guy in a pool of blood in the middle of the tunnel, the one who must have charged the girl in the dark, not knowing she'd found the other guy's weapon. Dumbass bastard. Then his gaze swung to the second guy, the one against the wall that he'd pounded to the ground with his fist.

Double fuck. Mihail was gone.

"Look, we don't have a lot of ti—"

Before he could even swivel back the girl's way, the pounding of footsteps against the hard ground met his ears. He looked in her direction just as she darted around a corner and disappeared from sight.

"Motherfucker," he muttered. "Don't be stupid!" he yelled. "Come back here before you get yourself lost!"

Silence echoed back at him.

He needed to go after her. There was no telling who else was in these tunnels. But he couldn't. Not until he made sure Blake wasn't dead.

"Son of a bitch motherfucker," he muttered louder, crossing quickly back to Blake, avoiding the body in the middle of the passageway and the pool of blood he was not about to let stain the soles of his boots.

That would just make his fucking year. Yeah, his parents would be super proud to know their son had been arrested for murder.

Stop thinking about that shit.

He dropped to one knee beside Blake. The woman was sprawled on her back on the dirt floor, her head tipped to the side, her dark hair fanned out around her, eyes closed as if she were sound asleep. Shining the light of his phone over her, he glanced down her body but couldn't see any obvious signs of injury. No blood staining her clothing anywhere. No bullet holes in her slim jeans. He tugged one side of her fitted black leather jacket open and checked her torso but still saw no wounds. Her two-inch chunky-heel gray boots weren't even broken.

Frowning because this was a delay he didn't need, he lifted his hand above her face and snapped his fingers. The dead guy must have shoved her against the wall when the lights went out, and in the chaos she'd bumped her head. Yeah, she was a tough one, all right. Couldn't even handle a single scuffle. "Wake up, Blake."

She didn't respond. Didn't even move a muscle.

His irritation shot up another notch. Tossing a glance over his shoulder, he listened to see if he could hear the girl. No sound met his ears. Not even an echo.

"I don't have fucking time for this." He looked back at Blake and snapped again.

Still no response.

He scowled. This woman was not his concern. The girl running scared through the tunnels was the only thing he cared about. And if he lost her . . .

"Dammit." He pressed his fingers against the far side of Blake's jaw and tilted her head his way, giving her chin a small shake. "This is—"

His words died away when he saw the gash in her temple and the blood covering the whole left side of her face. "Shit."

Frustration turned to a sickening feeling in the bottom of his gut. He had two choices now, and neither one was going to get him the girl he'd come after tonight.

And neither one, he had a strong hunch, was going to end well for him.

———

A groan roused Harper from the darkness. A groan she belatedly realized had come from her.

She blinked to clear the blurriness from her vision and tried to catch her bearings, but nothing in her line of sight was familiar.

A lamp. A side table. Something slightly swaying near a watery blue light. Curtains?

She blinked again, trying to figure out where she was, how she'd gotten here, and what had happened to her, but her mind was in a fog, memories and thoughts disjointed and out of order.

She rolled onto her back, groaning again with the movement. Her body was stiff, her muscles not moving right. What was wrong with her?

"Try to stay still," a voice said somewhere to her left.

A male voice.

She froze and stared wide-eyed into the darkness, trying to see who'd spoken, trying to figure out who was with her and where the hell she even was. All she could make out was the dark outline of a man looming over her.

A *big* man.

She shot upright only to regret it as pain stabbed at her skull from every direction like a thousand knives slashing right into her brain.

Her hands darted to her pounding head, and her eyes slammed shut. A groan—this time a groan she knew had come from her—echoed through the room, louder than the first two.

A heavy sigh met her ears. "You don't listen. Why am I not surprised?"

Footsteps sounded, and Harper desperately wanted to open her eyes and see where the mystery man was going—*who* the mystery man was—but the pain slicing through her gray matter was too intense for her to do anything but sit still and whimper.

"Here." Thick fingers wrapped around her left hand, pulling it away from her forehead. Two small round objects dropped into her palm. "Take these."

Pills. He was giving her some kind of pills. She hesitated, still unable to open her eyes and look up at him because the pain was too intense.

"Don't worry," he said in the darkness. "It's just acetaminophen."

She managed to pull her eyes open enough to look down at the pills in her hand, confirming what he said. Small white pills stamped with a familiar logo. Her instincts said not to trust him, but she was in too much pain to do anything but pop the pills in her mouth. As soon as her hand came away from her lips, he pressed a cool glass into her grip, and she lifted it, grateful for the water.

She swallowed the meds, and he took the glass from her before she could decide what to do with it. Something clicked to her left, and then a rustling sounded at her back. "You need to relax," he said from somewhere above her. "You're not going anywhere anytime soon in your condition."

Tearing her eyes open once more, she looked up at his silhouette not more than a foot away and realized something about him was familiar. Something about his shape and the sound of his voice. And the instant his woodsy scent hit her senses, the panic she'd felt inside before instantly melted and was replaced with a warmth that came out of nowhere and only confused her more.

It hit her all at once—who he was, when she'd last seen him, and what he'd been doing. Hit her hard like a swift punch to the gut, stealing her breath.

Russell McClane.

She should have been disgusted—her last memory of him was catching him in those tunnels trying to kidnap that underage girl. She should have been scared—he was the lead person of interest in another underage girl's disappearance. But she was neither. Her blood was continuing to warm, and her muscles were relaxing under his watchful stare one by one.

His silhouette moved closer, and realizing he was leaning toward her, she tensed. Not from fear, though. No, instead of reacting like a normal person in this situation, she was tensing at the thought of his big, masculine hands touching her—everywhere.

"Relax," McClane said in a low, irritated tone. A tone that shouldn't be sexy but was. *Really* was. "I'm just checking the stitches."

His last word echoed in her pain-riddled mind, and as she tried to make sense of it, something tugged at the skin on the left side of her forehead.

"These are fine. You need to keep the stitches covered for a few days, though."

He smoothed something back over her forehead, and belatedly, she realized it was a bandage.

"Stitches?" she managed to say as his fuzzy silhouette moved away from her and that intoxicatingly refreshing scent of his faded. "What stitches?"

"The stitches you needed when you cracked your skull open. Don't worry. I've stitched up wounds before. You might luck out and not even have a scar."

She blinked and stared after him, trying to make sense of his words. She was having trouble processing. Why was she having such trouble processing?

"You should try to get some sleep."

Sleep?

The word revolved in her head, and without even realizing what she was doing, she reclined back against a trio of pillows.

She was in a bed. Her gaze darted around the dark room, and she spotted the lamp and table she'd first seen when she'd awoken, a dark window with watery blue light covered by swaying thin curtains, a dresser opposite the queen-size bed, and to her right, a door that led . . . she didn't know where.

She still didn't know where she was. The only thing she knew for certain was this wasn't her bedroom. And she had no idea how she'd gotten here after she'd seen McClane in those tunnels with that girl.

"Wh-what happened?" she asked, struggling to remember. Why the hell couldn't she remember?

From the dresser where he was doing something she couldn't quite see, he turned and folded his arms over his chest. Then stared across the room at her as if she were a fly he wanted to squash against the window. "What happened?"

This time she didn't hear annoyance in his voice. She recognized the tone as anger. Very restrained anger. An anger that dampened the wicked attraction she had been feeling and reminded her she was in a very precarious situation. With a man she didn't know. Who could, in fact, be a killer.

"I'll tell you what happened. You fucked things up for me. Badly. And I'm not happy about that."

CHAPTER SIX

Rusty frowned, hating the way Blake seemed to shrink back into the pillows at his words.

He drew a deep breath, forcibly relaxing his shoulders so he wouldn't scare her any more than he already had. He knew he intimidated people with his size and presence. He was used to people avoiding him. But for some reason, he didn't like seeing that reaction from Blake now. And he disliked even more that he even cared what she thought of him.

Man-hater, he reminded himself. She'd pegged him as guilty from the moment she'd met him in Renwick's office. And he was sure she'd only followed him into those tunnels because she'd expected to catch him in the act.

He leaned back against the old dresser and crossed one foot over the other, hoping it made him look relaxed, but he couldn't keep from clenching his jaw when he said, "How long have you been following me?"

"I . . ." She glanced around the dark room again, only a sliver of moonlight shining over her on the bed. "I'm not sure." She lifted one hand to her forehead, careful near her bandage, and winced. "I can't quite remember."

Convenient excuse. He fought back a frown. "Could be the concussion. Could be a lie."

"Concussion?" Her head came up, and confusion clouded her hazel eyes when they locked on his. Hazel eyes that weren't the least bit alluring, dammit. "What concussion?"

Man, she was really drawing this out. "The one you got when you smacked your head against the tunnel wall."

Her gaze skipped over the room once more, then drifted back to his. "How . . . ?" She lowered her hand to her lap and drew her knees up under the thin blanket. "How did that happen? I don't remember."

He wasn't buying her act. She might not have seen the guy who plowed into her—even Rusty hadn't seen him until after the fact—but she'd seen Rusty in the tunnel just before the lights had gone out. "Let's cut the crap, why don't we? I know you were following me. I know you're a former cop and you probably have buddies still at PPD. Were you hoping to pin shit on me? Is that why you were down in those tunnels?"

She stared at him and slowly blinked. "No, I . . . I was trying to find Melony Strauss. I work for Renwick, remember? The easiest way for me to prove you had nothing to do with her disappearance is to find her."

"And you thought you'd find her by following me?"

"No, I . . ." She looked around again, and he could tell she was fighting hard to remember . . . or maybe just to find the right words to cover her ass. "I talked to a couple girls on the street. Showed them Melony's picture. They hadn't seen her, but one of them mentioned a man—you," she said, looking up, "having just been there asking about another girl. She's the one who told me you'd gone to that strip club."

Shit. Rusty drew a breath and stared at Blake across the room. The hookers had ratted him out. He needed to be more careful about covering his tracks, obviously.

"Who was that guy in the tunnel?" she asked. "The one with the gun?"

He was thankful she wasn't asking what he'd expected—like what the hell he was doing chasing an underage girl or what he planned to do with her when he found her. "Someone you don't want to run into again, trust me."

"What happened to him?"

Rusty shrugged. "Don't know. After the lights went out, he ran."

It wasn't a complete lie. He figured a half truth was better than nothing.

"Is he the one who hit me?"

"No." He was a little surprised she wasn't assuming he'd hit her. Considering what she already thought of him. "That was one of his business associates."

"And what happened to that guy?"

Since *that* guy was probably still lying facedown in that tunnel, Rusty decided to sidestep that question. A shooting—even if it was in self-defense—wasn't something he was about to implicate himself in with a former cop. "I don't know."

She blinked at him across the space, looking small and just the slightest bit fragile. Which was an asinine thought considering she'd been a cop who'd been fired for sexual harassment. "And what about the girl? Where is she now?"

"That I also don't know." With an edge of annoyance, he added, "When you showed up unexpectedly, everything kind of turned to shit."

Silence met his ears, then quietly she said, "Wait. Were you trying to *help* that girl?"

Why the surprise in her voice irritated him more than anything else, he'd never know. All he knew was that she was the last person he needed to waste time explaining himself to.

He pushed away from the dresser. "It's late. I'll arrange a ride for you in the morning."

He reached the open door before her voice stopped him. "Ride? From where? Where are we?"

Someplace he shouldn't have taken her. "My house. Since you didn't have any ID on you, I didn't have a whole lot of options." He tugged the door closed behind him as he left. "Don't cause any more trouble tonight. I've pretty much reached my limit."

The click of the door closing echoed in his ears in the dark hallway, as loud as that gunshot had sounded in that tunnel.

Shit. This was the dumbest thing he'd ever done. He should have dumped Blake at an ER and been done with the woman. No, better yet, he should have left her in that tunnel and gone after the girl. Thanks to tonight's antics, Blake was now a witness in her disappearance, and he had no doubt the woman wouldn't hold back from fingering him as the suspect if questioned. She'd decided long ago he was guilty. The skepticism in her question just moments ago told him loud and clear nothing she'd seen tonight had changed her opinion.

Shaking his head at his stupidity, he bypassed his bedroom—too close to the guest room where Blake would soon be sleeping—and instead headed down the stairs of his farmhouse and into the basement where he'd set up his study. He wasn't getting any sleep tonight. The smartest thing he could do was start researching where the girl from tonight might have gone.

Or which girl he was going after next.

———

Harper couldn't sleep. She'd tried clearing her mind. She'd tried the relaxation breathing technique her therapist had taught her. She'd even tried counting sheep, but nothing worked. Her brain couldn't stop spinning with thoughts of McClane and why he'd brought her to his house.

The man did not like her. She didn't need to be clairvoyant to pick up on his distaste. Then again, she hadn't done anything to earn his approval. Including, she realized, asking him if he'd been helping that girl tonight.

She threw back the covers so cool air could wash over her body. She was hot. Hot and bothered, and not just because she couldn't figure out McClane's motives. Now that her head wasn't so foggy, she remembered more of what she'd seen in that tunnel. McClane hadn't been touching that girl. He hadn't been the one holding a gun. The hooker on the street had said he was a good guy, not a bad one. Even the stripper he'd taken down to that room beneath the club had said . . . What had she said?

Harper stared up at the dark ceiling and racked her brain, thinking back to her conversation with Destiny. She'd said he hadn't done anything with her. That he'd just been after information. About a young girl. And Destiny had told him about the tunnels. That—

A memory flashed in her brain. *"That's how Mihail gets them out."*

Slowly, Harper sat up. The pounding in her skull was more a dull throb now, but she didn't let it deter her. Replaying that entire conversation again, she combined it with what she'd seen in that tunnel. And realized . . . "Shit."

McClane hadn't been transporting that girl out of the club for himself. He'd intercepted the bald guy with the gun who'd been taking her out for something—or some*one*—else.

She still wasn't sure why. She still didn't know what McClane had been doing there or how he'd known something like that would go down tonight. But she planned to find out.

A buzzing sound echoed through the room. Brow lowered, Harper glanced around, only to realize it was coming from her jacket, which was thrown over a plush chair in the corner of the small room.

Pushing out of the bed, she rose and held on to the mattress until the room stopped spinning, then crossed to the chair and tugged her phone from the pocket. Four texts popped up on the screen. All of them from Andy, wondering where she was and why she wasn't answering.

She thought about responding and telling him what had happened tonight but then decided not to. She didn't want to have to explain how she'd ended up at a client's house. Didn't want to get into the whole scenario with Andy when she still wasn't sure what had actually happened herself. And even though instinct told her to text someone and let them know where she was—just in case—something in the back of her mind told her she wasn't in any kind of danger. At least not from McClane.

"He's not a threat."

The redhead on the street had said that to her about McClane. At the time, she'd dismissed the words as naivety, but glancing toward the closed bedroom door now, thinking about the way McClane hadn't just gotten her out of that tunnel when she'd been knocked unconscious but stitched her wound, she believed it. The only question left was . . . why? Why had he done those things? Why hadn't he dropped her at a hospital or even on the street? Why hadn't he gotten rid of her as soon as he could? And why, especially when it was clear he didn't trust her, had he brought her to his house?

Her logical mind told her it was because he was covering his own ass, but that made even less sense. By bringing her here, he'd opened himself to more questions. He had to know that. Unless, of course, he didn't care about the questions or what she would do with the answers.

Unable to stay still, she reached for the door and pulled it open. Phone in hand—just in case—she quietly moved out into the dark hall, slowing when her footsteps caused the old hardwood to creak. Three doors were closed in the short hallway. She didn't know where they led but decided not to look. Moving for the stairs, she headed down to what she realized was the main level of the house and stopped when she reached the living room.

The room wasn't big, but it was cozy. A stone fireplace rose to the vaulted ceiling, topped by a thick wood mantel and a large scenic painting of a forest. Bookshelves flanked each side of the fireplace, filled with hardcover tomes of all kinds, from fiction to DIY gardening. The furnishings were oversize and leather, the tables wood and masculine and extremely clean. There wasn't a lot of clutter, just a single newspaper on the coffee table, a few knickknacks that looked store-bought, not personal, and a handful of pictures in frames she couldn't stop herself from studying.

She recognized McClane in some of the group shots of what she assumed must be his family—brothers, sister, parents. There was one of a young girl who looked about five, in a pink dress and holding a balloon. Another of a young couple decked out in bridal attire in front of a church. One of a man and woman in their fifties, the woman smiling, the man pressing a kiss to her cheek. In all of them, the people were happy, warm, friendly looking. In the ones that included McClane, he was standing in the background, never smiling.

Her hand closed around a framed photograph of five people, and she lifted it from the shelf and studied it closer. It had to be the McClane siblings. Three men—including McClane—one woman, and a teenage boy. McClane was in the middle, flanked by his sister and the teenager, and even though he was surrounded by people who were all smiling and laughing, and even though he had his arms around them as if he were an integral part of the group, his expression was blank. Somber. Almost . . . detached, as if he were haunted by something only the camera could see.

She studied his features in the photograph, trying to figure out where she'd seen that look before. It was familiar. She ran her fingers over the edge of the frame, trying to remember. And her mouth dropped open when it hit her.

She'd seen that look in the mirror staring back at her. Not recently, but not that long ago either. In the days and weeks after her father had died.

A creaking sound drew her head around. She froze and glanced to her right, only to realize the sound had come from a doorway on the other side of the staircase, from a door that was partway open, letting a sliver of light shine into the dark living room.

Her pulse picked up as she set the photo of McClane and his siblings back down. Common sense told her to go back to bed. That McClane wouldn't take kindly to her snooping around his house. But she didn't want to go back to bed. She needed to know what was really going on with the man. Not only for her job, she realized, but for her own sanity.

Quietly, she moved across the floor in nothing but her socks, belatedly realizing she had no idea where her shoes were or even what had happened to her gun. That might have been something she should have asked McClane: *What did you do with my gun?*

Reaching the door, she peered into the two-inch gap where it had been left open. Another set of stairs leading down to a basement. Silently, she tugged the door the rest of the way open and moved down the carpeted staircase, only to draw to a stop when it turned a corner and she discovered she wasn't alone.

McClane was seated on another leather couch, his back to her so he didn't immediately see her, in what was very clearly his man cave. It was some kind of daylight basement, with big wide glass doors that opened onto a patio. Unlike the living room upstairs, which had been uncluttered and fairly spotless, this room looked lived in. A desk stacked with folders and loose papers sat against a wall to the right. A worn recliner was kitty-corner to the couch, angled toward the big-screen TV hanging on the rocks above another fireplace and mantel. A dartboard was set up on the far wall, complete with darts sticking out all over the target, not far from a pool table scattered with pool balls. And just past the bottom three steps, there was even a bar complete with a shiny mahogany surface, three leather stools, and bottles lining the glass-front cabinets above.

But McClane wasn't watching the TV. He wasn't even staring into the fire. From where she stood, it looked as if he was studying a large bulletin board leaning against the hearth, one that was covered in pictures and notes and all kinds of clippings.

She narrowed her gaze, trying to see what he was looking at. The only image she could make out was that of a teenage girl in the center— what looked to be a school photo—with only the face and hair visible behind newspaper clippings and articles he'd pinned up all around her.

Ice clinked in his glass as he set his elbow on the armrest of the couch, and her gaze drifted from the dartboard to him as he leaned his head back against the leather cushions and sighed.

She had no idea if his eyes were open or closed. Had no idea what he was feeling or who he was thinking about. But in the center of her chest, she sensed an emptiness. Not in the room, not in his gaze like in the photos upstairs, but in him. An emptiness she recognized because she lived with it herself. Had most of her life. Not just since she'd lost her father a few years ago but from the day her mom had died when she'd been a kid.

An overwhelming urge to comfort him enveloped her, compelling her to move forward. But she resisted, easing back a half step instead.

Her skin grew hot; her hands trembled. Feeling something for a client—for a man she still wasn't sure was innocent—was not like her. She was rational. Unemotional. Not impulsive. And she knew why she was reacting to McClane this way when normally she wouldn't even think twice about someone like him.

Because she was attracted to him. Wildly attracted to the bad boy inside him and whatever dark and dangerous things he'd done to get him to this point in his life. And if she didn't get away from him, and fast, she was going to do something she'd regret massively in the morning.

Heart pounding hard, she quickly headed up the stairs and didn't stop until she was safely back in the guest room where he'd left her. Leaning against the wood door, she drew a deep breath and brushed her damp hands down the front of her dirty jeans, her mind tumbling with thoughts and questions and options.

It was dangerous for her to stay here, not because of McClane but because of her. Because it had been so long since she'd been attracted like this to someone, she didn't trust herself around him. And because she still didn't know if he was innocent or guilty or how he was linked to Melony Strauss.

"Find the girl, Harp."

Callahan was right. Strauss was the key. The only way she was going to get her answers was to find her. And the only way that was going to happen was if she got out of this house right freakin' now.

Before she did something she couldn't take back.

———

Rusty stomped the mud off his boots, wishing like hell the hour he'd spent walking through the vineyard checking the pruning job had improved his mood. It hadn't. Not only had it started raining—no, pouring—while he'd been out there, but he couldn't get his mind off that aggravating woman who'd slept in his guest room last night.

He'd fallen asleep on the couch in his study sometime after four a.m. and had awoken after seven to find her gone. He didn't know when she'd left. She hadn't left a note, not even a "thanks for stitching up my head." But one look in the guest room, and it was as if she'd never been there. She'd even made the bed and tidied up.

Why that irritated him more than everything else, he didn't know. Shaking the water off the hood of his jacket, he pushed the door to his portable office open, hoping he could stop thinking about the woman for ten freakin' minutes so he could get some work done today. He should be focused on the construction schedule, on the supply order he needed to put together, on checking the website to see if that girl had been posted again. But instead all he could think about was Harper Blake and what the hell she'd been thinking last night when she'd stared across the guest room and asked him if he'd been helping the girl.

He stepped into the main room of the portable, but before he could even close the door, Abby yelled, "Not with the boots! Take those muddy things off before you even think about coming any farther in here!"

Shooting her a look, Rusty kicked off his boots, leaving cakes of mud on the rug by the front door. He dropped his boots next to the ones Abby had worn in from her truck. "Happy?"

She grinned and smacked her hand against the stapler on her desk. "Very." As he rounded her desk, heading for the door to his office, she added, "But you won't be in about thirty seconds."

He stilled with one hand on the front of his door, a sense of fore-boding he didn't like rushing down his spine as he turned back to her. "Why not?"

She smirked and stapled another set of receipts together. "Because Tweedledee and Tweedledum are in your office, waiting for you."

"Shit." This was not what he needed today. He'd been so lost in his stupid head, thinking about Blake, he hadn't even seen their cars in the parking lot. "When did they get here?"

"'Bout twenty minutes ago. I told them you were out. They wanted to wait."

He glanced back at the thin wood door, able to hear them chatting now that he knew they were in there. Dammit, he wasn't in the mood for this.

"If they're not gone in ten minutes, come and rescue me. Make up some excuse like one of the construction guys up at the barn put a nail from a nail gun through his eye."

Abby chuckled. "Stop fantasizing ways to go. It's not healthy."

Rusty shot her another look. "You have no idea what kind of shit I have to deal with."

Her grin only widened as he braced himself for the coming onslaught and pushed his office door open.

Just as he'd expected, his brothers had made themselves at home and were going through his stuff just like they'd done when they were kids. "Get out of my desk," he said to Alec, who was currently rifling through the top drawer. "And get out of my chair. I don't need your stink all over my stuff."

Alec harrumphed but shoved the drawer closed and pushed the rolling chair back from Rusty's desk. As he stood, he held up the Rapunzel key chain he'd dug out of the back of Rusty's drawer. "Emma's gonna be really hurt when I tell her you shoved this in your desk and didn't put it on your key chain. She picked it out special for you at Disney World, you know."

"Nice try." Rusty frowned and dropped down into his desk chair. Emma hadn't picked the key chain out. Alec had in the hopes it would embarrass him.

Alec shook his head and sprawled on the couch against the paneled wall. "Breakin' the heart of a five-year-old. You've sunk to new lows, my man."

As if Rusty cared. He flipped his laptop open, hoping his brothers would take the hint and leave.

"You lost your shoes somewhere, you know," Ethan said from where he stood at the window, his hands in the front pockets of his slacks, his off-white dress shirt rolled up to his elbows.

"I was in the vineyard. They're covered in mud."

"Ah." Ethan glanced toward Alec on the couch. "You were right. He's still in a mood."

"Told ya." Alec threw an arm over the back of the sofa and grinned.

Rusty glanced from one brother to the other. They couldn't look more different if they'd tried. Alec was fair, dressed casually in jeans, a navy button-down, and boots, looking every bit the photojournalist that he was, and Ethan was dark and all business, having probably just come from court, where he'd tried to save yet another juvenile delinquent's future by convincing some judge the kid wasn't half as bad as he seemed. "Is there a reason you're both here bugging me? Or should I just start making up asinine excuses for your stupidity?"

Ethan grinned. Alec chuckled.

"At least you haven't lost your sense of humor," Ethan said.

Rusty rolled his eyes and pushed back from his desk, swiveling around to the file cabinet behind him to pull out his last purchase order. "Whatever it is, I really don't have time. Unlike both of you, some of us have to work."

Ethan perched a hip against the side of Rusty's desk and crossed his arms over his chest as Rusty swiveled back. "We gave you a day. Figured that was enough time."

Rusty knew better than to look up. He ran his fingers over his keyboard, feigning disinterest in whatever Ethan was hinting at—even though he knew *exactly* what he was hinting at. "Yeah? You were wrong."

Alec pushed up from the couch and stepped forward, his hands on his hips. "If you'd rather deal with Kelsey, we could go get her, bring her back. Have her grill you. She's still ticked at the way you went after Hunt last month. Pretty sure she'd love the chance for a little payback."

Rusty shot his brother a scathing look, remembering all too well how he'd jumped to conclusions when he'd overheard Hunt and Kelsey in the closet together at his parents' house, before he'd realized they were an item. "Don't even joke about that. I already apologized for that. And I'm not in the mood to deal with Kelsey right now." And he sure as shit didn't want her knowing what the fuck was happening with him.

Alec grinned.

"Then start talking," Ethan said, "because you've got us seriously worried. You've got Mom and Dad worried too. And trust me, it was all we could do to keep them from coming down here to grill you. Mom was beside herself when you were arrested the other day, then didn't even bother to call with an update. Your lawyer had to do that."

Growing more agitated by the second, Rusty leaned back in his chair. "I wasn't arrested. And I sent her a text and told her everything was okay."

"Yeah, but you didn't call," Alec said. "What the fuck is really going on? A missing stripper? Do you have any idea what kind of things are going through Mom's head?"

Rusty blew out a breath and raked a hand through his hair, wishing like hell he'd stayed outside in the downpour so he didn't have to deal with this conversation. "I hope you told her it wasn't a big deal. I don't even know the girl."

"Of course I told her that, but it hasn't stopped her from stressing over what you're into."

"She's worried about you," Ethan said calmly, shooting Alec a look that said "tone it down," taking on the role of peacemaker just like he always did during times of crisis in the family. "We all are." He looked down at Rusty again. "Cops showing up at the house tend to put everyone on edge. Does this have to do with Lily?"

"Shit." Rusty clenched his jaw and looked up at the ceiling, really wishing he'd stayed out in the mud and rain now. He'd been through this with his brothers before. As far as they knew, Lily was his biological sister who'd been abducted and was presumed dead before he'd joined the McClane family. What they didn't know was the truth, and he wasn't about to tell them any of that twisted shit now. "I'm not answering that again."

"Like hell you're not," Alec said. "It's a legitimate question, considering everything else. If you're looking for her again—"

Unable to sit still a second longer, Rusty pushed to his feet and crossed to the window to yank the damn thing open, needing air, wishing like hell Abby would get her ass in here about that emergency. "I'm not looking for her, all right? I know she's"—the word burned in his throat, but he pushed it out—"dead. This has nothing to do with her."

"Nothing?" Ethan's brow lifted. "Are you sure? Hunt told us the stripper who went missing was only fifteen."

Rusty glanced over his shoulder at Alec. "Hunt told you?"

Alec frowned. "His buddy Callahan fed him some info about the case. He told us. And he was right to tell us. This isn't looking good for you. A missing fifteen-year-old stripper, and you were the last one seen with her? The last time you were in a strip club you were looking for Lily."

Pressure built in Rusty's chest. They didn't have a clue when he was last in a strip club, and he didn't want them knowing any of what had gone down last night.

"Alec's right," Ethan said. "If you've gotten wrapped up in something you need help getting out of—"

Nope. No way. He did not need his brothers' help with this. Rusty held up a hand. "I get it. But trust me, it's not what you think. I've got it handled."

"Handled how?" Alec frowned. "By chasing ghosts?"

Rusty pinned him with a look.

"Look, we're just worried," Ethan said. "This isn't like you."

"I'm fine."

"Really?" Alec asked.

"Really."

"Then when was the last time you went on a date? Or hell, got laid?"

Rusty cringed at Alec's question and moved back to his desk. "What does that have to do with anything?"

"A lot if you're visiting strip clubs to get your rocks off."

Rusty dropped back into his chair with a huff. "The whole world doesn't revolve around sex, you know."

Alec and Ethan—both of whom were married—exchanged glances. Glancing down at him, Alec said, "And therein lies the problem with your thought process."

Rusty rolled his eyes and ran his fingers over his keypad again to bring up the screen.

"He has a point." Ethan pushed up from the desk and slipped his hands into his pockets once more. "In a blunt, obnoxious, Alec sort of way. You spend all your time out here at the vineyard. You need to get out and have some fun, live a little. Why don't you come over for dinner tonight? There's this new girl at Samantha's biotech company in research. Late twenties, blonde, totally your type."

Rusty wasn't interested. And blondes were totally *not* his type. His stupid brothers didn't even know what his type was. He liked brunettes. Feisty, hardass, frustrating brunettes. Like the one who'd run from his guest room this morning.

Thoughts of Blake circled in his mind, and he gave himself a mental shake. The woman despised him. Jesus, did he need to be hit over the head with that fact?

"I've got plans tonight." And he wasn't interested in a blind date set up by his sister-in-law, no matter how nice Samantha was.

"Come on," Ethan said.

"It'd be good for you," Alec said.

The last of his patience cracked. He looked up at Alec, then at Ethan, hoping they could see in his eyes that he was way past done with this conversation. "I appreciate what you're both trying to do, but I don't need it. I'm fine, okay? I'll call Mom and tell her the same thing. There's nothing for her or you to worry about."

His brothers exchanged looks that said they *so* didn't buy his line of bullshit, but when they faced him again, neither called him out on it.

"What about the date suggestion?" Ethan asked. "If you won't let Samantha set you up, then at least promise you'll get off this property and go do something fun."

"And by fun we don't mean a strip club," Alec added.

Images of Blake filled his mind again. Images of Blake in a little black dress, sitting across a candlelit table from him.

Shit. He scrubbed both hands over his face, wondering where the fuck that thought had come from. "Fine. Whatever. I'll think about it." *I'm so not thinking about that again . . .*

"Good. Then we're done here." Ethan glanced toward Alec. "Anything else you want to add?"

"Yeah." Alec held Rusty's gaze. "Don't go getting arrested again. This family needs a fucking break from all the drama."

Right. Like he was the problem here. These two and their antics had caused way more drama than he ever had. "You two were the juvenile delinquents, not me. Now get the hell out of my office, would you? I have work to do."

Alec smirked, reached for the door handle, and moved out toward Abby's desk, already chatting with her about something, forever the charmer. Before Ethan followed him out, though, he turned back and said, "Seriously. If you need anything, call one of us, would you? We're family. That's what we're here for. And whatever it is you're chasing, let it go. Let it go before it ruins you. It's the only way you're ever going to be free."

A lump built in Rusty's throat. He knew what Ethan was getting at even if he didn't like it. Unable to respond, he nodded. And as soon as the door snapped shut and he was alone, he leaned back in his chair and blew out a long breath that did shit to ease the knot twisting in his chest.

His brothers knew about Lily. They sort of knew what had happened to her even if he'd never given them all the ugly details. They knew he'd spent years hoping she was still alive. And they knew—as he did—that she wasn't. But Ethan didn't realize just how on-point his last comment was, not about Lily but about the secret vendetta that ruled Rusty's life, which he was afraid he'd never be able to ignore.

He dropped his hands to his lap and stared at the dark screen of his laptop, thinking about that date idea. He couldn't remember the last time he'd been on a date. Couldn't remember the last time he'd sat across from a woman at dinner. Couldn't remember even when he'd last been interested in a woman. Except . . . that wasn't entirely true. He knew when he'd last been interested.

The memory of Blake's heat seeping into his as he carried her into his house and up his stairs last night filled his mind. Memories of how soft her skin had been when he tugged off her jacket and the soft moaning sounds she'd made when he was tucking her into bed and tending to her wound.

He was definitely interested. Which was more than ironic because she would never be interested in him.

He hit a button on his keyboard and told himself not to get distracted. He'd probably never see her again, and if he did, all he could do was hope she didn't tell anyone what had gone down last night.

Or how he'd been involved.

CHAPTER SEVEN

"Andrew Renwick. You are such a snake. Don't steal my croutons." Andy's wife, Maureen, swatted at his fingers with her fork while shooting him an entirely unconvincing frown. "They're the best part of my salad."

Smirking because he knew his wife would give him anything he wanted after the diamond earrings he'd surprised her with for their anniversary, he leaned close and pressed a kiss to her cheek. "I'm your snake and you love me."

She rolled her eyes, picked up a crouton slathered in ranch dressing with her fingers, and slipped it into his mouth. "Yes, you are." Using her napkin, she swiped at the corner of his mouth. "Especially when you play hooky with me on a Tuesday afternoon. It feels positively scandalous being up here at the Portland City Grill during the middle of the day."

He grinned, loving that she was having fun, and chewed the crouton she'd given him. Some men wanted fresh and young, but not him. Andy was still as much in love with her as he'd been the day thirty-three years before when she'd married him. And he had her to thank for keeping him sane all these years.

Behind her, the view of the river and hills from the thirtieth floor of the US Bancorp Tower filled the wide windows. The waiter came and refilled their wineglasses, announcing that their entrees would be served in a matter of minutes. Reaching for her chardonnay, his wife said, "I still can't believe you were able to take the entire afternoon off. You're usually so busy at the office."

He brought her free hand to his lips and pressed a kiss against her soft skin. "Never too busy for you."

She smiled and went back to her salad. Just as he was reaching for his wineglass, the phone in his pocket buzzed, and he pulled it out and glanced at the screen.

Then wished he hadn't.

The good mood he'd been in since he'd decided to take the afternoon off dropped like a rock in the middle of his gut.

"Is everything all right, dear?"

"Fine." He covered quickly with a smile and pressed another kiss to Maureen's cheek as he pushed to his feet. "It's just Harper," he lied. "She was out this morning on a case. I need to take this. I won't be long, I promise"

"Oh, say hello to her from me. It's been so long since I've seen her. Tell her to stop by the house sometime soon so we can catch up."

"I will."

Hating that he was lying to his wife—again—he moved quickly away from the table and answered as he walked. In a low voice, so Maureen wouldn't hear him, he said, "This isn't a good time."

"I don't care if it's a good time," the icy voice said on the other end of the line. "You were supposed to call me with an update. I want to know where Robin Hood is."

Perspiration broke out on Andy's forehead. He moved into the men's room, thankful when he found it empty. Slipping into a stall, he hit the lock and leaned back against the marble wall. "I'm still looking into that. I don't quite—"

"You're not looking hard enough. He struck again last night. The package got away."

A wave of relief washed over Andy, one he knew he didn't deserve, and he closed his eyes and dropped his head into his hand, massaging his suddenly throbbing temple.

"We were lucky it was recovered undamaged," the voice added in a chilling tone, "but we weren't so lucky with the other materials."

Andy's head came up, and he stared at the veins in the marble wall on the opposite side of the stall. "What kind of material?"

"Transportation. Expired."

The air whooshed out of his lungs. Someone had been killed.

"I'm losing my patience, Renwick. Robin Hood has become more than a nuisance. Now he's eating into my profits. I want him found, I want him stopped, and then I want him dead. It's as simple as that."

"I-I'm working on it."

"Well, work harder. I've made you very rich over the years. I've paid for that lifestyle your fancy wife loves so much. I can take it away just as easily as I gave it to you. Remember that."

Andy swallowed hard.

"Enjoy the view up there with the rest of your lunch."

The phone clicked dead in his ear.

Hand shaking, Andy lowered the phone and stared at the screen. He didn't know what had happened last night, but he had a strong hunch Harper would. She had connections all over the city and on the force. If someone had been killed last night, someone somehow connected to this Robin Hood character, she'd have the info.

He dialed her number and lifted the phone back to his ear, waiting as it started to ring. And closing his eyes, he prayed she'd be able to tell him something—anything—that would get him off the hook. He'd taken on a client years ago he'd known was dirty. He'd told himself it was a one-time thing. But now he faced a bitter truth. There was no such thing as "one time" with people like this. And no matter how hard he tried to tell himself he wasn't as dirty as they were, the reality was . . . he was worse. Because he covered it all up and pretended as if it never happened.

———

Harper pulled to a stop at a gas station and killed her Acura's ignition. Her phone had buzzed as soon as she'd driven into Vernonia, and she lifted it from the console, only to frown when she saw the message from Andy telling her to give him a call.

Her boss didn't usually keep her on a short leash, but she knew because of his personal connection to the McClane family that he was anxious to hear what she'd found. Dropping the phone back onto her console without replying, she pushed her door open, not willing to give him anything—yet.

Cool March air surrounded her as she climbed out, making her shiver beneath her leather jacket. She'd driven all the way out here on a whim; one of the strippers at Leather and Lace she'd talked to the other day had given Harper the name of an Uber driver Melony Strauss often called when she needed a lift. Harper had finally located that driver this morning, and he—a nice, fiftysomething man—had told Harper he'd once driven the girl way out here to this tiny town over an hour outside Portland and nestled in the Coast Range. He hadn't driven her out here recently, but Harper was hoping someone—anyone—in this town might know the girl and give her an idea where she should look next.

"Find the girl, Harp." Callahan's advice wouldn't stop echoing in her head. She knew he was right. Melony Strauss was the key to everything.

The gas station attendant—a young kid probably no more than seventeen—ambled out of the building and lifted his chin in acknowledgement of her. "You need a fill?"

"Yes." Harper tugged her credit card from her pocket and handed it to the kid. "Thanks."

Shaggy hair fell into the boy's eyes as he reached for the hose from the pump. "Thought you were from out of the state for a minute when I saw you get out of your car. Was afraid you were going to start pumping your own gas. Everyone's all confused with the new law."

The kid set the nozzle in the gas tank, the pump clicked on, and the scent of gasoline filled the air. As one of only two states with laws prohibiting motorists from pumping their own gas, Oregonians were often the butts of jokes in the country. The reality was no laughing matter, though. Those laws created jobs for kids just like this one. And though a newly passed state law now allowed those in counties with fewer than forty thousand residents to pump their own gas, Vernonia didn't qualify. The small town might be out in the boondocks as far as Harper was concerned, but it was still in a populated county.

"No." Harper smiled. "Oregonian, through and through. I know the rules."

"You passing through or visiting?" the kid asked.

Harper glanced around the quiet town, thankful it wasn't raining so she had an excuse to be out where she could dig for information. "Little of both, I guess. Cute town. You lived here long?"

"If by long you mean my whole damn life, then yeah."

Harper tucked her hands in her coat pockets as the tank filled. "Do most people stick around or leave?"

He shrugged. "Depends. A lot leave. A lot come back."

She really hoped Melony Strauss was one of those who'd come back.

"I'm actually looking for someone. A girl, not a whole lot younger than you." She tugged the photo out of her pocket and handed it to him. "Any chance you recognize her?"

Warily, he took the photo. "You a cop or something?"

Harper worked up a smile she hoped relaxed the kid. "No. Just a friend of a friend. She was in Portland up until a few days ago. Her friends are worried."

He didn't answer, just looked down and studied the face, keeping one hand on the gas pump hooked to her car. After several seconds he handed the picture back to her. "No. Sorry. I don't know her. But she looks like she could be a couple years younger than me. I don't always pay attention to the younger kids at school."

Not a surprise. Harper slid the photo back into her pocket. Teenagers lived in their own little worlds. But she was disappointed nonetheless. She'd been hoping in a town this size that finding someone who'd known Strauss wouldn't be too hard.

The kid hooked the nozzle back on the pump, twisted the cap back on her tank, and shut the gas door. Punching buttons into the machine, he said, "You might try over at the Black Iron Grill, though. Sally, the owner, has a kid about that age."

"Thanks." Harper waited while the receipt printed, then took it from the kid and smiled. "Appreciate the help."

"Sure thing. Drive safe."

Climbing back into her car, she started the ignition again and pulled away, looking right and left for the restaurant the kid had mentioned. Her cell phone buzzed as she moved out onto the street. One glance at the screen told her Andy was in a mood and growing more anxious by the minute.

She ignored him as she had before—not wanting to talk to him about anything that had happened last night—and found a parking spot on the street. Five minutes later she was standing inside the restaurant's barnlike red building, looking for anyone who acted like an owner.

The sign said SEAT YOURSELF, so she found a table as close to the counter as she could and pulled out a chair. A middle-aged woman in an apron delivered food to a booth nearby, then rushed behind the counter, where a man who looked to be a bit older was ringing up bills on a cash register. The woman grabbed a fresh water and a menu and hustled to Harper's table.

"Welcome," she said, setting the water down and handing Harper the menu without looking at her face. She pulled out a notepad and pen from her apron pocket. "Special today is a patty melt with choice of sides, and our soup is minestrone. What can I get ya to drink?"

Harper glanced at the menu, scanning the page quickly. "Can you make a cappuccino?"

"Yup." The woman scribbled on her notepad. "Got a full espresso bar and the best coffee in town. Also have a full 'bar' bar on the other side of the restaurant if you want something stronger."

After last night, Harper could use a strong shot but knew better than to indulge. She lowered the menu to the table and eyed the name tag on the right side of the woman's apron that said JILL. "Cappuccino's strong enough for now. Thanks."

"Be right back."

Jill rushed off. As Harper waited, she glanced around the restaurant, taking in the mismatched wooden tables and chairs, the wagon-wheel decorations, the smattering of locals enjoying a late lunch, and the collection of old-time photos on the walls showing what the town had once looked like, way back when.

Long minutes later, Jill finally returned with a steaming mug of coffee and set it in front of Harper. "You ready to order?"

"Actually, I'm just going to have this. But I do have a question." She pulled the photo from her pocket and held it up. "I'm looking for this girl. The boy at the gas station said someone here might recognize her."

Jill stared down at the picture, and her lips thinned into a flat line. Without a word, she turned, picture in hand, and rushed back toward the kitchen.

Okay. Odd . . .

Harper swiveled in her chair and glanced toward the counter in the back. Jill stood next to the older man, whispering and pointing at the picture, then at Harper. The man's face paled, then he grasped the photo from Jill's hand and disappeared through the swinging doors into the kitchen with Jill not far behind.

Not odd. A definite sign these people knew something.

Gathering her bag, Harper pushed back from the table and moved toward the counter.

Just as she drew to a stop, another woman, this one older and heavier, with her gray hair gathered in a hairnet and her body draped with an apron that said SALLY on the right side, swung through the double doors with Harper's picture in hand and glared at her across the counter. "Who are you?"

Taken aback, Harper didn't immediately answer, but she figured honesty was the best way to go with these people. She drew her business card from her wallet and held it out. "I work for an attorney in Portland. I'm in town looking for the girl in that picture. An Uber driver I talked to drove her out here once a few months ago. I'm hoping maybe you recognize her?"

Sally didn't look down at the photo, just continued to eye Harper warily as if she were a snake about ready to strike. "What kind of attorney?"

"Wills and probate. That kind of thing." It wasn't a total lie. Andy did manage several wills. "Have you seen her recently?"

"Sounds like a pile of BS to me."

Voices quieted in the restaurant behind Harper. Without even looking, she knew all eyes were locked on her and the scene at the counter. "I work for Renwick and Associates. I'm a litigation investigator with the firm. If you want to call the offices to verify my identity, feel free. They'll tell you who I am."

Sally lifted the card. "And if I ask if this Renwick and Associates represents the Plague, they'll tell me what?"

Harper's brow lowered. She'd heard that name before—the Plague—she just wasn't sure where. Or how it was connected to Melony Strauss. "I'm not sure who or what the Plague is, but that's not why I'm here."

Sally's eyes narrowed. "Then why are you here?"

The animosity was palpable. Harper took a deep breath. "The girl in that picture has been missing for several days. Our firm represents a man who's been labeled a person of interest in her disappearance. I'm trying to locate her before the cops charge him with something he didn't do."

Holy shit. Had she actually said that? She still didn't know if McClane was innocent when it came to what had happened to this girl, but apparently her subconscious had already made up its mind, something she knew could end up burning her in the long run.

Sally pursed her lips and continued to eye Harper suspiciously. Long seconds passed in silence where Harper had no idea what the woman was thinking. Abruptly, the woman turned and called, "Wait here," over her shoulder.

Harper didn't have a clue what was going on or what the woman was doing, but she sure as hell planned to google the shit out of "the Plague" as soon as she got back to her car.

Quietly, the man who'd been running the cash register stepped back to the counter and rang up her coffee. "That'll be three fifty."

Three fifty for a coffee she hadn't drunk. Harper handed the man her credit card while Jill reappeared and quietly moved back into the dining room.

Long minutes filled with an awkward silence passed as the man waited for her receipt to print. Sally reappeared just as the man was sliding Harper's receipt across the counter to her.

"Here." Sally slapped a yellow note on top of her receipt. "That's all you're gonna get."

An address was scrawled across the paper. No name, no city, just a house number and street name. Harper looked up. "Is this here in town?"

"I got nothin' else to say. You want to know more, you find out on your own." Sally turned toward the man at the cash register. "Don't you give her more." Then she disappeared back into the kitchen.

"It's here in town," the man whispered.

"Thanks."

"Outside of town," he corrected, shooting a look over his shoulder toward the kitchen doors. "Be careful. They're even less friendly than she is."

Harper's nerves jangled as she thanked him again and tucked the address in her pocket. But as she turned and wove around tables, heading for the door, she knew he was watching her. Everyone in the restaurant was watching her.

"Sheesh." Harper didn't take a full breath until she was back in her sedan. "If everyone in town is this friendly, I can see why you ran," she muttered to the photo as she tossed it on the passenger's seat.

It took her about ten minutes to find the right road—her GPS kept disconnecting in the small town because of its spotty satellite signals. She might have turned around if the guy at the restaurant hadn't told her the address was really out of town, but she kept going even when the houses grew farther apart and the woods became denser.

She slowed as she approached a gravel road flanked on both sides by tall pines. There was no address sign, and with the fading light she couldn't see more than twenty or so yards down the long lane. Adrenaline pulsing, she turned off the highway and slowly crept down the lane, jostling in her seat as her tires dropped into potholes in the old gravel road.

Harper's instincts went on high alert as that name—the Plague—revolved in her mind. She hadn't taken the time to google it yet, but she knew she'd heard it before.

Glad she'd grabbed her replacement weapon this morning when she'd gone home, Harper drew a breath that did little to settle her nerves. The weight of the Glock against her hip beneath her jacket was reassuring, but even she knew it was stupid to be out here alone. Andy had warned her. Even the man at the restaurant had warned her. She could be walking into anything out here. Common sense told her this was a dumb idea and it would be best to come back with backup. Or at the very least, a witness.

She looked for a place to turn around but couldn't find one. The trees were thick right up to the road. Knowing she had to be closer to the end than she was to the road, she decided not to back up but to keep going.

"Shit." She hit the brake when the trees opened up and a house came into view—a small cabin with a long porch and a man already stepping off the last step with a shotgun in his hands, lifted and pointed right at her windshield as he moved toward her car. Shoving the car into "Park," she slowly pushed her door open, careful to duck down just in case. "Don't shoot," she called. "I'm not here for trouble."

"Turn your car right back around and get your ass out of here," the man yelled, still stalking toward her.

He looked to be in his late thirties, was dressed in jeans and a flannel work shirt, and his eyes were wild and defensive.

Harper scanned the house as she pulled her weapon, then climbed out and ducked behind the open door for protection. She couldn't see anyone else. No other threats lurking in the shadows. "Sally from the Black Iron Grill sent me out here. I'm looking for a girl. Melony Strauss. I'm not here to hurt her."

"Sally sent you?" The man's voice grew more tense. "Bullshit. Get the fuck off my property."

Shit. This was about to get bloody. Fast.

"It's true," Harper yelled, hoping for anything to defuse the situation. "I work for an attorney in Portland. I'm not a cop. I'm not with the Plague. I promise. I just want to make sure she's okay. They're trying to blame her disappearance on an innocent man. One who I think might have been trying to help her."

"I don't give a fuck about that. Get the hell back in your car, or I'm gonna shoot."

Holy shit. Harper's pulse went stratospheric.

"Daddy, don't!"

The panicked female voice from somewhere close echoed in Harper's head.

Gravel crunched, then the man yelled, "Get back in the house right now."

"No," the girl said, stronger this time. "I want to hear what she has to say."

"Nothing she says will make a difference," he snapped.

Confused, Harper lifted her head just enough so she could see over the door. The man was looking back toward the porch where a girl no more than fifteen with blonde hair and wide, scared eyes stood clutching a post near the stairs. A girl Harper recognized.

Excitement flared inside Harper. "Melony Strauss? My name's Harper Blake. I just want to ask you a few questions."

Harper stayed where she was, but on the other side of the car door she heard the man mutter, "Goddammit, Mel. I told you to stay the hell inside and let me handle it."

"Handle it by shooting someone?" She huffed. "Yeah, that wouldn't get you sent to jail or anything. And then where would I be?"

Footsteps sounded over gravel, moving closer, then the girl said, "Ms. Blake? I'm Melony. Who's looking for me?"

Slowly, because Harper still wasn't sure what the girl's father would do, Harper pushed to her feet, but she was careful to tuck her gun in her hip holster before she moved out from behind the car door so he couldn't see.

The man had lowered his weapon, but he stood only a few feet away with a scowl on his weathered face and a skeptical look in his eyes as he watched her closely.

Focusing on the girl, she tugged the picture of McClane from her pocket and held it up. "I work for an attorney. Do you recognize this guy?"

The girl took the photo and studied it, then warily glanced up at Harper. "You said he's been charged with my disappearance?"

"No, but he could be. My boss represents him. I need to know anything you can tell me about him."

"Mel," her father warned.

She shot him a look, then refocused on Harper. "I do know him. And you're right. He did try to help me."

"How?"

"He gave me a wad of cash and a bus ticket so I could get out of that hellhole and come home. If you represent him, don't you know who he is?"

"Yes, I know his name."

She shook her head. "I'm not talking about this real name. He's Robin Hood. He's the guy all the girls in the city have been whispering about. The one helping girls like me get away from the Plague before it's too late."

CHAPTER EIGHT

Harper's hands were vibrating by the time she slid back behind the wheel of her car over an hour later, this time not from fear but from excitement.

The lights were on in the house, and since dusk had fallen while she was inside talking to Melony and her father, she could see them clearly through the windows as he hugged the girl and pressed a kiss to the top of her head.

Harper didn't blame the man for being overly protective. His runaway daughter had just come home, escaping a nightmare of epic proportions in the city. No wonder he didn't want anyone from the outside coming near her.

Not wanting to worry them, she started her car, slowly backed around, and headed down the drive. But thoughts and information were pinging around in her brain like pool balls smacking into each other, and with them, her one chance for redemption.

Everything she'd learned from Melony Strauss had been disturbing on multiple levels. She still had a bunch of research to do, but the conversation with Melony had triggered her memory, and she remembered what she'd heard in passing about the Plague at the station.

The Plague was a dark-web, black-market group involved in human trafficking. They were connected to black market groups overseas. They had a website that often changed servers, but more disturbing than anything was Melony's story and the reality that the Plague was targeting runaway teens on the streets, posting photos of them online, and selling the unsuspecting kids off to the highest bidders.

McClane must have seen Melony's photo on that website, had figured out she was waiting tables at Leather and Lace, and intercepted the naive girl before the Plague's handlers—who Harper guessed had to be connected to the owners of that club—had been able to sell her or move her out of the country and into Europe. He'd protected that girl when her dick of a boss had come after her as she was leaving the club that night. Harper wasn't entirely sure what had gone down that night, but Melony had said he'd intervened, the two had gotten into a fight—which was how he'd banged up his hands—then McClane had gotten her to safety.

Harper thought back to McClane's stoic face during their first meeting, and she replayed his answer in her head when she asked him if he'd planned to meet Melony Strauss after he left her at that club.

"Whether I did or didn't doesn't change the fact I don't know where she went that night."

Harper had known he'd been holding back that day. She just hadn't looked hard enough to see why.

Her skin warmed and her blood hummed as she remembered him standing at the end of her bed last night, watching her warily with a look she hadn't been able to define. At the time, she'd thought he'd been watching her with distrust. Now she knew it was compassion. Even for someone he'd thought had already pegged him as guilty.

But he wasn't. Her instincts had been right last night. He was innocent. Innocent of everything.

She reached for her phone as she drove into Vernonia, the lights illuminating the dark pavement and the handful of cars out on the streets. As soon as it registered a signal, she pulled into a parking lot, killed the ignition, and dialed the one person in the world she swore she'd never speak to again.

The line rang three times before a voice she didn't recognize answered, "Detectives division. Officer Hock. How can I help you?"

"I need to speak with Captain Robinson."

"The captain's busy. You can leave a message if you—"

"He's not too busy for this." Harper knew Robinson was in his office, safely tucked behind that desk he delegated from, and that this newbie was feeding her a line of bullshit. "Go tell him Harper Blake is on the line and that I've got information he needs to hear."

"He won't—"

"My father saved his fucking life in the line of duty. Remind him of that. The least he can do is give me five damn minutes of his precious time. He owes my family that much."

Silence echoed back to her, then the officer said, "Hold on."

The line clicked to lousy elevator music, and as Harper waited, she brushed the hair back from her face, knowing this was her one chance to get her life back. It was her chance to give Rusty his back as well.

Moments later, a deep voice said, "Blake? I don't have time for whatever drama you—"

"You're going to make time. I know your officers are chasing their tails trying to shut down the Plague. I can bring you the major players."

Silence. Then in a low voice, Robinson said, "How?"

"I've got a connection. One who knows how they work."

"You never worked vice."

"No, but I'm aware of what the Plague is doing. Judging by your reaction, you are too. Do you want them stopped or not?"

"Of course we do. It's one of our main goals for the year. But I'm confused by your involvement here. What's in it for you? The credit?"

She shifted in her seat. "I don't want any credit. You and your department can have all of it."

"Then what?"

"I want to be reinstated."

Silence fell over the line, followed by a heavy sigh. "I can't make that happen."

"Yes. You can."

"The commander will never go for it."

"He will. If you convince him."

"Blake—"

"You owe me, Daryl. You know I didn't do a damn thing to Pierce. You know I was railroaded during that entire investigation. You *know* it would never have played out the way it did if my father was still alive."

Robinson sighed, and close to fifty miles away, she could picture him resting his elbow on his desk, rubbing his bald head with the palm of his big hand. "Bad things happen to good people, Blake. You know sometimes there's nothing we can d—"

"Bullshit. You can do this. I want my job back. You get it for me, and I'll bring you the head of the Plague in Portland. You and the commander can take all the credit. I don't care about that. I just want my job back. We both know I deserve that much after all the shit I've endured."

Silence echoed across the line again, then Robinson sighed once more. "I can't guarantee anything."

She'd won. Relief seeped deep into her chest. "No answer, no bust."

"I'll talk to the commander and text you."

"Tonight," she added before he could hang up. "I want an answer tonight."

"Fine. I'll text you tonight. But Harper," he said, his voice softening, "are you sure you can do this? These people are ruthless. This isn't just a local gang we're talking about. The Plague has connections all through Eastern Europe and into the Middle East. If they find out you're on to them—"

"They won't."

"You can't be sure."

She couldn't, but she knew one person who'd been fucking with them for years, and they still hadn't been able to find him. All she had to do was get him to help her. "I am. And I always deliver, Robinson. You know that. It's why I made a damn good cop."

He sighed again. "I remember. Just . . . be careful, okay? And keep your phone near you."

The line clicked dead in her ear. Stomach tight with excitement, she lowered the phone and stared at the screen in the darkness.

He'd taken the bait. She had one chance now. One chance to earn her old life back. And there was no way she was about to let that chance slip through her fingers.

She dropped her phone back in her console and shifted into "Reverse." And as she turned onto the dark highway heading back to Portland, she was already contemplating which club McClane planned to hit next, when that would be, and how she was going to convince him to partner up with her.

———

Rusty had kept to himself for three days. He'd done as he'd told his brothers he would: he'd called his mom, assured her he was not in any serious trouble, then laid low on the vineyard for three nights so as not to attract any other unnecessary attention. While he wasn't at all interested in being set up for a blind date, he'd even considered the "regular date" idea, then dismissed it. He couldn't think of a woman he had any desire to spend an entire dinner with. At least not one who didn't hate his guts.

By Friday, he needed to get out. His house felt too big and empty, his head too full of thoughts he shouldn't be thinking. And just his luck, the Plague had posted info to their website Thursday morning about a new auction. For an underage girl whose picture fit the profile of the girl who'd gotten away the night Blake had followed him into the tunnels.

He knew how to disguise himself on the network, making sure he used onion servers so nothing could be traced back to him, and had set up an account with the site long ago so his motives—in situations like this—wouldn't be questioned. All "members" were vetted, not with any kind of background search, since the whole point of the Plague's dealings was that they were anonymous, but with money. And he'd made sure to transfer a good chunk of his profits from the vineyard these last few years into a Bitcoin account they could verify was at the level expected for membership—meaning he had enough funds on hand to buy what they were selling.

Keeping that account high enough was part of the reason it had taken so long to gather the money to expand his winery, but he didn't regret it. Not if it saved some poor kid from a hell he didn't even want to imagine.

He posted his interest in the auction and waited. It didn't take long to be approved and for a separate message to come through telling him where the auction would take place late Friday night. Unlike the dealings he'd witnessed at seedy strip clubs in the past, though, this was happening at a very different kind of club. A club the cops steered clear of because it catered to the top echelon of society. To the really corrupt fuckers who had no problem buying people as if they were nothing more than chattel.

Disgust turned his stomach, but he was determined to do what he had to do to get that girl out of there. He owed her that much after the way everything had gone down the other night. But first, per the terms of the invitation, he needed a date.

For a moment he'd considered contacting Blake to see if she'd pose as his companion for the evening, then thought better of it. Not only did he not trust the woman, but the sultry images of her in his guest bed were still circling in his head from Tuesday, and he knew seeing her decked out in something slinky in that club just might make him lose his mind.

So he went with the second-best option. He took a chance and circled back to that alley a few blocks from Assets where he'd talked to that redhead. And by some stroke of luck, she was not only there but also said yes.

"You're sure no one's going to recognize me in there?" Brooklyn fixed the strap of her slinky black dress as they stood in the lobby of the posh building downtown and waited for the elevator.

"Not a hundred percent sure, but I'm pretty sure you're safe." In the slim-fitting dress that hit just above her knees and matching, tasteful heels, and with her red hair straightened and her makeup subtle, not flashy as it had been earlier, no one would ever take her for a street worker. In fact, looking at her now, Rusty had a hard time envisioning her on the street at all. He also had a hard time believing she was only twenty years old, a fact he'd wrangled out of her when they'd been at the mall picking out her dress for the evening.

"You hope."

The elevator doors opened, and he held out his hand to let her move into the small car in front of him. Her heels clicked as she stepped in and turned back to face him. Tugging at the sleeve of the purple dress shirt he'd worn, hating that he'd had to dig out a pair of slacks and a jacket for this place, he stepped in beside her, feeling old next to the young girl, feeling like a louse for taking her to this club. Of course, he was paying her, and this wasn't for fun, but he still felt like a douche. The only plus to the entire night was that he hadn't needed a tie. And that she'd said yes on such short notice.

"Here." He tugged the eye mask he'd picked up for her earlier from his jacket pocket and handed it to her.

"What's this?"

"Something to make sure no one recognizes you."

She smirked and slid the leopard-print eye mask on, fixing the strap so it tucked under her hair while he tugged on his black mask. "How do I look?" she asked when they were both done.

"Completely anonymous."

She chuckled and faced the doors.

"Did you think about my offer at all?" he asked as the car started to move down.

"You mean about the wine?" Gripping her clutch in front of her, she flashed him a look with green eyes that seemed so much darker here than they had on the street.

"Winery. The tasting room's opening in a few months. I need people who know how to deal with the public."

She huffed. "And you think a hooker is your best option?"

"No, I think someone who's smart and savvy is my best option. As for the 'hooker' part, I'm pretty sure that's what you're pretending to be, not what you really are."

She turned to face him, her eyes narrowing as if he'd belittled her. "I don't need you to save me, you know. I don't have any Cinderella fantasies in my head. I'm a realist."

"I know you are. And it's clear as day you can take care of yourself. But there's nothing wrong with accepting help now and then from people who are willing to give it."

"Why?"

"Why what?"

"Why do you want to help me? You don't even know me. I know you don't want sex; you already made that clear. So what's your deal? Do you have some knight-in-shining-armor syndrome?"

He knew she meant the question as a joke, but to him it wasn't funny. Not at all. He turned and looked down at her. "I knew someone like you once. No one helped her. Not even me when I should have. I don't want to see anyone else end up like her."

Her green gaze searched his for several seconds. "So that's why we're here?"

"Yes. That girl I asked you about the other night? She's going to be auctioned off to some pretty unsavory people in this club tonight. Unless someone stops it from happening."

"You're talking about that dick with the accent, aren't you?"

The one who'd pulled a gun on him in those tunnels. "Yes. You know him?"

"Not well. He approached me a few times. I told him to fuck off."

"See? I knew you were smart."

She rolled her eyes. "Not that smart. Look where I am."

"You can be anywhere you want to be, Brooklyn. Do anything you want to do. All you have to do is believe you can make it happen."

Hannah McClane had said that to him once. He'd never forgotten. It was part of the reason he was here now.

The look she shot him said she wasn't sure she believed that, but as she turned to face the elevator doors once more, she said, "I don't want to see any other young girls wind up like me either. And I definitely don't want them anywhere near that prick with the accent. But I still think you have some weird hero fetish."

He smirked.

"And I'll think about the winery. But you should know up front, I don't even like wine."

"Well, you're not old enough to drink it."

She flashed him another sly look that said she was way wiser than her age. "Touché."

The elevator doors opened, and he reached for her hand, playing the part of an older dude with a hot young girlfriend out for a night of fun. In a low voice he said, "Stay near me at all times. I don't want anyone getting any ideas about you."

"Don't worry." She gazed across the trendy club with its sparkling chandeliers and people in masks and suits and fancy dresses with a look that told him she wasn't nearly as confident as she'd seemed minutes before. "This is not my normal crowd. And I don't want these freaks getting any ideas about me either."

They moved into the fancy room, where a maître d' spoke quietly with Rusty and checked off the name he used online. Moving past the check-in station, they went down another set of steps and into the main club. A dance floor took up the central space. A popular beat echoed through the room, and couples were moving and dancing across the floor. U-shaped velvet booths were set up all around the perimeter, and off to the left stood a long, shiny bar, complete with every type of alcohol imaginable.

Brooklyn glanced around with wide eyes as they reached the main level and leaned close to his ear. "Have you been here before?"

"No, but they described it on the site. This is the tame part of the club."

"Tame?"

"Supposedly." Rusty nodded to the left, where a set of double doors kept opening and closing, admitting different couples. "I guess things get pretty wild back there."

"How wild?"

"Anything you can imagine."

"Like orgies and stuff?"

"And whips and chains if that's what you're into, depending on the night."

Her eyes narrowed. "You're pulling my leg."

"I'm actually not."

She glanced around the room again. Most of the men were Rusty's age and older. Most of the women were in their low twenties, like Brooklyn. "Depraved old fucks, aren't they?"

One corner of Rusty's mouth turned up in a half smile, her comment easing the pressure in his chest just a touch. "Thanks."

She looked back at him. "For what?"

"You just called me old."

She tipped her head. "Well. You are, kind of. How old are you?"

"Way too old for you. Trust me."

She rolled her eyes. "Please. You're not even my type."

He led her toward the bar, not wanting anyone to think they were acting odd standing around staring. "And what is your type?"

"Innocent. I like guys who aren't fucked up."

Rusty got the bartender's attention and ordered two club sodas.

"I also like skateboarders," she said when he handed her the drink. "Something tells me you aren't a skateboarder."

"Nope." He steered her away from the bar and into the shadows. "That'd be my younger brother."

"You have a brother?" She sipped her drink through the stirring straw, just as a kid would do.

"I have three. The youngest is close to your age."

"And he skateboards?" She took another sip. "Maybe I will think about that wine job."

"He's a little fucked up."

"If he boards I might be able to overlook that."

Rusty's grin widened. He liked this girl. Liked her a lot, in a friendly, big-brother kind of way. He just seriously hoped he wasn't about to screw up her life.

"So where's this girl we came to find?" she whispered, leaning into him as she glanced over the dance floor again. "Will she be out here?"

"No, she'll be somewhere in the back."

She drew back and looked up at him. "Then why are we wasting our time out here?"

Shit. This was the part he hadn't thought through. "I told you, it's supposed to be pretty bad back there."

She shot him a get-real look. "I've worked the streets. You think I haven't seen bad stuff?"

He knew she had. And he definitely didn't like that. "Yeah, I know, but—"

Her eyes narrowed. "Are you worried about being turned on by what you'll see back there?"

He nearly choked on a sip of his soda. "No." Using the napkin wrapped around his glass, he swiped at his lips. "That's not at all what I'm worried about."

"Because if you are, it's normal. I mean, people get turned on by the sounds and sights of sex all the time. It's biological. That's why porn's so popular."

His face heated. He knew she worked in the sex industry, but he really didn't want to be having this conversation with her. It made him feel . . . like a lech.

"Trust me. That's not the problem."

"Then what is?"

What was the problem? It hit him all at once. The problem was he didn't want to be in this club with her. He wanted to be here with a woman who was *his* type. One who was feisty and combative and tough and who'd run from his house before he'd had the chance to even check to see that she was okay.

"Why didn't you ask her to join you tonight?"

He blinked and looked down at Brooklyn. "What?"

"The woman you're thinking about," she said softly. "Why didn't you ask *her* instead of me?"

His face heated again. *Fuck.* Had he said all of that out loud?

"I . . ." Words wouldn't seem to form on his lips. He couldn't even think of an answer.

"You know, for a knight in shining armor, you're not all that smart when it comes to women."

He blinked again, knowing what she said was totally true. He had absolutely no idea how women worked. Especially Blake.

"Sometimes it's a curse having pinpoint intuition." She took the drink from his hand, turned and set both glasses on the end of the bar, then closed her fingers around his and pulled. "Enough stalling. That girl's waiting."

He let Brooklyn pull him toward the double doors, more confused than he'd been before. Not about her, though. About Blake. And what the hell he really wanted from the woman.

"Word to the wise, though," Brooklyn said as she looked back at him with a knowing grin. "I'm pretty sure you're gonna want to call that woman when you get home tonight because you're gonna be all kinds of out of sorts after you see what's behind these doors. And something tells me she'd be the only one who'd be able to fix that for you."

Well, fuck. He had a feeling this girl might be right. And he had no idea what the hell he was going to do about that, because he was fairly certain he was the last person Blake would ever want to fix that for.

————

Harper was operating on a hunch. A big hunch. One she hoped wasn't about to land her in serious trouble.

Or worse, dead.

After Robinson texted her back with confirmation her deal was a go, she'd spent the last three days researching the Plague and scanning the dark web for anything she could find on the group. What she'd uncovered was pretty disgusting. What she'd realized was happening right here in Portland was downright revolting.

The Plague was careful—she'd give them that. She'd had to do a lot of searching and hiding in chat rooms to get even a whiff of their site. But once she stumbled onto a chat about an auction in Portland tonight, she'd known where McClane would turn up next. And she'd known just how she could convince him she was on his side.

Sure, she could have stopped by his house since she knew where he lived, had a heart-to-heart with him about the whole thing, but she knew people. She knew someone like McClane would never go for that. The only way to convince him was to prove herself. And if this didn't do the trick, she didn't know what would.

Getting into the building was a definite problem. She knew where the auction would take place—in the lower levels of a swanky hotel downtown. But she couldn't get on the guest list. There wasn't enough time to be approved as a member, and she didn't have that kind of cash lying around for the approval anyway. So her second choice had been to get around the security she was sure would be tight for the event. And she'd done that by contacting a friend at the Portland Bureau of Planning and Sustainability and obtaining print maps for the tunnels that she knew still ran under all the buildings in the city.

Locating access to this particular building hadn't been that difficult. And after she got over her fear of rats in the tunnels below, it hadn't even been all that dangerous. A set of stairs had led up to the boiler room, and to her surprise, the lock on the aged steel door had been so old it hadn't taken much to jimmy it to get in.

Once inside, she'd tugged the clothes she'd brought with her out of a duffel, quickly changed, then stuffed everything else back in and hidden the bag behind a furnace. Smoothing her hand down the shimmery full-length emerald dress with spaghetti straps and a slit that ran right up to her thigh, she shook back her hair and told herself, hopefully, she wouldn't need to play the part of the rich and lecherous mistress about to get her freak on. But just in case anyone saw her slinking around the back rooms, she wanted to blend in, not stick out like a sore thumb in jeans, sneakers, and her go-to fitted black tee.

She had no idea if she'd chosen the right kind of dress. The website had said formal, but she'd gone for more conservative than slutty, figuring the people who could afford this kind of entertainment wouldn't look like they'd walked in from a strip club. She could have gone for something shorter. It would have been easier to move in. But "shorter" meant tighter, and "tighter" meant she wouldn't have been able to wear her thigh holster—which she was really grateful for now.

"Find the girl," she muttered to herself as she headed for the door. She pulled it open, then scanned the dark corridor that was—thankfully—empty. Nothing else mattered. She didn't even care if McClane was here or not. Once he realized she'd been the one to get the girl to safety, he'd know she meant business. And aside from that, part of her—a big part of her—wanted to find the girl to make up for the fact she was the reason McClane's rescue the other night had gone to shit.

She moved out into the corridor in her low, sparkly heels, clutch in hand, and turned to her right. The hallway wove around through the back of the building. Doors were spaced every so often along the corridor, but each one she checked was locked. Then she heard voices.

Male voices. Several. Coming in her direction. Speaking a language she didn't understand.

Her adrenaline pulsed. She didn't know who they were, but she wasn't about to be caught, especially down here. Heart in her throat, she quickly darted in the other direction, found another set of stairs that led up, grabbed the railing and took them two at a time until she found a swinging door and pushed herself through, only to draw up short when she realized she'd stumbled into a kitchen.

A man in a chef's hat turned her way and scowled. With a wave of his hand, he muttered a string of words in a language Harper didn't understand, then pointed to another door on the opposite side of the kitchen.

"I'm so sorry. I was looking for a restroom and got lost." Harper skirted the ovens and the long stainless counter in the middle of the industrial-size space where several other cooks stared at her as if she'd lost her head. "I'm really sorry. It won't happen again."

Hearing music and laughter and glasses clinking through the far door, Harper drew a breath and headed in that direction, hoping it was the main area of the party.

Fumbling for the eye mask from her clutch, she pushed the swinging door open and stepped out into what looked like a high-end club with sparkling chandeliers; plush, high-back, velvet banquette seating;

a trendy bar; and glitzy rich people dressed to the nines, all wearing masks, all drinking, dancing, and laughing to the heavy beat of some sultry dance music.

A woman and a man crossed right in front of her path as she stood there taking it all in. But instead of moving out of her line of sight, the man pulled back on the woman's hand and stopped, blocking her view. Slowly, as Harper tugged on her eye mask, her gaze shifted from the crowd to him. Then everything came to a screeching halt.

No, not just any man. It was *the* man. Her man. The one she'd been hoping to run into. Only tonight he wasn't decked out in loose jeans, a long-sleeve button-down, and work boots. Tonight, he wore fancy leather shoes, a pair of slim charcoal slacks that showed off the long length of his legs and the trim line of his hips, a deep-purple dress shirt, and a dark, fitted blazer. The collar of his dress shirt was open to show off a hint of chest hair, and the day's worth of stubble on his jaw made her itch to know what it felt like, running along her skin. And staring at her as if he'd seen a ghost, he looked very little like the rough and rugged bad boy who'd stared at her across that conference table at her office and everything like darkness and danger.

He let go of the woman's hand at his side and stepped toward Harper, and as he drew close, she picked up that scent—that clean, fresh, marine scent she'd smelled before and would forever associate with him.

"What the hell are you doing here?" he said in a low voice.

Okay, not exactly the reaction she'd hoped for, but she deserved that. She met his stare head-on. "The same thing you're doing here."

His dark gaze skipped over her features, assessing, calculating . . . disbelieving, she knew. "How did you find out about this?"

"The same way you did."

His eyes narrowed. "I doubt that."

"I found Melony Strauss. Alive. And she told me what you did for her."

He lifted his head, but he didn't step back. He didn't look away, and she took that as a good sign. And damn but she liked the way his body heat seeped into her, warming places inside her she hadn't realized had been cold.

She focused on the reason they were both here and not on how hot he looked. Or how good he smelled. Or how much better she was sure he probably tasted. "You need my help, and you know it."

A wary look passed over his eyes. And then he did step back. Not far, but far enough so his body heat was no longer washing over her, leaving her cold in all the places she'd just been warm. "I don't think that's a good idea. And I don't need your help." He moved a half step closer to the woman at his side. "I already have help."

For the first time since she'd seen him, Harper glanced toward the woman. It took a few seconds because she looked nothing like she had the last time Harper had seen her, but then recognition hit, and Harper's eyes widened. "Wait. You're not—"

"Not clueless, that's for sure." The redhead smirked and glanced from Harper to McClane, then back again. "And I'm definitely not getting in the middle of this." She turned toward McClane. "Turns out you're not going to need to call her after all."

"Whoa. Hold on." McClane's dark eyes widened as he turned to face the redhead. "You're not—"

"Yep. I am." Gripping the sleeve of his jacket, she pushed up to her toes, pressed a kiss against his cheek, then lowered to her heels with a knowing grin Harper couldn't decipher. "I'm outta here."

"Wait," McClane said. "You can't just leave."

The redhead chuckled. "I can do whatever I want, remember? Someone told me that. And thanks to that someone, I've got enough money for rent. Won't have to hit the street again this month."

Turning toward Harper, she said, "Go easy on him, honey. He's all kinds of out of sorts already."

With a wink, she moved behind McClane and headed for the stairs that led up to the elevator. McClane turned after her and called, "My secretary's name is Abby. I'm going to tell her to expect your call."

The redhead rolled her eyes and waved her clutch at him as she moved toward the open elevator door. "Yeah. Yeah. We'll see."

He watched her go, and only when the elevator doors were closed behind her did he face Harper again with a look that said he was as unsure about her as she was about him.

Harper had no idea what had just happened. She didn't quite understand McClane's relationship with that girl, or why his secretary would be waiting for a call from her, but something in her gut told her whatever was going on between them wasn't sexual. And for that she was thankful. And relieved on an entirely personal level.

"So . . ." She gripped her clutch in front of her, feeling awkward all of a sudden.

"So." He'd slipped his hands into the pockets of his slacks, but he didn't look calm and casual behind that leather eye mask. For some reason he looked like a firestorm just waiting to combust. One she suddenly wanted to set aflame.

"I guess that means you and I are partners tonight," she said.

"I guess it does."

"What's your plan?"

"To blend in and search the club."

"To blend in with your date," she clarified.

"Yes."

Which was her now.

Every inch of her skin felt as if it had come to life. But along with that came a host of nerves she hadn't expected.

Squaring her shoulders, she looked back at him and lifted her chin. "What are we waiting for, then?"

"Not so fast. I only need you to get me through the main doors. After that you can leave."

Her eyes narrowed. "I don't think so."

"I do. I don't work with partners."

Her first instinct was to be defensive, but then she realized what he was doing. Not being a misogynistic pig like some of the guys she'd worked with in the past. He was trying to protect her. The same way he'd tried to protect that girl the other night. The same way he had protected Melony Strauss.

"I'm not leaving you back there alone," she said, tipping her head and gazing up at him. "I don't leave partners behind."

"I already told you, I don't work wi—"

"I heard what you said. If you want to get behind those doors, though, you'll work with me." She turned to look out at the crowd again, searching for anyone she might recognize. The masks definitely did their job. She knew there had to be faces here from the city she'd know, but she couldn't decipher a single one from this distance. The only reason she'd recognized McClane was because he'd walked right in front of her . . . and because she'd been thinking about him way too much recently.

"You sure about this?" McClane asked quietly at her side. "It won't be like that strip club."

Memories of walking through that corridor, hearing those moans, thinking about him filled her mind. And with them came a rush of heat.

No, this wouldn't be like that at all. It'd be a thousand times more titillating because she'd be there with him.

With a man who was not a serial killer, not a predator, not even a pervert. He was innocent. And he was the hottest thing she'd seen in years.

Which meant her hunch had definitely led her straight into trouble. The worst kind of trouble there was. The temptation kind of trouble that hadn't just gotten her fired once before, it had nearly ruined her life.

CHAPTER NINE

When Blake didn't answer his question, Rusty knew they were in trouble.

"Wait here." He moved to the end of the bar and ordered two shots, figuring they both needed something strong and fast-working for what they were about to walk into. At least he did, now that his night had taken a dramatic turn.

While he waited for the bartender to make the drinks, he glanced back at Blake, who was eyeing the dance floor and the people swaying to the sultry music with a wary expression.

Damn, but that dress was a problem. Not only did it mold to all her curves, but the thin spaghetti straps crisscrossed over her shoulder blades and dropped to a low, scooped back that showed off the tiny pearls of her spine. And although the heart-shaped neckline had definitely drawn his attention, it was the slit up one leg that was going to do him in. The one that bared plenty of naked thigh and made him itch to slide his hand underneath the fabric and right between her legs.

The bartender set the drinks on the bar with a click, drawing Rusty's attention. Thankful for the distraction—for a moment, at least—he paid the bill, then grasped both glasses and headed back toward Blake.

She was still watching the couples out on the dance floor as if she wasn't sure what they might do. And though they weren't doing anything deviant—as far as Rusty had discovered during his research for this event, the rules stated this area was to remain tame—there were plenty of couples grinding against each other, way more explicitly than they would be in a normal club.

He stopped near Blake and handed her the glass. "Here. Drink."

She glanced down with a wary expression. "What's this?"

"Something we both need."

He downed his drink, savoring the burn as it spread down his chest and into his belly. Beside him, Blake tossed her drink back like a pro—not a prissy girl—then coughed and quickly pressed the back of her hand holding the glass to her lips. "Holy hell. What was that?"

"Three Wise Men." He took her empty glass and handed her a cocktail napkin.

The mixture of three whiskeys was already warming his blood and spreading through his limbs. Another shot would totally take the edge off, but he needed to keep his wits. Setting the empty glasses on the bar, he slipped one hand into the front pocket of his slacks, still unable to believe she was here, a whole lot distracted by that killer dress, and more than a little confused as to why she wanted to help him.

That little fact was still tripping him up as he moved back to stand next to Blake. She glanced his way with narrowed eyes—eyes that looked even more green than hazel, all because of that fucking hot dress. "Trying to get me drunk, McClane?"

"No." He might have laughed, but the situation wasn't the least bit funny. Not when he knew what they were about to walk into. "Just trying to help you relax. You were looking a little tense for the part."

"You mean the part of the randy date?"

This time he couldn't stop himself from smirking. "Yeah. That."

She glanced back out at the dance floor. "People are staring at us."

"Probably because neither of us looks like we're enjoying ourselves." Especially since anyone who took a close look could tell they were both extremely uncomfortable.

"Hmm." Blake pursed her lips. "Better fix that." She reached for his hand and tugged him with her out toward the dance floor. "Come on."

Rusty didn't fight her pull. He couldn't, because her silky-soft fingers felt way too good wrapped around his. And when she stopped in the middle of the dance floor and turned into him, pressing in close like all the other couples, his ability to think went up in flames.

She hooked her arm over his shoulder, grasped his hand, and tugged it in close to his chest. As he slid one arm around her, his fingers grazed the smooth skin of her lower back and the delicate line of her spine. But it was the plump curve of her breasts pressing against his chest and the wicked curve of her hips locked tight against his that were going to be his undoing. That and the mind-blowing, citrusy scent he couldn't decipher, not when his brain was already mush.

They turned in a slow circle, neither talking, then quietly, in his ear, she said, "So they're auctioning off one girl tonight?"

Her warm breath sent tingles all along his neck, but he fought from shivering. Fought from pulling her in closer as well. *Think, goddammit.* "Yeah. This party is a cover for it. Only a handful of the richest men here will be escorted down to the auction."

"It's somewhere in the back?"

"Supposedly."

"Sick fuckers."

They were. Rusty glanced around the dimly lit room, checking masked faces for any he recognized. He didn't see any.

"Do you think she's being held back there?"

"That'd be my guess. Probably in a lower level."

"I came in through a lower level. There was a corridor with several locked doors, but I didn't get a chance to check any."

For the first time, he realized she'd come in through a side door, not the elevator he and Brooklyn had used. "How did you get in here anyway?"

"The tunnels."

He drew back just enough to look down at her. "You're kidding, right?"

She shook her head. "A friend at the city got me a blueprint. From there I just had to jimmy a lock into the boiler room."

"Jimmy a lock," he muttered, looking over her head. "I don't know many girls who can do that. And I know even fewer who'd go into those tunnels alone."

"Well, I'm not a normal girl."

"No shit."

A smug little smile curled the edges of her lips. One he liked too damn much.

They swayed to the music for several more minutes, neither speaking, and neither making any move to pull apart. And damn but she felt good. It'd been so long since he was this close to a woman he was attracted to, he'd nearly forgotten how great it could feel.

"So our plan is to blend in with the crowd back there, sneak off and find the girl, then what? How were you planning to get her out of here?"

"I haven't figured that out yet."

She drew back and looked up at him with surprise. "Seriously? That's how people get caught."

"I was planning to wing it."

She laughed and slid in close again. "I don't know many guys who could wing that. And I know even fewer who would risk their life for someone they don't even know."

"Yeah, well. I'm not like most guys."

She drew back and looked up at him again, only this time there was no surprise in her eyes. Only warmth. A warmth that lit off a host of butterflies in his stomach. "I know. You're Robin Hood. I'm still not sure how or why, but I am sure if you'd told me that from the start, I wouldn't have screwed up your plans the other night. I also wouldn't have been such a bitch."

Shock hit him. That she knew who he was. That she was basically apologizing. But it was overridden by a heat that spread all through his body, making him hot, making him crave things he shouldn't be craving. "You weren't a bitch."

"Oh please." She rolled her eyes and pursed her lips in such an adorable way he itched to kiss the sarcastic expression from her face. "You thought I was a crazed man-hater when we met."

"Well . . . maybe not crazed."

She laughed and smacked her clutch against his shoulder. "Careful, buddy."

His lips twisted into a smile—the first full smile he could remember feeling in months—no, years. "Hey, watch it. That kind of stuff's restricted to the back rooms."

Her eyes widened just a touch. "Please tell me that is not what's back there. A little raunchiness I can handle, but the whole BDSM thing is not my scene."

A laugh tumbled from his lips—something else he hadn't done in years. "I think you're safe. BDSM night is on Thursdays."

She sent him another of those adorable little frowns. "You'd better be joking."

He was. And damn, but it felt good to have something to joke about.

She sighed and relaxed against him as they swayed a little more, each growing more comfortable against each other. After several bars of the music, she said, "So we find the girl and make for the tunnels."

"Yeah." It was as good a plan as any. But he suddenly wasn't ready to put it into motion. He wanted to stay here, doing just this a little while longer.

"I guess we should probably get on with it, then."

He swallowed the lump in his throat. "Yeah, I guess so."

Neither made any move to pull away.

"McClane?"

"Rusty."

"Rusty," she repeated with a warmth in her voice that told him she liked saying his name. "I was wrong about you. I'm not usually wrong about people, but I'm not above admitting my faults. Whatever happens back there, I just want you to know that I've got your back."

Pressure condensed beneath his ribs. A pressure that was completely foreign and nearly knocked him off-balance. No one had his back—no one but his brothers, and he was pretty sure if they knew the shit he was up to, even they wouldn't back him in this. But she knew. She knew and was standing here telling him she was on his side . . . and that she wasn't leaving.

He cleared his throat, unable to stop the rush of emotions that tumbled through him. "Thanks. That . . . that means a lot."

She leaned in close to his ear and, in a breathless voice, whispered, "I'm also carrying, so if any of those tartlets try anything with you, just let me know and I'll take care of them."

At what should have been one of the tensest moments of his life, Rusty laughed. And for the first time, he was glad he wasn't alone.

————

Harper wasn't sure what she'd expected to find behind the large double doors that led from the dance floor to the back rooms, but this wasn't it.

Still tingling from that dance that shouldn't have been so damn exciting but had been, she followed McClane—correction, Rusty—through the doors and into a dark corridor.

A woman dressed in a skimpy, black-silk dress that barely covered her ass and a black-leather bunny mask that covered the top part of her face and had ears sticking straight up, greeted them with a smile.

"Welcome to Club Euphoria." She held out her hand toward an arch-way illuminated by a red light. "This way to the introduction, please."

Harper's skin warmed as Rusty placed a hand at her lower back, just where her dress met her naked spine, and let her walk in front of him. The archway opened into a small room. The walls were black, the ceiling so dark she couldn't see it. Red lights created a sultry ambiance, and a raised, circular platform was set up in the middle of the room with ten or so plush chairs pushed up around it. There weren't very many couples in the room—maybe ten or twelve—but it was enough to make the place feel crowded, and when someone at her back pushed her forward, Harper stumbled and accidentally bumped into a woman at her right.

She mumbled an "Excuse me" to the blonde, then turned toward Rusty and said in a low voice, "What is this?"

"I don't know," he whispered back. "But I don't see any doors to escape through, so we better just hold tight for now."

"You're new, aren't you?" said the blonde on Harper's other side.

Trying not to be irritated the woman was eavesdropping, Harper checked her gut reaction and forced a smile as she said, "Yes. First time. The girl at the door said this is an introduction?"

The blonde smirked. "You could say that. It's where they set the stage for the night. Don't worry. You'll definitely enjoy it." She smoothed a well-manicured hand down the man's arm to her right—an older man, Harper noticed, who was checking out every other woman in the room and not paying any attention to his companion. "I still remember my first time." She shivered and let out an excited sigh. "You're in for quite a treat." She glanced past Harper to Rusty. "Both of you."

Wide-eyed, Harper turned toward Rusty with a we-should-get-out-of-here look she knew he didn't miss.

Wrapping his arm around her waist, he pulled her in front of him. In her hair, he whispered, "What do you say you and I stay in the back?"

Okay, she *really* liked his arm around her like that. "I'd say that sounds like a goo—"

Instead of pulling her back, he pushed her forward, his body coming up flush against her spine until she felt everything—hot and semi-hard and *big*. She sucked in a breath and turned to look at him, only to realize he was staring down at her. He mouthed the word "sorry" but didn't move back, and one glance was all she needed to see that he couldn't—another couple was pushing him forward.

Harper opened her mouth to tell the pushers to knock it off, but before she could even get a word out, the double doors at the archway slammed shut, and a male voice from the doors called out, "Masters and mistresses, the show is about to begin. Masters, take your seats and open your senses to a feast of pleasure."

Harper's nerves shot up all over again, and she glanced over her shoulder at Rusty with wide eyes. "Show?" she mouthed.

His lips thinned as he glanced over the crowd. People were already pushing them forward, and before she realized it, someone shoved Rusty into one of the plush chairs near the raised platform, and another set of hands maneuvered her down onto his lap.

Heat rushed to her face. She shifted quickly, trying not to make either of them more uncomfortable than they already were, and scooted over, perching herself on his thigh. He wrapped his arm around her waist and pulled her closer when she would have pushed away, and she realized it was because he thought she was about to fall. Her skin grew hot. Every inch of her body tingled. Beneath her, she heard him whisper, "Relax. Don't make a scene." And she was trying not to, dammit, but holy hell . . . this was not what she'd expected.

Bracing a hand on the back of his chair, she managed to sit upright so she wouldn't lean into him more than she had to, so she wouldn't get too comfortable. Because that was suddenly all she wanted to do. Slide fully onto his lap, melt into all his sultry heat, and get lost in the scent and feel of him right here in the middle of this room.

The lights went out. The voices around them quieted.

In the silence, Harper's heart picked up speed and she became hyperaware of everything—Rusty's big hand perched on her hip, holding her still, his muscular thigh beneath her ass, strong and thick, his chest brushing her side where she was trying not to lean into him, his breaths, not as slow and steady as they'd been when they were dancing, but faster now. Shallower. And his scent. His heady, sexy scent that was swirling around her, making her light-headed, making her envision things she shouldn't be envisioning.

A drum beat ahead of them. One drum. Then another to the right. And another to the left. The beat picked up speed until it was frantic rhythm, like war drums before a battle, vibrating through the floor, up through the chairs and into their bodies. Footsteps sounded in the darkness, circled the outside of the table in time to the beat, then echoed from the far side of the circle, coming closer until they stopped.

The drumbeats halted. A single light came on over the center of the platform. A woman stood in a hooded red cloak, her face and body hidden from view, the only thing visible her small bare feet. Slowly, she lowered to her knees, her features cast in shadows as she faced the crowd, then the light went out and another came on. The second light shone behind the raised platform, illuminating a man in a leather loincloth wearing a mask that covered all but his mouth and rose to two large bull horns on the sides of his head.

A primal feeling stirred inside Harper. One that sent a shiver she couldn't control straight down her spine. Against her hip, she felt Rusty's grip tighten, but she was unable to look his way. Unable to do anything but watch as the bull man climbed up onto the platform, stopped behind the woman, and reached down with one hand to draw her back against his lower body.

The hood fell from her face, revealing her delicate features and blonde hair pulled back into a ponytail. He gripped her jaw, then pressed his thumb along her lips until she opened and sucked on the digit. A groan echoed from the woman, and then the bull man whipped the cape from her body, revealing that she was dressed in nothing but a sequined bikini top that left nothing to the imagination and a gauzy skirt that looked like something straight out of a harem.

The man tugged the woman to her feet, and the two moved in a sultry dance around the platform that wasn't visually pornographic but was laced with so much heat and erotic foreshadowing Harper could barely look away. Their bodies undulated together in time to the music, pulled apart, then came back together. Fingers touched, arms and legs twisted around each other. Sighs and grunts filled the room along with the music, and the beat grew louder, faster, stirring up a frenzy between the two dancers and deep inside Harper's blood.

She tore her gaze away from the dancers and glanced down at Rusty to gauge his reaction, then drew in a surprised breath when she realized he wasn't watching the show. He was watching her. Closely. With a heat in his eyes that told her he was just as affected by the atmosphere as she was. His hand shifted from the arm of the chair where it was resting near her back, and his fingertips brushed the silk of her skirt near her outer thigh. Tingles raced up her leg and into her hip. Tingles and an awareness, the longer he stared at her, that maybe he wasn't reacting to the show at all. Maybe he was reacting to her.

Her blood ran hot. Her pulse picked up speed. Her gaze dropped to his lips, and she licked her own without realizing what she was doing, unable to keep from wondering if he tasted as good as he looked, if his mouth was as hot as his body heat seeping into hers—beneath her, against her, all around her. Wondering even more if he was thinking the same thing as her and just what he'd do if she leaned into him and kissed him as she suddenly couldn't stop thinking of doing.

The lights went out. Instinctively, Harper looked up and around even though she couldn't see anything. Mumbled voices echoed from the stage at her back. Followed by a sigh and a groan and the sound of fabric tearing. But before she could look over her shoulder to see what was going on, Rusty's arm wrapped around her waist, pulling her body up against his chest. And he whispered, "Stay with me."

His hot breath tickled her ear, her neck, sending shivers across her skin. She closed her eyes, lost in the sensation, and turned back to him. The sounds behind her faded. His scent, his heat, and the roar of her pulse overwhelmed every thought until the only thing she wanted was to get closer, to be touched, to give in to the *fire* seconds away from incinerating her.

This is a bad idea. Don't do anything stupid you'll regret later . . .

Her subconscious screamed at her to back away, to be smart, not to fall into the same bad-boy trap she'd fallen into once before. But she was past the point of listening. Biology took over. She shifted closer until his heat was all she felt. And when his arms tightened around her, she gave in and pressed her lips to his for a kiss that completely rocked her world.

———

Her lips were like candy, and he'd denied himself sweets for far too long. And when she opened and drew him into the heat and wetness of her mouth, he realized he'd been wrong. She was a drug—as strong as heroin—and he was never going to be satisfied with only one hit.

He tightened his hand against her bare thigh, loving the silky-smooth feel against his palm, and lifted his other hand to her jaw so he could tip her head slightly to the side, so he could taste her deeper and lose himself entirely in her kiss. She answered with a groan that rumbled from her chest into his and sent his blood singing, and when she shifted closer, when she pressed her breasts against his chest and licked into his mouth, it was all he could do not to tug her dress up to her hips, shift her fully onto his hips, and free himself so he could sink deep inside her.

She licked into his mouth again and again, lifted her hands to his face and tilted her head the other way, kissing him deeper, exploring his mouth as if it were her playground. And he let her. Let her do anything she wanted because this was the hottest kiss he'd had in . . . shit, forever.

Slowly, he became aware of sounds, coming not from the raised platform behind Harper but from around them. He tore his eyes open just as the lights came on and blinked several times in the red hue. Against him, Harper drew back a breath from his lips, but she didn't release her hold on his face, didn't move her sweet little body off his lap, didn't even put space between his chest and hers. And her eyes . . . her glittering green eyes stayed locked on his, glazed with a heat he felt everywhere as she stared down at him and licked her swollen, wet, succulent lips that had just been fused to his.

"The doors to Club Euphoria are now opening," the same man who'd ordered them to take their seats earlier announced in a booming voice. "We hope you enjoyed the show. Be sure to sample all the delicacies Club Euphoria has to offer."

People pushed chairs back and rose to their feet, but Harper still didn't move, and neither did Rusty. He was almost afraid to. Afraid to break the moment in case he'd only imagined it.

"Well," the blonde who'd been talking to them earlier said in a victorious voice. "I guess from the looks of you two, you enjoyed your first show. Maybe we'll run into you both later in one of the interactive rooms."

Rusty didn't want to break his gaze with Harper, but he couldn't stop himself from acknowledging the woman who was getting entirely too close, if for no other reason than to send her a back-off warning. She didn't take it. Only licked her lips and winked, then turned to catch up with her partner.

But that split second was enough to break whatever spell had enveloped Harper, and before he could stop her, she slid off his lap and nearly stumbled before righting herself.

He pushed to his feet and reached out to help her, but she stepped back and, without looking at him, said, "I'm fine." Smoothing a hand down her dress, she straightened her spine, then turned quickly for the door where everyone else had already exited. "Now's our chance to blend in."

A chill spread over him, one that dampened at least some of the heat he was feeling, at least enough so he could walk without pain. She was embarrassed by what had just happened. He could see it in the tense line of her back and the rigid set of her shoulders. But he knew she wanted him as much as he wanted her. He'd seen it in her eyes and felt it in her kiss. And even though he knew it was dangerous, even though he knew it wasn't smart, considering where they were and what they were supposed to be doing tonight, he was already plotting ways he could get close to her again. How he could feel that sinful body pressed up against his. How he could make her moan like she had when she'd been rocking against him in that chair.

He followed her out into the red-lit hallway. Music pulsed out of speakers hidden in the ceiling. The corridor opened to a large room complete with another bar and dance floor surrounded by plush velvet couches. But unlike the main dance floor, this one was occupied with couples in various stages of undress, some grinding and dancing obscenely together, others on the couches making out, not caring who could see, even more heading off in twos or threes to the interactive rooms past the second bar.

Debauchery was all around them. His blood heated as he envisioned pulling Harper into a dark room, pushing her over the arm of one of those velvet sofas, lifting the back of her dress. He glanced to his right to see what her reaction was to the scene, only to draw up short when he realized she was gone.

His gaze quickly skipped over the room, searching for anyone who could have grabbed her. And when he spotted her, pressed up against the wall with a guy in a leather bunny mask getting right in her face, every protective urge he had rushed right to the surface, destroying his control.

CHAPTER TEN

Rusty crossed the room in three strides, grasped the guy in the ridiculous bunny mask by the shoulder, and jerked him back. "Hey, buddy. Back off. She's spoken for."

The guy's gray eyes narrowed on Rusty. He was a couple of inches shorter but solid muscle, and even though Rusty knew he could take him, he didn't want to draw that kind of attention. Not unless he was forced to.

"Single woman alone in this place means she's available," the guy said in a low voice.

Oh, fuck that. This guy had predator written all over him. Rusty was just about to pop him in the nose to show him just what he could do with his "availability," but Harper sidled up to him, slid her arms around his waist beneath his jacket, and pressed in close. "My fault. Silly me, I got distracted by everything going on around me. I'm definitely not available."

She lifted her chin and pressed a kiss against the stubble on Rusty's jaw, and even though he was vibrating with the need to pound his fist into this guy's face, tingles rushed all through his skin at the silky-soft contact.

"See?" he said to the guy, wrapping his arm around her and holding her even closer. "Not available." He looked down at her. "You need to stay close to me, baby doll. I warned you about getting lost in here."

She narrowed her eyes in a way that said *Call me "baby doll" one more time, and you'll lose a testicle.* And the reaction was so *her* it defused his need for blood and pulled a smile from his lips.

He looked back at the dick in the bunny mask. "'Scuse us, would ya? We've got things to do."

He steered her around the scowling guy and out the doorway. She stayed plastered to his side until they reached the hall, and then she pulled back and smacked him on the arm with her clutch. "'Baby doll'? Don't even think of using that one again."

He chuckled at her reaction, then winced when she smacked him again. "Ow. Careful. I told you that was a Thursday-night thing."

"I have a feeling it's already going on in one of these rooms." She glowered his way. "We have to get out of here now. Before I pull out my gun and start shooting people."

She moved down the dark hallway, and he picked up his pace to keep up with her. "Just promise you won't shoot me."

"No deal if you call me baby doll again."

He smiled.

They passed a room where three women were going at it in the middle of a giant bed with several couples standing around to watch, and another room where groups of three and four were rolling around on mattresses laid out on the floor. Huffing, Harper moved faster, averting her gaze from every open doorway and only slowing down when she reached an intersection and had to decide which way to go.

Rusty watched her. The rigid line of her spine, the way her muscles flexed beneath her silky skin, and the flush to her face that told him she wasn't completely disgusted. She was turned on. Hopefully not by what she was seeing and hearing but by being close to him.

She turned the corner and whispered, "Finally," and as he followed, he saw what she'd already spotted: a dimly lit sign at the far end of the corridor that said Exit.

She pushed the steel door open and stepped into the dark stairwell that went both up and down. As the door snapped closed behind him, surrounding them in darkness, she fumbled through her clutch. "My phone's in here somewhere."

Maybe it wasn't smart. Maybe he should have just let things lie. But he couldn't seem to stop himself. Before she could flip on her light, he closed his hand over her wrist, stepped in front of her, and pushed her up against the cold stairwell wall.

"What are you—"

He couldn't see a damn thing, but he knew right where her mouth was, thanks to her protest, and he didn't even hesitate. He let go of her wrist, lifted both hands to her face, and lowered his mouth to hers.

She sucked in a surprised breath, and he used her shock to his advantage, tasting all that wicked heat that had nearly driven him mad only a handful of moments before.

Her protest died on her lips. Her clutch clattered to the floor at their feet. And then her hands were beneath his jacket, clawing at his dress shirt, her body straining toward his, her mouth wild and reckless and scorching beneath his.

He wanted her. Now, right now, right here in this stairwell. More than he'd wanted any other woman. And realizing he was seconds away from taking her, from shredding her dress and thrusting hard inside her, was the only thing that pulled him back from the edge of a control he'd very nearly lost.

Her breath was hard and hot and heavy against his lips when he released her. And damn but that felt good. *She* felt good. So much fucking better than he'd ever imagined.

"What . . . was that?" she breathed against his lips. But she didn't push him away. If anything her fingers were digging into the fabric of his shirt, pulling him closer.

Dear God, she wants me closer.

His legs felt weak. He lowered his lips to her shoulder and nipped at the tender flesh, then smoothed his tongue over the spot. "I don't know." He lifted his head and grazed her lips with his own. "But I really hope that's your gun beneath that fucking hot dress and not that you're happy to see me."

Her lips curled. She was so close he could feel her silky lips move against his. "Scared, handsome?"

"Terrified." But not of her. Of this wild, sizzling heat that was compelling him to give in to every one of his wanton urges.

He closed his mouth over hers again, and she sucked hard on his tongue and rocked her hips against his with a groan. And holy hell, he saw stars when she kissed him harder, when she rubbed her sinful body against his straining cock. Knew if she kept that up he was going to come. Right in his pants. Just like a freakin' randy teenager.

Voices echoed beyond the steel door, out in the hall. Several voices. Male voices. Voices that did not sound happy. They cut through the sexual haze, pulling Rusty back from the edge. "Did you hear that?"

Harper turned her head, her soft hair grazing his cheek, and went silent. Then she said, "Shit, they're coming this way."

He released her from the wall, stepped back so she could pick up her clutch, and then reached for her hand. "Come on. You need to stop distracting me so we can get out of here like you said."

She huffed in the darkness but didn't pull away from his hold as he tugged her quickly down the steps. "That's right. Blame me."

He grinned, enjoying the banter with her and the lighthearted moments even when they were conceivably in deep shit. "My baby doll? Done."

A soft chuckle met his ears. "I warned you, McClane."

They reached the lower level, and he tugged her toward the door, but she stopped him and said, "No, one more down. We're still two floors above the boiler room, and the hallway with the locked doors was only one level above that."

He let go so she could take the lead but stayed close. And when they descended to the next landing and she reached for the door, he placed a hand on her arm and said, "Let me."

She frowned. "Don't go getting all macho on me. I'm the one with the weapon, remember?"

"Like I could ever forget." He tugged the door open a crack and peered into the dimly lit hallway. Unlike the corridors above, this one wasn't lit by a red hue but by a few low-wattage bulbs high in the ceiling that spread light in cone shapes every fifteen feet or so.

"It's clear." He tugged the door open wider and stepped out into the space. As she'd said before, there was a scattering of black doors on both sides of the hall, spaced evenly apart. He stepped up to the closest one and knocked gently, listening for any kind of movement on the other side.

Silence met his ears.

"How are we going to figure out which one is hers?" Harper whispered.

He didn't answer, just moved to the next door and rapped softly. Still nothing.

"And once we find her," Harper continued, "how are we going to get her out? Do you have a key? Because I don't."

He stopped at the next door, lifted his gaze to hers, and smirked as he lightly knocked. Her answer was a frown and a tilt of her head that was so damn cute it was all he could do not to kiss her again.

He restrained himself, only because of where they were, and moved to the next door. This time when he knocked, a groan sounded from the other side.

"Bingo." He stepped back and reached into the inner pocket of his jacket.

"What are you doing?"

"Something my brothers and I learned to do a long time ago." He dropped to his knee, eyed the lock, then grabbed the tool that was closest to the right size.

"Is that a lock pick?"

"Yep." He slid the tool into the lock, searching for the tumbler.

"Were you and your brothers juvenile delinquents or something?"

"They were. I learned everything I could from them."

When she only shot him a disbelieving look, he looked up at her and smiled. "Serious. They both spent time in juvie when they were about thirteen. That's how our father met them both. He took time away from his practice to counsel kids in the system. He adopted each of them after they got out."

"He's either a saint or certifiable."

He chuckled. "Both." Feeling the pick catch, he pushed to his feet. "Got it."

The lock turned. He pulled the pick out, replaced it in his breast pocket, and pushed the door open.

Nothing but darkness met his eyes. "Harper, I need the li—"

"Here." She'd already turned the flashlight app on and was pushing her cell phone into his hand.

He lifted it and shone it over the room, then swore under his breath when he spotted the girl, lying in a heap on the floor in the corner.

"Wow," Harper whispered. "It really is the girl from the other night."

"You thought it was someone else?"

"I wasn't sure." Harper glanced his way. "I hoped it was her, but I didn't get a great look at her in the tunnel."

He crossed the room. "That's why this auction was so last-minute. They had to get rid of her." He knelt at her side and reached for the girl. "Help me."

They pulled the girl upright and moved her so she was sitting with her back against the wall with her legs out in front of her. Her eyes were half-closed, her head lolling to the side. One look was all Rusty needed to know she'd been drugged.

He shone the light over her eyes. "Megan? Can you hear me?"

Megan groaned as her head fell forward.

Harper pushed aside the sleeve of the girl's T-shirt and then the hem of her long shorts. "Doesn't look like she's been assaulted."

"No, they wouldn't have touched her. Not yet, at least. They get more for her if she's a virgin."

"God, these people are sick."

"I know." He wrapped his arms around the girl and pushed to his feet. "I'm going to have to carry her. How far to the tunnel?"

"Down another flight and through the boiler room."

The girl moaned again as he hefted her into his arms. "Let's just hope we don't run into any trouble between now and then."

Harper nodded and rose beside him. "Five minutes and we'll be in the tunnels. Then it's a straight shot to the bar I used to gain access."

Rusty sure the hell hoped so, because the sooner he got this girl to safety, the sooner he could get back to doing what he'd only barely been able to stop back there—which was getting lost in the tough-as-nails Harper Blake all over again.

———

Harper's heart raced as she led Rusty back through the dimly lit corridor, into the stairwell, and down to the lowest level. No sounds followed them. She hadn't heard any voices or footsteps, but she was still on high alert, her gun heavy in the holster against her thigh, her fingers itching to reach for it, just in case.

"Almost there," she said as she pushed the boiler-room door open and stepped into the sweltering heat.

"Jesus, it's hot in here," he said, shifting the girl in his arms as the door snapped closed behind him.

"This way." She crossed the large room quickly and rounded the boiler. Reaching for her duffel, she tossed the strap over her shoulder, then rushed toward the door, grasping her dress at the thigh so she wouldn't trip. "Here."

She tugged the door open and waited for him to step through. As he moved out onto the cement stairs, she pulled the door closed behind her and said, "Hold on a second."

She rifled through her bag and found her cell phone. After flipping it on so the tunnel was illuminated, she bent and yanked off her heels, then shoved her feet into her tennis shoes and threw the heels into her bag. "Okay, we're set."

He glanced down at the stairs. "Okay, Indiana Jones. Lead on."

When they reached the dirt floor of the tunnel, Harper shone the light ahead, then glanced back at Rusty, holding the girl upside down over his shoulder. "You okay carrying her several blocks?"

"This chick? She's light as a feather."

She scoffed.

"I work on a farm, remember?"

"A winery."

"Same diff."

God, he was cute. Too cute. She lifted the skirt of her dress up, keeping it out of the trickle of water in the middle of the tunnel as she walked, trying not to think about how cute he was. How *hot* he was. And what the man had done to her back there with his hands and lips and—holy hell—that smokin' body.

She was in serious trouble with this guy. Not just because she was wildly attracted to him but because she liked him. *Really* liked him. She liked his sarcastic sense of humor and the way he could cut the tension with one stupid joke . . . like the gun-beneath-her-dress crack back in that stairwell. She couldn't remember the last time she'd been with a guy who could not only make her panties melt but also make her want to laugh at the same time.

They rounded a corner. Her light shone over beams in the ceiling, the dirt floor, and scattered debris. When they turned down a second corridor, the girl over Rusty's shoulder groaned.

"She's starting to wake up," Rusty said. "How much farther?"

"Not much. A hundred yards, maybe? I came down a set of stairs from a red door. It's the back room of a dive bar on Sixth and—"

Shouts echoed at their backs down the dark tunnel. Angry male voices that drew Harper around and sent her adrenaline soaring.

"Motherfucker, they've realized she's gone." Rusty dropped the girl to her feet and grasped her by the shoulders. "Hey. Wake up." He shook her, then grasped her by the chin, forcing her head up. "Look at me. Megan, I need you to stand on your own."

The voices grew louder. As did their footsteps. Coming right toward them. "Uh, McClane."

The girl's eyes fluttered open. She looked at Rusty with a dazed expression. "Megan? I need you to go with Blake. Stay with her, don't slow her down." He twisted to look at Harper. "Take her and run."

His intention hit her like a swift punch to the gut. "What?" She grabbed hold just as he pushed the girl at her. "No. Are you crazy? Come with us."

"I'll hold them off as long as I can. Just get her the hell out of here." He quickly scanned the ground and reached for a two-by-four with a nail sticking out of the end of the wood. Swinging it around, he glanced back at her and yelled, "What are you waiting for? Go!"

Wide-eyed, Harper stared at him in horror as she steadied the girl on her feet. Then she spotted the bodies coming straight at them—two, at least. And her pulse went stratospheric. There was no time to give him her gun, no time to do anything but run.

"Come on, Megan." She grasped the girl by the arm and hauled her with her. "We have to go *now*."

She all but dragged Megan down the tunnel and around the next corner. The girl was like dead weight, struggling to keep up, her bare feet digging into the dirt as she slipped and stumbled. Twice she went down, and Harper had to haul her up with a yank she was afraid might jerk the girl's arm out of its socket. But she was too focused on what was going on behind them to care—on the unmistakable sounds of a fight—of fists slamming into bone, of grunts, of groans, of the thwack of what she hoped was Rusty's two-by-four doing damage to those fuckers.

Please let him get through this. Please let him be okay . . .

The pleas rang through her mind as she rounded the last turn, spotting the stairs and the red door. Hauling the struggling girl up the steps with her, she fumbled for the door handle, jerked it open, and pushed the girl through.

And froze when a gunshot echoed through the dark tunnel at her back.

CHAPTER ELEVEN

Harper's heart felt as if it had lurched into her throat. She stared into the darkness and waited, willing Rusty to come running around the corner toward her, praying for any sign or sound that told her he was okay.

Please, please, please, please, please . . .

Memories of the day her father had been shot flooded her memory, tightening her throat. The blood. The way he'd been lying in a pool of blood like an animal. She swallowed hard, not wanting to go through that again. Praying for history not to be repeating itself.

Come on, come on, come on . . .

The girl groaned at Harper's back. A shuffling sounded, and she heard a male voice say, "Hey, what's going on back here?"

Her entire body vibrated with the need to go back for Rusty, but she couldn't leave the girl. She had to get her to safety first. If she let something happen to her now, if Rusty found out . . .

Harper swallowed hard and turned toward Megan, lying on the floor like a sack of potatoes. The door to the tunnel snapped shut at her back. She quickly moved to Megan's side, where a man with a beard and a leather vest was eyeing her warily as if he wasn't sure if she was going to throw up or pass out.

Harper grasped the girl by the arms and pulled her to her feet. Sliding an arm around her waist, she said to the man, "Sorry. She had a little too much to drink, I'm afraid."

The man's gaze narrowed. "I don't remember seeing either of you in here before—"

"Just on our way out." She tugged Megan's arm over her shoulder and helped the girl through the bar and out onto the street.

Fresh air hit her, filling her lungs. Streetlights shone down around them, illuminating the wet pavement, but she didn't slow her pace, didn't give Megan a chance to rest. She hauled the girl down another block to her car, braced her against the side while she dug her keys from the duffel on her back, then yanked the back door open and pushed her in.

Her nerves hummed as she shut the door and glanced back the way they'd come, toward the bar with its flashing neon sign. "Come on, McClane," she whispered.

Long minutes passed with no sign of him. Her anxiety shot higher. She tugged the duffel free and tossed it in the trunk, then came back, crossed her arms over her chest, and paced the width of the sidewalk as she waited.

He was strong. He was tough. He could handle two thugs, right? He'd taken down the two in the tunnel the other night, right?

"Come on, come on, come on . . ."

When another few minutes passed with no sign of him, she stopped and glanced in the back window. The girl was dead asleep on the back seat of her car. Oblivious to everything going on around her.

She knew she shouldn't leave the girl, but she couldn't take it anymore. She hit the lock button on her fob. If he was hurt, if he was bleeding . . .

Her adrenaline spiked, and she pushed her feet into a jog. The bar door swooshed open halfway down the block, and Rusty stumbled out onto the sidewalk.

Her muscles shifted into overdrive. She reached him just as he lifted his head in her direction. Capturing him around the waist, she pulled him up against her, afraid he was about to fall. He was sweating, his hair dusty and rumpled, his jacket ripped at the shoulder, his clothing askew. And there was blood dripping down the side of his face. Blood that sent her heart into overdrive.

"I've got you. Are you okay?" Her hands streaked over his torso, searching for any signs of a bullet hole or more bleeding. "Where are you hurt?"

"I'm . . . fine." He staggered, then righted himself, pushing against her so he was standing upright. Closing his hand around her upper arm as if he needed something to keep himself steady, he gave his head a swift shake. "Just . . . got my bell rung."

She grasped his face in both of her hands and forced him to look her in the eye. "Let me see." Her gaze skipped over his face. "Your pupils are a little dilated. You could have a concussion. What happened down there?"

"Guy hit me. Hard."

That told her nothing. She let go of his face and grasped him by the arm. "Come on."

Carefully, she led him to her car, walked him around to the passenger side, and pulled the door open for him. Breathing easier knowing he was okay, she moved to the back of the vehicle, found her cell in the duffel, dialed, and held the phone up to her ear. "Hey," she said when the person on the other end picked up. "I need you to meet me at the circle on Montgomery, down by the water. Yeah. I'll be there in about three minutes."

She clicked "End," clutched the phone in her hand, and moved for the driver's door.

Once she was behind the wheel, Rusty glanced at her and said, "Who did you call?"

"Help."

"Mind expanding?"

"Someone I trust." She reached into the console between the seats and handed him a stack of tissues. "Just . . . sit still and try not to bleed all over the interior of my car."

He took the tissues as she pulled out onto the street, glancing once over his shoulder at the girl still sound asleep on her back seat.

Looking back at Harper as he pressed the tissue to his forehead, he asked, "Is she alive?"

"Yes. Thanks to you."

"No. Thanks to *us*. We make a pretty good team."

Her lips thinned as she made a turn, heading for the waterfront. Yes, they did, and that was going to be a problem for her. Not just because he was her ticket back to a life she thought she'd never have again but because she wanted him. She wanted him in her bed and between her thighs. And she had no idea how that was going to fuck up her plans in the long run.

———

Harper was quiet as they drove to the waterfront, and considering Rusty's ears were still ringing from that hit he'd taken to the side of the head, he was glad for it.

She slowed and pulled to a stop in the roundabout that faced South Waterfront Park. A hotel stood to their left above a closed steakhouse. At this hour, the street was deserted, and the lights from the Marquam Bridge illuminated the empty, damp sidewalks and the fancy yachts docked at the Riverplace Marina.

Rusty tugged the tissues away from his head and examined the bloodstain in the streetlights.

"How is it?" Harper asked.

"Fine." He pressed the tissues back against the corner of his forehead and glanced her way. "Guess we have matching injuries now. How's your head?"

She brushed the hair to the side of her forehead, pulling the locks away from the small red wound that had already healed quite a bit since the other night and was virtually hidden behind her bangs. "Better. You weren't kidding when you said you knew what you were doing with a needle and threa—"

Car lights shone in Harper's window, then moved behind her car as the vehicle slowed to a stop.

Reaching for the door handle, Harper said, "There he is. Right on time."

Rusty still wasn't sure what kind of "help" she'd called, and considering her connections with the police, he was more than a little concerned it might be one of those detectives who'd wanted to arrest him earlier in the week.

He watched through the rearview mirror as a man with dark hair dressed in jeans and a sweatshirt climbed out of the blue sedan. The man stopped at the hood of his car and perched his hands on his hips as Harper met him behind her car and spoke to him in a mumbled voice Rusty couldn't quite make out. Rusty didn't recognize the guy, and Harper didn't seem at all wary, so Rusty popped his side door open and climbed out.

The man's gaze flicked Rusty's way, then his eyes widened and he looked back at Harper. "Shit. You're working *with* him? After everything I told you? Are you insane?"

Rusty's back tightened as he shoved the bloody tissues into his pocket.

"Relax," Harper said. "I've got it handled."

The man glanced down at her evening gown, muddy and ripped around the bottom hem as she stood on the sidewalk in scuffed tennis shoes. "I'm starting to wonder just what that means. And how you've got it handled."

Whoa. That got Rusty's attention. He moved toward the back of the car. "Excuse me? Who are you?"

The man shot him a perturbed look. "Brett Callahan. Detective Brett Callahan."

Rusty recognized that name. He just didn't know from where. He came to a stop next to Harper, just in case this guy tried anything.

"I happen to be a friend of O'Donnell's." He looked back at Harper. "And you know better than to be anywhere alone with this guy. There's an open investigation going on."

Regardless of what this guy was saying, Rusty didn't like the tone in which he was saying it to Harper. He stepped forward. "Why don't you dial it down a no—"

Harper pressed a hand on his chest, stopping him from getting right in Callahan's face. "Calm down." She gazed up at him with a let-me-handle-this face. Then turning toward Callahan, she said, "I found Melony Strauss. She's alive and well and staying with her father. McClane here didn't have anything to do with her disappearance."

Callahan turned a skeptical look Rusty's way, then looked back at Harper. "It doesn't change any of what I told you before."

"I know that," Harper said. "But that's not why I called you. I called you because I need help with what's in the back of my car."

Callahan's lips thinned, and then he stepped around Rusty and moved to the passenger side of Harper's vehicle to peer into the back window. "Shit," he muttered. "That's Megan Christianson."

"You know her?" Harper asked, looking after him.

Callahan shook his head and moved back to stand on Rusty's other side. "She went missing up in Seattle about three weeks ago. Was ruled a runaway. And you found her tonight?"

Harper nodded.

"Where?" Callahan asked.

Harper glanced up at Rusty, then at Callahan. "I'm not sure you really want to know. All things considered." When he only shot her a blank look, she added, "At a party. A ritzy one downtown."

"Let me guess. A party the Plague was using as a cover."

"Are you working a case against the Plague?"

"No, but I don't need to be working a specific case to know what they're up to. Everyone in the division knows about the Plague, but it's not talked about because we don't have any leads to bring them down." He flicked a look Rusty's way. "Up until Robin Hood showed up on the scene, they've been operating two steps ahead of us. Which means—"

"Which means someone on the inside is feeding them information," Harper finished for him. "Damn. I hadn't considered that."

"Yeah." Callahan's lips thinned as he glanced once more at Rusty. "Which is why you having any connection whatsoever to anyone they think might be Robin Hood is not going to end well for you."

Rusty's chest tightened. If what Callahan was saying was true, then the cops already suspected his alias. And if a few of them were dirty, then the Plague suspected as well.

He looked down at Harper, realizing he was putting her in danger just by being near her.

"I'm not worried about me," Harper said. "I'm worried about girls like this. Can you help us out with her?"

"Yeah." Callahan glanced toward the back window of Harper's car, where the girl was still sound asleep. "Let's get her moved to my car."

It took all three of them to get her out, then Rusty and Callahan carried her to Callahan's back seat and laid her down. The girl didn't even move a muscle. Grabbing a blanket from her trunk, Harper tossed it over her, then stepped back as Callahan closed the door.

"Are you going to take her downtown and file a report about this?" she asked.

"No. I've got her parents' address. I'll drive her up to Seattle myself tonight. I don't want anyone realizing she was found."

Which meant he didn't want anyone at the station to know he'd had anything to do with her discovery.

Harper crossed her arms over her chest and shivered in the cool night air. "I appreciate this, Brett."

"Yeah, I know you do." He moved around his car to the driver-side door and flicked one last look at Rusty. "Just do me a favor. Go home and try to stay out of trouble. I'll try to cover for you as much as I can. Just remember what I told you before."

"I will. Thanks."

He climbed into his car, started the ignition, and slowly pulled away from the curb. And as they watched him go, a sinking feeling of guilt Rusty didn't like slid through him.

Harper turned and looked up at him. "Dang. You're bleeding again. Where are those tissues?"

Swiping his fingers over the oozing wound, Rusty glanced at the blood on his hand, then wiped it on his pant leg. "It's fine."

"It's not fine." She stepped off the curb and moved for her car. "Get in. You need that taken care of."

"You should go home like your friend said. I can find my way back on my own."

"What?" She stopped with one hand on her open door and looked over the car at him. "I'm not leaving you down here like that. Get in."

"Blake—"

"Harper," she corrected, staring at him with a get-over-it expression that was so damn alluring it was all he could do not to walk around and kiss it from her face.

And damn but he liked the way her first name sounded. Wanted to say it. When he was kissing her. Or touching her. Or taking her.

He sighed, pushing that thought out of his head because it was never going to happen. "Look, I appreciate the help tonight, but Callahan's right. I'm not someone you should be around."

"Get in the car, McClane. I'm still armed, and I'm not in the mood to repeat myself."

She slid behind the wheel and pulled her door shut with a snap. As he stood there staring after her, he frowned at her bossiness. Then that frown turned to a curl of his lips he couldn't stop because he *liked* that bossiness way more than he knew he should.

He made his way to the passenger side, opened the front door, and climbed in. She didn't look at him as she pulled away from the curb, but as soon as she turned he knew they weren't heading back downtown where he'd left a rental vehicle in a parking garage several blocks from the party.

He sat in silence as she drove, then finally said, "So are you going to tell me what that was all about back there?"

"It was about the girl."

He frowned. "Not that. Whatever Callahan told you about me before. That thing he kept reminding you of."

"Oh. That." Her jaw tensed. "When your name turned up in connection with the Strauss disappearance, the department received some . . . pressure from the city to connect you to the case."

"Pressure from whom?"

"The mayor."

Rusty's mind spun. "I don't know the mayor." In fact, he couldn't remember who the mayor of Portland even was.

"Not a surprise." She made a turn. "But the mayor knows you. Or your family, I should say. Miriam Kasdan was a huge donor to his political campaign."

"Holy shit." His eyes widened when he realized where she was leading him.

"Yep. Your brother was responsible for her incarceration and the end of those donations. Which means the mayor isn't particularly thrilled with anyone with the McClane last name."

Rusty rested his elbow on the windowsill and rubbed a hand over his dusty hair. This was definitely not good news. It didn't matter that Melony Strauss was alive and well. If what Harper said was true, the police were still going to be looking for any connection they could make between him and any of the other missing girls. Even if they thought the Plague might actually be responsible.

"They're not going to tie you to anything." She glanced his way, the dashboard lights illuminating her features in the dark. "So don't worry."

"If they think I'm Robin Hood, then the Plague likely does as well." He met her gaze head-on. "You're putting yourself at risk not just with them but also with the police now. I don't want them to connect you to anything I've done."

"They won't." She pulled into the drive of a cute little English Tudor set back from the road in the Hillside neighborhood of Northeast Portland and killed the engine. "Besides. I like to live dangerously."

"Harper—"

She climbed out of the car before he could try to talk some sense into her and slammed the door.

Sighing, he got out as well and looked at her over the hood of the car. "I didn't ask you to get involved in this."

"Nope. But I am. Stop complaining and come on."

She grabbed her duffel bag from the trunk and headed up the front walk to the arched, covered entryway. Flipping the keys around, she found the right one, slid it into the lock, and pushed the old red door open.

He stepped into the house after her and looked around. Three archways led to different rooms on each side of him. One opened to a living room with a big white wood-burning fireplace and plush white furnishings. One to a narrow hallway that led to the back of the house and a set of stairs that went up. And the last to a formal dining room with an antique wooden table and six upholstered chairs.

She turned on the overhead light, closed the door at his back, and flipped the lock. Kicking off her sneakers in the entryway, she motioned with her hand for him to follow. "This way. I have bandages in the kitchen."

The hallway ended in a long galley kitchen in the back that had red tile counters and a breakfast nook with a round white table and four wooden chairs. French doors looked out onto a wooded darkness, and to the left, he spotted a kitchen desk and a laundry room.

She pulled out a chair at the table, turned it to face the kitchen, and said, "Sit."

He did as she said, eyeing her bare feet on the old wood floor, her pink-painted toenails catching the light as she moved, and the muddy edge of her dress dragging behind her. "I should have taken my shoes off out fro—"

"You're fine." She tugged a cabinet open and pushed to her toes for a box of bandages and a bottle of alcohol.

Feeling out of place and unsure why she'd brought him to her house when she could have just cut him free after they met with Callahan, he searched for something to fill the silence. "This is a nice place."

"Thanks. It was my parents'."

"Did they downsize?" As he watched the muscles in her shoulders flex while she found the supplies she needed, it occurred to him he knew virtually nothing about her. Nothing except the taste of her wicked lips and how curvy she was beneath that sinful dress.

"No. They left it to me in the will."

Shit.

She turned toward him. "Take that ripped jacket off."

Feeling like a heel, he shrugged out of the jacket and folded it over the back of the chair. She stepped up next to him and brushed the hair back from his forehead. "This might sting."

She ran a cold cotton ball over his cut, and he sucked in a breath. "Sorry."

"It's fine." She smelled like tangerines. That was the scent he hadn't been able to identify before, he realized as she blew gently over the spot, then rubbed the cotton ball against his wound again. Tangerines and honey and vanilla. A dangerous combination.

"Sorry about your parents."

"You don't need to be. You weren't responsible."

He chanced a look up and saw that she was intently focused on cleaning his wound. And though he knew it was probably a sore subject he should steer clear of, he wanted to know more about her. Wanted to know what made her the tough-as-nails investigator who'd stared him down during their first meeting. "How did they die?"

Her eyes narrowed on his forehead. "My mom passed away when I was a kid. Cancer. My dad"—she blew against his wound again, her warm breath sending a shiver of awareness down his spine—"was killed almost two years ago in the line of duty."

"Your father was a cop?"

"Deputy chief of police."

Even worse. "What happened?"

She dropped the bloody cotton ball on the counter at her side and looked at the wound from different angles. "He was on patrol with a rookie. Observing. They got a call about a domestic abuse situation. Went to check it out. The guy inside the house pulled a gun and shot him through the window as he was approaching the front door."

"Jesus."

She shrugged and reached back to the counter. "It happens."

"Shouldn't happen, though," he said softly, watching her carefully. "No, but it does. He knew the risks of the job. We all did. I don't think this needs stitches. It's not that deep. A couple Steri-Strips should do the trick."

He nodded, and she went to work applying the tape to hold the skin together, then covered it with a bandage. "There. You'll be good as new in a couple days."

She turned, grabbed the wrappers from the bandages, and moved to toss them in the garbage under the sink. And watching her carefully, he realized she was acting standoffish all of a sudden. Nervous. Not at all how she'd been acting when they'd met with Callahan or on the drive over here.

"Are you okay, Harper?"

"Me? I'm fine. I told you. It was a long time ago."

Two years wasn't that long, but that wasn't what he was talking about. "I meant right now. After everything that happened tonight."

She froze with one hand on the edge of the sink, and even though she was facing away from him, toward the window, he didn't miss the blush that rose in her cheeks. A blush that told him she was remembering everything that had happened between them at the club.

"Tonight? Sure. I'm fine." Not looking at him, she stepped close once more, grabbed the extra bandages from the counter, and stuffed them back in the box. "It was all just an act."

Bullshit. Her hands were shaking as she hastily tried to close that box.

She replaced the box in the cupboard, then dropped to her heels. "If you're hungry, I could—"

He grasped her by the hand before she could get another step away and gently tugged. She landed on his lap with a grunt.

Her hand pressed against his chest, but he didn't let her lean back. He wrapped his arm around her, pulling her closer against him.

"What are you doing, McClane?"

"Rusty," he corrected, liking that she was so damn nervous. He was nervous too, but not for the same reason. "And as for what I'm doing? Something I probably shouldn't."

He pressed his mouth to hers and kissed her. And the second her mouth opened in a cute little *O* of surprise, he ignored every instinct telling him this was a bad idea and dove in to taste her all over again.

CHAPTER TWELVE

Harper sucked in a breath the second Rusty kissed her, unsure of what she should do. Had she brought him here because she'd wanted this to happen? Yes. But it still wasn't smart. It still wouldn't help her in the long run. But damn, the man tasted good—like heat and life and heaven all rolled into one. And he knew just how to kiss to make a woman's knees turn to complete jelly.

She groaned and opened to his kiss, unable to hold back. And then she was glad she was sitting on his lap and that he was holding her up because he kissed her deeper and all but rocked the world right out from under her.

When she was breathless, when she could hardly see straight, he drew back, nipped at her bottom lip, and grinned down at her. "I think I really need to know what's under this dress and why it keeps pressing into me."

She couldn't stop herself. She laughed, wrapped her arm around his back, and dropped her forehead against his shoulder. "It's my weapon. There are no surprises under this dress. At least not that kind."

"Thank God. I really wasn't in the mood for *The Crying Game*."

She leaned back slightly, glad he was still holding her up, pushed the skirt of her dress over, and unhooked the holster from her thigh. Pulling it out from under her, she set her weapon on the counter at her side. "Better?"

"Much."

He pulled her closer and leaned in to kiss her, but she stopped him with a finger against his lips. "Wait."

Instead of kissing her lips, he settled for kissing her finger. "Yes?"

Oh man. She wanted this. Wanted *him.* But wasn't sure. "This is a bad idea."

"My life is an exercise in bad ideas." He nipped at the side of her finger, sending a thrill through her she liked way too much.

"So is mine, which is why we should both double-think this."

"Harper." He lifted his hand, closed it around hers, and easily tugged her forward, forcing her to slide her arm around his neck once more. "Two wrongs can sometimes make a right."

Her eyes narrowed. "Are you getting all mathematical on me?"

"If it works? Absolutely."

She smiled as he kissed the corner of her mouth. "I was never very good at math."

"Well, lucky for you, I was an A student." He swept one arm under her knees and pushed to his feet, lifting her as he shifted her around and propped her up on the kitchen counter.

She immediately reached for him, opening her legs so he could slide in close. "So, Mr. Mathematician. Just what did you have in mind?"

He slid one hand under the fabric of her skirt. "First, I'm going to see for myself what's really under here. It's been driving me crazy all night."

She laughed, but when he drew her skirt aside and glanced down at her panties and his eyes filled with heat, her laughter turned to a shiver she felt everywhere. "Well? Surprised? Or happy?"

"Oh, baby doll." He placed the pad of his thumb right between her legs. Right over her panties, to press against that already tingling bundle of nerves. "You're soaked already. I'm definitely both."

He opened his mouth over hers and slid his tongue between her lips in a passionate kiss as he gently brushed his thumb back and forth over her clit. And gasping at the wicked-hot sensation, she wrapped her arms around his neck and pulled him closer and kissed him back, suddenly ravenous for him. All of him. Regardless of the consequences.

"Rusty . . ."

He tipped his head the other way. Kissed her deeper. Applied a tiny bit more pressure that made her whole body tremble. "Yes?"

Her knees pressed tight against his sides, and she gripped the sides of his face, taking charge of the kiss that had already destroyed the last bit of her resolve. "You're torturing me." She licked into his mouth and nipped at his bottom lip, loving the groan he made in response. "You've been torturing me since the club."

"I'm only getting started."

She shivered as he kissed the corner of her mouth, her jaw, as he worked his way to her ear and breathed against her neck. Between her legs, he teased her clit until she groaned. Then, lifting his free hand, he tugged the strap of her dress down her arm, inched his lips across her throat, and nipped at her sensitive shoulder as his hand came around to palm her exposed breast.

She shivered again, but it was the heat in his dark eyes as he lifted his head and looked at her, as he pulled his hand from between her legs and pushed the other strap down to free both her breasts, that made her wet. Made her ache. Made her ready for whatever he wanted to do to her.

His sultry gaze dropped to her breasts, and he palmed both in his big, scarred hands, rolling the tips of her nipples between his thumbs and forefingers. "You are absolutely gorgeous, Harper. I can't wait to see all of you." He lifted her left breast with his hand and lowered his head. "I can't wait to taste every inch of you."

His tongue was wet and soft and electric as it laved against the tip of her breast, and unable to stop herself, she dropped her head back against the upper cabinet, threaded one hand into his hair, and moaned as he licked and nipped and sucked until her whole body felt ready to combust in flames.

He wasn't satisfied with tasting only part of her. He moved to the other breast and repeated the process until she saw stars, continuing to torment her other wet nipple until she arched her back, all but begging for more. And then he moved to the valley between her breasts and kissed a trail of heat down her belly, over the dress bunched at her waist, until he was breathing, hot and wicked, right against her mound.

He pushed her legs wide and nuzzled her damp panties with the tip of his nose. "Oh, baby doll. How did you know green was my favorite color?"

That nickname sounded ridiculous, especially for a girl like her, but part of her liked it. And holy hell, she really liked what he was doing right now and wasn't about to say anything to make him stop. "Rusty . . ."

Her hands slipped from his shoulders to the edge of the counter as he lowered to his knees. And before she could even get the plea out of her throat, he tugged her thong to the side and licked a path of fire straight up her center.

She gasped, fumbled to find her footing on the drawer pulls beside her feet. Holding her firmly at the thighs so she wouldn't fall, Rusty ran his tongue over her again, circling her clit until she groaned and lifted her hands to the cabinets beside her so she could arch against his mouth and savor every single swirl and lick and brush of his talented tongue.

"Oh yes . . ." Pleasure streaked down her spine. Groaning at the sensations he was building inside her, she shifted one hand to his hair again, pulling him closer so she could arch harder against his mouth.

His tongue moved faster. One hand moved from her inner thigh and brushed her wetness, and then she felt one thick digit press deep inside her, finding that perfect spot on the very first try.

"Oh shit . . ." Her eyes slammed shut. She arched against him again and again while he slowly stroked that spot in a come-hither move that drove her absolutely fucking wild. "Yes, yes, oh fuck, there, right *theeeeere* . . ."

The orgasm slammed into her without warning, stealing her breath, her sight, her hearing, consuming her in a tidal wave of pleasure she hadn't seen coming. And even when it should have stopped, it went on, making her twitch and groan and cry out until her voice gave out on its own and she slumped against the cabinets at her back.

A soft chuckle met her ears, bringing sound back into play around her. Sweaty, dazed, she blinked several times and opened her eyes to Rusty pressing soft, tantalizing kisses against her inner thighs, her belly, over her breasts, until he found her mouth and dove in to devour her.

He tasted like sin and the tangy sweetness of her own arousal, and as she opened to him, desire came rushing back, making her hungry for more, making her greedy for him.

She pushed away from the cabinets so she was upright, wrapped her arms around his shoulders, and her legs around his waist, and kissed him hard and deep. "I want you," she whispered. "I want you right now."

He chuckled against her mouth, then sucked gently on her bottom lip. "You don't need a break? I was afraid you blacked out there for a second."

She was pretty sure she had. And she wanted to do it again.

She licked into his mouth again and dropped her hands to his belt. "I want you now."

He captured her hands before he could pull the button free and drew back from her lips. "I think I need a cold shower first."

"You're kidding, right?"

A nervous smile curled the edge of his lips. "Actually, no. You've got me pretty hot." He pressed his mouth to hers in a swift kiss once more. "I need something to cool me down, or this is going to be over too fast. It's been a while for me."

It had been a while for her too. And after what he'd just done to her, she did not want him anywhere near a cold shower.

Pressing a hand against his chest, she pushed him back and dropped to her bare feet on the kitchen floor. "I've got something way better than a cold shower. Guaranteed to take the edge off."

She pushed him back another step until he was leaning against the opposite counter in the galley kitchen, then lowered to her knees and reached for his buckle.

He sucked in a breath and stared down at her with smoldering eyes as she moved to the button on his slacks, then slowly worked the zipper down.

"Harper . . ."

"Yes?" He was already hard. Hard and hot and pulsing beneath his black boxer briefs. She nuzzled his package as she lifted her hands and worked the buttons on his shirt free, wanting to see all of him when she looked up. He helped her, pulling his shirttails out of the back of his slacks and slipping the top buttons free. And as he did, she reached inside his boxers and drew his magnificent erection into the light, licking her lips at how thick and long and ready he was for her already.

She wrapped her hand around the base, slid it up to cuff the head and back down. And he watched her the entire time with pure lust, his face flushed, his carved stomach tight and quivering with every touch. Her own body responded to his show of pleasure. Between her legs, her sex throbbed with the need for another release. But she held back, wanting to pleasure him the way he'd pleasured her. Wanting to take him where no other woman ever had.

She licked the tip of his cock, loving the way he groaned at the contact. Looking up, she did it again, and whispered, "Do you like that?"

"Yes." A muscle in his neck flexed, and his hand moved to the counter at his side, gripping it until his knuckles turned white.

"Do you want me to do it again?"

"Oh yes."

She ran the flat of her tongue all along the flared underside of the head, absolutely riveted by the way he trembled. "Do you want more?"

"Fuck yes."

She did it again. "Tell me, then. Tell me exactly what you want me to do to you."

His other hand wrapped around the back of her neck, and his thick fingers slid up into her hair. "I want you to wrap your lips around my cock and take me deep into that hot little mouth."

Fire erupted inside her. His sultry words, the hunger in his glazed eyes, even the hand at the back of her head pulling her closer, made her feel desired, wicked, powerful, and erotic. She closed her mouth around him, sucking hard, taking him all the way on the first thrust. And he groaned long and deep as he hit the back of her throat, held still a split second, then drew his hips back. Massaging the underside of his cock as he pulled away, she focused on giving him as much pleasure as possible, captured her breath when he almost slipped free of her lips, then sucked all over again as he drove into her mouth once more.

His moans grew louder. She wrapped her arms around his thighs, holding herself up as she worked him over with her mouth, not wanting to let him go until he came. He tried to pull away, and she knew he was trying to be gentle, but she didn't want gentle. She wanted to taste his release. She wanted to watch him shake when he came. She wanted to know what he sounded like in the throes of blinding ecstasy, and then she wanted him to remember that she'd taken him there.

She sucked harder. Moved her head faster. Took him even deeper. And she sensed his reaction between her lips as he grew harder. Felt it in his body where she held him, and in his muscles trembling faster. And she tasted it in her mouth where the first drops of his pre-come coated her tongue and set off a frenzy of need in her blood.

"*Fuck.* Harper." His other hand closed over the back of her head. The muscles in his throat strained as he looked down at her. "I'm not going to be able to hold back."

She let him slip free of her mouth long enough to gasp, "Don't. Use my mouth. I want you to do it. I want to feel you explode across my tongue. I want to taste your come."

She drew him deep again, and whether it was her dirty words or her aggressiveness as she sucked hard and swallowed around the head of his cock, she'd never know. But something primal broke free inside him. She felt it as he grasped both sides of her head and thrust deep again and again. She heard it in the animalistic groan that rose in his throat. And she tasted it when he swelled in her mouth and erupted in a burst of pleasure that she swallowed again and again and again until he let go of her head, collapsed back against the counter, and twitched from the power of his release.

Pure satisfaction whipped through her. A victory she'd never known she could feel from giving oral sex. Licking up the last of his release, she finally let go of his heavenly, still very hard erection and smiled up at him. "Well? Better than a cold shower?"

His skin was slicked with sweat, his face still flushed from his arousal, his eyes as dark as they'd been before, and when he groaned, grasped her upper arms, and pulled her to her feet with a smile that was all her doing, that victory only swelled stronger inside her.

"Way better." He pressed his mouth to hers and kissed her hard. "Dear God, you wrecked me."

Smiling, she closed her hand around his erection and gently stroked him from base to tip again. "Hopefully not. I still have plans for you."

He groaned again and pushed her lips apart with his tongue, dipping in for an erotic, wet, scorching kiss she felt everywhere. "I don't have a condom."

"I do." She lifted her arms around his neck and kissed him back.

"Where?" he asked against her lips.

"Upstairs. In my nightstand."

He tucked his erection back in his boxers, and then his hands streaked down to her butt and hefted her up, lifting her so her legs could slide right around his waist.

She gasped in surprise and held on tight to his shoulders as he moved out of the kitchen, headed down the hall, then turned for the stairs.

His mouth closed over hers again, licking fire across her tongue, and then he drew back and nipped at her bottom lip. "If I trip going up these stairs, we're both in trouble."

She giggled and tightened her legs around him, hefting herself higher in his arms as she kissed him again, shaking with the need to feel him on top of her, inside of her, to give herself over to everything he wanted.

"Turn right," she mumbled as he reached the top of the stairs. "End of the hall."

His kisses turned frenzied, his hands kneading her ass, making her tremble as he carried her. She felt her back hit the door, smelled the lilac diffuser she'd set up in her room, but didn't let go of him as he carried her in, didn't want to release him for even a second, not even to turn on a light.

"Hurry," she whispered.

He groaned as he kissed her, and then she was falling, the soft mattress brushing her spine. But it was the hard, hot, erotic man at her front she couldn't get enough of.

With one knee on the bed between her legs, he drew back and wrestled to get his shirt all the way off. Twisting to her side, not wanting to waste any time, she leaned over the side of the bed, jerked the nightstand drawer open, and grabbed a condom from the box in the back.

His magnificent erection was already out, catching the moonlight shining through the arched windows, his slacks and boxers pushed down just enough to set him free. She sat up and tore the condom wrapper open with her teeth, but before she could reach for him and roll it on, he pushed her back, grasped the thong between her legs, and pulled until the fabric snapped in two.

The arousal burning inside her flared white-hot. And when he leaned forward, she stared into his smoldering eyes and rolled the condom down his straining length, then wrapped her hand around the thick base and drew him toward her. "Come here."

He groaned as his mouth lowered to hers, as his tongue pushed between her lips, as his hard length thrust deep inside her in one slick move. And gasping at the tight fit, at the way he filled her so perfectly, she rose up to meet him, contracting around him when he drew back, wrapping her hand around his neck to hold his mouth close to hers, moaning against his lips when he drove in deep all over again.

They found a rhythm that made her absolutely wild, and as her body softened, as her sex grew wetter, she gave herself over to the wicked sensations and tightened even more against every thrust, knowing her climax was rushing toward her fast, not wanting it to engulf her in a wave of bliss until it engulfed him too.

"Ah God," she panted against his lips, holding on to him with aching muscles as he drove into her, harder, faster, his thrusts striking that perfect spot again and again. "More." She kissed him. "There, more. Oh *yes*, Rusty, right there. I'm about to come. Come with me."

He grunted, lifted his elbow from the mattress where he was leaning, braced his hand near her head, and gripped the comforter in his fist as he pounded into her with a force that pushed her directly to the edge and dragged a scream from her throat.

"Oh, fuck yes." He grunted. "I *feel* you coming. Do it. Yes. Come all around me, Harper."

She couldn't stop from doing just that. Her climax slammed into her and ricocheted through every cell, blinding her with mind-numbing pleasure. Vaguely, she felt him swell inside her, felt his erection thicken and lengthen. Heard him grunt with exertion as he drew back and shoved in even deeper. And then he groaned long and deep, holding still as he twitched and his orgasm claimed him. But she was too lost in another orgasm to savor it. Completely spellbound by him and the almost frenzied way he'd fucked her into complete and utter bliss.

She was limp when she finally tore her eyes open. Limp and sweaty and pinned beneath him on the mattress. But she didn't care. Dear God, she didn't care at all because that was the most incredible orgasm—two orgasms—she'd ever had.

"Holy hell, McClane." Though her arms ached—every muscle in her body ached—she lifted her hands to his sweaty shoulders and ran her fingertips down his slick and tempting skin. "This time you wrecked me."

He sucked in a breath, then rolled, tugging her with him until they were both on their sides. Lifting a hand to her face, he brushed the damp hair back from her cheek. "Sorry if I got a little aggressive there."

"You're kidding, right?" She gripped his arm at the elbow, loving the way he was playing with her hair, loving even more the way he was looking at her. As if he wasn't close to being done with her. "I like aggressive. I like it a lot."

"Christ." His lips curled at the edges in a devastating smile, one that tightened her chest in a way she didn't expect, and then he leaned in and kissed her. "You can't say things like that to me." He breathed hot over her lips. "I told you I haven't had sex in a while. I'm like a teenager right now. You keep that up and I'm going to be attacking you again in a matter of minutes."

Oh hell yes . . .

She tightened her grip on his elbow and lifted her lips to his, sliding her knee between his so his erection pressed against her thigh. "No one's stopping you."

He leaned forward and kissed her again. And knowing she had him, that he wasn't going anywhere tonight but exactly where she planned to lead him, she let him taste his fill, let him kiss her sweetly. Then she smiled when he drew back and stared deep into his eyes.

"This time, though," she whispered, "I was thinking you could try out some of those bull-man moves."

His eyes darkened. "Before or after the lights went out?"

"Your choice."

A primal groan echoed from his chest. Then he rolled her onto her back and kissed her. Hard. "Please tell me that wasn't just a three-pack of condoms in your drawer."

She grinned up at him. "It was a dozen. And it was a new box."

"Eleven might be enough. But I doubt it. Especially if you expect me to play bull man tonight."

Her laughter echoed through the room as he lowered his head and nipped at her throat. But it turned to a groan when he found her mouth again and kissed her. A groan she didn't dare hold back from a man she wasn't even close to being done with.

———

Andrew Renwick jerked awake at the sound of his cell phone buzzing on the nightstand and quickly grabbed it so it wouldn't wake Maureen. The number on the screen sent his blood pressure straight through the roof.

"Oh, Andy. Let it go to voice mail," Maureen groaned into her pillow at his side.

He ran a hand over her arm and then pushed out of bed. "I can't. It's Harper. I have to take it."

Maureen sighed and shifted her head the other direction with a mumbled, "Tell her hi from me."

Drawing a calming breath, Andy hit "Answer," stepped out into the hall of his West Hills home, and lifted the phone to his ear. "Yes. I'm here."

"You son of a bitch. He struck again."

Andy's heart dropped like a stone into his belly. "When?"

"Tonight. At the auction. He took the girl before it even started."

Relief filled his chest, but he knew better than to let it show in his voice. Moving quickly down the stairs, he crossed into his home office, shut the door and locked it, then moved to his desk. "Did anyone see him?"

"They were all in masks," he growled.

Andy closed his eyes and perched his elbow on his desk. Of course they were all in masks. Privacy for the buyers was the point.

"There was one person we identified. She snuck into the party through the kitchen."

Andy's heart nearly stopped, and his head came up. *Please, no . . .*

"She's become a liability, Renwick. Just like her father."

"No." He pushed to his feet. He might be guilty of a great many things, but he wasn't going to let his mistakes hurt Harper. "I-I'll talk to her. I'll make sure she backs off."

"If she's working with him, we have no problem killing her, just as we plan to kill him."

"That isn't the case. I promise. I-I'm sure she was looking for him, that's all. She wouldn't help someone like him. She's convinced he's a predator."

"You'd better hope you're right because if you're wrong, she won't be the only one we come after."

Andy swallowed hard, knowing he meant every word he said and that he wasn't just threatening Andy's life, he was threatening Maureen's as well.

"Bring me confirmation of Robin Hood's identity. I'm tired of waiting."

CHAPTER THIRTEEN

"All I've got is chocolate."

From his spot sprawled on the kitchen floor, leaning back against the cupboards in nothing but his slacks, Rusty watched Harper standing in front of the open freezer door, the interior light illuminating her shapely legs as she turned and looked down at him.

"Chocolate's great."

She shut the freezer door, the tails of his purple dress shirt fluttering around her thighs, and grabbed two spoons from a drawer. Dropping to her butt beside him on the hardwood, she handed him a spoon and tugged the top off the ice cream carton. "God, I'm famished."

So was he. And he was hoping the sugar would give him the energy hit he needed because he wasn't anywhere near ready to fall asleep.

She tipped the carton his way, and he dipped his spoon in for a scoop, loving the way she smiled up at him in the moonlight. Loving even more the way she looked right now—delightfully rumpled and sexually satisfied.

"What are you smirking at?" she asked as he savored the ice cream.

"You. In my shirt."

She scooped up a bite of the ice cream. "It's way more comfortable than that dress. And it was the closest thing I could find."

"Uh-huh."

She rolled her eyes. "Don't read anything into it."

"A guy's shirt on a woman's naked body is like a flag on a conquered fortress."

She shook her head and grinned even wider. "Oh my God, that's so sexist."

"It's true." He leaned close and pressed his lips against her cold and sugary ones. "It's also sexy as hell."

She chuckled and went back to eating her ice cream. "Speaking of sexy as hell." She glanced at him as he scooped up another bite. "You were quite the animal tonight."

"You told me to be the bull man."

She bit into her lip and glanced at his mouth. "Yes, I did." Something hot smoldered in her eyes. A fire he sensed was not the least bit extinguished. *Thank God . . .*

"But I wasn't talking about that. I was talking about in general." She glanced sideways at him and licked her spoon. "You said it's been a while for you. And I'm kinda curious . . . just how long is 'a while'?"

He tensed, even though he'd known there was a good chance this topic would come up.

"You don't have to answer if you don't want to," she said quickly, looking down at the ice cream in her lap. "I mean, it's none of my business. Forget I said anything."

She was nervous. Seeing how she suddenly wouldn't meet his eyes relaxed him in a way he didn't expect.

"Harper." He reached for her hand, curling his fingers around hers and drawing their entwined fingers over to his thigh so she would know he wasn't upset. "It's fine if you want to ask. I'm the one who brought it up."

"Yes, but you don't have to tell me if you don't want to. That's like a fourth-date kind of question, and this is just . . ." Her brows drew together as she looked down at their hands. "Well, this isn't even a date. It's . . ."

When her lips thinned and her voice trailed off again, he knew what she was thinking and afraid to say. "Just sex?"

Slowly, her hazel eyes lifted to his. "Well, yeah."

"Really good sex."

She smirked. "Yeah, that too."

He tightened his hand around hers. "It's probably reckless, considering how we met and what happened tonight, but I'm kinda hoping it's more than just really good sex."

"You are?"

Oh, man, he really liked that hopeful lift to her sexy little voice. And the way she was looking at him . . . Desire flared in his blood all over again. A desire he definitely wasn't close to extinguishing.

"Absolutely." He leaned her way and brushed his lips over hers. "I'm crazy about you, Harper Blake. I tried not to be. I tried to keep my distance from you, but you've been stuck in my head since our very first meeting."

"I have?"

"You absolutely have."

She drew in a breath and said, "You've been stuck in my head since then as well. It's more than a little irritating."

He chuckled, relaxing even further with her admission.

"And I really wasn't trying to pry into something I wasn't willing to share myself," she said. "I know 'a while' for a guy is anywhere from a few days to a month, tops. It's just that I haven't been with anyone in over a year. You're the first guy that I've been interested since that jer—"

"Longer."

"What?"

"It's been longer than a year for me."

She stared at him, almost as if she thought she'd heard him wrong. "Longer than a year?"

He nodded.

"How much longer?"

"A lot longer." When she only blinked at him, he thought back and realized, *shit* . . . Had it really been that long? "At least four years."

Her eyes widened.

No, that wasn't right. "Probably closer to five."

"W-why?" Her gaze slid down his bare chest, then lifted back to his face. "You're hot as hell."

He chuckled, *loving* that response. "Thanks. I'll take that as a compliment." He shrugged, feeling self-conscious about the answer but not wanting to hide anything from her. Not when she was being open about how she felt regarding him and this crazy relationship that had sprung up out of nowhere. "I don't know. Somewhere along the way, with my extracurricular activities on the weekends, I kinda lost interest in sex. The things I've seen in a lot of these clubs are not sexy."

"I get that. But still . . . you're a guy. You have to have . . . urges."

He smirked. "I have urges. It's just easier to take care of them in the shower than to deal with the whole dating, getting-to-know-someone, is-this-worth-my-time bullshit, you know?"

She studied him for several seconds in the moonlight, then softly said, "Who was she?"

"Who was who?"

"The woman who hurt you."

Every muscle in his body tensed, and a familiar feeling of guilt settled deep in his chest. One he didn't want to feel now. One he didn't really want to explain to her. He leaned his head back against the cabinet. "What makes you think it was a woman?"

"Because there's a reason you're Robin Hood. And knowing what I know about you now, I'm confident it wasn't a man who broke your heart and turned you into a vigilante."

One corner of his lips tipped up, but it wasn't an amused smile. It was a sad smile. And a little of an amazed smile that she could read him so easily.

He looked down at their joined hands against his thigh, wondering how much he could tell her, wondering what her reaction would be when she learned the truth.

Quietly, she took the spoon from his other hand, dropped it and her spoon into the carton, then set the ice cream on the floor at her side. Without a word, she straddled his lap and rested her hands against his chest as she stared at him with soft, warm hazel eyes, not pushing him even though he knew she was waiting for an answer.

"She was my stepsister," he heard himself say before he even realized the words were out. "She was a year older than me, way more mature, and a lifetime worldlier. I was thirteen when my mother first married her wealthy father and we had to move into his stuffy mansion, and I hated her because I thought she was a snob. She hated me too because up until we moved in, she and her father had been fairly close. He'd taken her everywhere with him. After he married my mother . . . he kind of abandoned her. I realized pretty quickly that she was a loner like me. Struggling to get by. We became friends."

"Sounds like you both needed that."

He nodded, unable to stop now. Wanting Harper to understand, even if he was taking a giant risk. "She was the first girl I ever cared about. The first I . . ."

He blew out a breath and glanced down at Harper's lips and remembered that first night Lily had climbed into his bed in the middle of the night, shaking and crying, asking for him to hold her. He hadn't liked seeing her so scared. Hadn't liked the sound of her sobs. So he'd scooted over, wrapped his arms around her, and held her just like she'd wanted, and nothing had ever been the same.

"My siblings . . . they all know about her. But they think she was my biological sister. I never told them she was my stepsister. I never told them about our relationship. I never told them she was the first girl I ever . . . loved."

"You were involved with her."

"Yeah. But it wasn't sexual. I mean, it might have been if things had turned out differently, but we were just kids. Anything that happened between us was purely innocent—we kissed, we held hands, and at night when she had nightmares, I'd hold her until she fell asleep. It wasn't dirty or wrong, it was just . . ."

"Pure."

There was no judgment in Harper's voice, and when he lifted his gaze to hers, he saw only warmth and encouragement for him to keep going. A flood of relief he didn't deserve rushed through him. "Yeah, that."

She smiled. "I can see you like that. At thirteen, being all protective. A miniature version of you now."

This woman knew exactly what to say to put him at ease. He couldn't remember a time he felt so relaxed around a woman, when he was this crazy about one. He lifted his hands from the floor where he'd been bracing them—just in case—and rested them on Harper's sexy bare thighs, needing to touch her anywhere he could before he went on.

"I didn't know it at the time," he said, "but about three months after we moved in, her father started taking her to these late-night meetings he'd go to now and then. Lily was . . . well developed for her age, and she was strikingly beautiful. One night, after she came back from one of these meetings, I could tell she was upset. She'd normally go into her room and hide for a day or two after the meetings, but this night she didn't. She broke down into tears and told me what happened there. They were at some fancy men's club where women aren't allowed. The men were all old, she said. All drinking and smoking cigars. At first her father told her to just be friendly to the men at the meetings, to help serve drinks and smile. He told her it relaxed his business partners so they could talk shop. But every time he took her, he asked her to do more. 'Don't just be friendly, flirt. Don't just touch their arms when you serve their drink, sit on their laps. Don't say no if one of them wants to touch you. Do whatever they ask, whenever they ask it.' It was all for the good of his career. Which was good for her, according to him."

"Jesus."

"Yeah." He cleared his throat. "I was so shocked and disgusted by what she was insinuating that I lost it. I lost it with her, and I lost it with him too. And that didn't go over well, as I'm sure you can imagine."

"What happened?" Harper asked quietly.

That night flashed in his mind. The rain, the screaming, the fight . . .

"I went after him. Told him she was never going to any of his deranged meetings again. He was in his study, and he never expected this skinny, hundred-and-forty-pound teenage boy to throw a punch at him. I was tall, but I wasn't all that strong, and we were both surprised when I knocked him on his ass. I got out of there as fast as I could. And I thought I'd won when he didn't come after me." He swallowed hard, forcing himself to go on. "She stayed in my room that night, and we made plans to run away together when we left for school the next day, but when I woke, she was already gone."

"He came and took her in the night, didn't he?"

He nodded, staring down at a mole on her thigh near his hand, remembering the panic he'd felt then. The shock when he'd realized what had happened. "They were both gone. I looked everywhere for her—everywhere I could think—but I couldn't find her. And when he came back that night, she wasn't with him."

"What did he do with her?" Harper asked softly.

He braced himself for the shot of pain he always felt when he remembered that night, but it didn't come. And he wasn't sure if that was because he was here with Harper now, or if he'd finally just grown numb to it over the years.

Lifting his gaze to hers, he said, "He sold her. To one of his business partners. To one of the men at the fancy, depraved meetings he used to take her to. He told me because I'd touched her he wouldn't keep her anymore. He must have assumed we were sleeping together. He said she was his, not mine, and he could do whatever he wanted with her. And then he told me not to bother looking for her because I'd never see her again."

"Oh, Rusty."

He ignored her sympathy—didn't need it—and kept going. "I flew into a rage. I don't remember much about that night, just that one minute I was standing there, staring at him in total shock, and the next I was pounding my fists against his face. He was bigger than me, though, and this time he was ready for me. He easily overpowered me and pretty much beat the shit out of me. By the time my mother heard what was happening from the other room and came rushing in, I was bloodied and bruised and writhing on the floor. She made the mistake of stepping between us then. I remember hearing him scream at her to get out. I remember her shrieking at him that she was going to call the police. My eyes were pretty well swollen shut from the beating at that point, but I remember prying them apart and looking up just as he grabbed her and hurled her to the side to get her out of his way so he could go after me again. And as long as I live I will never forget the sound of her head hitting the hearth of the fireplace or the way her body dropped to the ground with a thunk and then went still."

"Oh my God." Harper covered her mouth with her hand. "Did he—"

"Kill her? Yeah. Her skull cracked open. There was blood everywhere."

"I'm so sorry."

He shrugged, looking down at her thigh again. "My biological mother was not an overly affectionate woman. She cared way more about her status and money and rich friends than she ever did about me. I was a burden—a planned one, but still a burden. She got pregnant with me to trap her second husband, and it worked. He married her, and when he died of a heart attack three years later, she inherited a ton of money. But I got in the way of her parties and her romances and jet-setting life, and I had more of a relationship with my nannies than I ever did with her. I like to think she loved me in some way, especially since she died because of me, but I'll never really know."

"She didn't die because of you. She died protecting you. There's a very big difference."

He wasn't entirely sure. And since he hadn't planned to tell her nearly this much, he now just wanted to get it finished.

"He panicked when he realized she was dead. I mean full-on, complete, meltdown panic. To the point where he pretty much forgot about me. I didn't want him to start beating on me again, so I shifted behind the desk where he couldn't see me and just lay there and went still like her, hoping he'd think I was dead too. I waited for him to leave, to get the hell out of there, but he just continued to panic and pace. At some point I heard him on the phone talking to someone, but I was drifting in and out of consciousness at that point, and I honestly have no idea how long that went on. Then I heard voices. Someone had come into the room. A man. They argued. I tried to open my eyes to see who he was, but the swelling was so bad I couldn't make out anything more than fuzzy, dark shapes. Then a gunshot exploded in the room, and I heard a thud, and then the man's voice saying Jordan, my stepfather, was a stupid motherfucker."

"Holy shit."

"It gets better." This part he had no trouble getting through. Shifting against the cabinet, he said, "He crossed the room, checked my mother's pulse, and when he realized she was dead, he lit a match and dropped it on the couch before leaving. The sofa immediately went up in flames. In seconds, the curtains, bookshelves, everything was on fire. I knew I was dead if I didn't get myself out of there, so I struggled to my hands and knees and crawled toward the door. And that's when I heard Jordan call my name. He wasn't dead. Not yet. He was lying on the floor in the middle of that room, his head tipped my way, his arm reaching out to me, begging for me to help him, but I ignored him. I just stared at him as the flames inched their way across the carpet toward his body and ignited his clothing. He screamed, but I stayed and watched. I wanted to see him suffer after everything he'd done. I wanted it so much I didn't even notice that the carpet under me was on fire as well."

"That's what the scars on your arms and stomach are from, aren't they?"

He nodded. "Watching that fire eat him alive was the only thing that jolted me out of that trance. Somehow I made it out of that room, but that's all I remember. The smoke was too thick. I think I collapsed in the foyer. I'm not sure. I remember coughing. Trying to breathe. And then the next thing I knew, I was waking up in the ER, and a woman in hospital scrubs and a white doctor coat was talking to me. She smelled like lilies. It's the only reason I let her touch me. Her name was Hannah McClane."

Harper's eyes slid closed for a second, but when she opened them and met his gaze he saw they were damp with emotion. "And you never found her? Lily?"

"No. I looked for a long time. When I was old enough to hit the clubs, I looked in every one in the Portland area, hoping whoever her father had sold her to was making her work here. But I never saw her. And I know in my gut that I never will. She's dead."

"You don't know that."

"Yeah, I do. She told me once, before all this happened, that she couldn't take it anymore. If he kept making her do those things at those parties, she was going to kill herself. She would have followed through with that. I'm sure of it."

"That's awful. I'm so sorry, Rusty."

"I didn't tell you any of this because I wanted your sympathy. I told you so you'd understand. I'm not a normal guy. The shit I've done and seen and the things I'm still involved in are fucked up. You asked me why it's been so long since I've been with a woman. It's not because I hold out any hope that Lily's still alive. Even if she were, she would not be anything close to the girl I remember. The truth is I haven't been with anyone in a long-ass time because I've been so focused on making sure what happened to her didn't happen to any other girls that I haven't let myself feel anything for anyone else. But my brothers are right. It's not healthy. It's definitely not helping me. And the minute I saw you in that green dress tonight at that party, I knew I didn't want to go on living like that."

He pressed his fingers against her thighs as he stared into her sexy hazel eyes. "I want you and a chance to see where this reckless, impulsive, superhot relationship can go."

Her eyes darkened with a heat he felt everywhere. And then her mouth was on his, her slick tongue sliding between his lips to kiss him deeply, her arms wrapping around his neck, and her sinful body pressing against him everywhere.

He was absolutely breathless when she eased back just a touch and whispered, "I want you too." Breathless and absolutely aching to taste her everywhere all over again.

He pushed away from the cabinet at his back, wrapped his arms around her, and scooted forward on the floor with her on his lap.

"What are you doing?" she asked, glancing toward the floor at her side.

"Getting you right where I want you most." He laid back on the floor so the top of his head was only a few inches from the cabinets he'd just been reclined against, and tugged on her toward him. "Straddle my face, baby doll. I'm starving for you."

Lust flushed her cheeks, and a moan slipped from her lips. But she did as he said, climbing over him until her knees were braced on both sides of his head and his hands were hooked around her thighs, holding her still.

He looked up her gorgeous body and smiled, loving that she was still here, that she hadn't been horrified by what he'd told her. That she still wanted him just as much as he wanted her. "Hold on to that countertop so you don't fall."

She bit her lip and stared down at him with wonder and excitement as she gripped the edge of the counter until her knuckles turned white.

And drawing in a deep whiff of her sultry scent, he finally let go of everything in his past that he'd been holding on tightly to for so very long. Then he parted her with his fingers, tasted her, and took them both straight to heaven.

———

Every muscle in Harper's body was sore as she rolled over in the watery light of morning and peered toward the clock on her nightstand.

Eight thirty-two a.m.

Groaning, glad it was a Saturday and not a workday, she rolled onto her back and tossed an arm over her eyes to block the light. The enticing scent of bacon frying wafted through the air, bringing her senses to life and her eyes wide open.

She pushed up on her elbows, looked toward her open bedroom door, and listened. She could hear the sound of the bacon sizzling, of pans scraping the burner, and someone moving around downstairs in her kitchen.

No, not *someone*. Russell McClane.

Memories of the things he'd done to her last night—in this bed and downstairs in the kitchen—flooded her mind, bringing a rush of warmth to every inch of her body. She shifted her legs, then groaned at her stiff muscles all over again. But this was a good stiffness. The kind that came from a wild night she'd thoroughly enjoyed, and as the muffled sound of his voice—humming—drifted to her ears, she had an uncontrollable urge to go down there and do it all again with him.

Holy hell, she was completely crazy about the man. And when she remembered the things he'd told her last night in the kitchen, she was also awed by his resilience. Awed and more than a little impressed that he hadn't just lived through all that horror but dedicated his life to helping other young girls, right here in Portland.

Ironically, that helping was the one thing that kept her from rushing right down to kiss him good morning. Sitting up slowly, she swiped the hair back from her face and realized . . . she'd crossed a line last night. Instead of reporting the entire ordeal to the cops, she'd participated in stealing from the Plague. And she'd also gotten personally involved with a client. Something that was not allowed in her firm.

Her cell phone buzzed on the nightstand beside her. Holding the sheet to her breasts, she twisted to the side and grabbed it, then frowned when she looked at the screen.

"How the hell did you know I was thinking about the office?" she mumbled down at her phone as she read the text from Andy.

I left four messages for you last night, and you didn't answer any. I'm starting to worry. Call me.—A

Knowing she couldn't leave him hanging, she hit "Call." He answered on the very first ring, which told her—wow—he really was worried.

"You've been MIA for three days, Harper. Is everything all right?"

"Yes, I'm fine. You can stop stressing, Andy."

"Did you find anything on McClane?"

And that was the real reason he was calling, she realized. Harper tried not to be irritated by that little fact as she tugged her knees up under the sheet and wrapped her arm around her legs. She liked Andy— they were friendly—and she really liked his wife, Maureen. And as far as jobs went outside the department, this was a good one. She needed to remember that and not let her irritation show.

"Yeah, I did, actually." Since the last time she'd spoken to Andy was on Monday when she'd left the office to run some leads on Rusty, she knew it was way past time to fill him in. But she had to be careful about not giving too much away. "I found Melony Strauss."

"And?"

"And she's alive and well."

He was silent on the other end of the phone, and the silence struck her as odd. "You're not happy about that?"

"No. Of course. I'm relieved. Where is she?"

Something in his tone had the hairs on her nape standing to attention. "Safe," she heard herself say, though she wasn't entirely sure why she wasn't telling him where she'd found the girl.

"That's good news."

"Yes, it is." Then why didn't he sound as if it were good news?

"So what happened with McClane? How did she get away from him?"

Harper didn't like what he was insinuating. Or where her thoughts were leading as to why he was insinuating it. "Nothing," she lied into the phone. "Nothing happened with McClane. She was never with him after leaving that club."

"Hmm . . ."

He was definitely not happy with that answer. Something was going on. Something she was bound and determined to get to the bottom of.

"Well," Andy said. "I guess that's that, then."

Now he was lying through his teeth.

"Listen, Harper, I know today is a Saturday, but I need you to stop by the office and fill out some paperwork. You've been out of the office all week, and I need your signature on a few things."

"Sure. I can do that."

"I'll be here until about four."

"Okay. I'll stop by early afternoon."

"Good. See you then."

The line clicked off in her ear. Drawing her phone away, she stared down at the screen, an odd feeling rolling through her stomach.

Rusty's humming drifted her way again, and she glanced through the open door toward the stairs. She should probably tell him about the weird conversation she'd just had, but she wasn't sure what to say. And she wanted a little time to do some digging to find out what she could come up with. She also needed to find out more about his extracurricular activities, as he called them, namely how long he'd been doing this, how he'd first learned about the Plague, and who else might be targeting the two of them as well. Then—somehow—she needed to find a way to convince him to let her work with him, not just to rescue more of those girls but to bring down the entire organization so they stopped victimizing girls altogether.

She bit her lip and pressed the end of her phone to her chin. She should also probably tell him about the deal she'd made with the commissioner. But she wasn't sure how to do that and convince him to work with her *and* not make it look like what had happened between them last night had anything to do with trying to get her job back at the department.

"One fine corner you've backed yourself into, Harper." Shaking her head, she threw back the covers and climbed out of bed, then reached for Rusty's dress shirt from the floor and tugged it on. "Better figure out fast how you're going to get out of it."

She fluffed her hair, headed for the stairs, and moved quietly into the kitchen, only to still when she caught sight of Rusty wearing nothing but his boxers and her pink apron, flipping bacon in a pan at her stove.

Her stomach pitched. And pressure—one she'd never felt before—compressed her chest until it felt as if an elephant were sitting right on top of her. A pink phantasmagoric elephant, like the one in her childhood VHS copy of *Fantasia*, dancing and singing around her, trying to reach inside her chest and steal something right from between her ribs.

Her heart, she realized. This heffalump didn't want honey. He was after the one thing she'd vowed long ago never to give away to anyone.

———

Rusty's stomach tightened as he reached for his coffee and eyed Harper next to him at the table. She had been oddly quiet through breakfast. Quiet and strangely detached. So detached, in fact, if Rusty didn't know her better—which he honestly didn't—he'd think she'd changed her mind about seeing where their relationship could go.

He really hoped that wasn't the case. Considering she was wearing his shirt again this morning, he didn't think it really could be, but women were a mystery to him. The only woman—hell, she hadn't even been a woman, she'd been a girl—he'd had any kind of relationship with was Lily. And that had been twenty years ago. He definitely wasn't up to speed on female reactions and moods and what the heck their silences meant, especially in this situation.

After fifteen minutes of her pushing the food around on her plate, barely eating any of it, he figured enough was enough.

"It's not going to magically jump into your mouth, you know."

"Sorry." She set her fork down with a sigh and reached for her coffee. "I guess I'm not that hungry. It's really good, though."

"Uh-huh." He watched her carefully as she sipped, two hands wrapped around her mug, her face devoid of makeup, her hair messy but adorable. More than anything he wanted to kiss her like he had last night, but he wasn't sure how she'd react in her current mood, and he didn't want to do anything to set them back. "Everything okay?"

"Yes. Why, don't I look okay?"

"You look . . ." *Sexy as hell, gorgeous, like every guy's wet dream.* But he knew not to say any of those things right now. So he settled for, "Uneasy."

"Oh." She glanced his way for a brief second and smiled. But it wasn't the warm, flirty smile she'd given him last night. It was reserved. The kind of smile you flashed to a friend.

His stomach tightened, and to keep from saying anything he'd regret, he reached for his own coffee and sipped. If she launched into a "we should just be friends" conversation, he wasn't sure he'd be able to handle it, let alone sit here and listen.

She tucked a lock of hair behind her ear. "I was just thinking about the Plague."

A breath he hadn't realized he'd been holding whooshed out of his lungs, easing the knot that had grown in his gut. Okay, yeah. He could see how thinking about the Plague could dampen any good mood. Letting go of his coffee, he slid his hand across the table and closed it over hers. "Are you worried they'll figure out who you are?"

Except . . . as soon as those words were out of his mouth that knot twisted right back together. *Please don't say you changed your mind about us because of my connection to the Plague.*

"No, of course not."

Again that pressure eased, allowing him to fill his lungs with sweet, blessed air.

"Then what?"

She looked down at their joined hands, then drew a breath and turned in her seat to face him. "I guess I'm curious. How did you stumble on the Plague, and what they were doing?"

"Kinda by chance. Several years ago I was in a club with some buddies. They were all drinking and having a good time, flirting with the dancers, but I wasn't. I hadn't been in a strip club since I'd given up looking for Lily in my midtwenties. Back then I'd spent a lot of time in clubs like that and online, searching for any sign of her. There have been rumors for years that black market groups use the web for human trafficking. That night I found myself searching the faces of all the girls in that club, looking for Lily again, even though in my head I knew she was never going to be there. When I realized what I was doing, I got up and left, told myself I wasn't doing that again, and went back to working in my vineyard. A few days later, though, my curiosity got the best of me, and I ran a search on the dark net, looking for her once more. I didn't find her, but I did come across a listing for a young girl I'd seen waiting tables at that club. I went back to that strip club to find her, only she was gone. Couple dancers I talked to said she was a street kid, that she'd only started working there recently, and that she'd up and vanished recently with no word. No one found that odd except for me. I went back to the website, tried to find that listing again, but it had disappeared as well. I don't know what happened to her. The more I looked, the more I researched this online group that I later learned was the Plague, the more I realized whatever they did with her wasn't good."

"That's awful."

"Yeah." He looked down at their joined hands, liking her touch and the way she didn't pull away from him.

"And that spurred you on to helping other girls."

"The ones I could, yeah."

She stared at him for several seconds as he lifted his coffee with his free hand and sipped, a calculating expression he recognized brewing in her hazel eyes as she tipped her head. "What?"

"I don't know. Considering all that, I guess I'm just wondering what you're really trying to accomplish with these extracurricular activities, as you call them."

"I'm not sure I get the question."

"What's your endgame?"

He glanced around the kitchen, confused by her question because he thought he'd just answered that. "To help whoever I can help."

"That's admirable, of course, but it's not really solving the problem, is it?"

Unsure where she was going, he let go of her hand and leaned back in his chair. "It is for the girls I'm able to help."

"I know. And it is. I'm not diminishing that at all. But . . . what if you didn't have to help any of these girls? What if there weren't any girls to help?"

"I'm still not sure what you're saying."

"I'm saying . . . what if there was no more Plague? Then those girls wouldn't need you anymore."

Understanding hit him. He slowly crossed his arms over his chest and eyed her warily. "You want to take down the entire organization."

"Yes."

Yes. Just like that. With no fear in her eyes and no worry about the consequences to her personally. "You're nuts. It can't be done. It's too big. Trust me. I've thought about it—a lot. It's just not feasible for one—or even two—people."

"Listen to me." She sat forward. "You heard Callahan last night. The cops haven't been able to nail the ringleaders. I worked for the department for years. I only heard whispers about the Plague. Callahan confirmed it's being kept quiet, which means someone in the department knows what they're doing and who's involved, and they don't want them brought down. You and I have acquired more leads in the last week than anyone assigned to the case. Wouldn't it be better to stop these people from ever traumatizing another girl than to try to rescue her after the fact? We could make that happen. Together."

He stared at her, completely confused as to why she'd put her life on the line like that. "Why?"

"Why what?"

"Why do you care? This isn't personal for you. Be honest, Harper. Five days ago when you found out about Melony Strauss's disappearance, you weren't overly concerned with rescuing her. You were interested in bringing me down if I'd done anything to hurt her."

"You're right." She bit her lip and rested her elbows on the table. "But it wasn't because I wasn't concerned for her safety. It was because I thought you were the threat." She dropped her hands into her lap and looked at him. "I was wrong about that. Very wrong. But you are also wrong about this not being personal for me. It is. Not the way it is for you, but I know what it's like to be victimized. I've never been victimized the way these girls have, but I know what it's like to be taken advantage of. I know what it's like not to have anyone you can turn to for help. I know how powerless that feeling is."

"You're talking about the reason you left the department, aren't you?"

Her lips thinned. "I guess I shouldn't be surprised you know about that."

"I looked you up online."

"Ah." She nodded. "Then you know I was accused of sexually harassing my partner and that my former partner came forward to corroborate his story and accuse me of the same thing."

"Yeah, that's what I read. Sounds like you have a different version."

"Yes. I do." She smoothed the hair back from her face. "I just . . . never told anyone about it because I knew I wouldn't be believed."

"Do you think I won't believe you?"

"No. I know you will," she said in a small voice. "It's just . . . it's not something I'm particularly proud of."

He leaned forward and took her hand in his again. "Proud like . . . frequenting-strip-clubs proud?"

A soft chuckle slipped from her mouth, and the edges of her lips curled in a winsome smile. "Okay, maybe not that bad."

He rubbed his thumb over the back of her hand. "You don't have to tell me if you don't want to."

"No, I do want to. I . . ." She drew in a breath. "I was involved with my partner. The same one who accused me of sexual harassment. We had an affair that lasted about six months. An affair I went into even knowing he was married."

She didn't pull her hand away, and he took that as a good sign, so he kept on rubbing her skin gently with his thumb, waiting for her to go on.

"It was stupid. I wasn't even that attracted to him. It's just that after my dad died, I was struggling, and one night when I was in bad shape, he was there to comfort me. One thing led to another, and before I knew it we were seeing each other after hours and sneaking around. I didn't like it. I knew it was wrong, and I wanted to put a stop to it, but . . ." She shrugged. "I was lonely."

"No one blames you for that, Harper."

"Tell that to his wife." She sighed. "When I finally came to my senses and broke things off with him, he got upset. I think he was worried I'd tell people what had happened between us, but I had no intention of ever doing that. It's not easy being a female cop. You have to be twice as tough as the men, and you have to put up with the constant misogyny and demeaning jokes on a daily basis. I didn't want to be known as the ho who'd slept with her partner. So I asked my captain to be reassigned. And that didn't go over well at all. When our captain went to him and asked him what had happened between us, he assumed I'd ratted him out, and he accused me of coming on to him, of using my legacy with the department to pressure him into having an affair with me. Only none of it was true."

"What did you do?" he asked softly.

"I fought back, of course. Which only made things worse because then word of our affair got out and his wife heard about it. It got ugly. They eventually reassigned me to a new partner, but I felt like shit. Every day at work was a nightmare. I still had to see him in the office. But then things slowly died down, and I thought . . . okay, it's all going to work out. Until, that is, my ex-partner from patrol—someone I'd never had anything but a platonic working relationship with—claimed I'd done the same thing to him."

"Why did he do that?"

"I still have no idea. The only thing I can figure is that regardless of what year it is and all the advancement that has happened in the women's movement, law enforcement is still a good ol' boys' club. I crossed an invisible line when I requested that transfer, and I learned quickly that the people I thought were my friends really weren't. They rallied around him."

When she only frowned, he sighed and said, "I hear what you're saying. And I think it's admirable that you want to help these girls with the Plague. But it doesn't change the fact that what you're talking about doing is dangerous."

"I'm not afraid of the Plague."

"You should be. Look what happened last night."

"We beat them last night."

"Yeah, but they could have just as easily beaten us. You could have been killed last night, Harper."

Something in her eyes softened. Something that hit him hard, right in the center of his chest.

She slid off her chair, crossed to him, straddled his lap, and, placing both hands on his bare shoulders, stared deep into his eyes. "You are absolutely irresistible when you are in macho, protective mode."

He inched his fingertips up her back, loving the way she fit against him, loving the warmth seeping from her into him—not just from where she was touching him but from the way she made him feel— wanted, cherished . . . *home.*

His throat grew thick. He only wanted more of that feeling. Wanted more of *her.* "I'm not kidding. I'd never forgive myself if something happened to you because of me."

She slid her arms around his neck and kissed him. "The only thing that's going to happen to me right now is you. Hopefully on this table."

She pressed her lips to his and squeezed her knees against his sides. "I'm not going anywhere."

Instead of unwinding that knot of worry inside him, her words only tightened the noose on his emotions. Because he was suddenly terrified at the thought of losing her right when he'd finally found her.

He drew back before she could lure him into a mind-numbing kiss that made him forget his own name. "I'm not built for casual flings, Harper. You need to know that right now. And 'macho, protective mode' is pretty much who I am."

"I know it is."

He stared into her eyes, knowing from her admission that she didn't have regular relationships. But he didn't want to be a fling or an affair for her. He wanted to be everything. And he had no idea if she was ready for that, or even if she wanted the same.

"Good thing I like macho, protective mode," she whispered, leaning in to kiss him again. "I like it way more than I ever thought I could."

Dammit, he liked *her* way more than he ever thought he could. As he opened to her kiss and let her draw him into all her silky heat, he realized he didn't just like her. He was falling for her. Falling fast, judging by the way he was already giving in to every single thing she wanted.

He just didn't know how that was going to impact his dealings with the Plague, or what that would mean for either of them in the long run.

CHAPTER FOURTEEN

By the time Harper finished up at the office, the good mood she'd been in from her tryst with Rusty in her kitchen was long gone. What she'd found in the office records didn't implicate Andy per se, but it hadn't made her feel any better about her current job.

As the sun sank in the western sky, she pulled her Acura off the highway and turned onto the long drive that wound up a gradual hill to Rusty's property near the top of the rise. He still hadn't completely agreed to her whole bringing-down-the-Plague idea, but he hadn't said no, and when she'd suggested they meet for dinner to discuss their strategy, he'd invited her to his place with a, "We'll discuss it more later."

As far as she was concerned, there was nothing to discuss, but she wasn't opposed to using her feminine wiles to convince him. Her belly warmed as she remembered the way she'd seduced him in the kitchen just this morning. It was crazy to be so wild about the man after such a short amount of time, but she didn't care. For once she was doing what she wanted and ignoring the consequences. And for the moment she was also going to ignore that little voice in the back of her head telling her she needed to tell him about her deal with the commissioner. In all honesty, it really wasn't even a big deal. And it had absolutely nothing to do with her relationship with the rough and sexy Russell McClane.

She passed the sign that read BLACK SHEEP VINEYARDS and smirked at his joke. When she'd called that Uber earlier in the week and slipped out of his house in the wee hours of morning, she hadn't paid much attention to his property. She'd just wanted to get away as fast as she could. Now she was anxious to see all of it because it was clearly important to him.

She pulled to a stop next to his truck in the drive of his house. It was an older Craftsman-style farmhouse, with light-gray siding and white trim that looked as if it had been remodeled. Three steps led up to the wide, wraparound porch and old, red-painted door, and a couple of old wine barrels were placed on each side of the door, probably to hold plants, she realized, in the warmer months.

She moved up the steps and knocked, but when he didn't answer, she glanced back through the vineyard toward the old barn and the small, portable building next to it.

He was probably still working. He'd told her before he'd left her house that he needed to check on the construction process for the winery this afternoon. Since it wasn't raining, she decided to walk and drew in a breath of fresh air as she tucked her hands into the pockets of her leather jacket, relaxing more with every passing second.

She liked the hustle and bustle of the city, but she had to admit, there was something about life in the country that had its appeal. It was quiet, for one. Traffic was a helluva lot easier to deal with. And the clean air was a definite plus.

Hammering sounded from the direction of the barn. It was a gigantic structure with sharp rooflines and an enormous deck that looked down the hillside toward what she suspected was an incredible view. Two large doors were rolled open, and voices echoed from somewhere inside. She followed the sound and stepped into the massive space, glancing across the empty cement floor, searching for Rusty.

She recognized his voice coming from somewhere above. Turning toward a wide set of stairs, she grabbed the temporary handrail and headed up, following the sexy timbre, remembering with a shiver she couldn't control just what it had felt like when that sultry voice whispered naughty things in her ear last night.

He was standing on the far side of the huge room, talking to a man in a yellow hard hat with a tool belt around his waist, both of them looking up at something on the ceiling. Tools and extension cords were strewn across the dusty, bare floorboards, and two sawhorses and a slab of wood were set up like a workbench in the far corner.

For a second, she just stood there watching him, admiring the way he moved and that incredible voice that did crazy things to her blood. God, he was sexy in those loose jeans that hugged his ass perfectly and sat low on his hips. And the way the muscles in his shoulders and back flexed beneath the long-sleeved Henley as he lifted his arm and waved his hand toward whatever they were looking at only reminded her just how strong he was, how easily he'd picked her up last night, carried her upstairs, and done wicked things to her she couldn't wait for him to do again.

That pressure she'd felt in her chest this morning when she'd come downstairs and seen him in her kitchen in nothing but his boxers and that ridiculous apron squeezed her lungs all over again, stealing her breath, making her feel things she wasn't sure she was ready for. She was in serious trouble with this man. Not just because he ignited a craving in her she'd never felt before but also because he made her want things she'd never even considered until right now . . . a life away from death and crime, a home—a real home—and a family of her own.

Her skin grew hot. Her head, light. Reaching a shaky hand out, she searched for the wall, afraid her legs might go out from under her.

A family of her own? Where had that thought come from?

Across the room, almost as if he'd sensed her mini panic attack, Rusty turned, spotted her, and slowly smiled. And just that fast, whatever anxiety had tried to claim her slowly faded until all she felt was heat. Everywhere. And a burning need to feel him close.

He said something to the man at his side she didn't hear, then he crossed the floor to her and reached for her hand. "Hey. Sorry I wasn't at the house when you got here. We were trying to figure out what to do with the doors that will lead out to the de—"

She slid her hands up his chest and around his neck, then lifted to her toes and kissed him, cutting off his words, not even paying attention to what he'd been saying, just needing this. Him. For reasons she didn't even want to question.

He sucked in one surprised breath, then opened to her kiss and wrapped his arms around her lower back, pulling her up against him, right where she wanted to be most.

When she was breathless, he drew back and looked down at her with a sexy grin. "I guess that means you missed me."

"Maybe a little."

He laughed and kissed the tip of her nose.

"This is a great space."

He released her, but he didn't go far, and he didn't let go of her hand as he said, "Thanks. It's coming along. Still needs walls. And doors. And windows."

"All in good time," the guy in the yellow hard hat called, making a mark on the floor where he and Rusty had been standing before.

Rusty chuckled, then looked down at Harper. "That's Matt, my contractor. Who promises we're going to come in on time and under budget," he called over his shoulder.

"Then you better get out of my hair and let me work," Matt answered, not looking back at Rusty.

Rusty turned back to Harper. "Want a tour?"

"Sure."

He showed her all around the barn, pointing out where the tasting counter would be, the tasting room with couches and tables and chairs, and the deck; then he led her downstairs and showed her the processing facility and, finally, where his office would be.

"What about storage?" she asked, having a hard time imagining it all finished. Right now, it was just a giant, open space, but the excitement in his voice told her he already had every inch of it mapped out.

"Don't need it up here. That's what the caves are for."

"Caves?"

"Yeah. They're the whole reason I bought this property. There were two small caves in the hillside that I excavated early on. The bigger one will be used for storage and aging, the smaller one for tastings and events. Eventually I want to do wine pairings and dinners. Tourists will eat that up."

This was his passion, she realized. The way his eyes lit up when he talked about the winery and new tasting room made him look like a kid on Christmas morning. And it softened the lines around his eyes and took away some of that dark, brooding mystery that had seemed to hover around him from the moment they met.

"Do you wanna go down and see the caves?" he asked.

Her stomach grumbled before she could answer.

He smiled and reached for her hand. "Don't answer that. Let's eat first. Lots of time to see the caves."

Good. She was suddenly famished. She hadn't eaten since breakfast, she realized.

The sun was almost behind the mountains by the time they left the barn and headed back to his farmhouse. As they stepped into the foyer, he let go of her hand and took her coat, turning to hang it on a coat tree to the right of the door. "Are you hungry? I've got steaks out of the freezer."

"Mm. The fastest way into this woman's pants is straight through her stomach."

He chuckled and pressed a kiss to her temple before reaching for her hand and leading her past the staircase and into the kitchen. "There's wine on the counter. Why don't you pour two glasses while I go start the barbecue on the deck?"

The kitchen opened to a great room with wide windows that looked out over the deck and provided a view across the valley. It wasn't quite as spectacular as the one from the upper tier of the barn, but it was still pretty amazing, and as Rusty moved toward the big sliding doors in the dining area and stepped out onto the deck, she could totally see him relaxing here. She could totally see *herself* relaxing here.

"Slow down, girlfriend," she muttered to herself before finding two wineglasses in the cupboard and bringing them back to the counter. They barely knew each other. Sizzling-hot sexual chemistry was one thing, but that wasn't something to build a relationship on. First they had to plan their takedown of the Plague. Then she'd focus on whatever this thing was simmering between them.

They ate dinner at the dining table that sat in the corner of the room, in the fading daylight. He hadn't just taken steaks out of the freezer, Harper learned rather quickly. He'd put potatoes on to bake at some point while he'd also been working, and he'd made a salad. She couldn't remember the last time a man had cooked for her. Wasn't sure one ever had, aside from her father.

When their dinner was over, Rusty told her to refill her wine and take her glass downstairs where he kept his research while he cleaned up. They hadn't spoken about the Plague during dinner—she'd purposely kept the topics light, not wanting to ruin the romantic mood. But part of her was anxious to find out just what he'd already uncovered. And to compare it with what she'd found. Another part was nervous about what she needed to tell him.

Twenty minutes later, she was sitting on the floor in front of the coffee table, her eyes wide as she flipped through a notebook he'd used to record each of his interactions with the Plague, when he came down the stairs.

He set his wineglass on the coffee table next to hers as he sat on the leather sofa. "I see you found my stuff."

"This notebook goes back five years."

"Yeah."

"You've been doing this for *five* years?"

"More like six. I didn't keep track at the beginning."

Her mouth fell open. "Every weekend?"

"Not every weekend."

No, just whenever he got a tip or heard about a missing girl. "How many have you rescued?"

He shrugged and leaned back against the cushions. "I'm not sure."

"Rusty, there are over a hundred entries in here."

"I didn't get to most of them."

No, but he'd gotten to a lot. At least twenty.

The meticulous details, and the regret she heard in his voice, tumbled through her mind, telling her this might not be his passion like the winery, but it was important to him. His way of making up for what he hadn't been able to do for Lily.

Her nerves jangled, and slowly, she sat back on her heels and looked down at the notebook in front of her, not wanting to show him what she'd found today, yet knowing she had to. "I have to tell you something."

"Okay," he said warily.

She drew in a breath, unsure how to handle this. Figuring straightforward was best, she said, "I did some digging today while I was at the office. I didn't tell you before, but I talked to Andy this morning before I came down for breakfast. There was something in his line of questioning that hit me as . . . off."

"That's why you were acting so odd at breakfast?"

"Yeah, I was trying to work it all out in my head."

"Okay." He eyed her skeptically when she didn't go on. "I'm not sure how to read that. What about his questioning felt off?"

"All of it. I got this strange feeling he wasn't being truthful with me about your entire case."

Rusty leaned forward to rest his forearms on his knees and clasped his hands. "Go on."

She reached for the folder from her bag on the floor at her side and pulled it out. "Your stepfather was James Jordan, is that correct? He was a hotelier from Portland."

"Yeah. He owned Majestic Hotels, a chain of midlevel hotels throughout the country. But his pride and joy was the five-star Imperial Hotel in downtown Portland."

She set the folder on the table in front of her and flipped it open. "Andrew Renwick was his personal attorney in a few specific cases."

"That's not a surprise. Renwick's firm handled my trust fund after my mother and Jordan died in that fire. That's why Michael and Hannah McClane called Renwick and set up that meeting for me when I was questioned by the cops about Strauss's disappearance. They figured since he already knew me, he'd be on my side. Are you saying he's not?"

"I'm not sure. Andy didn't seem thrilled when I told him Strauss was alive and well. He still assumed you did something to her."

"And what did you tell him?"

"Nothing. Red flags were going up all over while I was talking to him, so I decided to keep quiet. I did a little digging at the office this afternoon after he was gone. So I could try to figure out what was going on." She flipped another paper. "I didn't find anything concrete, but this surprised me."

She handed him the paper and waited while he studied it. "Jordan's primary attorney for personal and business dealings was Howard Bradbury. Not Andrew Renwick. But about three years before your mother married Jordan, Andy handled the paperwork and tax filings for a big donation Jordan made to a local charity here in Portland. He also signed the paperwork as a representative of Jordan's estate."

"Wow. A hundred and fifty thousand. The man was a miser. I never knew him to be so generous."

That didn't surprise Harper. And it didn't make what she was about to tell him any easier.

"CAOF." Rusty's dark eyes narrowed on the paperwork in his hands. "That name's familiar, but I'm not sure where I've heard it."

"It's a children's charity. They help at-risk youth in the city."

He frowned. "Jordan was never concerned with at-risk youth."

"Neither is Andy as far as I'm concerned."

"Did you run a check on this place?"

"Yes, but the charity shut down about a year ago, and everything on the web regarding it has been scrubbed. I didn't get very far."

"Hmm. That doesn't look fishy at all." After several seconds study-ing the paper, he reached for the cell from his pocket and pulled it out.

"Who are you calling?"

"My sister's fiancé, Hunter O'Donnell. He runs a security company in town, and he's got a few IT guys who can dig deeper than either of us right now."

"Good idea."

She waited while he dialed and drew a deep breath, almost afraid to tell him the rest. After several seconds he started speaking into the phone, but it was clear from his end of the conversation that it had gone right to voice mail.

He hung up after he left a message and set his phone on the coffee table. "He didn't answer, but he'll call back. Hunt's good about that."

She nodded and glanced back down at her papers. "There's more."

"Okay," he said skeptically again.

She drew a deep breath and knew she had to tell him. "James Jordan traveled a lot."

"Yeah. He didn't particularly like being stuck in one place."

"He was married twice before he married your mother."

"I know. The first was his college sweetheart. She left him after he had an affair with his secretary. The second was his secretary."

"Neither marriage lasted more than a few years."

"Right," he said, drawing the word out. "I know this already."

No, she was pretty sure he didn't know *this*. "Neither woman gave him any children."

His brow lowered. "Yes, the secretary did. That was Lily's mother. She gave up custody of Lily to him after the divorce."

"No, she didn't." Harper drew out the other paperwork she'd uncovered at the office and handed it to him. "This is the other case Andy handled for Jordan immediately after that large donation to CAOF."

Rusty's confused gaze skipped over her face as he took the paper she held out. But when he glanced down at it, every muscle in his body went still. "This is a petition for an adoption."

"Yes," she said quietly. "About three years before you and your mother moved in with him. Look at the age of the child."

He stared at the paper without moving, without showing any kind of reaction, and as she sat on her knees on the carpet watching him, something in her heart broke open wide for him. For the turmoil she knew he was feeling and the knowledge there was nothing he could do about any of it now.

"She was . . . twelve." A vein in his neck pulsed, and he cleared his throat, lifting one hand to run over his mouth. "She told me he was her father."

"I guess by the time you met her, legally he was."

He stared at the paper another few seconds in silence, then dropped it on the coffee table as if it had burned him, pushed to his feet, and went straight to the bar near the wall, where he grabbed a glass from the cupboard and a bottle of Johnnie Walker and poured himself a generous shot.

"He bought her?" He tossed back the shot and didn't even hesitate to pour another. "You're telling me that he bought a twelve-year-old girl. That was years before he started taking her to those meetings."

"I know," she said quietly, pushing one hand against the couch cushion, moving to sit so she could see him near the bar, knowing he needed space and that she shouldn't try to comfort him right now.

But she wanted to. She didn't like that wild look in his eyes. She didn't like seeing every muscle in his body tense and straining as if he were holding back a firestorm.

He tossed back the second shot. "Motherfucker. He bought a twelve-year-old girl like a fucking piece of meat. And he kept her with him every minute of every day like a goddamn . . ." He braced both hands on the end of the bar and dropped his head. "I always knew he was a sick son of a bitch, but I never thought he . . . goddamn mother-*fucker*. It was going on right under my nose, and I didn't even know."

She pushed to her feet, unable to sit still any longer, hating that she was the one who had caused him this much pain, especially when there was nothing either of them could do about it now. "Rusty." She gently laid her palm on his back where he was hunched over the counter. "It wasn't your fault. There was nothing you could have do—"

"I need some air." He pushed away from her as if her touch repelled him and crossed to the sliding glass doors that opened to the patio. Jerking the left side open with a hiss, he stepped out into the darkness and slammed the glass door at his back.

Her heart contracted as she watched his silhouette disappear into the night, and she sank onto a barstool, unsure if she should go after him or let him have some space. She didn't know him well enough to know if he was the kind of guy who wanted comfort in times of stress and turmoil or if trying would only push him further away. And she hated that she didn't know that because she didn't want to do anything to damage what had started between them, especially now, when she knew it could be something amazing.

Tears burned the backs of her eyes. Tears she fought because she didn't want to be weak. But more than anything she wished that she hadn't brought any of this up. That she'd kept that one piece of information secret. That she hadn't been the one to tell him the girl he'd once loved had been bought and sold as a sex slave long before he'd ever met her.

———

Rusty couldn't get the image of Lily as a naive twelve-year-old girl out of his mind. Of what the man who'd bought her like a piece of meat had done to her.

He'd seen pictures of her at twelve years old. There had been snapshots of her in frames all over Jordan's mansion. At twelve, she hadn't looked a thing like she had at fifteen when Rusty had met her. She'd been prepubescent at twelve—flat-chested, no curves, with a body that could have been mistaken as that of a little boy instead of a girl.

Bile shot up his throat, and he slammed his eyes shut in the dim light of the wine cave where he was sitting with his back against the curved wall, swallowing hard to hold it back. Normally, the caves relaxed him. He could come here and think, calm down, find that fucking inner peace his brother Ethan was always yammering on about. But not today. Today he couldn't stop thinking about Lily. He'd thought she was a snob when he'd first met her. He hadn't realized that blank look in her eyes had been the haunted sign of abuse. Years of sexual abuse at the hands of the man he'd believed was her father.

He'd always hated Jordan. He'd never liked his slick personality, not even from the start. And after he'd learned how Jordan was exploiting Lily and what he'd done to get rid of her, he'd hated the son of a bitch even more. But nothing compared with what he felt now. The urge to wrap his hands around Jordan's thick neck, to watch the life fade from his eyes, overwhelmed Rusty. So much so he curled his hands into fists against his thighs. He'd do it now if he could. He wouldn't even think twice about the consequences or going to prison. But he couldn't even have that satisfaction because the motherfucker was already dead.

A creaking sound echoed through the cave, and without even looking, Rusty knew who'd found him. Knew and didn't want her here. Not when he was hovering close to the edge of a meltdown he wasn't sure he could stop.

Footsteps sounded across the polished cement floor. Footsteps that echoed like cannon fire in his head. Harper rounded the corner, stepping around a pallet of wooden wine-bottle racks he'd ordered but had yet to set up, and moved into the light shining down from the round, iron candle chandelier.

Her steps slowed when she spotted him sitting on the floor against the wall. "There you are," she breathed. "I've been looking everywhere for you."

He ground his teeth together, just wanting her gone. "I didn't ask you to look for me."

"I know." She tugged the blanket she must have grabbed from the back of his couch tighter around her shoulders and stared down at him with worry and regret in her hazel eyes. "It's just . . . you've been gone awhile. I was worried."

He drew a calming breath that did little to settle his raging pulse, and pushed to his feet. "I'm really not in the mood for company anymore."

"Rusty, I know you're upset—"

He exhaled a sound that was a half laugh, half huff of disgust, he wasn't sure which, and rubbed a hand across his forehead, fighting back the urge to scream. Or pound his fist right into the rocks around him. "Upset doesn't even begin to describe what I am. Which is why you need to leave and head home where you're safe."

She stared at him for several seconds, but instead of turning and running like he'd hoped, her lips thinned. "I'm not afraid of you."

He lifted his head, knowing he wasn't really mad at her but unable to keep the animosity from his voice when he said, "Well, maybe you should be. There's a reason I'm thirty-five and single. There's a reason I don't date."

"I know there is. Because you don't think you deserve to be happy. But you're wrong."

He huffed and turned away from her. "I don't need to listen to this. I can get the psychobabble bullshit from my brother anytime I want it." He pressed both hands against the rock wall and dropped his head, wishing, praying she'd give him time to deal with the conflicting emotions swirling inside him before he lost his shaky hold on control. "I'm asking you to leave."

She took a step toward him. "Rusty, it was twenty years ago. It wasn't your fault, and there was nothing you could have done to stop it then."

The cap on his temper started to wobble. He closed his eyes and curled his fingers against the rocks, every muscle in his body flexed and rigid. "Get out, Harper. Get out right now before I decide not to ask."

"What are you going to do? Throw me out?"

He lifted his head and glanced toward her, the edges of his vision dark from his vibrating emotions, seeing nothing but her defiant hazel eyes and her sharp chin lifted in challenge. "Yeah. That's exactly what I'll do."

One side of her lips curled in a smirk. "Try it. You won't get very far." When he only stared at her in shock, she added, "I'm not leaving you like this. You need me whether you realize it or not."

She was wrong. He'd never needed anyone but himself. He'd proved that time and again, hadn't he? Without even realizing what he was doing, he stepped toward her, intent on proving to her he didn't need her or anyone. Needing people only fucked you over in the end. It left you raw and exposed. It came back to bite you in the ass twenty years later.

He stopped in front of her, leaned down, and wrapped one arm around her legs, planning to toss her over his shoulder and haul her out of his cave if he had to. But she surprised him when she jerked one leg from his grip before he could immobilize her and hooked her foot behind him, knocking him off balance.

Her hands pressed against his shoulders. His weight shifted back. He stumbled, tried to right himself, but couldn't keep from hitting the ground on his butt and falling back on the cave floor.

The blanket broke his fall, but it didn't completely keep him from cracking the back of his head against the hard floor. "What the *hell*, Blake?" he managed as pain shot across the back of his scalp.

Harper straddled his waist before he could sit up and pressed her palms hard against his chest, holding him down. "It's Harper. And I'll tell you what's what, mister. You're not getting rid of me. I told you I'm not leaving you, and I'm not."

"Jesus Christ." He dropped his head back against the blanket and stared up at the ceiling, fighting for control, wishing like hell he could just be alone. Everyone was always trying to drag him out of the shadows and into the world—his siblings, his parents, *her*. But life was safer alone. Cleaner. Way fucking easier.

"It wasn't your fault," she said, staring down at him, not releasing him, not easing up on the pressure on his chest either. "You have to stop blaming yourself for what happened to her. You were just a kid too. You didn't know."

He didn't like what she was saying. Didn't want to hear it. But at some point in the last ten seconds, the fight had whooshed out of him, and he didn't have the strength to push her off him or even try to get up. The backs of his eyes grew hot. Hot and tingly, and he closed them tightly, wishing—*shit*—he didn't know what he wished anymore.

"You couldn't have saved her then," Harper went on, gentling her voice. "Nothing you do now can save her either. You have to let her go, Rusty. You have to let all of it go before it destroys you."

His conversation with Ethan days before echoed in his head, melding with the words Harper was saying now. *"Whatever it is you're chasing, let it go. Let it go before it ruins you. It's the only way you're ever going to be free."*

"Fuck." The burn behind his eyes intensified, spread to his nose. He tossed an arm over his face, not wanting Harper to see his epic breakdown, fighting to hold up the crumbling wall that held back his emotions because he knew what would happen if that wall broke. Those emotions—the things he hadn't let himself feel in years—would drag him down into a darkness it would take weeks, probably months, to claw himself free from.

"I'll help you," Harper whispered somewhere close. "Whatever you need, however you need it. I won't leave you alone to deal with it all. I'll help you get through it. I promise."

He swiped at his damn eyes with the back of his arm, focused on breathing, tried to protect himself, but the emotions broke through, pummeling him from every side, stealing his breath, his thoughts, sending a jarring burst of pain straight through his chest.

Soft lips skimmed his damp temple, his cheek, brushed against his hairline. In a daze, he felt Harper's warm breath tickling his cheek. Felt her body shifting over his, felt her hands cupping his face as she whispered words that made no sense and kissed his temple, his forehead, his cheek, the corner of his mouth—

A new wave of emotion slammed into him, this one stronger, more immediate, and all-consuming.

He lowered his arm, turned his head, found her mouth, and kissed her, needing her heat to warm the cold chill inside him, needing her strength to lift him out of this funk. She groaned and opened to him, licking into his mouth with the same hunger suddenly consuming him. And then she lowered her hips to his, pressing the heat between her legs right over his cock, shoving aside every thought until only one need remained. A need so hot it was all he could see and feel and hear and crave . . .

His arms closed around her. He shifted his weight and rolled her onto her back, never once moving away from her mouth, continuing to kiss and nip and lick and savor every bit of her on his tongue. Her legs fell open. Her hands streaked up into his hair as she tipped her head and kissed him deeper. His hands rushed to the buttons down the front of her white blouse, but his need was too insistent, his craving too fierce. Unable to wait, he grasped the two sides of her shirt and yanked.

Buttons went flying, skittering across the concrete. She kissed him harder. He made quick work of the clasp on the front of her bra, flicking it free, then dragged his mouth from hers and closed his lips over her left nipple.

She groaned his name, arched into his mouth, and threaded her fingers into his hair. He wasn't gentle. He couldn't be gentle when every inch of his body was on fire. He circled the nipple with his tongue as she moaned beneath him, then bit down with his teeth. She cried out and lifted her hips against his, grinding against his swollen cock. The sound fueled the fire inside him, made it rage higher. He moved to her other breast, tortured it with the same motions, and when she was writhing against him, he shifted back, found the snap on her jeans, then wrenched the garment from her legs in one swift move.

She gasped in a shocked breath, pushing up on her elbows, but he didn't give her a chance to get up. Wrapping both arms around her legs to hold her still, he lowered his mouth to her sex and feasted.

"Oh *fuck*, Rusty . . ." She collapsed back on the blanket, bucking against him. And the sound of her pleasure was like a drug, pushing him harder, making him hungry for more, drowning out every other thought and sound and need.

He drove her right to the edge, and when her climax consumed her, he swallowed every drop. She collapsed against the ground, but he didn't give her time to relax. He licked and sucked and swirled again and again, needing more, needing everything, driving her to the peak again and again.

"Please," she panted after three strong orgasms had decimated her. Her trembling hand landed against the back of his head. "Please . . . I can't . . . No more. I want . . . you."

Her words were like gasoline to a spark. He tore his mouth from her dripping sex, wrenched the snap on his jeans open and finally freed his aching cock. She lay still and breathing heavily below him, but he wasn't done with her yet. Not even close. He made quick use of the condom in his pocket—slid it on, then hooked his arms around her thighs and jerked her toward him.

"Again." He pressed into the ground with his knees, lifting her with his arms so he could line her sex up perfectly with his cock. "Come for me again, Harper."

She lifted her head, her face slicked with sweat, her lips trembling, and the moment her glazed eyes met his, he drove in deep, filling her completely in one thrust. She groaned. Then her whole body shuddered as her sex tightened around his length, holding him as close as she possibly could. "Oh God, yes . . . ."

He drew out, shoved back in harder, tightened his hold on her legs as he held her up and plunged into her again and again, driving them both closer to the edge of something neither of them could see.

"Come," he growled, fucking into her faster, deeper. "Come *now.*" His need to feel her release all around him was a blinding obsession, fueled by something he didn't understand. All he knew was that he needed this. Needed her. Couldn't think of anything else.

He hammered into her, watching her body, the way she clawed at the blanket beneath her, focusing on her tightly closed eyes, knowing she was close, feeling his own orgasm barreling toward him. Fuck, he was going to come, was so close . . .

"Now." Every muscle in his body contracted, and electricity streaked down his spine. "Fucking come *now* . . ."

Her body tensed. Around his length, her sex spasmed uncontrollably. And just as she arched her back and cried out, that electricity ignited in his balls and exploded, shoving aside every last bit of pain he'd been feeling, leaving behind nothing but blinding pleasure.

He wasn't sure what happened next, but when sound slowly returned, he heard fast, heavy breaths and realized they weren't his own. They were Harper's, right below him. At some point he'd collapsed against her, but he didn't remember it. He didn't remember anything except the all-consuming power of that release. He didn't want to remember anything but that. That and the way her soft fingers were threading through his hair now, the silky feel of her damp skin against his, the citrusy scent he'd always associate with her, and the way she was holding him everywhere—with her arms wound possessively around his shoulders and her legs locked tight against his lower back.

He drew in a deep breath and let it out, shifting his head slightly so he could press his lips against her shoulder, the only part of her he could reach at the moment. Because his body was completely wrecked.

"Are you alive?" she whispered.

He swallowed the lump that seemed permanently wedged in his throat and managed to find the strength to say, "Yeah." But his voice was raspy, thick, and he knew she heard it. But he didn't care. For the first time in his life, he was glad he wasn't alone.

"Did I hurt you?" He knew he was crushing her, but he couldn't quite move yet, and she didn't seem to want to let him go. And the honest truth was he didn't want to leave the heat of her body or the warmth of her embrace.

"No. Unless you call making me climax four times hurting me. I think I understand now why the French call it *la petite mort*, the little death."

One side of his lips curled, relief sliding through him. He pressed another kiss against her silky-smooth skin.

"And I think I hurt you. Sorry about your leg. And knocking you down. I was just trying to get your attention, not, you know, really hurt you."

He knew that. Emotions flooded his chest again, but they weren't the dark, painful, agonizing emotions he'd felt earlier. These were sweet, from a place of light, from knowing she cared.

He shifted his hand to the concrete and pushed up on his arm, just enough so he could look down at her. At her captivating face in the flickering light, staring up at him with so much affection his heart contracted.

"Thank you," he rasped. "For getting my attention. I needed it."

She lifted one hand to his face and caressed his cheek, and without even thinking, he leaned into her touch. Savored it.

"I meant what I said, Rusty. I'm not going anywhere."

His heart pinched harder, and he turned his face to press a kiss against her palm. And in a shaky breath, he said, "I need that too. I was on the edge of a dark place, spiraling, and you stopped it from taking me. I won't forget that."

"Good." She lowered her hand to the blanket, pushed up on her elbows, and pressed her lips against his in a hard, swift kiss. "I won't let you forget it either."

Out of nowhere, a laugh pushed up his chest, one he only felt when he was with her. In the middle of the shitstorm that was his life, she was there, making him happy, making him whole, reminding him he was alive.

He dropped his forehead to her shoulder, drew in another shaky breath, then gently climbed off her.

He pushed to his feet and pulled up his pants. After disposing of the condom in a trashcan near the entrance to the cave, he came back to find her sitting upright in her jeans, her hair a mess around her gorgeous face, her hands fumbling with the two halves of her ruined blouse.

"This is a lost cause." She dropped her hands in her lap and frowned up at him. "Gimme your shirt."

He reached back and tugged off his T-shirt, then watched with rapt attention as she pulled it on and the black garment all but swallowed her whole. "I'm tellin' ya. A flag on a conquered fortress."

She rolled her eyes and pushed to her feet. "Now I see. That was your plan from the start. Sneaky."

He captured her hand when she drew close and tugged her into him. Surprise registered in her eyes as she lifted both hands to his chest, but he didn't let it deter him. He wrapped his arms around her back and closed her tight in his embrace. "No plan. I never have a plan with you. Just a craving I can't ever seem to sate."

Softly, he pressed his lips to hers, so thankful she was here, wanting to tell her just how much she meant to him, but wary because he didn't want to do anything to scare her away. Especially after that epic meltdown he'd nearly had.

She sighed and kissed him back, then rested her cheek against his chest and just let him hold her. And God, that felt good. Everything he hadn't known he'd needed or even wanted until this week.

"I like this cave," she said against him. "It's the one you'll hold events in, isn't it?"

"Yeah." But he really wasn't in the mood to talk about the winery. Or anything, really. He just wanted to go on holding her.

"Where did you get the condom?" she asked long moments later.

"I stopped at the store on my way home."

Her lips curled against his bare skin. "Wishful thinking, huh?"

"No. Hopeful. You have that effect on me. Making me feel hopeful." He tightened his arms around her and lowered his face into her hair. "I don't want you to leave," he whispered. *I don't want you to ever leave.* "I want you to stay with me tonight."

Her fingertips pressed against the muscles in his chest. "I want that too."

Thank God . . .

He drew back just enough so he could kiss her again, then said, "Let's go back to the house. It's warmer there. And I've been dying to have you in my bed."

"Hmm. Another *petite mort*? Okay, you talked me into it."

Laughing, knowing he didn't deserve this woman but unable to let her go, he wrapped his arm around her waist and steered her toward the cave doors. "Great. Now the pressure's on."

The hand wrapped around his waist dropped to slap his butt. "You bet your cute ass it is. No rest for the weary here."

Nope. And he wouldn't have it any other way. He just hoped she didn't change her mind after she got to know him better. Or that by choosing to stay with him, her life wasn't in any kind of danger.

CHAPTER FIFTEEN

Andy was running out of time.

He paced back and forth in his home office in the early-morning hours, running his hands through his hair again and again, trying to figure out what he could do, how he could spin this, what steps he needed to take to make sure the people he cared about were safe.

Harper had not taken his advice yesterday at the office. When he'd given her another case to work on, she'd said she'd get to it but that she was still looking into McClane's activities, building a case for him in the event the cops decided to charge him with something. Only Andy had known she was lying to him. She was a bloodhound when she had her mind set on a case, just like her father. He'd foolishly thought he could use that to his advantage when she'd been pushed off the force, but now . . .

He chewed on his lip as he turned near his desk and paced the other way, thoughts of both Harper and McClane swirling in his head. He'd been stupid to have Harper check into McClane's activities. Even if the man was Robin Hood, Andy already knew everything there was to know about McClane's past.

He'd thought he was protecting her by hiring her to come work for him. Had thought if he kept her close, she wouldn't fall into the same trouble her father had stumbled into, that if he could do one good thing for her, it would make up for some of the shit he'd done in the past. But he was wrong. He could barely protect himself. And even though the secret he knew about McClane could be Andy's get-out-of-jail-free card, he wasn't going to pull it.

It was time to take a stand. It was time to keep all the shit from happening again. He wasn't going to let the Plague get to McClane or Harper. Not when he knew they were both innocent. And not when it was clear if something happened to either one of them, he'd be in even deeper shit—this time with the authorities.

Decision made, he moved to his computer, opened his laptop, and booked flights and hotels for Maureen and their daughter with a Visa gift card he'd previously purchased so the Plague wouldn't know what he was planning. The girls wouldn't question this surprise. His daughter, Cindy, a sophomore in college, would jump on the chance to spend a week or more in Paris. And it would get them out of the country and somewhere safe while he attended to matters here.

When he was finished making travel arrangements, he sent a text to his daughter, asking her to stop over for lunch today. Then he drew a deep breath and dialed Harper.

Everything hinged on her going along with his plan. On her listening for once and not being so damn stubborn.

Because he wasn't sure what he'd do if she didn't cooperate.

———

Harper smiled as she snuggled against Rusty beneath the covers. The man was right. His bed, it turned out, was way more comfortable than hers.

She sighed, loving his warmth, and told herself to remember to ask him what brand this mattress was when they were both fully awake. She needed to get one. She'd slept better last night than she had in years.

A lingering voice in the back of her head said she'd slept so well because Rusty had been curled around her, holding her close and making her feel safe all night long, but she ignored it. Just as she'd ignored the other voice, insisting that she'd better tell him sooner or later about the deal she'd made with the commissioner.

A buzzing sound echoed through the room. At her back, Rusty mumbled, "You better not have set an alarm," into her hair.

"Are you kidding?" she answered in a sleepy voice, eyes still closed. "It's Sunday. I don't set alarms on Sundays."

The buzzing stopped, and his arm around her waist tightened, pulling her back against a—*oh, wow*—very aroused erection.

"Good," he muttered in her hair. "Because I've got a better way for you to wake up."

She chuckled, then groaned when he pressed that magnificent erection between her legs and bit down on her throat.

Oh my, yes . . .

The buzzing sounded again, stilling Rusty's movements at her back. Lifting his lips from her throat, he said, "I think that's a phone. Can't be mine. I left mine downstairs. Must be yours."

There was only one person who could be calling her on a Sunday morning, and she really didn't want to take his call. She wasn't in the mood to talk to him about anything.

She reached for Rusty's hand at her waist and scooted back against him. "Let it go to voice mail. It's probably just Andy."

He didn't rub against her again, and his silence told her he was thinking. That just her one comment had burst the bubble of happiness around them.

Rolling onto her back, she looked over at him in the hazy morning light. "Are you okay?"

He perched his elbow on his pillow and rested his head against his hand. "Yeah, I'm fine."

He didn't look fine, though. He was staring down at the pillow beside her, looking . . . troubled. Like he had last night when he'd been staring at that paper she'd given him, trying to convince himself it didn't mean what he knew it meant.

She reached for his other hand against her belly and lifted it to her lips, pressing a kiss to his palm. "Don't go there."

His dark gaze lifted to hers. "I'm not. I'm thinking about you and Renwick. You don't like working for him, do you?"

She lowered his hand to her chest, liking the weight of his touch. "It's fine."

"But you don't love it."

"Do many people love their jobs?"

"A lot do. I do."

She rolled her eyes and toyed with his fingers. "You're one of the lucky few."

"Why don't you like it? Aside from the fact Renwick is a dick?"

She chuckled and studied his fingernails. He had great hands. Big, rugged, with nice long fingers and clean, short nails. "You make it sound as if I hate it. I don't hate it. I just don't love it."

"Isn't it similar to what you were doing before? Investigative work?"

"Sort of. But then I was investigating the bad guys. Now I'm defending them."

"Or helping to keep the good ones free."

She smirked and looked up at him. "True. But you're an exception. Most of the people who come through Renwick's doors are there because they've done something that needs to be defended. And most of it isn't good."

"So it's the moral aspect of your job you don't like."

She shrugged and looked back at his hand. "I guess."

"What about the innocent people the police put away? You didn't have any problem with that?"

"I wasn't involved in anything like that when I was a cop."

"Never? Nothing you investigated was ever used to falsely accuse someone?"

She suddenly didn't like where this conversation was heading. Letting go of his hand, she pushed back against the mattress so she could sit up in the pillows and tug the sheet up over her breasts. "What are you getting at?"

"Nothing."

She crossed her arms over her chest. "Doesn't sound like nothing."

He sighed. "I know how the police work. My brother Ethan was falsely accused of something he didn't do and sent to juvenile detention as a kid, all because the cops needed to pin a crime on someone. You yourself told me that the mayor is putting pressure on the department to pin Strauss's disappearance on me because he's ticked a McClane caused his political donations to take a sharp drop. I believe in what the police do to protect the people, but I also know not every single cop is honest. If someone at PPD is covering up for the Plague, you know it too."

An uncomfortable feeling gathered in her belly. She believed in what the police did as well, yet she also knew he was right. There was corruption in everything. And now that the blinders were off and she was aware of all the shady deals being spun behind the scenes, could she go back to that world? Would she even be able to make a difference? Or would she forever question if her investigations and reports were being twisted to fit whatever narrative someone higher up wanted them to fit?

Her cell phone buzzed again on the nightstand next to her, and happy for the distraction—even if it was Andy on the other end of the line—she grabbed it and pressed "Answer."

"Yeah," she said into the phone. "I'm here."

"Jesus, Harper," Andy exclaimed on the other end of the line. "I've been calling you all morning."

"Sorry. I was"—she glanced at Rusty, watching her carefully at her side, then quickly looked away—"distracted. What do you need?"

"Nothing. Nothing for me. But I need you to get out of your house. Take a vacation. Leave the state. Go . . . anywhere. Just disappear for a while."

She pushed away from the pillows and sat up straight. "Why? What's going on, Andy? And don't even think about lying to me again."

He exhaled a long breath. "They know, Harper. They have security footage of you at that . . . that club. They know you were there when that girl disappeared. They're coming after you."

Harper's breath caught. Wide-eyed, she turned toward Rusty, who, from the intense look in his eyes and the fact he was already throwing the covers back, had heard what Andy had said.

"Get out of there," Andy said. "Disappear. Let things cool down. I'll call you when it's safe to come back."

"No." Harper pushed to her feet, reaching for her jeans as Rusty hurriedly dressed across the room. "I'll call you from a safe location when I get there. And you better answer, Andy, because you owe me a much better explanation than this."

He was silent a moment. "I will. I'm sorry, Harper. I'm so sorry I dragged you into this."

She wasn't sure she believed that. And realizing he knew way more about the Plague than he'd ever let on, she had no idea if she could trust him.

———

Thirty minutes later, Rusty wanted to swear. The best he could do was curl his hand around the steering wheel of his truck and clench his jaw so he wouldn't freak Harper out any more than she was already.

"Slow down, would you?" Harper glanced up from her phone and shot him a look from the passenger seat. "No one's chasing us."

She was right. No one was chasing them . . . yet. But that didn't mean they wouldn't come after them soon. Easing his foot off the gas a touch, he turned the wheel as the road curved to the left, his mind spinning with how he was going to protect her now that the Plague knew about her. He didn't care if they knew about him or not. All he cared about was her. She'd said she knew how to protect herself, but this was different. *The Plague* was different. Risking his life was one thing, but risking hers . . . that wasn't an option for him.

"Well, here's some good news for you." She lowered the phone and breathed out a sigh. "Callahan just texted me. Megan Christianson was happily reunited with her family. No matter what happens, we did the right thing."

Rusty didn't answer, just kept his eyes on the road. Yeah, that girl making it home was definitely a good thing, but that was the only good he could see. He didn't even know where they were heading. His brain was such mush he hadn't formed a plan yet. After calling Abby and telling her to inform everyone not to come to work today—even the construction guys, just to be safe—he'd pushed Harper into his truck and torn off the farm. A motel seemed like the only option at this point—he didn't want to lead the Plague to anyone in his family—but then what? What the fuck were they going to do now that the Plague knew who she was?

His cell phone rang. Glancing at the screen, he spotted Hunt's number and hit the button on his steering wheel to take the call over Bluetooth. "Hunt. There you are. Thanks for calling me back."

"I called you twice last night. You didn't pick up or return my calls."

Damn. He hadn't even checked his phone last night or this morning. "Sorry. Distracted. Were you able to find anything?"

"You're kidding, right?"

Rusty glanced toward Harper, the hairs on his nape tingling, only he didn't know why. "No, I'm not. Should I be?"

"Shit. I can't believe you don't remember this. CAOF—Children Are Our Future—is the charity started by Walter Kasdan, Miriam Kasdan, and their son, Arnold. The same three people who were abducting and selling small children in the Pacific Northwest. The same ones who abducted Emma."

"Holy shit." Connections fired off in Rusty's brain. A hundred and fifty thousand dollars' worth of connections.

He hit the brakes and swerved off onto the gravel on the side of the country road. Beside him Harper grabbed the handhold above her seat with wide eyes as the truck came to a stop.

Rusty looked toward his phone. "I need to meet with you and Alec today. Can you call him?"

"Yeah. What's going on?"

Rusty met Harper's curious hazel eyes. "A lot more than any of us thought. I think CAOF wasn't just selling small children to childless couples. I think they were selling older kids and teenage girls to pedophiles as well."

"You're fucking kidding."

"I wish I were. I'm also pretty sure they were linked to a black market group called the Plague that's selling teenage girls on the dark web."

"Shit," Hunt muttered. "And let me guess. Your knowledge of that is why the cops were at Hannah and Michael's house last weekend."

"Yeah." Rusty held Harper's gaze. "I want to bring them down, Hunt. All of them."

"Then get your ass over to my place ASAP, and we'll figure out how to do that."

———

An hour later, Harper still couldn't believe what she'd heard.

Rusty had agreed to help her bring down the Plague. All without her having to do a single thing to convince him.

That fact should have thrilled Harper. Instead it set off a weird vibration in her chest. One she didn't understand and liked even less.

And considering where she was and who she was surrounded by, it was one more odd reaction she wasn't ready for.

From her spot at the big table in Hunter O'Donnell's high-tech apartment on the top floor of his privately owned building, she glanced warily toward the group congregated in the center of the room discussing CAOF and the Kasdans. Currently, Rusty was sitting in the middle of the giant, U-shaped couch of the living area, seated beside his sister, Kelsey, while his other siblings—Alec and Ethan—and their significant others were rallying around Rusty in a way she suspected he didn't even realize. All were eager to help him figure out who was behind the Plague and how they could bring them down. All except her.

She was on the fringe of the discussion, feeling like a complete outsider, pretending to run searches on her laptop, all the while wishing for some air because the big-family dynamic was not something she was used to or even liked.

"Hold on," Rusty said, lifting his hands as he leaned forward. "You're telling me Miriam Kasdan had nothing at all to do with older missing kids?"

"No." Raegan, Alec's wife, met Rusty's eyes and flipped her auburn hair over her shoulder. "We're saying we never found any proof that she had anything to do with any children over the age of five who went missing."

"That doesn't mean she wasn't involved," Alec said from where he was perched on the armrest next to his wife, his arms tightly crossed over his chest.

Raegan reached out and laid her hand on his thigh, and Harper watched as he uncrossed his arms and closed his hand over hers, as if just her touch relaxed him. "Miriam Kasdan was working with the Department of Human Services to identify at-risk youth in the community. The older children were often sent to CAOF for services."

"Legitimate services," Alec cut in, "which is why the charity operated for so long under the radar."

"Right." Raegan nodded up at him and looked back at Rusty. "She wasn't interested in the older kids. In her mind, the older children were lost causes. She was interested in any younger siblings. Those she could save, the same way she saved her adopted son, Arnold, from the family she took him from in Washington."

"Took." Alec huffed. "She kidnapped the son of a bitch. Then she twisted him up until he was as fucked in the head as she was."

Raegan shot him a look. "Your daughter's in the next room."

"She's sleeping."

"Hopefully."

Alec leaned down and kissed the top of Raegan's head. "Okay. I'll tone it down. Any talk of the Kasdans makes me see red, though."

"I know." She squeezed his hand.

"What about Lily?" Rusty asked. "Did you find anything in the Kasdans' files about her?"

Alec and Raegan shared a somber look, then both met Rusty's gaze. "No," Raegan said. "Nothing."

"There were no kids in those files over the age of five," Alec told him.

"Lily was what, twelve when Jordan filed that adoption paperwork?" Ethan asked from across the room where he was standing next to his wife, Samantha, an arm around her shoulder and a somber look on his face. When Rusty nodded, he said, "That's the age CAOF would have been providing services to." He glanced toward the stack of files Alec had brought in, encompassing all the research Raegan had done on the Kasdans and CAOF for the book she was writing about their experience. "Instead of focusing on the Kasdans, we need to be looking at CAOF's files on the kids they serviced."

"We don't have all of them," Raegan said. "Just the ones that were linked to the younger children found in the Kasdans' files."

"That's a start," Hunter said, reaching for the top folder from where he sat on the sectional next to Rusty's sister, Kelsey.

Harper turned back to her computer as each of Rusty's siblings reached for a folder and everyone started going through the files. She knew why they were doing this: if they could find a link between CAOF, the Kasdans, and the Plague, they'd have something solid to take to the police. It made sense. The problem was, they still didn't know who was running the Plague.

She and Rusty had talked about it in the car on the way over. The man who'd shot Jordan and set that fire twenty years ago had likely done it to seize control of the group. But since Rusty had never seen the man's face and couldn't remember his voice, that could be anyone. Up until this point, they'd dealt with low-level thugs like that asshat Mihail, who grabbed the girls and transported them to points of sale. They had no idea who was sitting at the top, and they were never going to stop the organization until they figured that part out.

She skimmed through the Kasdans' financial holdings, which Hunter had provided her with, and compared them with those Jordan had invested in. One stood out. A research science facility in Hillsboro, outside Portland.

She opened a new window and ran a search on the facility. A website popped up.

She scanned the page, then opened another window and ran a search on the facility's investors. Her gaze skipped over the list, stopping when she spotted a very familiar name.

Holy shit.

"Um," she said aloud to the room. "I have a question."

Papers shuffled at her back. Glancing over her shoulder, she saw they were all looking at her curiously, but she focused on Alec and Raegan. "Did CAOF work with homeless kids?"

Alec looked at his wife, then back at Harper. "I'm not sure. We never focused on that. Why?"

Harper glanced toward Rusty in the middle of the couch, his dark eyes already narrowed on her as if he knew what she was about to say. "Because homeless youth aren't often reported as missing."

"That's true." Ethan closed the file folder in his hands. "The statistics are pretty dismal. And Portland has a huge homeless-youth problem. There are a lot of reasons, but the biggest is because the city's become known as a place where the homeless, in general, won't be kicked out."

"It's also a city with a huge sex-trafficking problem," Rusty said in a low voice, still watching Harper. "And homeless youth are a prime target for trafficking. They go missing, and no one cares."

Hunt turned his attention Rusty's way. "You sound like you know that from personal experience."

"I do."

When he didn't elaborate, and it was clear everyone was waiting, Harper decided enough was enough. Rusty might think he was keeping his family safe by staying silent about his extracurricular activities, but he wasn't. Not now when they were all here helping him. And even though he'd decided long ago he didn't need anyone to lean on in his life, one look at this room told her they'd all leaned on him in the past and that they were here because that's what family did—they had your back even when you didn't want them to. "He's been rescuing as many as he can from the Plague before they can sell them. That's why the cops were after him. They thought he was the one taking them. They didn't know he was trying to save them."

Alec's eyes widened as he looked from Harper back to his brother. "She's kidding, right?"

Rusty scowled her way and mouthed "thanks" and leaned back against the couch cushions without answering.

"You were right," Alec said to Ethan across the room. "Just not completely right."

Ethan turned wide eyes on Rusty. "We thought you were still trying to save Lily."

"Lily's dead." Rusty didn't meet either of his brothers' questioning gazes, he only stared at Harper. And though part of her knew he was probably ticked she'd spilled his secret, she didn't care. They deserved to know. They loved him. Didn't he realize that when people loved you the way these people loved him, it meant they believed in you, they trusted you, they'd do anything they had to do to keep you safe?

A memory slammed into her—one of him yelling at her in that tunnel to take the girl and run, to leave him. Of that gunshot going off in the darkness. Of standing on that damp, dark sidewalk, waiting, praying for him to come out that tavern door.

The breath caught in her lungs. A rush of emotion she didn't expect hit her from all sides, squeezing her chest. Looking quickly away from him, she turned toward her computer and focused on her screen, clenching and relaxing her fists, trying to figure out why they were suddenly damp and what the hell was wrong with her.

She didn't want him to die either. That was it. Except . . . her heart contracted again, and this time, visions of last night flooded her mind. Of how distraught he'd looked in that cave, of the turmoil in his eyes. Of the way he'd completely melted into her after she'd made it clear she wasn't leaving, followed by the way she'd felt utterly complete with him. Safe. As if she was finally *home*.

Kelsey pushed to her feet and punched Rusty in the upper arm. "You big jerk." She dropped to the couch cushions next to him. "You could have been killed."

Rusty wrapped his arms around her, pulled her in close, and in low voice said, "Me? Never. Too stubborn for that."

Kelsey sniffled and whispered something Harper couldn't hear, and she was still too rattled by her emotions to try to listen closer.

"Sorry," Hunt said. "I still don't see the connection. What do homeless kids being preyed on by the Plague have to do with CAOF or the Kasdans?"

Hunt's question knocked Harper's brain back into gear, and, blinking away the memories and weird feelings swirling inside her, she cleared her throat. "A lot, I think." She pushed her computer to the side so they could see the news article she'd found, but she still wasn't ready to turn and look at any of them. "This is an article about the mayor, Gabriel Rossi, and his vow to clean up the streets and rid Portland of its homeless epidemic. It was published just before the Kasdans were arrested. Look at the picture."

Fabric rustled, and she sensed all of them pushing off the couch and coming her way. Her stomach tightened.

"That's good ol' Miriam and her son, Arnold," Alec muttered.

"Yep." Harper flipped screens. "And this picture is from some twenty years ago, when the mayor was nothing but a city councilman. Recognize anyone besides the Kasdans and Rossi?"

"Fuck me," Rusty muttered. "That's Jordan. And my lying-ass attorney." *Her* boss.

"Yep," Harper said again. "Miriam and Arnold Kasdan, Gabriel Rossi, James Jordan, and Andrew Renwick, all together. This photo was taken at a charity ball for at-risk youth, hosted by a research facility in Hillsboro that had just opened at the time. According to what I found, all four of them were investors in the company."

"What kind of company?" Ethan asked.

Harper flipped screens one last time and sat back in her seat as the company's web page came up. "This kind."

"What is it?" Raegan asked.

"I'm not sure." Harper pursed her lips, eyeing the medical facility's web page, which touted the company as one dedicated to research and development in the areas of infection and disease. "But something tells me it's more than just a place where they try to find the cure for cancer. Especially if it involves the Kasdans, Rossi, Jordan, and Renwick."

Silence echoed at her back, then in a low voice, Alec said, "I think someone needs to look into this research facility so we know exactly how it connects to the Plague and the Kasdans."

"Agree," Hunt said, "but we definitely need to look into Renwick's association with Rossi more. He could also have warned you to see what you'd do next."

A sick feeling settled in Harper's stomach. She didn't want to think it was possible—her dad had known Andrew Renwick personally before his death. She knew their friendship was the reason Andy had offered her a job at his firm after her father had died and she'd left the department. But if Hunt was right, it meant that Renwick had been working for the Plague the whole time. He'd been using her to lure Rusty into a trap. And she'd very nearly given all of them exactly what they wanted.

Guilt stabbed at her. A guilt that made it hard to breathe. But with it came the knowledge she could fix some of the mess she'd created by figuring out who was really running the Plague.

"A stakeout sounds like cop work." She closed the laptop on the table and pushed to her feet. "I'll check out this research facility. The rest of you keep digging into the link between the major players."

Harper made it two steps toward the kitchen before Rusty called, "Not so fast. You're not going anywhere without me."

Her feet froze seconds away from freedom. She didn't turn to look at him. Couldn't. Because her heart was pumping so hard she was afraid he'd see the truth in her eyes the minute she met his gaze.

She wasn't volunteering to leave because she felt guilty. She wasn't trying to get out of this apartment because she needed space from his family. She needed to run because she'd realized two seconds before just why the thought of him being hurt stabbed like a knife right through her heart.

Because she was in love with him. Wildly, completely, head over heels in love with a man she'd really only just met a handful of days ago. And that scared her. Scared her more than any thug or criminal or black market gang because love was something she had very little experience with. And love—in her experience—only ended one way.

With the person you couldn't live without dying and leaving you all alone.

CHAPTER SIXTEEN

Rusty was trying not to be frustrated with Harper. She'd argued with him repeatedly that she didn't need him to come with her to check out the research facility. That she could handle it on her own, that nothing bad would happen. That he should stay with his siblings and keep researching. Argued so much he was starting to think she was trying to get rid of him.

Did she not think he could handle what they'd find? Or that he'd mess up her stakeout? He didn't want to jump to conclusions—not after last night—but he didn't like the thought of her trying to sideline him in any way when it came to the Plague. Especially when there was no way in hell he'd ever let her get near the Plague alone.

"Are you okay?" he asked.

"Yeah, I'm fine. Why wouldn't I be?"

"You've been quiet since we left O'Donnell's."

"Just thinking. I've a pretty strong hunch this research facility isn't so much into research and is way more into donations."

He shot her a look across the console. "What do you mean?"

"I mean, there was a tab on the site with instructions on how to donate your body to science."

"That's pretty normal, isn't it?"

"Yes. But in this case, I can't find any link between this company and any major research studies published anywhere on the web. I've spent the last fifteen minutes looking."

"So what does that mean?"

"It means," she said on another sigh, "that this might not be a research facility at all but a body broker."

"Like where they sell off body parts to other scientific facilities?"

"Yes."

"That's not illegal, is it?"

"No. Legitimate body brokers accept donations from individuals and hospitals, then transport the parts to different research facilities that use the donations to promote medical research. But there are no government regulations in the acceptance and sale of cadavers as there are in organ donations. Legitimate companies, however, often offer free cremation services to facilitate donations from families who are cash-strapped for funeral expenses."

"So families donate organs and tissues from the deceased to companies like this, and the facility cremates the rest for free?" Rusty asked.

"Yes. It's a way for families to offset funeral costs. Companies like this advertise free cremation services with morticians, hospitals, and institutions that deal with death on a daily basis. This facility, though? I can't find any info on it aside from their website. No ads online, no articles about their services, no mention of them anywhere on the web."

That was definitely odd.

"On top of that"—Harper turned in her seat to face him—"a friend at PPD told me in confidence that there have been a number of missing girls in Portland recently. It's possible most of them were picked up by the Plague and sold. But what happens to the ones they can't sell? No business operates at one hundred percent sales. Where do those girls go? And if the Plague is killing them, why haven't their bodies been found? It's almost as if . . ."

When her voice trailed off, Rusty turned to look at her. "As if what? Don't stop now. You've totally got my attention."

Her shoulders tensed. "It's almost as if those girls have completely disappeared. And as soon as I saw that website today, and who was in those pictures, all I could think was . . . how do you get rid of a body without any kind of evidence?"

Rusty sucked in a breath. "You get rid of every part of the body by donating it to science."

"Right." She looked over at him. "It's only a theory. But if that's the case here, there would be records. Forged records, at least. Every person who donates a body has to file a written consent donating their body to science, which has to be signed by the donor prior to death. In most states it can't be signed by anyone who has a power of attorney. This facility would know that and would have forms on hand in case they were ever investigated."

"So we need to somehow see their files and compare signatures."

"Yeah." She blew out a breath and looked ahead again. "That would be my suggestion. If several of them are similar, then we'll know they're being forged. Though I'm not quite sure how to get inside to see those files. I think our best bet right now is to stake the place out and see who comes and goes."

It was as good a plan as any, and he nodded to tell her he agreed, but he couldn't shake the feeling she still wasn't telling him everything. There was something else she was holding back. Something she didn't want him to know.

Before this night was over, he was going to find out what that something was. And how—or if—it pertained to them.

———

Harper couldn't stop thinking about Andy and the Plague and their connection to this facility as Rusty pulled his truck to a stop across the street from the research facility. There were only a handful of cars in the parking lot. Through the lobby windows, Harper spotted a receptionist sitting behind a counter, and behind her, file cabinets and a door that led to the back rooms.

"Surveillance everywhere." Rusty pointed to the cameras on the light poles in the small parking lot and the ones they could see through the glass windows in the lobby.

"Yeah. Must be something important inside they don't want people to see. You find it odd they have a secretary here on a Sunday? This is a research facility. Not a medical clinic."

"Yeah, a little." Reaching for his door handle, he said, "Let's go see what we can find out."

"No." She stopped him with a hand on his arm. "Let's just wait and see who comes out. If they're linked to the Plague like we think and they see my face on the camera, it might spook them."

"Good point."

They sat in silence. Dusk turned to darkness, and the lights across the street in the parking lot came on. A few people in hospital scrubs came out, climbed into their cars, and drove away. Not many, but enough to make her wonder what was going on in this place on a weekend. When only one car remained in the parking lot, they watched as the secretary tidied up her desk, then flipped off the main lights, locked the door after herself, found her car, and drove away too.

"Did Jordan donate his body to science?" Harper asked, watching the building closely.

"No idea."

"Hmm." She lapsed into silence again.

Twenty minutes later, when the place had grown quiet, he sighed. "What do you think?"

"I don't know." She glanced over her shoulder, down the empty street. "I think we should wait awhile longer and see if anyone else leaves or shows up."

He nodded, sinking down in his seat a bit. As silence crept back over them, he laid his hand on the thigh of his jeans and tapped his fingers against the worn cotton until she glanced his way.

He stopped tapping and shot her a sheepish look. "Sorry. I'm new to the whole stakeout thing."

God, he was cute. And as their eyes met across the dark vehicle, her chest pinched with that same shot of fear she'd felt back at O'Donnell's apartment.

"I told you that you didn't need to come with me." She looked quickly back toward the research facility, breathing deeply, hoping it would make the pain dissipate, hoping he wouldn't notice. Messing around with him was one thing, but loving him was just going to hurt her in the long run. Had she learned nothing from her parents? From her own failed dating history? Cops didn't have lasting relationships. The statistics proved it.

But you're not a cop anymore . . .

That was true. She still wanted to be one, though . . . didn't she?

"Sit here with you, or spend the time being hounded by my siblings. Hmm. Trust me. That wasn't even a choice."

Rusty's comment pulled her away from the swirling thoughts in her head. "What?"

He glanced at her with narrowed eyes. "My siblings?" When she only blinked, completely unsure why he was talking about his family, he said, "Are you okay? You look confused."

She *was* confused. Way the hell confused. Because suddenly she wasn't sure what she wanted. Did she want to go back to that life? To putting her life on the line every day, to being an outcast in the good ol' boys' club, to keeping her distance from relationships and basically having no life—no future—because she was afraid she'd one day end up like her dad?

She'd been so focused on proving to everyone—especially herself— that she wasn't a quitter, that she hadn't stopped to consider everything her new life was giving her. She'd only been thinking about what she'd lost the day she'd been asked to resign.

She opened her mouth to try to tell him all of that when a white van passed his window. It slowed as it approached the facility, then turned into the parking lot. But it didn't stop out front, it disappeared around the back of the building.

Rusty sat up straighter in his seat. "Did that driver look familiar to you?"

"Yeah." He looked eerily similar to the guy from that first night in the tunnels. The one who'd held a gun on Rusty and the girl he'd been trying to rescue. "Way too familiar."

His gaze met hers. "What now?"

Right now she needed to stop focusing on what-ifs and start focusing on what was. She reached for her door handle. "Now we see what they're really up to."

———

"Harper," Rusty hissed, crossing the street in the dark after her.

She ducked into the brush on the side of the building so the cameras couldn't pick her up and disappeared from sight.

He pushed a blackberry vine away that snagged his denim jacket and looked up to make sure she wasn't too far ahead. He could just see the bushes waving behind her where she'd already gone through.

She was crouched in the brush when he caught up with her, peering through the leaves and twigs toward the back of the building.

"Shh," she whispered when he drew up next to her. She nodded toward the van, backing up to what looked like a loading dock. "That's him all right. Destiny said his name was Mihail."

"Destiny?"

"The stripper you paid in that bedroom beneath Assets."

"You caught her name?"

She tipped her head to see better through the brush. "She was a wealth of information."

Yeah, she had been.

He looked sideways at Harper. "I need to tell you something."

"Hmm?"

"I'm glad I waited five years for you."

She went still, then slowly turned toward him with a look that was a cross between confusion and something else.

But he didn't let it deter him. He reached for her hand and whispered, "If I'd known you were out there, I'd have waited a helluva lot longer than five years."

Harper's mouth fell open, but before she could respond, Mihail climbed out of the driver's seat and moved to the back of the van. The loading-dock doors went up, and another man stepped into the light as Mihail climbed up on the dock and opened the van's doors. But the man's face was cast in shadows—all they could see was his dark silhouette against the lights of the loading dock.

"What have you got?" the dark silhouette asked in a low voice.

"A bitch who can't keep her mouth shut." Mihail reached inside the back of the truck. Seconds later he stepped back with something big wrapped in a black plastic bag. The other man crossed in front of Mihail, then grabbed the opposite end of what Rusty realized was a body bag being unloaded from the truck. They disappeared inside, but not before the sound of a muffled groan reached Rusty's ears.

"Holy shit," Harper whispered. "Did you hear that?"

Fuck. "Yeah. Whoever's in there is still alive."

"She won't be if we don't do something fast." She tugged her hand from his and pushed through the brush.

CHAPTER SEVENTEEN

Harper drew her gun, her senses on high alert.

She recognized Rusty's footsteps behind her, knew he was close, but she didn't slow her steps. Whoever was in that body bag was alive, which meant her instinct had been right. This place wasn't at all what it seemed to be.

Her pulse pounded hard as she stopped near the door to the facility. They hadn't closed it completely. Pushing it open a little more, she checked right and left into the hallway. Finding it clear, she nodded for Rusty to join her. He moved up at her back and in her ear hissed, "I thought this was a stakeout."

"I'm improvising."

"Harp—"

"You know whoever's in that bag doesn't have a lot of time. If we wait for help, it'll probably be too late by the time they get here. This is no different from what you've been doing for six years." When he didn't argue, she knew she had him. "Stay close."

"Don't worry. You're not getting away from me."

Something warmed inside her. Something she liked. She'd never needed a man to protect her, but she liked that Rusty wanted to. Liked even more that he wasn't threatened by her assertiveness. If anything, he seemed to appreciate it. Which made her like—love—him even more.

She moved down the left side of the hallway, keeping her gun in front of her, checking rooms they passed. The hall was dark, with only a few lights every twenty feet or so on low, casting an eerie glow over them as they inched along. The scent of heavy industrial cleaners filled the corridor.

Voices echoed from a room at the end of the hall. The same voices she'd heard on the loading dock. She glanced back at Rusty and lifted her finger to her lips. He nodded and peered into a doorway left partially open. Tapping her shoulder, he pointed toward the door that looked as if it led into some kind of operating room. She had no idea what he was doing, but she nodded and waited while he pushed the door open wider, then disappeared into the room. Seconds later, he reappeared with a scalpel and a long metal instrument that was flat at one end and curved like the letter *L*. Harper had no idea what it was for but remembered seeing something similar on a medical drama when the actors had pried open a patient's chest.

He gripped the instrument in one hand like a club and held the scalpel, blade facing out, in the other. Smirking at what he'd chosen to use to protect her, she turned and inched closer to the voices and the light spilling out of the door at the end of the hall.

"Open it up," a third voice said, this one unknown to Harper.

The sound of a zipper came from across the hall, followed by a muffled groan.

"This isn't what you usually bring me," the unknown voice said. "This one's old."

"Doesn't matter," Mihail answered in his thick Eastern European accent. "The boss wants her eliminated."

The unknown voice chuckled. "He didn't want to try to sell this one online?"

"No one would buy this one," the third voice said. "She's damaged goods."

Harper's breath caught. She recognized the third voice. Recognized it well. As soon as she'd heard it on the dock, she'd suspected it was him, but now she knew for sure. Knew because she'd worked alongside that voice for almost a year. Had stupidly trusted that voice. And had spent the last damn year plotting all the ways she was going to make the man behind that voice pay for pushing her off the force.

"All the ones you bring me are damaged goods," the unknown voice said. "What did she do to the boss man?"

"She couldn't keep her mouth shut," Noah Pierce answered, just as smug and vile as he'd always been.

"Stupid woman," the unknown voice muttered. "Then again, most of them aren't very smart. Good for only one thing."

The soft chuckling that met Harper's ears only made her vision blur red even more.

"How much did you give her?" the unknown man asked.

"Twice what we normally do," Mihail answered.

"Shit."

"We had to hit her twice," Pierce muttered. "She's used to the easy stuff."

"Hmm. We'll have to give the drugs time to get out of her system." Another groan echoed from the open doorway. "Put another strip of tape over her mouth, zip up the bag, and strap her to the table. We'll check on her in a bit to see how she's doing."

Footsteps sounded in the room. Harper turned back to Rusty and motioned toward the open doorway where he'd snagged those instruments. He nodded and moved silently in that direction. Following him, she ducked into the dark room and moved behind an instrument cart where she went still and waited.

A lifetime seemed to tick by in the silence. Her heart raced as she waited for them to finish whatever they were doing and leave. Metal scraped metal. Footsteps sounded. Then she heard a click, like a door shutting, and she sucked in a breath, relieved they were finally going.

Voices echoed in the hallway, then footsteps. She held her breath as they passed. But the unknown voice called, "Wait. Did one of you go in here?"

Footsteps drew closer, and a click sounded, followed by light flooding the room where she and Rusty were hiding.

She went still as stone, afraid to move, afraid to breathe. The gun grew heavy in her hand at her side. The man with the unknown voice stepped farther into the room and glanced around. From where she was hiding behind the instrument tray, Harper could just barely see his feet—encased in black dress shoes—his slacks, and the bottom of what looked like a white doctor's coat.

Moving her head very slowly, Harper glanced to her right where she knew Rusty was hiding behind a refrigeration unit. She couldn't see him. She hoped to God this man couldn't see him either. She had no doubt Pierce was armed. He was always armed. Mihail she wasn't sure about, but considering he'd pulled a gun on Rusty in that tunnel, odds were good he was armed too. This man in the doctor's coat was a wild card.

"Jesus," Pierce called. "You left that door open earlier. Come on, Johnson, I'm starving. If you want my help with that harvest tonight, I need food."

"Fine, whatever," Johnson muttered. "There's sushi in the staff room."

"I fucking hate sushi," Pierce muttered.

Johnson flipped the light off and closed the door. A click sounded, then his muffled voice chuckled. "That's because you have no class, Pierce."

Their footsteps faded down the hall along with their voices, but Harper didn't move for several minutes, just in case.

Rusty was the first to make a sound. He stepped out from behind the refrigerator and was at her side in seconds. "Motherfucker," he whispered. "They're harvesting organs from the girls they can't sell."

Yeah, she'd already figured that out. "We have bigger problems at the moment. I think they locked us in here."

He moved toward the door, closed his hand around the knob, and muttered, "Fuck."

"Can you pick it?"

He knelt and studied the lock. "I don't know. I don't have my pick kit with me."

"There has to be something in here you can use."

He glanced behind him at the drawers in the cabinets along the wall. "Look for any small instruments with a long, pointed end."

They both went to work, pulling drawers open as quietly as they could. When she found what he'd described, she drew it out and said, "Got it." She met him at the door and handed it to him. "Will this work?"

"We'll find out."

He dropped to his knees and inserted the instrument into the lock hole, moving it back and forth and up and down. Her pulse picked up. She glanced through the window in the door, out into the hall, hoping and praying Pierce and his friends weren't on their way back.

"Relax," Rusty muttered. "I got this."

"We need to get that girl out of here before they come back."

"If they drugged her, it's going to take several hours for the drugs to wear off."

"That's not what I'm worried about."

"No?"

"If she starts making noise, like I suspect she's about to do, I don't put it past them to find a way to shut her up without drugs. They only need her alive enough to take her organs."

Rusty's hands stilled against the lock. "Shit."

Yeah. Big-time shit.

He worked faster. And when the lock clicked several minutes later, Harper silently rejoiced.

"Good job." As she pulled the door open, a groan sounded from across the hall. "She's waking up."

Harper checked the corridor. Finding it clear, they made their way across the industrial tile floor, where she breathed a sigh of relief that Pierce and the others hadn't locked this door.

The room was dark when they stepped inside. Only a single light was on over a sink on the far wall. Rusty moved quickly for the body bag strapped to the gurney in the middle of the room and pointed toward the door. "Lock that, just in case."

Harper holstered her gun at her lower back and flipped the lock. When she turned back, Rusty was already unzipping the bag. The girl inside groaned again, this time louder.

"Oh shit," Rusty muttered.

"What?" Harper moved to his side, and her eyes grew wide when she looked down. "Oh my God, it's Destiny."

The stripper who'd helped them both moaned beneath the tape covering her mouth, her eyes tightly shut, and tried to move. But with the bag strapped to the gurney, all she did was shake the table.

Harper's gaze shot to Rusty. "They know she helped us."

"That'd be my guess." Rusty went to work on the closest strap. "Get that one. We have to get her out of here."

Harper fumbled with the buckle on the second strap and silently hoped they could do that without causing any commotion. Their lives hinged on Destiny staying quiet and cooperating.

Considering she was drugged and that whoever had grabbed her wanted her dead, there was no guarantee one way or the other.

———

Rusty's pulse was a roar in his ears as he followed Harper back down the dimly lit hallway with a limp stripper dressed in nothing but a ripped and flimsy T-shirt dress over his shoulder.

Gun drawn in front of her, Harper paused twice and held up her hand, telling him to stop, making his heart beat even faster because he was sure they were about to be overrun by the three goons from before. Each time though, Harper lowered her hand, then nodded for him to follow her closely as they headed back toward the loading dock.

Thankfully, Destiny stayed quiet until they reached their destination. When he tried to climb down with her slung over his shoulder, she let out a loud groan. Sure she was about to set off some silent alarm, he went still as stone. But when nothing happened, he told himself to stop being so jumpy and hustled to catch up with Harper.

They managed to get Destiny loaded into the back seat of his truck. Pulling a blanket out from under the seat, he handed it to Harper, who climbed in the back with her, then he jumped in the driver's seat and pulled away from the facility as slowly and quietly as he could.

Harper didn't talk as he drove, but he checked his rearview mirror to make sure both women were okay. Destiny lapsed in and out of consciousness as she lay sprawled across Harper's lap, wrapped in the blanket. Harper was still on high alert, checking car lights behind and in front of them, just to make sure they weren't being followed.

Now that they were out of immediate danger, he couldn't help but think about what he'd seen back there. Harper had been right. They were using the facility to get rid of evidence. This went way beyond human trafficking. It dipped into black market organ trade and he didn't know what else.

Twenty minutes later, he pulled to a stop in front of St. Vincent's ER. After flagging down assistance, he helped two orderlies haul Destiny out of his truck and into a wheelchair. He didn't want to have to file a report, so he gave them the bare basics, told them they didn't know what kind of drugs she'd taken, then split as soon as they turned to wheel Destiny inside the hospital.

Harper was sitting in the passenger seat of his cab when he came back out, the phone pressed to her ear. As he put the truck in "Drive," he whispered, "Who are you talking to?"

"Callahan," she mouthed. "Yeah," she said into the phone, "I'm here."

Their conversation was brief. She gave him an abbreviated summary of what they'd found at the body broker, then asked him to send someone to watch over Destiny in the ER. Rusty was just coming out of the tunnel on Highway 26, heading toward downtown, when she hung up and said, "I need to make a stop before we head back to O'Donnell's."

"What kind of stop?"

"A police kind of stop." When he eyed her skeptically, she added, "Don't worry. I won't be long. But I recognized more than just Mihail at that facility."

"You did? Who?"

"The second guy. The one who met Mihail on the loading dock. It was my ex-partner, Noah Pierce. The same detective who questioned you after Melony Strauss went missing."

"Shit. That's why his voice seemed so familiar."

"I need to let my former captain know. That's not something I can sit on."

He understood that.

He parked across the street from the department on Second Street. Lights shone down over the smattering of cars on the road at this hour and the trees trying to leaf out in late March.

Harper popped her door as soon as he pulled to a stop and jumped out. "I won't be long."

"I'll g—"

He didn't get the words out before she slammed the door and rushed across the street.

He climbed out, hit the lock button on his fob, and hustled after her. Catching up with her just as she yanked the front door open, he grabbed it above her head and held it for her. She looked up in surprise and said, "I thought you were going to wait in the truck?"

"And miss all the fun? No way."

She frowned but didn't seem too bothered. "This won't take long, I promise."

He waited behind her while she crossed to the reception counter and checked in with the officer on duty. Short minutes later, she handed him a visitor badge, then turned toward the elevators with her own badge. "This way."

Three officers were waiting for the elevator when they reached it. They nodded at Harper as if they knew her, and she did the same in response, but there was no spark of friendship. He couldn't help but wonder if she'd been close to anyone in the department besides Pierce— the man he wished he'd been able to take one good swing at with a crowbar, like the weapon back at the facility.

They rode the elevator up in silence. When the doors opened with a ping, he followed her off the car and into a large room filled with cubicles and officers and a flurry of activity, even at the late hour.

She pointed toward a trio of plastic chairs along the wall. "Have a seat; I'll be right back."

He wasn't thrilled with being relegated to the waiting area, but he could tell she was slightly stressed, so he did as she said with a nod. She wove around desks and cubicles, heading for a door on the far side of the room. As she passed, a few officers took notice of her, but no one called out her name or muttered hellos, and Harper didn't acknowledge them either.

She stopped near an office on the far side with a wall of glass windows blocked by drawn shutters. The sign over the door said CAPTAIN; she didn't bother to knock. Just twisted the knob and walked straight in as if she owned the place.

The door slapped shut. Rusty eyed its dark wood, knowing he should stay put as Harper had told him but curious about what kind of reception Harper would get from this captain. She'd told him the department was a good ol' boys' club. He knew her captain hadn't believed her before and that he'd forced her out of the department. What if he didn't believe her now? What if he took Pierce's side over hers?

Instinct pushed him to his feet. He skirted the edge of the room, around the outside of the cubicles, following the path she'd taken.

A couple of officers eyed him speculatively, but after glancing at his visitor badge they went back to their work. He slowed his steps as he approached the door he'd seen Harper march through. Voices echoed from inside, sending his pulse up. Forceful voices. Hers and a man's.

"You're absolutely sure of this," the man said.

"Without a doubt. I saw him. What the hell is going on, Daryl? He wasn't working undercover, was he? Do you even have control over what's happening in your division?"

"Watch it, Blake."

"Why? People are dying out there. They're killing those girls and selling off their body parts as if they're nothing but livestock. You've got a mole here in the department, and I just told you who it is, and you don't seem to even care."

"I care, goddammit. It's just not that easy."

"'Not that easy'?" Her voice lifted an octave. "He lied to the review committee about me. I knew it, he knew it, and you even knew. I got fired, and here he is a year later, still working for the department, all the while participating in a black-market organization that abducts, sells, and murders innocent women and girls. He needs to be fucking brought in *now*."

"I understand your anger," the man said in a placating tone. "But I would have thought you'd use this to your advantage, not come barging in here all bent out of shape about it."

"What does that mean?"

"It means," he said with a sigh. "This is what you wanted, isn't it? Your connection to the head of the Plague? If we take Pierce down now, you risk losing that connection. You risk letting the head of the organization off the hook. The commissioner is never going to live up to his end of your deal if you don't bring him the mastermind. He won't give a rat's ass about Pierce, and you won't be reinstated."

Rusty sucked in a breath when he realized what they were discussing. Somehow, at some point, she'd made a deal with the police commissioner to get her old job back. A deal that hinged on her bringing the department information on the head of the Plague. A deal she could only follow through on after convincing Rusty to help her bring down the organization.

Their conversation in the kitchen the morning after they'd rescued Megan Christianson slammed into him. As did her words just before she'd slid onto his lap and lured him into hot sex right on her kitchen table.

"Wouldn't it be better to stop these people from ever traumatizing another girl than to try to rescue her after the fact? We could make that happen. Together."

The blood drained from his face. He didn't hear any more of her conversation inside that room, couldn't focus on the words. All he could focus on was the fact she'd used him. Used him to get what she wanted, which was her job back. She didn't care about saving those girls. She didn't really care about bringing down the Plague. And she didn't care about him. He'd been a means to an end, and he'd fallen right into her trap.

The realization that he'd been stupid whipped through him. And the bitter reality that he'd been duped. The "something else" he'd seen in her eyes tonight wasn't anything related to their relationship. It was pure and simple deception. A deception he should have picked up on a long time ago.

He wasn't sure how he made it down the elevator and out of the building. Didn't remember handing in his badge or crossing the road to his truck. All he could focus on was the sour taste of betrayal and the painful bite of his own foolishness as he drove. He should have known better.

Happy endings didn't happen for people like him. And he had no one to blame for getting his hopes up but himself.

CHAPTER EIGHTEEN

The cell phone on the edge of Andy Renwick's desk buzzed, jolting him in his seat as he'd been trying to read a brief.

He hadn't been able to sleep. After he'd dropped Maureen at the airport for her red-eye, he'd come back to the office and decided he'd get some work done. But now he wished he hadn't. Now, as he eyed the buzzing phone as if it might burst into flames at any moment, he wished he'd stayed home, thrown the covers over his head, and ignored everything outside the safety of his walls.

There was no ignoring it, though. Swallowing hard, he reached for the phone with a shaking hand and flipped it over. One look at the number told him just who it was. Just as it told him he couldn't ignore the call.

"Yes," he said as he pressed the phone to his ear, trying to keep his voice level and smooth, cringing internally when he heard it crack.

"They know, goddammit!" the voice screamed into his ear. "They were at the facility in Hillsboro tonight! They took that fucking whore out of there before she was processed."

Panic pushed Andy out of his seat. "Who knows? Who took her?"

"Your fucking assistant and your fucking client."

The blood drained from Andy's face. "H-how do you know it was them?"

"Because security cameras outside the facility picked them up leaving the damn place. You had one job, Renwick. One measly job. To keep that bitch under control. But you failed."

"I-I'll talk to her. I'll make sure she knows how serious this is."

"Don't bother. We're handling it from here on out."

"No." That panic turned to full-on terror. "I'll warn her again. Sh-she must not have understood me yesterday. She—"

"She's a liability, Renwick."

"No, please. This isn't her fault. It's McClane—"

"We should have taken care of her two years ago when we took care of her father. That's on you as well, convincing us she'd never be an issue. You were wrong on both counts."

"Please, listen. I'll do whatever you want. Just don't hurt her. This isn't her fau—"

"Stop fucking whining. It's unbecoming of a man in your position. Both of them will be dead by morning. Unless we decide to sell Blake to one of our investors instead. In which case, she'll wish she was dead."

The line clicked in his ear. Pulling the phone away from his ear, Andy stared at the screen in horror. Hand shaking, he dropped it on his desk, scrambled for his personal phone in his top drawer, and dialed Harper's number.

"Please," he whispered, "please pick up."

It rang three times and went to voice mail.

"No. God no." He dropped into his chair, rested his elbow against the desk, and swiped the sweat forming on his brow as he dialed again. "Answer, Harper. Goddammit, just answer."

Rusty didn't feel like going back to Hunt's place. He knew if his brothers took one look at him, they'd know something was wrong. And he wasn't in the mood for sympathy or the inevitable what-did-you-expect-getting-involved-with-a-cop looks he knew he'd get from Alec.

His gut said Harper shouldn't be alone, not if the Plague knew about her. But he couldn't make himself stay, so as he walked out of the station, he pulled his phone from his pocket, sent her a text, then told himself the woman could take care of herself. Hell, she could easily kick his ass. She had, both physically and emotionally.

Maybe it was stupid to go home, but no one had followed him today. No one at the station had spared him more than an annoyed glance. Pierce hadn't seen him at the research facility, and if Renwick had told the Plague he was Robin Hood, he'd already be dead. But just to be safe, he decided to grab a blanket and a bottle of scotch and lock himself in the wine cave for the night. No one would find him there. And there was no sense taking stupid chances. God knew, he'd taken enough stupid chances in his life, especially during the last week.

Feeling like a schmuck, a grade-A asshole, and an idiot all rolled into one, he turned onto the vineyard and bypassed his house. It was still standing, still in one piece, not a single thing out of place. Parking in front of the barn, he grabbed his car keys and slammed the door.

The barn was dark and deserted, just the way it was supposed to be. He'd gotten in the habit of leaving his keys to the caves hanging on a hook in the loft for the contractor so the crew could get to the building fixtures he'd stored out of the weather, and as he jogged up the temporary stairs to the upper deck, he hoped they were still where he'd left them. Work tools were scattered across the naked floorboards—hammers, triangles, crowbars, a nail gun, the stapler he'd left out after hanging a sign warning the construction crew about some rotten floorboards. The makeshift table was stacked with plans, pencils, squares, and used paper coffee cups no one had thrown away yet.

He turned in a slow circle in the middle of the massive space, seeing it all in his mind's eye. It was going to be perfect when it was done. Rustic, classy, everything he'd imagined for nearly fifteen years. Except the one person he'd started envisioning here in the space with him wasn't ever going to be here. Not now. Not when he knew the truth.

"Moron," he muttered, shaking her from his head as he pushed his feet forward. The sound his boots made on the wood echoed as he crossed to the far side and looked up at the markings Matt had made both on the header above and the floorboards below. He'd do exactly what he'd always done. He'd focus on work. On the property. On getting by with what he had. He'd made it this far on his own. Being alone was what was familiar to him.

Shuffling sounded on the stairs. And he frowned when he realized he wasn't alone. If Harper had followed him, he wasn't sure what the hell he was going to say to her. He turned toward the stairs, then froze.

Not Harper. Not even close.

Two men stepped into the moonlight coming through the open wall. Two men he recognized because he'd seen them only an hour ago at the facility.

Harper wasn't sure if she wanted to vomit or if flames were about to shoot straight out of her ears.

As she left Robinson's office and turned to skirt the edge of the cubicles in the middle of the room, she realized there was a chance both could happen.

He wasn't going to arrest Pierce. She understood the reasoning, but she didn't like it. And she hated that she doubted Robinson would do the right thing and let Pierce lead them to the head of the Plague. What if Robinson was corrupt too? Hell, he hadn't believed her once before, why would he believe her now?

She rounded the corner and stared at the empty bank of chairs where she'd told Rusty to wait. Slowing her steps, she glanced right and left, looking for him. All she saw was the normal chaos of the department, officers answering calls, typing on keyboards, moving around with papers and coffee cups.

"Jessica," she said when she recognized a young officer in a blue uniform with her auburn hair pulled back in a slick ponytail, moving toward her, heading for the elevators.

"Hey, Blake. Haven't seen you around here lately. You meeting someone for drinks after their shift?"

"No, I had a meeting with Robinson. There was a guy sitting here a few minutes ago. Civilian. Tall, dark, wearing Romeos, jeans, black Henley, and a jean jacket. Did you see him?"

"Oh yeah, he was cute. All dark and brooding, just my type. Was he with you?"

Yes, absolutely he was with me, she wanted to yell, but forced herself to stay calm and instead said, "Yeah. Did you see where he went?"

"Yeah. Where you just were. He was over here for a while, then he got up and moved toward Robinson's door. Stood there for a few minutes and left. That was only a few minutes ago. I didn't realize you were inside."

"Left?" Panic surged inside her. "What do you mean, 'left'?"

She chuckled. "'Left,' as in, he walked this way, got on the elevator, and left."

"Dammit." Harper's mind spun as she glanced down at the floor. If he'd stood outside Robinson's door and was gone now, she could think of only one thing that would make him leave with no word.

"Shit." She pressed a hand against her forehead as sickness swirled in her stomach.

He'd overheard Robinson discussing her deal with the commissioner.

"Hey, you okay?" Jessica asked, placing a hand on Harper's arm. "You don't look so well all of a sudden."

"I-I'm fine. Thanks." But she wasn't. She was freaking the hell out.

Swiveling around, she rushed to the elevators, hit the "Call" button again and again, and stared up at the lights above the doors as she waited, willing the damn car to get here.

She knew exactly what he was thinking. Exactly why he'd left. And he wasn't wrong. He just didn't know that between the time she'd made that deal and now, she'd completely changed her mind about what she wanted.

The elevator doors opened, and she rushed inside and hit "Lobby." Minutes later she burst through the front doors of the building and scanned the dark street.

Rusty's truck was gone.

"Dammit."

Her phone buzzed, and she quickly tugged it out, hoping it was from Rusty. It was, but not the words she'd wanted to see.

Something came up. Call O'Donnell. He'll take you back to his place where you'll be safe. Don't be stupid and try to go home. They know where you live.

Her stomach rolled. She knew without even calling O'Donnell that Rusty wasn't at his apartment. She could all but hear the hurt in the words on her phone. Glancing right and left, she quickly scanned the street for a cab. A yellow vehicle idled two blocks down near a restaurant.

She pushed her legs into a run and waved her arm to get the driver's attention. He didn't seem to notice her. Heart thundering, she raced toward the corner. Just as she passed a dark doorway, a hand reached out of the shadows.

An arm snaked around her waist and yanked her into the darkness. Harper gasped but didn't have time to scream. Another hand closed over her mouth and jerked her up against a hard male body.

Something cold pressed against her throat. Something sharp. And in her ear a menacing voice whispered, "Don't move."

CHAPTER NINETEEN

Rusty stared across the room at Pierce and the Eastern European they called Mihail, listening for any sounds that anyone else was with them. He couldn't hear anything, but that didn't mean they were alone.

"You're missing your little bodyguard," Pierce said, resting his hands on his hips. "Lucky us."

Instead of the cheap suit he'd been wearing last week when he'd questioned Rusty, tonight he was decked out in dark jeans and a black turtleneck. Mihail was wearing the same, except the prick had added a stocking cap to protect his bald head.

"Guess you should have arrested me then," Rusty answered, watching both of them closely in case they made any kind of move for the holsters at their hips. They were armed, he wasn't, but he knew this construction site and they didn't. If they came at him, he'd give them a few surprises they wouldn't forget, even if he died in the process.

"Guess I should have."

"How do we want to do this?" Mihail asked.

"Suicide would be best," Pierce answered. "Fewer questions. It won't be hard to stage the scene. Get close, though."

Fuck that. Rusty bolted for the sawhorses. His shoulder slammed into the hard surface as he flipped the make-shift worktable over, ducking behind the hardwood they'd nailed to the top.

A gunshot went off, echoing through the space.

"Motherfucker!" Pierce screamed. "Are you an idiot? Don't start shooting up the place. It'll look too damn suspicious!"

"Oh. But you said—"

"Just fucking go get him," Pierce hissed.

Footsteps pounded close. Rusty glanced right and left, searching for a weapon. Mihail yelled, "Come out from behind there, you dickhead, and take it like a man."

Rusty wrapped one hand around the handheld work light that had been hanging from a pole on the side of the worktable and which was still plugged in. Then he gripped the nail gun that had flown off the table when he'd flipped it over and breathed hard as he waited.

"I said," Mihail growled only feet away, "come *out.*"

His head popped over the edge of the table. Rusty looked up just in time to see the barrel of the gun. Lifting the work light, he flipped the switch, illuminating the room. Mihail grunted and stumbled back. Rusty didn't hesitate. He popped up, lifted the nail gun, and pulled the trigger.

A hiss sounded as the nails left the gun, followed by a series of thwacks as they struck Mihail right in the forehead, not more than a foot away.

Wide-eyed, Rusty stared at the blood oozing from the man's face. In front of him, Mihail swayed, grunted, then collapsed against the ground, lying limp with his eyes wide open.

Rusty's stomach pitched, and bile shot straight up his throat.

"Motherfucker." Across the room where he'd been watching, Pierce reached for his weapon.

Knowing he didn't have time to deal with what he'd just done, Rusty swiveled and pointed the nail gun at Pierce. But when he depressed the trigger, nothing happened. Gunshots echoed through the barn. Rusty dropped the nail gun and light and dove back behind the table. The *thwack, thwack, thwack* of bullets digging into the wood at his back sounded all around him.

He scanned the ground, spotted the cord to the light, and yanked the plug from the outlet, dousing the room in darkness.

"You think you're tough?" Pierce yelled. "You think that nail gun's gonna save your sorry ass? You don't know shit."

Rusty's heart beat hard. Sweat broke out all over his body. He looked around, searching for something—anything—he could use as a weapon. The closest objects were a crowbar and a sander.

"I did some research on you," Pierce growled. "Found out what kind of sick fuck you really are. You like young girls just as much as our clients, don't you? I think we'll have to make sure your whole family knows just what kind of shit you like. We can find that nice doctor mother of yours and fill her in. And your slutty little sister, and all those pretty little wives those bastards you call brothers managed to fuck. Bet they'll be a hotter lay than Blake. You've taken a liking to her, haven't you? I get the appeal. Trust me. But she's not worth the effort. If she's not dead yet, she will be in a matter of minutes."

Rusty's vision turned red. Grasping the crowbar in one hand, he reached for the sander, jerked to his feet, and hurled it straight at the sound of Pierce's voice in the darkness.

The man grunted and stumbled back. Something whacked the floor. Scrambling over the table, Rusty hurled himself straight at him and swung out with the crowbar, nailing him in the side of the head.

A crack echoed through the large space. Pierce groaned and rolled across the floor. Muscles vibrating, Rusty gripped the crowbar and went after him.

"You son of a bitch." He swung out just as Pierce found his footing. The crowbar smacked against the side of his face.

Pierce went flying. His body hit the ground. He groaned, writhed against the ground in pain, and tried to push up on his hands and knees.

Breathing heavily, Rusty watched him, fighting the urge to finish the son of a bitch off. Pierce managed to push to his feet, then stumbled to the left, like a dazed fighter, his head lolling on his neck, and hit the ground with a grunt.

He wasn't worth it. Rusty released the weapon at his side. It clattered against the floorboards.

He reached into his pocket and pulled out his cell phone to check on Harper. He only got in three numbers before Pierce lurched to his feet, screamed, and rushed right at him.

Rusty only had a split second to decide what to do. He lifted his fists to defend himself, and then he realized where he was standing.

On the markings Matt had made for the door tracks. Two feet from the drop-off that was more like three stories up instead of two. Where the deck would eventually be but wasn't yet.

Every muscle in his body tensed as Pierce's enraged face shot toward him. But just before the man's fist made contact, Rusty ducked to the side and stepped to the left. Pierce's eyes grew wide when he saw nothing but darkness, but it was already too late. He went sailing over the edge of the old barn loft and smacked with a thud against the concrete far below.

Rusty's heart raced as he turned to look. Pierce was facedown, not moving. Bending forward, Rusty rested his hands on his knees and sucked back air. Far below, a cell phone rang. Rusty lifted his head and peered over the edge as it rang again, realizing it must be coming from the phone in Pierce's pocket. The man still didn't move a muscle.

The ring died out, leaving an eerie silence in its wake. Dropping his head, Rusty focused on breathing, on filling his lungs with air and slowing his racing heart. Behind him, another phone shrilled.

He whipped around and scanned the space. It was coming from the middle of the room. From Mihail's pocket. It too rang four times, then died out.

Shit. The Plague was checking their progress. He had minutes before someone else showed up.

He fumbled for his cell phone, hit Hunt's number, and reached for the keys in his pocket as he raced toward the stairs.

"Hey," Hunt said, picking up on the first ring. "Where are you? We thought you two were coming back here tonight. Kelsey made din—"

"Harper didn't make it back?" Panic pushed his voice an octave higher.

"No. Was she coming here alone?"

"Goddammit. I thought he was baiting me."

"Whoa. Slow down and tell me what happened."

"They have her, Hunt." Rusty hit the concrete floor, darted for his truck, and jerked open the driver-side door. Jumping inside and starting the engine, he said, "Harper and I went to the facility, and when we were there—"

His phone beeped with an incoming message as he was backing around the sedan Pierce and Mihail must have driven. Heart in his throat, he hit the brakes, hoping maybe it was her and that Pierce had been lying. "Hold on."

He yanked the phone away from his face and looked down at the message. And felt his heart shoot right into his throat.

It was a picture. Of Harper. Bound, with duct tape around her ankles, her knees, and her wrists, which were trapped behind her back. Her eyes were open but only partway, and the dazed look reflected in their hazel depths told him she'd been drugged. Another strip of silver duct tape was secured over her mouth.

He couldn't tell if she was conscious or unconscious since it was a still photograph. But he saw the blood dripping down her face and oozing from beneath the tight tape. And inside, all he knew was rage. White-hot, blistering rage.

His phone dinged again, only this time it wasn't a picture that came through; it was a text. A text that told him they knew he'd escaped death. And that they were using her as bait.

Her life is in your hands. If you want her to live, follow these instructions very carefully.

Harper groaned and tried to roll to her side, but something was preventing her from moving.

She struggled, tried to sit up, couldn't. Tried to move her legs, couldn't. Tried to move her arms, still couldn't.

Panic set in, stealing her breath as she opened her eyes and blinked. Nothing but darkness met her eyes. She opened her mouth to yell, but only a muffled sound met her ears. And her head . . .

Blinding pain was stabbing at her skull. At her fuzzy skull, she belatedly realized. She felt as if she were moving in slow motion, in water. If she could move.

Something was wrong. Something was very wrong.

She sucked air in through her nose and screamed as loud as she could. Her muffled voice echoed back at her, followed by a rush of warmth that felt like . . . her breath.

In a daze, she realized why it was so dark, why she couldn't move, and why her breath was rebounding over her. She lifted her head—the only part of her that wasn't strapped down—and discovered in a rush of horror she was right.

She was in a body bag. She was drugged and strapped down, just as Destiny had been. Oh God . . . she was back in that facility where that monster carved up bodies and stole organs.

"Now, now," a familiar voice said somewhere close. "You've woken up, I see. Let's just have a look, shall we?"

She froze, recognizing that voice as the doctor she and Rusty had heard when they'd been here earlier tonight. The one Pierce had called Jones, or Jackson or . . . no, *Johnson*.

A zipper sounded, and then light shone down a single line in the center of her vision. Plastic crackled, and then the light grew stronger, blinding her as the two halves of the bag were pulled open.

"My, my. They did a number on you, didn't they?"

He spoke as if he were talking to a child. Harper squinted and tried to see his face. All she could make out were fuzzy shapes and . . . Glasses, he was wearing glasses.

"Let's just see where we're at, shall we?" He moved out of her line of sight. Rustling echoed from the right. Plastic clicking. Then he returned, filling her vision with his shadowy, fuzzy shape as he lifted an object in his hand and moved it over her, lowering it near her arms, which were strapped together against her torso. "Hold still now." Something tight closed around her upper arm, then he pressed his finger against the crook of her elbow and said, "This might hurt."

He stabbed a needle into the crook of her elbow, and she cried out as pain ripped up her arm.

"Hmm, not a very good patient." He tugged something off the end of the needle—a vial she realized, a vial of her blood—and pressed another in its place, waiting for it to fill. "Don't worry. This will all be over soon. They didn't have to give you too much to sedate you. It'll be out of your system soon enough. Then you'll have a nice long sleep."

She winced as he yanked the needle free, not bothering to be gentle, not bothering to cover the spot with a bandage. As he took the vials to the counter near the foot of the gurney she was strapped to and started testing her blood—for what, she didn't know—he hummed as if there was nothing fucking wrong with this situation. As if she were a lab rat and not even human.

"Oh, this is wonderful, wonderful," the man crooned. "You're a universal donor. Your organs will be easy to place. Very easy. But the drug isn't quite out of your system. We'll have to wait a little bit longer."

He turned and grinned down at her, and now that her vision was clearing, she could see the evil gleam in his eyes. And the fact the man had no soul.

"As it is, turns out the boss wants to watch." He nodded to his left. "I've got a camera set up when he's ready. He's dealing with your boyfriend first. But when that's done . . ." He clucked his tongue. "Then it's showtime."

Harper's heart rate shot up. He was talking about Rusty. They had Rusty. She screamed behind the tape over her mouth and kicked her arms and legs as hard as she could.

"Oh, you are a wildcat, aren't you?" He sighed and stepped to the end of the gurney, shaking as if he couldn't contain his excitement. "I can't wait to see what surprises you have inside."

———

Every muscle in Rusty's body vibrated with pent-up restraint as he was escorted into the fancy mansion on the outskirts of the city where the text had told him to come to—alone, with no weapons and no witnesses.

If he contacted the police, Harper was dead. If they saw any evidence he'd brought backup, she was dead. They'd made it clear they were watching him. He wasn't sure when they'd put eyes on him, but he was holding on to hope it hadn't been when he'd left his vineyard. His money was on the moment he'd turned onto the freeway. That was when he'd noticed the lights following him, all the way through the city and out to this desolate estate. Which meant they didn't know the plans he'd made with Hunt before that.

At least he prayed they didn't.

Two bouncer-size bodyguards in black suits had patted him down as soon as he'd arrived. They'd taken his phone, but finding him unarmed, had led him through a series of fancy rooms and down a set of curved stairs to a lower level. Another bodyguard followed closely at his back. None of the three spoke, and as they moved, Rusty prayed again and again that he'd made the right decision.

They wouldn't try to auction Harper off. He was sure of that. She wasn't a teenager. She wasn't a virgin. They could make a few bucks off her by selling her on the black market, but they knew she was a cop. And she could defend herself. They'd never risk the chance she might escape from whatever fucking piece of shit purchased her as a slave because she knew too much about their organization to be left alive.

Which meant they were going to kill her. Just the thought sent bile rushing up his throat, but he forced it down and reminded himself they had time. These men might be monsters, but they were also business-men. Harper was a healthy, fit woman in the prime of her life. If they'd gone to all the trouble of kidnapping and binding her up like they had in that picture, they were planning something else. They were going to harvest her organs first.

The two men in suits ahead of him stopped at a set of double doors and turned to face him. Stone-faced, the one on the left reached for the door handle and pushed it open, moving into the space ahead of him. The other stayed at the door.

It was an office, he realized as he stepped into the room. A big office with dark wood paneling, an entire wall filled with shelves and old books, a mahogany fireplace fronted by a couch and several side chairs, and a big old desk on the far side that was immaculately clean except for a phone, a lamp, and a single pen.

The bodyguard moved to the desk and stopped there, turning sideways and clasping his hands in front of him in silence. Ignoring him, Rusty glanced over the paintings on the walls, knowing they were spendy too, not recognizing the artists or even caring. Jordan had once had expensive paintings like that on the walls of his office. The same office where he'd beat Rusty to a pulp the day he'd revealed Lily was gone. Disgust burned in Rusty's gut. Some men craved possessions.

He was going to do whatever it took to make sure Harper was no one's possession, ever.

A door to the left of the big desk opened, and a tall, dark-haired man in his late fifties entered the room, wearing slacks, a striped dress shirt unbuttoned at the collar, and a jacket that was clearly custom-made to fit his tall frame. A man Rusty recognized from a photograph Harper had shown him.

"Mr. McClane," he said, moving behind the desk and reaching for the fancy leather rolling chair. "We finally meet." He nodded toward the bodyguard.

The bodyguard nodded back in response, set Rusty's cell phone on the edge of the desk, and moved for the door. Behind him, the door clicked closed.

His jaw clenched down hard as he stared at Gabriel Rossi. The mayor of Portland. "I'm here, like you asked. I followed your instructions. Tell your thugs to let Blake go."

"I would love to, but"—he reached for Rusty's cell phone, turning it over in his hands as he studied the screen, then leaned back in the chair—"she's caused all sorts of problems."

Rusty's vision turned red all over again, but he forced himself to stay in control. Losing it now wouldn't help Harper. And he'd known this prick wouldn't live up to his end of the deal. "I'm the one you want and you know it. You have me. Let her go."

Rossi sighed, powered down Rusty's phone, and dropped it on the desk as if he were bored. "Sadly, that's not up to me anymore. I tried to get Renwick to keep her in line, but . . . the man has no spine."

The door opened again, and Andrew Renwick stepped into the room, his head hanging, his shoulders slumped, every part of him somber and nearly defeated.

Rusty ground his teeth together to keep from lunging at Renwick, and then a third person moved into the room, accompanied by the hum of an electric wheelchair.

Rusty's mouth fell open as he stared at the heavyset man dressed in a suit. He was bald on top with a fringe of white hair around, and he was wearing a pair of wire-rimmed glasses that made his dark eyes appear almost beady. But he was familiar. And with one look as he used a hand to maneuver the machine into the room, Rusty knew who he was.

"You look as if you've seen a ghost," the man said with a note of glee in his strained voice. "Never expected me to be alive, did you, son?"

Rusty stared at James Jordan, unable to piece together the past with what he was seeing. Jordan was alive? He'd made it out of that fire? He'd survived? Rusty stared at him, seeing no burn marks. No signs he'd ever even been in a fire.

It wasn't possible. The air contracted in his lungs, making his chest tight and achy. Jordan had been alive all this time?

Head spinning, feeling like he was in some kind of sick dream, he glanced toward Rossi, who was seated behind the desk, eyes narrowed, lips thin, watching Rusty closely, then to Renwick, cowering in the corner, and finally back to Jordan in the wheelchair.

A very much *alive* Jordan. And very much in control of this room and the men Rusty had thought were running the Plague.

"I don't . . . How did you . . . " Rusty blinked, staring at Jordan again in disbelief. "Who shot you?"

"A cop. One who was working undercover at the time when we were first starting up. He surprised me, I'll say that much." His swollen lips curled just a touch in a twisted smile. "But he got what was coming to him. Took a few years, but we got him back. He'd figured out I was still alive, you see. He was getting too close again. Damn cops are always doing that. Playing hero and getting in the way. But we took care of him. Just like we're going to take care of his pretty little daughter."

Holy shit. He was talking about Harper's father.

"B-but there was a fire. I saw you burn." A fire the man who'd shot Jordan had started. *Double shit . . .* Harper's father had done that too.

"You saw a body burn. Just not mine. It was what we call a convenient cover-up. My men were easily able to toss a homeless man into that blaze in my place. The fire definitely took care of the matter of your mother. Would have taken care of you too, if I'd been coherent enough to tell them you were hiding behind that desk."

No, that wasn't right. Rusty's brow lowered. He remembered seeing the same man who'd shot Jordan start that fire. Only . . . The more he thought about it, the more he wondered if that was accurate. His eyes had been swollen. He'd definitely been concussed. It was possible he'd blacked out behind that desk. That the fire had started later. His memories from that night weren't as clear as he'd once thought.

"Now." Jordan seemed to sit up straighter in his chair. "Enough with the walk down memory lane. I always knew you were alive. I just had no idea they'd hide you right under my fucking nose. The situation is very simple. You fucked with the one thing I cared about most in this world. Now I'm going to fuck with the one thing you care most about."

Harper. He was talking about Harper. In that moment, Rusty knew that nothing he'd done in the past could have saved Lily. He'd been a kid back then. He couldn't have stopped Jordan because he'd had no idea what kind of true evil lurked in this man's soul. But he did now. He knew how this man thought and what he wanted and how he planned. And if it was the last thing he did, he was going to make sure he didn't ruin another life ever again.

Jordan turned toward Rossi. But instead of giving him any kind of signal like Rusty expected, he pulled a gun from a space between his hip and the inside of his wheelchair, pointed the long-nosed barrel capped with a silencer toward the corner of the room, and fired.

Rusty jerked back and stared wide-eyed toward Renwick. A hole in his chest spread blood all across his white shirt.

Rossi swiveled in his seat at the desk and shook his head as he glanced toward Renwick. "Stupid son of a bitch," Rossi mumbled.

"Gave him one job and he couldn't do it. All you had to do was keep the bitch under control," he yelled at Renwick.

Renwick's legs gave out, and his body slid to the floor. Just before he died, Rusty heard him whisper, "I'm—sorry. Tell her, I'm . . . sorry."

Rusty's hands were shaking as he held them up, his heart pounding like a thoroughbred's as he waited for Jordan to turn the gun on him. But he didn't. Instead, he lowered it to his lap, let go of it to rest his fat hand on the controls of the wheelchair, and turned the contraption toward Rossi at the desk. "Make the call. And get the remote. I want him to watch as they carve her up."

"There's something you need to know," Rusty said quickly as Rossi reached for the phone.

Rossi's hand froze against the receiver.

He was out of time. He had one shot to save Harper's life. All he could do was hope and pray he'd made the right choice and that Hunt was already there.

"I thought you might double-cross me," he said, staring at Jordan. "Which is why I gathered all my research on the Plague and left it for my brother. You know who he is, don't you? A journalist. The same journalist who brought down your friends, the Kasdans. By now Alec's already uploaded all of it to the internet and triggered a dead man's switch. If Harper dies, it goes out. If your thugs carve her up, it goes out. If they do anything to hurt her, six years of research, documenting everything I've seen and every person involved, will hit the papers by morning and be the biggest scandal Portland has seen in years."

Silence filled the room.

Jordan's beady eyes narrowed with veiled hatred. "The world already thinks I'm dead."

"Jordan . . ." Panic rose in Rossi's voice as he pushed to his feet.

"Shut up," Jordan snapped, staring at Rusty. "I don't give a flying fuck about a scandal," Jordan said in a low voice.

"Oh, you will." Rusty met his stare head-on. "You'll care because you'll lose millions of dollars and everything you've built. And because my cell phone over there that you think is turned off was recently loaded with some fancy software by my sister's fiancé that has been broadcasting this conversation right to my brother the whole time you've been talking."

CHAPTER TWENTY

"He's got my name," Rossi screamed at Jordan. "He'll ruin me." He grasped Rusty's phone and hurled it toward the far wall. It cracked against the wood and hit the floor with a thunk.

"You're panicking," Jordan growled. "Stop fucking panicking."

"I'm not going down for this. I'm not going down for you . . ." Rossi lurched around the desk and dove for the gun in Jordan's lap.

He was too slow, though. Jordan grasped the gun and lifted it. A popping sound echoed though the room, and Rossi grunted as the bullet struck his stomach and he fell.

Rusty knew this was his only chance. He lurched forward, but Jordan lifted the gun and pointed it at him, stopping his movement.

"Not yet." Shifting the gun to his other hand so he could keep it trained on Rusty, he wrapped his sausagelike fingers around the wheelchair's joystick and backed the wheelchair up to the side of the desk. Then he reached for the phone from the corner of the surface, laid it on his lap, and dialed.

He lifted the phone to his ear and waited. "Yes," he said, holding the gun steady, the barrel pointed at Rusty. "Go ahead. Start. No, I don't care if the feed isn't working. She'll scream loud enough. He can listen through the phone."

Rusty's vision turned red. "You son of a bitch. If you even think of—"

"This is my favorite part." Jordan pulled the phone two inches away from his ear and turned it so the receiver was pointed Rusty's way. "When he makes the first cut. You're going to love the sound she makes."

Rusty's heart lurched into his throat, and his gaze zeroed in on the receiver. A crackling sound echoed over the line, followed by a groan. Sickness surged up his throat, and his heart rate shot into the triple digits, but his feet were cemented in place, every muscle in his body flexed and ready to pounce but useless to Harper from so far away.

Please, please, please . . .

More crackling sounded over the line. Metal scraped. His breathing sped up as he listened. There was some kind of commotion happening on the other end of the line. A banging sound echoed. And then he heard a whispered, "No, no, don't you dare . . ."

Rusty jerked forward a step. "Harper!"

A scream ripped through the line, echoing in the room like cannon fire.

In his wheelchair, a satisfied smile curled the edges of Jordan's fat lips. "I told you you'd like that first sound."

Rage was a firestorm inside Rusty, one he couldn't control. One he could no longer hold back.

A series of pops echoed over the line. Jordan jerked back from the phone and dropped the receiver as if it had burned him. And Rusty didn't hesitate. He hurled himself at Jordan, surprising him.

The gun went off, but Rusty had already knocked it to the side, and it went flying. His body slammed into Jordan, sending the wheelchair straight back and down to the ground with a thud.

Jordan grunted as Rusty climbed over him and started swinging. His fist slammed into the man's face. Blood spurted from his mouth, his nose. He screamed, but Rusty didn't stop. All he felt was hate. All he knew was vengeance. He swung again and again, until his knuckles were bloody and his arms were aching.

Jordan went still beneath him. It was the only thing that slowed Rusty's punches. One look told him Jordan was unconscious but still breathing.

He staggered off the man and lurched for the phone Jordan had dropped. Lifting it to his ear with shaking hands, he yelled, "Harper! Harper, talk to me!"

"Shit," a voice mumbled. His heart was in his throat. His nerves were frayed beyond belief. Some kind of commotion was taking place outside the doors of the office, and he turned that way, but he couldn't focus on what was happening there. He had to find out if Harper was okay. Needed to hear her voice . . .

"Harper, dammit, talk to me!"

"Rusty? Is that you?"

"Hunt?" *Thank God* . . . "Please tell me you got there in time."

"We got her. She's already on the way to the hospital."

He swallowed hard. "Is she okay?"

"They drugged her. She's pretty banged up, and—"

The door to the office burst open, and three armed police officers stormed into the room with weapons drawn. "Hands up where we can see them!"

Rusty's hands went straight up, and he dropped the phone. A sea of police swept into the room.

An officer in full riot gear pointed his weapon at Rusty and said, "On the ground. Now. Arms out."

"Not him," a voice called. "Let me through, dammit." Footsteps sounded across the hardwood floor, then the voice said, "Not him; he's one of the good guys."

Rusty lifted his head as Callahan bent and held out his hand to help him up. "You okay?"

"Yeah." He nodded toward Jordan, lying on the floor near his over-turned wheelchair. "He shot both of them."

"We heard."

Thanks to Hunt's fancy software.

"He's still alive."

"Good. He's more valuable to us alive. Don't worry. He won't ever see the light of day again."

"He'd better not."

Callahan glanced toward Renwick slumped over in the corner and shook his head. "Stupid son of a bitch. He left a message at the station yesterday. Sounded like he wanted to make a deal. I didn't know it was about this case. Too little, too late."

Rusty wasn't sure if that was a just result for Renwick's shady deal-ing, or if he felt sorry for the man.

"Go on, get out of here," Callahan said, nodding toward the door. "Something tells me she'll want you to be there when she wakes up."

Rusty nodded, a lump in his throat, and moved for the door. And as he wove around police spilling into the house and jogged up the stairs to the main level, moving faster as he headed toward the open front door, he pushed thoughts of Jordan and Rossi and Renwick aside for good. And hoped like hell Callahan was right.

Because he wasn't about to leave her again.

———

Harper jerked awake and stared wide-eyed into the darkness with a gasp. Her heart raced, her hands grew sweaty, her chest rose and fell with deep, painful breaths.

"Hey," a familiar voice said softly to her left. "Relax. Breathe. You're okay. You're safe."

She knew that voice. Knew it really well. She looked to her left in the dimly lit room to see Rusty's smiling face as he leaned forward in the chair beside her and ran a hand down her arm in a gentle, calming motion.

"Rusty?"

"Yeah. It's me. You're in the hospital. Everything's fine. Hunter and his team got to you before anything happened. You're okay."

"Oh my God." The memories came rushing back—the blinding light, that psycho doctor with the scalpel coming at her, the sound of gunfire, shouts, and the screams . . . *his* screams, muffled and frantic and coming from far away.

A tremor she couldn't control racked her body, and tears spilled over her lashes before she could stop them.

"Hey." Rusty pushed out of his seat and perched a hip on the side of her bed, wrapping an arm around her and pulling her up against his familiar warmth. "It's okay. Everything's okay."

She turned into him, clinging to his dirty T-shirt as she pressed her face against his chest. "I-I was so scared."

"I know. But it's over now. That doctor's never going to touch you again. The facility's been shut down. They can't hurt anyone else like that again. And neither can the Plague. We got 'em."

"No." She pushed against his chest and sat up, staring at him though blurry vision. "You don't get it. I don't care about that or what they were going to do to me. I was scared about you." She clenched his shirt tightly in her fist as the emotions slammed into her again, as hard and sharp and painful as they had when she'd heard him scream her name and that gun go off. "I thought—"

Her voice hitched.

"Hey." He lifted a hand to her face, swiping the tears from one side and then the other. "I'm fine. Look at me. No worse for the wear."

She blinked several times. Sniffled. Stared at him through watery eyes. "How . . . I don't . . . What happened?" she finally managed.

"They sent me a message. Told me if I wanted to save your life, I had to meet with them. I called Hunt. I had a hunch they'd taken you to that research facility. He and his men got you out."

"I know, but what . . ." She looked down at her hand, still holding tightly to his shirt. "What happened with you?"

"They made me drive out to this fancy mansion in the hills outside the city. Rossi and Renwick were there."

She sucked in a breath. "Renwick really was working with them."

"According to Callahan, he was a small-time player. He covered up a few things for Jordan, like you found early on. That was enough to rope him in. They had him then. Forced him to cover other things up over the years. I don't think he was a willing participant, if that helps."

She shook her head, swallowing the bile as she stared down at his shirt. "It still makes him an accomplice." And she'd still worked for him.

Rusty's hand dropped to the mattress. "He's dead, Harper." When she lifted her gaze back to his, he said, "Jordan shot him right in front of me."

Her eyes widened. "Jordan? But he's de—"

"No. He's very much alive. He fooled everyone."

Her gaze skipped over his face. "I thought Rossi—"

"He was there too. He was the front man. But Jordan was running the entire thing from his cushy mansion in the hills. He survived that fire. I don't know how, but he did."

"My God."

"There's more."

"More?"

"Yeah." A somber look filled his eyes. He wasn't touching her anymore. The arm that had been around her was perched on the bed railing at her side. His other hand was resting against his thigh, and she didn't know what that meant. Was afraid to ask when he was staring at her like he had something truly horrible to say.

"What? Tell me."

"Remember when I was telling you about the night my mother died?"

She nodded.

"I told you I got into a fight with Jordan. That he beat me to a pulp."

"I remember."

"I managed to crawl behind his desk after he killed my mother. And then someone came into the room and shot him."

"Yes. You said you never saw his face, but he's the one who lit the house on fire."

"Yeah."

He was torturing her by not elaborating and just staring at her with those worried eyes. "What, Rusty? Just say it."

"It was your dad. He was working undercover vice back then. Jordan and his cronies were just starting up the Plague. That's what those meetings were about, the ones he took Lily to. Your dad tried to stop him. He had to have met Lily at some point. If he was at any of those meetings, he had to have seen her. All I can figure is that he'd found out Jordan had sold her, and he confronted him about it."

Harper let go of his shirt and lifted her hand to her mouth.

"I know," he said softly, shifting his hand from the railing to cover hers perched on the mattress at her side. "I know that's not what you expected." He curled his fingers around hers and swallowed. "And I don't want to be the one to tell you this, but your dad wasn't killed on a routine domestic violence call. He was still trying to stop the Plague, almost twenty years later. He'd found out Jordan was still alive. They killed him because he got too close."

"Oh my God," she whispered, the shock of everything swirling in her head.

Tears sprang to her eyes all over again. Tears she couldn't contain. Everything she'd been told about her dad's death ricocheted through her mind, and with it, the reality that it had all been a lie.

Rusty leaned forward, closed his arms around her, and held her close. "I'm sorry," he whispered. "I'm so sorry this has all been so fucked up and connected."

It was. Completely fucked up and insanely interconnected in a way she'd never thought possible. She sank into him and let him hold her as memories ignited behind her closed eyelids, mingling with what he'd told her and the realization that her dad had known Lily. He'd been trying to stop the Plague.

"He was a good cop," she whispered, sniffling against him.

"Yeah. He was."

"He tried to help people."

"Just like you."

She squeezed her eyes shut as a bittersweet pain stabbed at her heart. And then it hit her.

Wide-eyed, she pushed back and stared at his arms, covered by the long-sleeved shirt, visualizing the burn scars on his forearms he'd gotten trying to escape that fire. "Oh my God, he started that fire."

"No, he didn't. Someone else did. I was wrong about that. One of Jordan's men set that fire to fake his death so your dad would think he was dead."

Tears filled her eyes again. Tears because she could have lost him then, long before she'd ever known him. And she could have lost him today, when she'd finally realized she didn't want to live without him. "I'm sorry," she whispered, gripping his forearms over his scars. "I'm so sorry. I should have told you about the deal I made with the police commissioner. I don't know why I didn't. I think I was just scared . . . I didn't know what I—"

"Yeah, you're right. You should have told me."

Her lips snapped closed, and she blinked damp lashes at him. "I know," she whispered. "And I wanted to. I just . . . I was afraid. I didn't want you to think that's why I was with you."

"Is it?"

Her heart contracted, and fear wrapped around her heart as she looked down at his arms and swallowed hard. She didn't want to lie to him, not about this. Not about anything ever again. "At first, yes. I mean, I didn't sleep with you to try to get my job back, if that's what you think. I went to that masquerade party intending to meet up with you, hoping we could work together so that, yeah, maybe I could find a way to get my job back. I know you can't understand this, but being a cop is all I know. It's what I thought I wanted again. But then everything happened between us, and I realized—"

"That I'm irresistible."

Heart racing, she slowly looked up at him only to discover he wasn't upset. He didn't even look mad. He was watching her carefully with narrowed, amused eyes, almost as if he knew a secret.

Almost as if he knew *her* secret.

Her pulse pounded hard in her ears, and she swallowed again, knowing this was her chance not to get her old life back but to reach for one she'd never thought she could ever have.

"Yes," she whispered. "Completely irresistible. I didn't plan to fall in love with you, but I did. And it changed everything."

He stared at her for several seconds in silence, and as the clock ticked on the wall and she watched his gaze skipping over her features, she had no idea what he was thinking or feeling or what he would say in response. All she knew was that she couldn't lose him. Not now, not after she'd finally realized he was everything she'd never known she'd wanted.

She gathered her courage. "Rusty—"

"No more secrets."

She blinked, unsure what he was saying. "What?"

"From now on, if you want something, just come out and say it. I knew you were keeping something from me. If you want to go back to being a cop, I don't care. That's your choice, and I'll support you in whatever you want to do. But I do care that you couldn't just come out and tell me. I would have said yes if you'd just asked me to help you straight up. In case you haven't figured it out by now, I can't seem to say no to you no matter how hard I try."

Warmth flooded her chest, and tears burst free of her lashes, but they were the good kind, the happy kind, the oh-my-God-I-didn't-fuck-this-up kind of tears.

She threw her arms around his shoulders and held on tightly, and as his arms closed around her back and she turned her face against his throat, she whispered, "I will. I promise. I love you."

He pressed his lips against the soft skin behind her ear, then said, "I love you more."

Joy burst inside her when his mouth found hers, and as he kissed her and tightened his arms around her like steel bands, she knew he would always be her safe haven. And that anywhere with him was exactly where she wanted to be.

When she was breathless, when she knew he wasn't going anywhere, she drew back and looked up at him, taking a good look now that her heart wasn't about to lurch out of her chest.

She brushed her fingers down his cheek. "You're a mess, you know."

"So are you."

She smirked and pressed her lips to his. "We make quite a pair."

"Yes, we do." His gaze skipped over her face. "And I meant what I said about the department. I want you to do whatever makes you happy."

"You make me happy." She skimmed the stubble on his jaw. "And to be honest, I don't really know what I want to do. I mean, I thought I wanted to go back to law enforcement, but with everything that's happened, I don't know if my heart's in it anymore. I kinda like being able to set my own hours. Means I can spend more time with you."

He smirked. "That does have its advantages."

She laid her head against his shoulder. "I also want to work for someone I believe in. Someone I know is doing good."

He ran a hand down her hair. "I've got an almost brother-in-law who runs a security and PI firm."

"Yeah?" God, she loved being close to him like this. "How does he feel about hiring women?"

"I'm gonna guess he's just fine with hiring women. Plus, if he lets you do something reckless, I can go yell at him and not you."

She laughed and snuggled closer.

A knock sounded at the door. Rusty lifted his head. Harper glanced over her shoulder.

"Who is it?" Rusty called.

The door pushed open a tiny bit, and from behind the curtain that was drawn, a female voice said, "The cavalry. Is she up for visitors?"

"Shit," Rusty muttered. "Hold on."

"Who is that?" Harper asked.

"My mother and the rest of the family." Rusty let go of her and pushed off her bed so she could sit up. "I'll get rid of them."

"No, don't." She grabbed his hand, stopping him. "Let them in. I want to meet your mom."

"Are you sure?"

"Yeah, why not." Harper let go of his hand and fluffed her hair even though she knew it was probably a lost cause, then swiped at her eyes just in case her mascara was sliding down her cheeks. "Are you afraid for them to see me like this?"

A warm smile curled his mouth just before it lowered and pressed a quick kiss to hers. "Not a bit. I just don't want them to overwhelm you."

She reached for his hand again. "I need to get used to them at some point, right? Better now than later."

"God, I love you." He kissed her again, then said, "When you want them to leave, squeeze my hand."

"Got it."

"Okay, come in," Rusty called.

Voices sounded, footsteps echoed, and then the room was filled with more people than Harper could count.

Most she recognized—Ethan and Samantha, Kelsey and Hunter, Raegan and Alec, with little Emma perched on Alec's hip—but there were a few she didn't recognize . . . the lanky teen in the corner shaking the shaggy hair out of his eyes, and a man and woman, both in their fifties, moving up on the side of her bed.

Rusty cleared his throat. "Harper, you know most of the rat pack. That goofy-looking kid over there in the corner is my youngest brother, Thomas, and these are my parents, Michael and Hannah."

Michael McClane smiled down at Harper with warm eyes and reached for her hand. "It's very nice to meet you, Harper. The kids filled us in on what you did for our son. We're very thankful. And we're very happy to hear you're all right."

"Th-thanks." A lump formed in Harper's throat. She wasn't used to praise. At least not from strangers.

"We're also very proud of both of you." Rusty's father glanced up at his son on the other side of Harper's bed. "Though if we'd known what you were up to all this time, my reaction might have been very different."

Rusty smirked and squeezed Harper's hand. Harper glanced his way, imagining just what kind of lecture he would have gotten if his father had known what he'd been doing late at night in seedy strip clubs around town.

Soft fingers closed around Harper's other hand resting on the top of her blanket, and she looked up to see Rusty's mother smiling down at her with shimmering amber eyes. "You are absolutely beautiful. I had no idea. If I had known . . ." She turned and looked up at her husband, then back down at Harper and finally to Rusty. "If we had known . . ." A tear spilled over her lashes. "I always wanted Rusty to find a nice girl. I had no idea it would be you. It was meant to be."

"Come on now, Hannah." Michael squeezed her shoulders. "Don't start crying again. You'll make poor Harper uncomfortable."

Too late. Harper turned wide eyes up at Rusty, afraid to pull her hand away from his mom, completely confused about what was going on. From the confused look on Rusty's face, he was just as clueless as her.

"Mom, what are you talking about?"

When Hannah only sniffled and swiped at her nose with a tissue in her free hand, Rusty glanced at his father. "What is she talking about?"

Alec chuckled at the end of the bed. Ethan smirked. Kelsey elbowed both of them and whispered, "Knock it off. This is sweet."

"I'm hungry," Thomas muttered at the back of the group. "Is anybody else hungry? There has to be a cafeteria in here somewhere."

"I hugry, Unca Thomas."

"Cool. Let's go, squirt." Thomas reached for Emma from Alec's arms while Michael comforted Hannah, and Rusty and Harper tried to figure out what was going on.

"Keep an eye on her, Thomas," Alec said. "Don't let her run off."

"I will." He turned for the door with Emma on his hip. "Sheesh. It's like he's afraid you're gonna disappear or something."

Emma threw her little head back and laughed as they slipped through the curtain and headed down the hall.

"Would someone please tell us what's going on?" Rusty asked.

Hannah sniffled one more time and dabbed at her eyes, looking across Harper's bed at her son. "Johnathon Blake is what's going on."

Harper glanced up at her. "That was my dad."

"I know, honey." Hannah squeezed her hand and smiled down at her. "He also saved Rusty's life."

"He did what?" Rusty asked.

Hannah looked back at her son. "Detective Johnathon Blake is the one who pulled you out of that fire. He was one of the first people on the scene when you were trapped in the fire. He told me later that he was on patrol in the neighborhood when the call came in. A neighbor had called nine-one-one, told the dispatcher there were children in the house. He rushed over, heard you coughing from the entryway where you'd managed to crawl before collapsing. Then he ran into the fire and pulled you out. He's the one who got you to the hospital, who brought you to me. And he didn't leave your side the entire time you were there. He wouldn't let anyone but me and a nurse in your room either."

"Oh my God," Harper muttered, looking up at Rusty, understanding dawning. Her father hadn't just been in the neighborhood. He'd been driving away from the scene, from shooting Jordan. He hadn't known Rusty was there. When he'd heard the nine-one-one call, he'd rushed back. "He knew if the Plague realized you were still alive, they'd come after you."

"Yes," Michael said. "He knew he had to hide you somewhere, and after your mother told him we'd recently adopted Ethan and Alec, he arranged it so you could come live with us."

"The report he filed said you'd died in that fire," Hannah continued. "He hid you with us, and he checked in on you every year to make sure you were okay."

"Of course he did." Tears filled Harper's eyes all over again as a rush of emotions swept through her. She squeezed Rusty's hand and glanced up at him. He looked shell-shocked, but not in a bad way.

"He was so proud of you, Rusty," Hannah said, sniffling again. "Of your vineyard and your plans for the winery."

"He knew about that?" Rusty asked, stunned.

"Yes." Hannah swiped at her eyes. "He knew everything." She looked down at Harper. "And he was very, very proud of you. He talked about you all the time."

Tears pushed past Harper's lashes, but she didn't care. This was the best day. The best end to a day she could ever imagine. She squeezed Hannah's hand, and Rusty's again.

"Why didn't he ever talk to me?" Rusty asked. "Why didn't he ever tell me—"

"Because he couldn't." Harper smiled up at him. "Because he was still keeping you safe, even at the end." Rusty's shocked gaze met hers.

She smiled wider and turned toward Hannah. "Thank you. Thank you for telling me. For telling us."

Hannah grinned. "This was meant to be." She glanced up at her son. "You two were meant to find each other."

They were. Harper believed it. She'd never believed anything more strongly.

"Come on." Michael squeezed his wife's arms one more time. "Let's leave these two alone now that you've thoroughly shocked them both."

Hannah released Harper's hand and leaned down and hugged her while Michael shooed everyone else out of the room. "Welcome to our family," she whispered into Harper's ear. "And thank you for saving my boy."

Harper's throat grew thick as she hugged Rusty's mother back. "I-I didn't."

"Yes, you did." Hannah eased back and grinned. "You gave him a reason to save himself."

She turned out of the room with a wave, and when the door drifted closed, Harper turned to look up at Rusty.

"Wow," he muttered, sinking to the edge of her bed.

She scooted over to make room for him, glad when he stretched out beside her on the narrow mattress. "Yeah, wow."

He wrapped an arm around her, and she snuggled into him. Silence filled the room as he ran his hand up and down her arm in a lazy motion, and then he said, "I'm not sure what we're supposed to do with that."

She chuckled and pushed up to look down at him. "How does living happily ever after sound?"

A wide smile broke across his face as he lifted one hand and brushed the hair back from her eyes. "I think that sounds pretty damn perfect."

He slid his hand through her hair and gently tugged her face to his, and as he kissed her, she sighed.

It sounded pretty damn perfect to her too.

EPILOGUE

Summer was Rusty's favorite season. And this summer was the very best one of his life.

Rusty pushed back from the table in the brand-new tasting room of the Black Sheep Winery in late August and lifted his glass as he looked over the small group of people who'd gathered for this preopening opening—his family, his assistant Abby, Callahan, and Brooklyn, who'd finally agreed to work for him. Currently, Brooklyn was standing behind the counter, drying wineglasses as she rolled her eyes at Thomas, who was perched on a stool trying to hit on the older girl. "Okay, settle down. Especially you over there, mister hormones."

Thomas grinned.

Rusty smirked. "I don't do this often, but I'm about to make a toast."

"Make a fool out of yourself is more like it," Alec muttered across the round table.

Rusty shot him a look, but it was half-assed, because even Alec's taunting couldn't ruin his good mood.

"This winery has been a vision of mine for a long time," he started, reminding himself not to get choked up. No one liked a pussy who cried. Especially tough chicks. They liked manly guys. He glanced down at Harper seated next to him in a sexy yellow sundress he couldn't wait to tear off her when they were alone.

A smile curled his lips as he went on. "A lot of years that were filled with struggles—some good, some bad; a lot of them I don't want to remember." Soft laughter echoed through the space. "But the one thing I could always count on, whether times were good or bad or just plain crazy, was the people in this room. Every single one of you has supported me . . ."

His throat grew thick, and he paused, working like hell not to cry. At his side, Harper grasped his hand and squeezed, and it was exactly what he needed to keep going.

He looked at her and smiled, drawing on her strength just as he did every single day. "And that support means more to me than any of you will ever know." He looked back over the small group. "Which is why I'm giving you each a small percentage of the winery."

Gasps filled the room. From the tasting counter on the far side, Thomas said, "Did he just say he's giving us money?"

Rusty laughed. "Don't get excited. It's not worth anything yet."

"But it will be," Alec cut in. "I always knew Rusty was my favorite sibling."

Kelsey smacked him on the arm.

"That's very generous of you, son," Michael said. "And unnecessary."

"I know it's not necessary, but it's something that I want to do. You've all pitched in around here when I needed it. I know you'll do it again whenever I ask. I want to share this with you. My vision was always that this would be a family winery, and there's no family more special to me than the one in this room."

"Hear! Hear!" Ethan said, lifting his glass.

Someone yelled, "Cheers!" and they all clinked glasses. And before they could get too rowdy, Rusty said, "One more thing. When we harvest this year's crop and bottle our first chardonnay"—he looked down at Harper—"it's going to be called the Golden Harp, after this incredible woman who worked her ass off to make sure I wasn't arrested. More valuable to me than any piece of gold."

Harper tipped her head and smiled that for-him-only smile, then reached for him when he leaned down and kissed her. *Ahs* rose up in the room, intermixed with Thomas making puking sounds from the tasting counter, but Rusty ignored him.

Grinning, he lifted his lips from Harper's and stood upright, thinking back to their romantic evening on a blanket between the rows of vines in the vineyard last night and the private celebration they'd had under all those stars. "Oh yeah, and she said yes. Finally."

Kelsey was the first to screech and jump out of her chair, run around, and grab Harper in a hug. And then the entire family was swarming, hugging, and congratulating both of them.

"Another wedding," his mom said with a beaming smile as she kissed his cheek. "I can't wait."

"We want to do it here on the vineyard," Harper said, standing next to him. "Sometime this fall."

"Oh, you have to let me design your gown," Kelsey exclaimed. "I can do anything you want."

While the girls circled around Harper, ogling the two-carat ring she'd kept hidden from them earlier and launching into wedding discussions, his brothers each hugged him and made jokes about being part of the old ball-and-chain club, and his dad patted him on the back with a broad grin. "Not too bad, son. Not too bad at all."

"Thanks, Dad."

Hunt stepped in front of him with a smirk, with Kelsey at his side.

"What are you grinning at?" Rusty asked. "You're gonna be joining that club in a matter of days."

"I know." He handed Rusty a manila envelope. "Consider this an engagement present."

Not sure what he was talking about, Rusty turned the envelope over. The outside was blank. Beside him, he sensed Harper stepping close, curious about what was in his hands.

"Open it," she said.

He pried the metal tabs open and shook the contents into his hands, watching Hunt's peculiar smile the whole time. "He looks goofy right now," Rusty said to his sister.

"I know." Kelsey only grinned and kissed Hunt's cheek.

Shaking his head, Rusty pulled the papers out of the envelope and flipped them over. Only they weren't papers. They were photographs. Glossy eight-by-ten photographs of a woman in her midthirties with warm brown hair and shimmering brown eyes.

"Oh my God." His eyes grew wide.

"What?" Harper asked, looking down at the photo of the woman standing in the front yard of a small house with a child who looked about two on her hip. "Who is that?"

Rusty flipped to the next photo. In it, the woman was standing on the sidelines of a football field, her hair in a ponytail, holding the hand of a small girl who looked about five on one side, and the hand of a two-year-old on the other side. And she was grinning up at a man in a baseball hat and a blue nylon jacket that said COACH on the right breast, while a third child, a boy who was probably ten, leaned against the man's side.

"It's Lily," he muttered. His gaze shot to Hunt. "She's alive?"

"Alive, very well, and very happily married in Michigan with her football-coach husband and her three little kids."

Rusty stared down at the picture again, barely believing what he was seeing. "H-how . . . When? How did you . . ."

"After we learned that Harper's dad was working undercover and had infiltrated the Plague, I started digging." Rusty looked back up at Hunt, who'd shifted his gaze to Harper. "Turns out Johnathon Blake was the one who bought her. Cashed in his pension to do it. Then he got her out of Portland, set her up with a new family on the East Coast where Jordan would never find her, and made sure she was safe. Flip to the last photo."

Rusty did and was shocked to see a picture of Lily—as an adult—with her arms wrapped around the waist of an older man—Harper's father.

"That was right before he died." Harper stared at the photo with wonder.

"Yeah," Hunt said. "He went out to visit her about once a year, just to check on her. Like a surrogate father."

Harper's shimmering eyes lifted to Rusty. "Like he did with you."

Holy shit. Exactly as he'd done with him.

"My guy who found her saw that in her house and took a snapshot of it." Hunt nodded at the photo. "Thought you'd like to have that, Harper."

Harper ran her fingertips over her father's smiling face. "I would. Thank you."

"My guy didn't tell her who he was or who he worked for or why he was looking for her, just in case you were wondering," Hunt said. "But her address is in there. Just in case you want it."

Rusty was still too stunned to speak. He swallowed hard and nodded.

"Thank you, Hunter." Harper reached out and hugged him. "This was the best engagement present anyone could have given us."

"You're welcome," Hunter said, hugging her back. "You're coming to the office on Monday, right?"

"Yep. Bright and early."

"Good. We're excited about having you on the team."

"So am I."

Rusty cleared his throat, knowing they were talking about Harper's new job with Hunter's company but still trying to process everything he'd learned about Lily. "Th-thanks, Hunt."

"No problem." Hunt wrapped an arm around Kelsey's waist and headed toward the counter where most of the rest of the family had already moved to drink more wine and talk.

But Harper stayed close, knowing Rusty needed her. Always knowing what he needed, even when he didn't.

Quietly, she said, "Do you want to go see her?"

A wave of emotion slammed into him, and he closed his arms around her, pulling her into him, letting the pictures dangle from his fingers at her back. He shook his head into her hair.

"Are you sure?" She ran her fingers up and down his spine. "Because I want you to see her if you need to see her."

"No." His throat was thick, but he didn't care. He didn't even care that tears were spilling over his lashes. He only held her tighter. "I don't need that. I'd only be a bad memory for her, and I don't want that. I want her to be happy."

"She is, Rusty."

She was. He couldn't believe it.

Easing back, he looked down at Harper through watery vision, knowing he could never love anyone more than he loved her. "My mom was right—you and me—we were meant to be. He saved her life. Your dad saved her life, just like you saved mine."

She smiled. "I didn't save your life."

"Yeah, you did." Tears filled his eyes all over again as he lowered his forehead to hers. "In the best way you ever could. You gave me a reason to let go of the past. You gave me a reason to truly want to live. And I'm going to spend the rest of my life showing you just how much that means to me."

"Oh well." She lifted her lips to his, smiling wider. "In that case, I will happily take all the credit. Especially if it means a repeat of what you did to me last night on that blanket in the vineyard."

He laughed as he kissed her. "Oh, baby doll. It means a whole lot more than that."

She sighed and sank into him. And as he kissed her deeper and the pictures fluttered from his fingertips to land softly on the floor, he knew everything he'd been through, even all the struggle and pain and heartache, had been preparing him for this moment. For this life, with her and the future they were meant to build together.